praise

Provocative … Clare animates her tale with elegant prose. Evading killers sets the groundwork for a sublimely written story of love and passion.

— *Kirkus Reviews*

Kelleigh Clare brings a fresh new voice to the genre, and her debut delivers a sensual, riveting romantic thriller filled with intrigue and surprises.

— *New York Times* bestselling author J. Kenner

Dark, intriguing, and scorchingly sexy. The premise is electrifying, the romance is sizzling, and the storytelling is top-notch.

— *New York Times* bestselling author Julie Ann Walker

Captivating and provocative. This fast-paced story will wrap you up and not let go until the last satisfying paragraph.

— *Wall Street Journal* bestselling author Kerry Lonsdale

A propulsive, thrilling read filled with action, romance, and intrigue. Passion and lies make this book irresistible. Loved it!

— *USA Today* bestselling author Kaira Rouda

A gripping romantic thriller that will capture readers from the onset. Clare deftly blends danger and romance in an exciting way that will keep readers turning the pages.

— RT Book Reviews

Kelleigh Clare hooks you on the first page with a story of captivating characters and follows up with a gripping plot.

— Independent Book Publishing Professionals Group

The wholly original contemporary romance plot combines the best part of modern fiction with something close to the best elements of the fantasy genre.

— The BookLife Prize

International Book Awards
Cross-Genre Fiction Winner

Next Generation Indie Book Awards
Romance Winner

Foreword Indies Book-of-the-Year Awards
Romance Winner

National Indie Excellence Awards
Romance Winner

TWISTED BEAUTIFUL LIES

also by kelleigh clare

HASTINGS BROTHERS NOVELS

Twisted Beautiful Lies (duet, book one)

Twisted Beautiful Lies: Extended Epilogue

Her Lovely Lies (duet, book two)

Two Pretty Lies (standalone)

Two Pretty Lies: Extended Epilogue

SAVAGE SYNDICATE NOVELS

Wicked Rivals

Merciless Empire

Cruel Vows

For more info, visit

www.klclare.com.

TWISTED BEAUTIFUL LIES

HASTINGS BROTHERS

USA TODAY BESTSELLING AUTHOR

KELLEIGH CLARE

WHITE ROSE PRESS

www.klclare.com

Twisted Beautiful Lies is a work of fiction. Names, characters, places, and incidents are products of the author's imagination or are used fictitiously. Any resemblance to actual persons, living or dead, events, or locations is coincidental.

Published by White Rose Press

www.whiterose.press

978-1-958110-09-6

March 2022 Edition

Editors: Elizabeth Kracht, Jaime Brockway, Jovana Shirley

Cover design: © The Pretty Little Design Co.

Photo: © Michelle Lancaster

Previously published as *Lies That Bind Us*.

For my grandmothers in heaven, my mom, my dream-chasing daughter, and the many other strong women who've touched my life in ways big and small.

acknowledgments

To the many beautiful, brave souls who took a chance on this novel, read the ugly first drafts and reinforced my confidence with generous feedback, and provided encouragement, guidance, and big-hearted endorsements—you forever have my gratitude.

Thank you, Liz Kracht, for showing me how to push the boundaries gracefully as we developed the premise of this story.

Julie Kenner, I'm blessed to have somehow earned your thoughtful support. Your passion for this industry is unrivaled, and you give back far more than you could ever owe.

To Jennifer Longenberger, who never complains about my nonstop talk about this story and provides me with sound advice, you are a wonderful friend, and I'm thankful for you.

Special thanks and all my love to my parents and my two brilliant children: the four of you allow me to live inside my head and patiently wait for me while I travel between my two worlds.

one

THE FIRST SIGHT OF WILL'S FACE STUNNED ME. HIS INTENSE eyes burned into mine, and for a minute, we were more than two strangers at a small-town parade. Our connection was something undefined and painful and beautiful. A love story.

People cheered as a traditional highland band arrived, marching through the center of the boulevard, filling the air with one last song to honor those lost at sea. As the procession ended, the crowd shifted, providing me with an unobstructed view of him.

He stepped into the street, and my breath caught.

Neither of us looked away.

I forced myself to breathe.

I'd never seen a man so tall, with shoulders so broad. I absorbed every detail, noting the width of his chest, the thickness of his dark blond hair. His jawline was strong and commanding, reminding me of paintings I had studied in college of ancient Roman gladiators.

The word *magnificent* danced on my tongue.

He wore close-fitting jeans. His cut biceps emerged from the sleeves of his faded indigo T-shirt, and when he moved his right arm, a slight amount of ink played peekaboo with the edge of the sleeve.

While the celebration continued to clear out, Jess and I stayed at the curb for a few more minutes, where we'd been for the better part of an hour. My best friend released her pretty red hair from a ponytail and lifted her face to the late morning sun with a peaceful sigh.

I continued staring at him, the man who had commanded my full attention.

The street itself was narrow, and with the pageantry and most spectators gone, every move he made was visible to me. His hands flexed at his sides. A smile slowly touched his lips as he dropped his gaze to my mouth, driving a sensual shiver through me.

I was stuck in the moment, our moment, in that something undefined.

Jess elbowed me. "Who's the guy, Ellie, and why are you staring at each other like that?"

I turned to her, narrowing my eyes. "Like what? I don't know him. Maybe he's the one who followed me home the other night. But I could be wrong about that whole thing. Gran mentioned this morning that a family rented the house behind ours for the season, so maybe the follower was just going there."

When I refocused on the street, my perfect stranger had disappeared.

"Maybe you should say something, just in case, report it to the police."

"Paranoia is my sister's thing, not mine. You know that. Make up your mind, Jess. You're always telling me to let new people into my life."

"Well, not a stalker," she teased. "You haven't been curious in a long time, and I do kind of like it. You need to get out of your artsy little head more often. Anyway, be careful. If you think someone is following you again, promise me you'll do something about it."

True or not, Jess was the one person who wouldn't judge me for thinking it.

"I will. I promise."

Most likely, no one had followed me. My imagination had misled me, I thought.

My hometown was a summer destination after all, bursting at the seams with tourists because it occupied the best of Connecticut's coastline, facing the open Atlantic waters. People milled around the historic town and its waterfront parks by day and wandered through the streets in the quiet darkness of night. Some even came to work for the commercial fishing fleet.

Still, as beautiful as Stonington was, posing picture-perfect for visitors, its residents fought addiction and crime under the cover of that same darkness.

"I'm going to head over to the art studio. The kids chose today to make up the day-camp session we missed over the holiday. Catch up with you later?" I asked.

Jess closed her eyes and nodded, lifting her freckled face back to the sun.

AFTER THE LAST OF MY STUDENTS HAD GONE, I LOCKED THE studio door and walked to the fishing pier on the southwest side of the peninsula to sketch. It was that or go home and listen to my sister rattle on about my refusal to test the waters in the local pool of single men. The pool was small, and I didn't need to dip in a toe to know there was nothing more left in it for me.

Time alone with my art in quiet places around town kept me sane, made me feel connected to my life. It allowed me to escape my sister's and grandmother's intrusiveness. At twenty-seven, I was quite capable of shaping my own future. Isobel and Gran often overcomplicated matters, but they were all I'd ever had, and I knew they meant well.

Gran still mourned her only child, my father, even after all the years he'd been gone, and we both dreamed of him. She would tell me of her pleasant dreams, but in the same breath—and only God knew why—she would curse at my father for the wealth he'd left us. Isobel seemed to suffer our mother's death more. She never talked about either one.

I looked out over the harbor and inhaled, pulling in brine and seaweed and hints of sunscreen, and spotted *Neptune* trudging her way in. The sailboats beyond paled in her presence. I didn't know what it was about that old fishing boat, but I loved her. The emerald-green hull had become chalky over time, and the once-black hoists and white booms were bathed in rust. Still, she was glorious against the backdrop of the sea.

Sitting in my usual spot, I lost myself in the sketch.

Ten or fifteen minutes had passed when the pier thrummed with the pounding steps of a docking crew as they hurried to meet *Neptune*. With a soft curse, I covered my drawing and watched them secure the lines.

"Hello."

My shoulders jerked. I arched my neck back and blinked at the man looming above.

"I didn't mean to startle you," he said.

I wasn't sure which was more surprising—his thunderous tone or the British accent. A rich, masculine scent rolled down his arm when he offered his hand.

Without taking it, I stood and dusted off my backside. I lifted my chin to meet his eyes. He was close, so close, towering a foot above me. I studied him, explored his eyes. They were pale blue, but there was nothing cold about his gaze as it warmed my skin.

"Hi. It's you. I mean, from the street. You were staring."

The tall man from the parade offered no apology. He offered his hand again instead, palm facing up this time. "I'm Will Hastings." A seductive smile played with the corners of his mouth, one side curving higher than the other. His commanding presence saturated the surrounding space.

Power. He was power.

I bit my lip and gave him my hand this time. "Ellie James."

He held my fingers while inspecting my eyes, my lips, my body. "Christ, you're lovely."

The texture layered in his voice captivated me, as did his choice of words. My pulse sped. No words came to me, nothing intelligent anyway.

Will Hastings pressed his lips to my knuckles. "I'll see you again, Ellie." His eyes moved over my body again, and then he released my hand and walked away.

"Hey, wait," I called through the heat of my blush.

"See you soon," he said over his shoulder with absolute confidence.

Watching him go, I reminded myself to breathe. His movements stirred something deep inside me, the way he walked, the swing of his powerful arms. It was alarming. And beautiful.

The daylight and evening had vanished without notice, and midnight had arrived.

I couldn't sleep. I climbed out of bed, switched on the lamp over my drawing table, and began to rework my sketch from the pier, using only memory to coerce life into the fishing boat. After finishing *Neptune*, I flipped the page and allowed my mind to create whatever it wanted to see at the moment.

Will's eyes soon stared back at me. I held up the sketch and angled it left and right, considering the penciled likeness. Something unexpected revealed itself. Even though I had gently shaded his light blue eyes, a clear expression of darkness was present.

The darkness drew me to him, even on paper. And what was more, it also ignited an alluring energy within me that drove images into my head of tangled sheets and sweating, entwined bodies.

I shook my head to clear it, deciding I'd go to my family's beach house at the end of the week to catch up on some sleep and start on my art curriculum for the upcoming school year.

No one else used the place anymore but me. The beach there was quaint and private, almost forgotten. Stepping directly into the Atlantic to ease my soul was as necessary as the air that I breathed. The ocean soothed me, softening the edges of the void that lingered in my spirit with comforting messages of home.

Maybe the strength of the sea would help me rid the seductive stranger from my mind. Perhaps its whispers would replace his voice, and its beauty might erase his handsome face, make me forget his imposing stare.

two

Several days later, powerless to clear Will Hastings from my thoughts, I walked along the pier again, hoping to run into him. He wasn't there, but honestly, it came as no surprise to me. His polished demeanor had suggested that he wasn't a longshoreman in for the season.

My curiosity was becoming a preoccupation, his eyes haunting me. As I walked to and from work, the art studio, Jess's place, I searched the streets for him. I needed to find him to ease the ache low in my abdomen that assured me of his presence.

God, I needed to get past this thing, whatever it was.

While dressing for an evening shift at Nick's Restaurant, preoccupied and growing irritable, a text message from Jess hit my phone. She was running late. Together, we tended bar at Nick's three nights a week, sometimes four, to pass the time. Neither of us needed a second job.

Another message from Jess.

Don't forget. Busy night. It's the
big party.

An annual event celebrating the restaurant's long run in the community. It drew people for miles throughout New London County, and the timing was perfect. I hadn't forgotten.

If my gut was right and Will Hastings was still around town, he would show up, as he had at the parade. I'd get a chance to talk to him, and then the possessed mood taking over my life might let go.

I pulled on a T-shirt with my employer's latest crimson-and-yellow logo, remembering for a moment how my niece, Lissie, had mentioned how it resembled the Superman emblem, tucked it into my cutoff denim shorts, and added a soft peachy-rose gloss to my lips.

Without a word to Isobel or Gran, I slipped out the front door and headed for Nick's.

Only minutes into my shift, the crowd growing with each swing of the restaurant's signature blue-painted door, Josh Mendes came inside from the terrace. He stood before the bar, not speaking, watching while I mixed two skinny margaritas and a whiskey smash.

"I'm a little busy, Josh. Can I grab you another beer?"

"Yeah." He held on to my wrist when I reached for his empty. "Come back to me, Ellie. Give us one more shot. Please."

We had dated on and off in the three years since I'd come home from the University of Connecticut, though we'd never gotten it right. He was a good man, a lieutenant with the local police department. I wanted to love him, but it never came to me, the collision of fiery emotional and physical bliss that I refused to live without.

Josh needed consistent encouragement for some reason, and I'd grown tired of managing the intimacy between us.

Pulling back, dropping my chin, I reached for a clean glass and filled it with Guinness. "It's been months, and nothing has changed for me. I'm sorry."

"If there's something I can do to change your mind, you know I'll do it."

"I know." I offered his beer with the one thing I could give him, a friendly smile, before turning away.

When I glanced at the wall of mirrors to see if he'd moved on, it was Will Hastings I found staring back at me. Every part of me tensed, my pulse quickening from the intensity of Will's focused eyes. I spun, scanned the crowd. I couldn't let him get away.

We locked stares again, and I searched for the dark, menacing trait that had nagged at my subconscious. It was there, but it didn't frighten me. It filled my senses and fueled my curiosity. This man would never need encouraging.

Canting his head, Will signaled for me to follow him out the rear exit.

"Cover me for a bit, Jess," I said, watching him go.

"What are you up to, Ells?"

"Just a short break, that's all. I'll be on the patio. Text if you need me back inside."

She bumped her hip against mine as she passed. "Got it."

Twenty- and thirty-somethings packed the terrace, though Will was easy to find. He leaned against the building's brick structure with his arms crossed over his chest and his feet spread wide. I pushed my way through the sweating mob of drinking and dancing revelers, staying along the wall, but lost sight of him when someone pulled me into the mix. The guy who'd snatched my arm abruptly released me and stepped away, looking behind me.

Will was there. "Turn round, beautiful," he said close to my ear, so close. The warmth of his breath on my neck caused goose bumps. His words held no hint of intonation. It was a command.

I turned to meet his eyes.

He flashed his brows and rubbed his chin, a glimmer from one of the sun's last rays bouncing off his platinum Patek Philippe watch.

I ignored the odd fluttering in my stomach and waited.

He stepped closer to me, compelling me to put my back to the wall. One of his hands rested against the bricks near my head. His eyes never left mine.

"Who are you?" I asked.

"I told you my name."

"Yes, but why are you here, in Stonington?"

"Business. I have a job to do."

"Not at the pier?"

A smirk dominated his lips, his face. "No, not at the pier."

That assuming smile made him impossibly more handsome, and it almost unmade me.

I wiped my sweating palms on my hips. "Why did you introduce yourself to me, then just walk away?"

He shrugged but never broke eye contact. "I shouldn't have."

"Shouldn't have introduced yourself or shouldn't have walked away?"

"I shouldn't have done either."

"But you wanted to, so you did both. Have you followed me, Will?"

"Yes."

"Why? You're clearly not a shy man."

"You should talk to your sister about that. I'd rather she filled you in," he said.

"What does that mean? How do you know my sister?"

"I haven't met her."

"You're making no sense."

Another shrug. As he glanced at my mouth, his eyes grew possessive, and I became mesmerized. I wanted to reach up and drag my nails along his scruffy jawline. His scent overwhelmed me with notes of sandalwood and spicy toffee, sensual and earthy and sweet. I was certain he drank scotch.

He cocked his head and flashed a satisfied smile.

"Where can I find you?" I asked.

His smile dissolved, and his eyes burned deeper into mine. "Stop looking for me."

I matched his determined stare. "Stop following me."

"You don't need to look for me. I know where you are, Ellie. Talk to your sister. Give her my name. Tell her I'm here."

"What?" I whispered.

Neither of us moved. Was I breathing?

To dismiss me, he dropped his arm and stepped back. "It's getting dark. You should go inside."

My body submitted to his suggestion before my brain could catch it. I stopped and looked back after several steps. He was still there, watching me with his arms folded against his chest. Our eyes connected again, and I knew he'd be back.

When I reached the door, I glanced over my shoulder, but he was gone.

I spent the rest of my shift caught up inside my head, confused by what had happened on the patio. One thing was clear to me. I wanted to see Will again.

Jess gripped my shoulders, causing me to spill the beer in my hand. "Ellie, did you hear me? I have to go. The emergency department needs all surgical nursing staff at the hospital. There's been some kind of street fight on the north side of town. The police dispatched Josh to the scene. It's time to close anyway. You'll wait for Isobel?"

"Yes, go. I'll close out your receipts." I sent a quick text message to Isobel, asking if she knew Will Hastings and if she planned to meet me after closing, as she often did, but my sister never replied.

three

MY STREET AND HOME WERE QUIET AS USUAL WHEN I ARRIVED. I waved good-bye as I turned the key, unlocking the front door. Given the chaos around town, Josh had sent one of the rookies to drive me home. She gave a nod and accelerated. The patrol car sped down the street, heading north with its red and blue emergency lights engaged.

It was dark inside the house.

The usual aromatic bouquet from Gran's evening chamomile didn't greet me.

No one was there to witness my terror when I switched on the light in the foyer and found my sister and my grandmother lying on the floor, holding hands. A deep red pool beneath them widened.

They'd been shot.

Gran had already passed.

Isobel blinked her hazel eyes, horror marking her beautiful face. She tugged on a scrap of paper sticking out of her pocket until exhausting her strength, and her arm fell to the floor. Her fading whisper floated away with one last breath. "Find Lissie and get out now," she managed.

I shouted at her, disobeying her orders, as I always had,

demanding that she stay with me, and fell to my knees between my dead grandmother and dying sister, clutching their hands in mine.

Then, they were both gone.

A wail pushed hard at my lungs for release, but I wouldn't allow it. Stinging tears flooded my eyes. Pain-filled moments that felt like an eternity dragged on through my heart until Gran's old clock chimed eleven times, forcing me to dismiss it all. Fear for my life and for Lissie's took its place. I had to find her.

I grabbed the paper from my sister's jeans. Not a scrap at all, but a thick sheet, and when I unfolded it, Will Hastings's eyes stared back at me. Something senseless, something I couldn't rationalize that was neither right nor wrong, skipped through my mind and banged around inside my skull.

Isobel had taken my sketch. Beneath his picture, she'd written the name Ethan and some numbers. I put the drawing into my pocket and jumped up, causing myself to slip, righting myself, only to stumble and fall onto the round entryway table. I anchored there for a moment to catch my breath.

My mind reeled, sorting through frenzied thoughts, seeking answers, though there were none. One of those deliberations made sense. Only one. *Run.*

I rushed up the old Victorian staircase and called out for Lissie. Her bedroom was at the back of the house, and her door was already open. I pounded the side of my fist against the light switch. The room spun. I reached for the doorframe and pulled in a deep breath to fight the sickening rush of adrenaline.

"Lissie, are you here?" I called out again, but there was no reply, no sound at all.

After searching beneath the bed and in the closet, I hit the hallway and headed for Isobel's room. Lissie wasn't there either, and my room was just as empty. A sob pushed upward into the back of my throat. I ran down the hall to the last bedroom, to

Gran's room. There, I heard a thump against the wall. Everything in me froze. It came again—another soft thump against the far wall.

I sprinted across the room to the walk-in closet and heard my niece scream.

Lissie was crouched in the corner of the secret room at the back of the closet, her hands covering her head. She'd hidden in the place where Isobel and I had hosted tea parties with our dolls when we were children. The same little room in which we'd giggled about boys and sworn we'd seen the ghosts of our parents. I didn't know my sister had shown Lissie our hiding place, but I thanked God she had.

"Lissie, sweetheart," I whispered, lowered myself, peeling her hands away from her face so she could see me. She lunged like a wild animal, wrapping her arms tightly around my neck.

We were in danger. The best course of action would have been to get out of the house, but for several moments, I could do nothing more than hold the one person that I had left in the world.

Isobel's words meant something. She'd been clear that I should find her daughter and leave.

I listened carefully for sounds anomalous to the old house. Soft whistling from the air ducts, a dog barking in the distance.

"I need to call for help, then we'll leave, Lissie," I told her. "You stay here while I get a phone. Understand? Wait here for me. I won't leave this house without you. I promise."

I didn't want Lissie to see her mother's lifeless body. I didn't want it to be the last image of Isobel that she burned into her memory forever.

After hugging Lissie, I exited the secret room and dragged my fingers along the door casing inside the closet, searching for the key to Gran's storage trunk. I rummaged through the old wooden chest for the metal box that I had never imagined I might someday need.

Secured inside was a pretty little .25 caliber automatic pistol, a wedding gift to my mother from my father once upon a time. Pearl, named so for the grip, had a silver frame, embellished with floral engraving with natural patina. Gran had tried to give it to me a few times, but I'd refused her.

Isobel would have taken it.

"Why can't you listen for once?" Isobel had scolded after our grandmother tattled on me. "Take the gun. After you learn the basics, we'll get you something more useful. Do it, Ellie."

My sister had guns of her own, and she'd practiced each week at the local shooting range.

We'd celebrated her thirtieth birthday two weeks earlier.

I pushed the preloaded magazine into the gun, slid it ignorantly into the back of my shorts for lack of a better plan, and pulled the closet door shut, listening before entering the hallway. In Lissie's room, I stuffed a backpack with some of her things before hurrying to mine, where I grabbed my Stella McCartney bag, phone charger, and keys.

My smartphone was in the foyer. The one landline phone we'd maintained wasn't any closer, so I sidled down the wooden stair treads with my eyes focused on the wrought iron chandelier. I crawled past the ornate entry door. Vomit burned my throat. I forced it back down and reached out, fumbling around until I made contact with my phone. Once it was in my hand, I dropped my head for a moment and fought my body's overwhelming urge to give in.

I needed to get onto my feet, get us out of the house.

A floorboard creaked behind me. The sound of my thrashing heart flooded through my ears.

Someone was inside the house again. I'd screwed up. We shouldn't still be there.

"You shouldn't be here," an intruder's voice echoed.

four

THE INTRUDER PULLED THE GUN OUT OF MY WAISTBAND AND lifted me from the floor, covering my mouth with his hand so I couldn't scream, and carried me from the foyer into the living room.

My back was pressed tightly against his chest, and my wrists were restrained in one of his hands. The power surging through his body was undeniable. He refused to remove his hand from my mouth or allow me to face him, but I had known who it was the moment he first spoke.

"I'll let go if you assure me that you won't scream or run from me," he added.

That voice.

Will Hastings. *Ethan.*

"Be quiet and as calm as possible. All right?"

I didn't know if he was Will or Ethan, as my sister had written, a murderer or not, and I did want to run away from him. But I nodded in agreement to his terms instead.

God, I'd left Lissie alone.

I was alone.

My mind gave over to the shock, to the pain that I was trying to control, and my knees buckled.

Will caught me, lifting me into his arms, and I rested the side of my face against his chest to catch my breath. His steady heart thundered in my ear. I lifted my eyes, and his gaze burned into mine.

"The men who did this, they'll come back for you, Ellie. You must come with me. Say you'll walk out of this house with me now."

"I'm not sure I have another choice," I half-whispered.

"Good. That's good." He steadied me on my feet, cradling my face in his hands and meeting my eyes again with his. "I know you're confused, but understand that I'm here to protect you, not hurt you."

"So, you weren't part of this?"

This. The deaths of my sister and my grandmother.

"No, not this." Fierce, wild emotion stirred in his eyes, but it was tempered by a beautiful contrast of concern and honesty.

I'd misread him. This man was driven by an intense, protective instinct, not by menace.

"Lissie. She's still upstairs," I blurted out.

"What? There's someone else in the house?"

"My niece is upstairs. She can't see this. Please, she's just a little girl."

"We'll get her out." He released me, nodding toward the staircase. "Go to her."

I grabbed my bags from the floor and hooked them on my shoulder as we headed up to get Lissie from Gran's closet. The tired staircase groaned under Will's weight as we climbed.

He spoke into a communication device that I couldn't see, "Move the car to the front. Be ready to roll. I need cover in here. There's another survivor."

When we reached Lissie, she curled into a ball with her hands covering her head again. I squatted to pull her into me, but she resisted.

"It's time for us to go, sweetheart, Lissie," I whispered to her.

But she wouldn't come to me.

"There's no time. Move aside," Will said.

I searched his eyes for reassurance and then stepped aside.

He lifted Lissie with a firm gentleness, and after she curled back into her fetal ball, he shifted her into one arm. My niece was smaller than average for her seven years, and she looked like an infant against his broad chest. She whimpered when we covered her with a blanket and pushed out her hand, seeking mine.

Will's other hand covered the small of my back. "Stay close to me, Ellie."

A large man with a buzz cut arrived at the bottom of the stairs with a pistol drawn.

I stiffened as my heart gave up another second of my life.

Will nudged me forward. "It's all right. Ben is with me."

As we descended, I concentrated on Ben's appearance to keep from looking at the sight of my family. Black hair. A thick, oblique scar slashed across his forehead, and he was dressed like a soldier, wearing a black T-shirt, military trousers, and combat boots.

The two men flanked me, shielding me with their bodies as they moved us from the house to the dark SUV waiting in the otherwise empty street. Will opened the door and pushed me into the back, slid Lissie onto the seat next to me, and climbed in.

"Drive north, get us out of town, and take the southbound motorway. Move," he said, cuffing the driver on the shoulder.

I pulled Lissie onto my lap and held her against my chest as she cried for Isobel. Once the car was moving, I closed my eyes and battled for control of my own emotions.

"You'll be safe for a short time at your beach house," Will said.

I nodded. It was exactly where I would have gone anyway. I had no one left, nowhere else to go.

We rode in deafening silence until reaching the main highway, though I could feel his eyes on me, watching as I fought to keep myself together, as if he were waiting for me to break.

Finally, he spoke, "I'll keep you safe, Ellie. Both of you."

I turned away and fixed my gaze on the blurred passing terrain outside the window. One word was all it would take. One word, or maybe the right combination of two or three words, escaping my mouth, and I would fall apart.

Will slid across the seat, narrowing the gap between us, and placed his hand on the back of my head. "Look at me," he ordered.

I turned to meet his eyes, but neither of us said anything. I dropped mine then and swallowed against the thickness in my throat. The pressure of his hand remained as he lowered it to the nape of my neck. When I lifted my eyes, his were still there, waiting for mine to come back.

"You have my word that I'll protect you," he said in a softer tone.

Avoiding his words and the reason for them, I offered something that wouldn't break me. "Who's Ethan?"

"He's my brother." Will let his hand drop. The strength it had provided went with it.

"Did he know my sister?"

"Yes, quite well. They met in London."

Isobel had spent an entire summer in London eight years earlier.

I dug beneath Lissie to get the sketch from my pocket and held it so he could see only the name and numbers Isobel had written. "Is this his phone number?"

"It is."

"None of this makes sense." The first of my tears fell, and more followed in an unbroken stream.

Tears like that came only with trust. I trusted him, as crazy as it was. Isobel had ties, and I'd always had blind faith in her. In an unguarded, vulnerable moment, I'd transferred that to him, I thought. What would I do without her?

I choked on the silent panic strangling me.

The back of Will's fingers lingered near my cheek before he lowered his hand again. "When you're safe, we'll talk. I'll explain everything, fill in the pieces you seem to be missing."

I wiped at the tears, tilting my head toward the driver. "Who's this?"

"John, my youngest brother."

"How many brothers do you have?"

"There're four of us. John is seventeen. Thomas is twenty-eight. Ethan's thirty-four."

"And you?" I asked.

"Thirty-two."

John peered into the rearview mirror and revealed eyes almost identical to Will's. The difference was John's youthful innocence. My breath caught for a moment, and my gape was drawn to the little girl on my lap. I looked back at the mirror, comparing his eyes to hers. I'd been staring at the same eyes on my niece since her birth.

Will watched me. He shifted his weight. "How old is she?" he asked.

I studied his pale blue eyes and made the same comparison. "She was seven in April."

He turned and cursed under his breath. When he came back to me, he found a single tear clinging to my cheek and wiped it away with his thumb.

His touch unleashed new tears, and as the watery pain streaked down my face, something more crushing struck me. I was responsible for Lissie, her life, but I had no idea how to be that person for her.

"What's going to happen? To our family, I mean?" I asked.

"They'll be held at the medical examiner's office while police look for you. Ben will go back to make certain authorities have found them." He tucked his forefinger under my chin and pulled me close as he leaned in with his chest. "Hey, I won't leave you alone in this."

Though it was fleeting, relief washed over me.

Moments later, we pulled up in front of my seaside second home, to my safe place. To the haven where I always ran when something in my world failed, when I was broken.

But this time, I wasn't alone.

five

THE EDGE OF THE SEA REACHED UP TO SOOTHE ME, CLEANSING the dried blood from my knees. My mind drifted above its body, above mine, lost in heartache.

I stood in the water with my arms outstretched and my eyes clenched shut, inhaling the brackish gusts of air as they whipped my hair about. Breaking waves rolled in and pushed me back as if to save me.

"How do I get through this?" I whispered into the briny depths.

Will stood nearby. He'd refused to let me out of his sight, refused to allow me beyond arm's reach. He'd tried to convince me to stay inside, but I'd needed to feel the sea.

Two hundred feet behind us were several vacation homes, nestled high among boulders and stones. At the foot of the hill, sea oats grew tall along weatherworn fencing. The houses had white cedar shake siding, as was traditional for Lords Point, but each had varying patterns of gray and brown, caused by winter beatings.

"We should go inside and talk while Lissie is sleeping. There's something you should have been told a long time ago," Will said.

The moment I stepped out of the water, his hand was low on my back, guiding me up the rocky hill path. His touch was warm and strong, filled with energy, similar to the summer storm about to hit the beach. His presence was powerful. It tugged at me, drawing me to him.

Inside, Will leaned forward from his position on the edge of the sofa and raked his long fingers through his hair as he stared at me. "You noticed the cross of St. George?"

I sat at the opposite end with my legs pulled up and the side of my face resting against the soft back cushion. "Yes." I would never forget the sight. In blood, a cross drawn on the wood floor.

"It's a signature, a calling card."

I lifted my head and swallowed a ragged breath. "You know who did this?"

"What do you know of your lineage?"

"What? My sister was murdered, and you want to discuss my lineage?"

He raised a brow and waited.

"I know my grandparents were English. My grandfather's parents settled here before the turn of the twentieth century."

"Tell me about your parents," he said.

I shrugged. I never knew my parents. "There was an accident. I was two. They'd taken a trip abroad without Isobel and me. The plane went down. My grandmother raised us."

"I'm sorry for that, for the losses you've suffered. You're English as well. Raised here, but your bloodline is pure. What do you know about your surname?"

"It's a damn name," I snapped. "What's there to know? Look, it's pretty clear I'm uninformed where my family tree is concerned, so if you know something that will help, please just tell me."

His eyes shifted to the floor, and he shook his head, cursing under his breath, as he had in the car. It was his thing, raking his hair and cursing beneath his breath. I couldn't help but get caught up in it.

When I realized he was watching me stare at him, it jolted me from my head, and I snapped at him again, "What does this have to do with what happened tonight?"

Will took my hand, his attempt at patience. A deep breath through his nose. An exhale. "Christ, did they tell you anything at all?"

I watched his every move, studied him, waiting for him to say something more. His moods shifted fast and without warning.

Another call on my smartphone from Josh went to voice mail.

"This will sound mad, but I give you my word it's the truth." He locked on to my eyes with his. "Fuck."

"Just say it," I demanded.

"Your family name was changed at some point, and the bloodline has been hunted for generations."

"What? What do you mean, *hunted?*"

"An order of British assassins believes your family could be a threat to the Crown." He went on after assessing my silent, emotional deliberations. "Our families made a pact that's been in play for a very long time. Mine was contracted to defend yours."

I pulled my hand away. Was he joking? What he'd said was insane, even as he'd said it with absolute conviction. "You're right. It sounds ridiculous, like a story by the Brothers Grimm, but go on."

"My job is to keep you alive."

And he'd done that.

"So, I guess you'll be leaving now."

"I won't be going anywhere without you." Sharp words. He meant it.

"You're telling me that my life has been a lie—some tragic, untold fairy tale—and Prince Charming has at last been dispatched to rescue me. What do you expect me to do with that?"

"Never confuse me with the good guy. I'm not some fucking prince, and this has nothing to do with fantasy." He paused. The same hand he'd held mine with was now clenched. "Don't doubt my word when I give it." His anger was palpable. He'd absorbed mine and made it his.

I had an impulsive urge to soothe him. Touching the inside of his wrist, I encouraged him to open his fist, and when he did, I slipped my hand back into his. "Suppose I believe. Why is this important? Does the Crown even hold power in the present?"

"Most don't realize the Crown quietly makes countless moves by way of royal prerogative. But it doesn't matter in this case. They aren't behind this." His thumb caressed the bright blue veins on the inside of my wrist. "Jesus, you're delicate."

I narrowed my eyes.

"The heir is seen as a self-indulgent arse. The prince's outspoken positions are quite unpopular. Public mood could become unstable when he inherits. That's the driving force behind the Order's current objective."

"To be clear, that objective is preservation of the prince's position."

"Yes. Elimination of any threats."

"Political complicity. I get that. It's everywhere. But an order of assassins that executes families—" I swallowed hard— "my family? It feels Shakespearean, medieval."

Will nodded. "American culture is in its infancy compared to most civilizations, and most Americans know nothing about their heritage or its history."

The remark might have offended others, but he was right. I'd studied art history for six years before earning my master's, and ancient European cultures were esoteric. "How far back does this conflict go?"

He hesitated in thought, something dark filling his eyes.

"Tell me everything, Will." I touched his forearm and dragged my fingers to his palm.

He stiffened, his gaze now locked on my hand. "I believe the first group of assassins emerged after the death of Queen Anne."

"So, this Order has survived centuries—"

"It doesn't survive," he interrupted. "It reforms. There's quite a difference."

"This reformation," I corrected, "wants to make certain the prince inherits, feels just in safeguarding his accession even though public opinion is low. There's worry about a referendum or maybe another heir coming forward. Got it. But why would my family be a threat? Please, I need to know."

"You do." His fingers curled onto mine. "Your father was the last successor of patrilineal descent to Edward IV."

"Patrilineal descent?" I stretched my brain to recall the significance of Edward's reign. It had been eclipsed by the Cousins' War. York versus Lancaster and then the Tudors, I thought. "But none of his sons survived."

"One survived. Your English history lessons here in America are wrong."

"Well then, I'm sure many descendants still live."

"None like you, Ellie. You're a direct descendant of the last pure, successive line."

"And I guess because my father had no sons, that makes me the end of the line."

"Yes, in the eyes of the Order, when you're gone, it's over."

"This is insane," I said, denying it all. "And by the way, that presumption is archaic and sexist."

The corners of his mouth twitched as if he were amused. "You asked for the truth."

"My sister, she died for this?" I asked, the last three words fading to a whisper. The image of Isobel and our grandmother lying on the floor filled my head, and I winced with pain.

"I won't allow it to happen to you."

“This can’t be right.” I shook my pounding head, holding it between my hands, pushing away the gruesome image.

Will’s hand went to my arm, his touch soft and hesitant as he tested my reaction. “I’m here.”

I don’t know what to do. I don’t know what to say. I don’t know where to go.

That was what I wanted to tell him, but the sob that had been trapped in my chest broke free, releasing my heartache. I closed my eyes. Tears raced down my cheeks. I trembled.

My family was gone.

He gathered me onto his lap, pressing the side of my face to his chest. “I’m here now. I’ll never leave you again,” he said, purring the words against my hair.

six

I PADDED ACROSS THE WOOD FLOOR AND SLID OPEN THE WHITE draperies across the French doors. Golden beams of sunlight radiated through the east-facing panes of glass. My throbbing head tortured me, allowing thoughts and images from the day before to collide into one another as they whirled around inside my mind.

Ben was on the other side of the glass on the veranda, standing guard. He raised one hand in greeting and gave a nod. I stared stupidly before opening a door to step outside next to him.

"Where is Will? I need to see him."

Both of Ben's hands were on an impressive-looking rifle strapped to his shoulder. His muscled body seemed tense. "He'll be back soon. Please stay inside until he returns." When I nodded in agreement, his face and his shoulders relaxed.

"Why don't you sit down? There's no need to stand," I said.

He shook his head, pulled his phone out of his pocket, and removed his dark sunglasses to read a text message. His eyes scrunched, and a smile lifted his entire face, causing the scar on his forehead to pucker. I turned to go inside, but he stopped me. "Hold on." Extending his phone, he revealed a picture.

"She's beautiful. What's her name?"

"Chelsea."

"Well, Chelsea is just gorgeous. You must miss her. She's your daughter?"

"She is. I miss her quite a lot. She's three." He looked down at his boots and forced his feelings to retreat.

His empty mug was sitting on the side table.

"More coffee?" I asked. If I pumped him with caffeine, maybe he'd talk. I wanted to know more about everything, more about Will.

He nodded. "Yes, thank you."

"I'll be right back."

I went inside and pulled the curtains back across the doors for privacy. Lissie was still sleeping. It was close to seven, but she was used to sleeping until nine or later during the summer months. I brushed my teeth and changed out of the dirty clothes I'd slept in.

John was in the kitchen, and a handgun was on the counter in front of him. His broad shoulders, his eyes, his dark blond hair all made him look so much like Will, though he stood only about five-eleven.

"Ellie," he said by way of greeting before stuffing his mouth with sausage.

Finding him in my kitchen surprised me, and for some reason, it also warmed my heart.

"Where's Will?"

"Taking care of a few things. He thought he'd get back before you woke." He smiled then. It was so handsome, warm, fraternal. "You're safe. We're not leaving you and Lissie."

I composed a meager smile. He was kind and deserved more than that. I touched his shoulder in thanks, then busied myself, making coffee. It was my morning essential, always. A fresh pour over, hot and strong.

Determined to continue my conversation with Ben, I headed back to the veranda with fresh coffee and cups in hand.

"When did the three of you arrive in Stonington?" I asked, handing him both cups, filling them. "I should have asked if you wanted sugar or cream."

He gave a cup back and immediately drew a sip from his. "I take it black. Thanks again. Will came over in May. Ethan sent John and me round the beginning of July to bring him back."

"Yet a month has passed, and you're all still here."

He shrugged his free shoulder, the other still supporting a rifle. "An army couldn't move him."

"How does this work for you guys?" I sat and invited him to do the same.

He remained on his feet, nailing me with his dark eyes by pulling his sunglasses down just enough. "It's not my place to have this conversation with you. You need to wait for Will."

"Is he going to?"

I'd been lied to by my family, not trusted with my own truth. They had left me. He was gone after promising not to leave me alone.

"Yeah, he will. Just give him a minute," Ben said.

We stared out to the sea and drank our coffee. A gull's raucous call filled the air as it swooped down to pluck a dead fish from the seaweed that had been washed ashore by the storm the night before. The smell of decaying algae came in with the breeze. I wrinkled my nose.

"Look, Ellie. I can't give you his story, only mine. Our fathers were close, as we are now. I manage security operations for his family."

But before I had an opportunity to explore Ben's remarks, John came through the door.

"Mate, there's a policeman in the drive," he said.

"Get back inside and guard Lissie's room," Ben told him. "Ellie, you must get the door, but don't allow him in. I'll stay close, but don't give me away. We can't allow the police to know we're here with you."

"What if I don't get the door?"

"If you don't, then the police will get a warrant to come inside. Do it now, damn it."

"Okay," I snapped.

Ben stayed close on my heels as I went to the front door. He rotated his rifle so that it rested on his back and drew a pistol from his belt, hiding just out of view with his gun sighted on the policeman.

I swallowed and opened the door.

After flashing his badge and identification, Detective Parker apologized for the early hour and told me that he'd recently transferred to Stonington from Mystic's police department. One of his hands gripped the doorframe, and the other was pushed down into his trouser pocket, jangling keys or coins or something metal.

"Of course, you're new," I said. "I don't remember seeing you at Nick's."

He squinted.

"You know, Nick's Restaurant, the force's favorite burgers? We see the entire department once or twice a week. I've worked there for years."

"Yes, that's right. I mean to stop in soon." His eyes shifted to see beyond the open door.

Confused now, I stared at Parker and waited for him to speak again. He hadn't stated the reason for his visit, and considering the circumstances, I found it unsettling that he hadn't yet mentioned my family. Where was his damn compassion?

"Would it be all right if I came in, Miss James?"

"Can you tell me anything at all about my family? Should I come to the station?"

"Are you alone?" he asked, his question the one, the only one, that could break me.

"Yes, I'm alone."

He again jangled whatever he carried in his pocket. "No need to come to the station yet. In fact, if you plan to come back from the beach, call me first. We'll see that it's safe." The detective handed me a Stonington Police Department business card with his number handwritten on it. "Maybe you need to see to some arrangements. I can escort you."

"That's very generous, but I'd rather have you focused on the investigation."

"We're doing all we can, Miss James." The detective stared behind me again.

"If there's nothing else for now, I'd like to rest."

"Of course. You have my number." Parker extended his hand, and I gave him mine. His grip was uncomfortable, meant to intimidate me. "A word of advice: don't go too far."

I closed the door and watched Ben put away his pistol. A stinging sensation gnawed at the pit of my stomach. And I knew. If they didn't already, the police would soon consider me a suspect.

seven

Lissie peeked into the shower. "Aunt Ellie, I'm hungry." Then, she sat on the toilet seat lid and waited for me to finish. I'd seen her sit in the bathroom with Isobel that way hundreds of times.

"Okay, sweet girl, I'm almost done, then we'll have breakfast. Wait for me. Don't leave the bedroom without me. How are you feeling?"

"I don't know. I wanna cry."

"It's okay to cry." I quickly rinsed out my hair. "It's okay to be sad. I'm sad too. You do know that, right?"

"Are those guys still here?" she asked, skating over my failed attempt to talk about her feelings.

"Yes. Do you remember their names?"

"Will."

"Will, yes. Ben is the one with dark hair. John is the youngest, who looks like Will."

"Are they good guys? Like superheroes?"

I pulled back the shower curtain and slipped into my bathrobe. "Well, not exactly, but they are here to help us." I took hold of her chin, thumbing the little dimple there, and placed a kiss on her forehead. "I know you're sad and scared. Me too. I don't have answers yet, but I promise I'll figure this out. For now, I think we're safer if they stay. I'll never leave you, Lissie. I love you."

It was the first time those last three words had ever left my lips in that order.

I knew nothing about being a mother, and I couldn't have been more unprepared to be her guardian. Isobel had once told me you needed only to know love to be a parent.

"That counts me out," I'd said, confessing to never having loved anyone other than her and our gran. And that had never been close, affectionate love.

Maybe it was my fault. Maybe my heart didn't know how to love because I never gave it a chance, choosing to paint my view of life within the boundaries of my mind rather than live it. I'd been raised without parents by a preoccupied English grandmother. Perhaps it was their fault for abandoning me. Could be that I was just a cold bitch and didn't have it in me.

I closed my eyes and shook my head to clear it all away. "Let's get you something to eat now." I had to smile when she looked up at me with those beautiful eyes.

Inside of thirty minutes, I'd scrambled some eggs, and Lissie had finished them. But as we were about to leave the kitchen, she broke into tears. She was a child abandoned, left with nothing more than pain and the idea of solitude, and that was something I understood well.

"Mama's never coming back ... she's never coming back ... my mama," Lissie cried, her words disjointed, heartbreak wrecking her. It was the worst thing I'd ever seen.

I dropped onto my knees and held her as tightly as I could.

God, tell me what to do. Please help me help her.

Her sobs eventually slowed to soft weeping.

Will walked in as I used a kitchen towel to dry the last of Lissie's tears. His jaw dropped and his eyes widened when she turned to him and fixed her puffy gaze on his. They stared at each other—with eyes the same.

When she turned back to me, her eyes revealed the same striking intensity as his. I wanted to ask what she'd found in his, wanted to know what it felt like for her. Did she recognize a small piece of herself? Instead, I hid my surprise behind a reticent smile. "I have art supplies in my closet. Go to my room, choose your favorite colors from the shelf, and wait for me. I'll be there soon."

She stared at Will as she skipped from the kitchen, resilient and cheerful once again.

"Are you all right, Ellie?"

I nodded but avoided his eyes. I'd fallen apart on him the night before.

He came around the center island. "You're sure?" The tenderness in his voice was soothing. I shut my eyes to absorb it. "Hey." He lifted my chin to force eye contact, likely expecting more tears. There were none.

"Ben told you about Detective Parker?" I asked.

"He did. And you're all right?"

"I'm fine. He thinks I had something to do with it."

"Did he accuse you?"

"It's the way he looked at me."

"I'll check into it. He hasn't reported your location yet. When he does, police will be all over this place, so stay close to me. I'll handle the authorities. Local media hasn't taken an interest yet either, and I want it to stay that way until we're gone. I have someone conducting surveillance in town, but still, we can't stay here long. You understand, right? I need you to trust me."

I studied his eyes as they studied mine. I didn't know what to say. Where could I go? Pain, confusion, and loneliness haunted me, but when he was close, when he touched me, my mind rested. I would stay close to him. And I would trust him. So, I nodded.

"Lissie's beautiful," Will said.

"Her eyes. She looks a lot like—"

"Ethan," he finished. "I don't believe my brother would bail on his own child." He shook his head. "Not if he knew she was his. Let's keep this between us for now. I need to talk to him before we assume anything further."

GOOSE BUMPS RAN UP MY ARMS AS I SAT OUTSIDE ON THE BEACH with Will, even as the rays of sunshine heated my skin. Will's spice mingled with the seaside scents and drifted on the ocean breeze, whirling around me. We watched Lissie sort through her collection of shells and stones and color them with her paints.

"How long have you been here, Will?" I wanted to hear it from him.

"Since round the first of May."

"To watch us."

"You," he corrected, straightening his back, meeting my eyes. "I've been here before. You've seen me."

"What do you mean?"

"You deserve the truth, Elle."

"When?"

"The first time, there was no imminent danger. You were seventeen. My father had forbidden it, but I needed to see for myself that you were real, that the training had purpose. He reminded me often that I was meant to protect you. The whole thing, the pact between our families, the reason behind it, it all seemed mad to me then, as it does for you now."

Sincerity burned in his eyes, and his words captivated me.

I wanted more, so I encouraged him. "Go on. Tell me, Will."

"You were walking along Water Street, laughing and eating

ice cream with some friends. There was a celebration, the town was crowded. You were shoved, and I caught you." He moved his stare to the horizon. His eyes appeared unfocused, and his lips curved with a self-indulgent smile. "You looked up at me and apologized. I could never forget those green eyes."

A sharp breath caught in my throat. I remembered.

When he looked at me again, the smile was gone. "Four years after that, I looked in again. It was impulsive, ego-driven that time. I beat a man for following you across your university campus."

"You did that," I whispered.

His eyes charged with emotion. "You should know, if you hadn't turned back, he would be dead."

The guy had threatened to find me later because I'd refused him at a house party. Jess and I had found him later, brutally beaten, and called campus police.

"How long did you stay?"

"Six or seven days. Ethan and I had recently executed the partnership agreement for our private equity company. It was a critical time for me to be present." Will stood and offered his hand. "Back inside. It's getting late."

IN MY ROOM, AFTER I CHECKED ON LISSIE ONCE MORE FOR THE night, I could only stare at my bed. Going near it would be to fall into a dark, isolated hole with no way out, a feeling that had begun to haunt me during my last year at college.

Panic slunk around my neck, suffocating me. I put out a hand, reaching for the wall, the doorframe, anything. I needed fresh air, the sea, something to make it go away.

Will appeared on the other side of the glass-paned doors, as though he were responding to my silent plea. He opened one and extended his hand, waiting without a word to see if his offer would be accepted. It was. I did. I placed my hand into his. He led me to the double-wide chaise, where he gestured with his head for me to sit, and handed me an opened bottle of red wine.

I wriggled into an awkward position on the edge. "Thanks. Staying inside can be challenging."

"Unless you're with me, you must not come outside."

"I know." I tipped the wine bottle, sipping politely at first, then gulped until I had to let up for air.

When I offered him the next drink, the corners of his mouth twitched. He took a swig and returned it to me, then watched me pull deep from the bottle a few more times. I sank into the downy cushions with a light head. His lips curved into a full, crooked smile as he grabbed a throw blanket from one of the other chairs and covered me.

I was tipsy, liquid courage flowing through me, so with a flirty smile, I offered the wine bottle but without extending my arm. It was an invitation. I needed the peace his closeness provided. With a brow raised, he accepted, placing the bottle on the table before he dropped into the cushions next to me. He lifted his arm, and without hesitation, I rolled into his side and placed my head on his chest.

"Go to sleep," he commanded.

Settled against the warmth of Will's body, I did sleep for a few hours in the cool night air. No doubt, the rolling and crashing of waves had been a lullaby, but he'd been my anchor.

I woke before him and stared at his rugged, beautiful face. Golden stubble highlighted his jawline, and long lashes touched his cheekbones. I remembered the younger Will Hastings who I'd bumped into ten years earlier. His hair had been lighter and his face clean-shaven, but the same charged eyes had held mine. He'd been well-built even then and stood at the same imposing height. My strawberry ice cream had dotted his black T-shirt.

He stirred, twisting from his back to his side, pulling me against the front of his body. I could feel that he was aroused. As he shifted his weight and settled, the chaise's wood frame creaked in complaint.

"Will?"

"Yeah?" He opened his eyes and stared back at me.

"Tell me what's going to happen. I don't know what to do."

"Let me take you back to England. I have unmatched resources there to keep you safe."

"What? But my life is here. I don't know how to live anywhere else, without the beach, my work with the kids and at the gallery, my friends." I winced. None of it mattered without my family.

Will tightened his embrace and waited, aware that I was pushing away my grief.

"You must have a life of your own that you'd like to get back to," I said.

He lifted his head and snapped, "Your protection is my priority. I'll be with you or near you—"

"For how long? When will this end, Will?"

He shrugged. "It might never end."

"That's insane."

"It's who we are. We're bound together by this shit, Elle, and neither one of us can change it. I understand you haven't had quite enough time to come to terms with it, but I'm warning you all the same—if you run, I'll follow. If you stay here, I'll fucking stay. Assassins will come again, here or there—your location makes no difference. England provides me with advantages. You and Lissie will be safest at Eastridge."

"That's a lot to take in," I whispered. "What is Eastridge?"

Will softened his tone. "It's the name of the house."

"How long will you give me to consider it?"

"There isn't much time."

Time. I closed my eyes, one syllable echoing in my head. I was overwhelmed by the thought of anything beyond the moment we were in. The future was more than I wanted to consider. I wanted only to lie there with Will near the sea, soothed and protected.

"What's this?" His fingertip traced the white butterfly-shaped birthmark on my neck.

My eyes flew open. His touch was rousing and unexpected. "It's a butterfly. I mean, the silhouette is, but it's a birthmark."

He traced it several times, sending shivers along my spine. "It's not a butterfly," he said, guiding his long finger away from my birthmark, over my cheek, to my bottom lip. His eyes met mine, and then he moved his fingertip, replacing it with a warm, soft kiss.

It was easy to let go, to allow myself to melt into his body. He already held me in his arms. I touched his cheek. "Do it again, Will."

But he didn't kiss me again. He threw his legs over the side of the chaise with a hoarse curse and gave me his back. "Get inside and stay there."

"What? No." I was confused, defiant.

He lowered his head into his hands. "Go."

I stood, folded the blanket, dropped the wine bottle into the recycle bin, and then went back inside, where I stared at my bed once again.

The door was still open. *Let him close it*, I thought.

We both knew he was planning to lock it anyway.

eight

On the next morning, Will came back from an exhausting shoreline run and kept his back to me as he crouched with his elbows against his thighs to catch his breath. I watched the muscles in his back expand and contract and his shoulders rise and fall, and for whatever reason, it was the catalyst that caused my anger to progress.

I needed either a good fight or maybe to be taken hard in bed. He'd made it clear that he wasn't even going to kiss me again, so a fight he would get. "Where's my gun?"

His head snapped in my direction. "I'll manage the weapons."

I narrowed my eyes. "It's mine, and I want it back."

Rising to his full height, he turned and stood with his feet wide and his arms folded over his chest. "Do you know how to use it?"

"How hard can it be?"

He darted onto the veranda and hovered over me like a storm. "You will not carry a gun. You'll not touch one or even look at one unless you have learned to use it properly. When you're quite finished behaving like a fucking brat, we'll talk about what happens next."

"Me? You're the big bastard."

"Fucking brat," he repeated.

He was sweating, and, God, his spiced, scorching heat turned me on. Recognizing the distraction, I stifled a moan and vowed to fight harder.

"Your move." He cocked his head.

I considered slapping the smug expression off his face.

He shook his head in warning before jerking me to his chest and resting his cheek on top of my head. "I know you're scared and grieving. Let me bear the weight of this burden. You don't need to worry about protection detail. I won't let anyone hurt you."

I clutched his sweat-soaked shirt in both hands. I thought I should cry, but tears would not fall. I couldn't feel sorrow or pain, not as I had a few nights before, not at that moment when I was in his arms.

"I know you're worried for Lissie, but she'll be fine. You are my concern."

"Fine?" I glanced inside, beyond the glass doors, where she lounged on my bed with her tablet.

"When she's discovered, it won't be an issue. Her lineage is completely matrilineal."

My fingers still clutched his shirt, and his arms still held me. I lay my head against his chest, thinking. "Do you really believe it?"

"I do. We'll be cautious to be sure."

"I could never risk her precious life," I said.

IT WAS UNUSUALLY WARM THAT EVENING, THOUGH THE SUN HAD set hours before, but the cooling sea breeze was enough to balance the heat.

Lissie was sleeping when I approached Will from behind the

chair in which he sat and whispered near his ear, "Take me down to the beach." Then, I breathed, "Please."

He surprised me, taking my hand, leading me through the kitchen and down the rocky hill path to the beach without an objection, telling me, "Just stay close to me, Elle."

Elle, not Ellie. The intimate version of my name that he used, the one he shared with no one.

As we walked along the shoreline, I could tell something troubled his mind.

"Has something happened, Will? Tell me," I said.

"Listen, it would be easier if you chose to leave with me for England, but goddamn it, we're running out of time. It's wrong for me to gamble with your life, to comfort you. You have forty-eight hours to settle on the idea. Then, we're leaving."

"Oh." I set the matter aside with that.

I was still thinking about what needed to be done, and what was best for Lissie. His words were a decree anyway, not an attempt at conversation.

We'd gone far enough from the beach house, so we stopped and sat at the water's edge for a while. Some moments we filled with relaxed exchanges, some with a contented silence.

I leaned back on my elbows and lifted my face to the moon. The tide swept over my legs.

"You should roll up your pant legs, Will. The water feels amazing."

He'd already taken off his T-shirt.

I couldn't stop looking, imagining how it would feel to drag my fingertips over his skin.

Will's sculpted body seduced my creativity on more than one level. His chest stretched wide into a smooth canvas, beautifully flawed by two scars. The longest slashed about four inches in length across his right pectoral muscle. The other was smaller and higher, on the left side.

The tattoo on his right shoulder was striking. A medieval-style shield, blooming roses, a heraldic lion, and the Latin word *defensor*. The ink was dark, no color, but nevertheless, it was beautiful artwork.

When I moved my eyes back to his, I realized he'd been watching me inspect his body. I smiled at him. "Even defenders need to have a little fun now and then, right?" Leaning forward, I slipped my hand into the water and splashed him.

He wiped the drops from his cheek and grinned. And winked. "Careful, woman. I'm not quite sure you'll like my brand of fun." It was the first time he'd allowed me to see how light-hearted and charming he could be.

I wanted more of that Will.

As he rolled up his jeans, I splashed him again. But instead of extending his legs into the water with mine or retaliating with a splash, he got to his feet and pulled me up with him. The wide grin returned to his face, and he held my arms as his eyes moved out over the water.

"You wouldn't dare!" I pulled back, laughing, but his grip was firm. I shrieked as he swept me up into his arms and stepped into the sea.

He kept walking, grinning, walking. "I would."

"Will," I shouted through my laughter, beating on his chest with my fist.

He put me down in water that reached the hem of my shorts. His jeans were soaked above the knee. I stepped back and found a shallow spot, where I kicked water up at him. Lunging, he swept me back up again and headed toward a large, rolling wave.

"Okay, go back! You win!"

Moving in close to the beach, beating that wave, he let me slide down the front of his body, his hands gripping my waist. "I always win, Elle. That's something you should never forget."

I didn't want him to let go of me, not ever.

"We'll see," I told him.

Gentle, tumbling waves struck my knees. He watched my

eyes as they followed my fingers while I dragged them over the scars on his chest, along the curves of his biceps. I couldn't stop touching him, tracing the ink on his shoulder, caressing the length of his neck.

"Kiss me, Will."

The hunger was there, burning in his eyes as he leaned in and erased the distance between us. He wanted the kiss as much as I did. He stopped close to my lips, so close. "You're exposed out here, and I need to remain focused." His breath touched my skin.

"So then, kiss me inside."

He led me out of the water and let go.

Will found ways to touch me, to put his arms around me, making it part of his job to console me. But when he stretched the justification as far as he could, he pulled back and punished us both. He denied his desire for me, though we both felt its constant pull.

I was ready to push him. "Why do you pull away?"

He stilled, his mouth open but no words forming.

"Save all of me. Kiss me."

Glints of moonlight played in his eyes as he stared at me. "You believe I'm one of the good guys that you belong with. You're mistaken. I'm not that, not heroic. I destroy lives. I take what I want, and others are ruined in the process."

He takes what he wants. He doesn't want me. The words were wrong, twisting around in my head, but I couldn't shut them out. I eyed the sand and tightened my arms around the middle of my abdomen.

"Look at me, Elle," he said, coming close, leaning in over me.

I moved my gaze up to his.

"Ask me how many lives I've taken. I won't hesitate to do it again whenever I need to. How many lives do you think I've damaged with my business transactions? Ask me."

"I won't ask. I don't care," I said.

He grasped my chin between his forefinger and his thumb. "Well, you should care." His fiery eyes burned into mine.

"I don't."

"You're quite determined."

"Yes."

His lips parted as he stared at mine. "I hurt people, Elle. But you can rest, knowing that I'll never hurt you. Not you, not ever." He ran his thumb over my bottom lip.

"It's your duty to keep me alive and unharmed."

"It is."

I pushed his hand away. He'd taken something from me, and I planned to take it back. "Like you said, we're bound in a way that can't be undone, not until one of us is dead. So, what difference does any of that make? Only one thing matters, and that's how you see me. If you see me as an obligation and I'm so undesirable to you, then it makes sense for you to keep your distance. Because after all, you take what you do want."

"What? You don't know what you're saying." Will raked a hand through his hair. He cursed and paced on the sand in a wide circle around me, calming himself. "I don't want to hurt you. I can't let that happen."

It would've been easier to walk away and let him have his win, easier to guard my heart against the danger of more wreckage. But it was too late. My heart had already invested in him, and it wanted to know him. I needed to know him. I eliminated the remaining space between us.

Will retreated, and I advanced. Again. When he accepted my resolve, he stopped, and I rested my hands against his abs. He glared at me, his eyes mirroring my own determination.

"Tell me, Will. How do you believe you'll hurt me?" I met his stare from beneath my lashes.

His eyes narrowed. "What are you doing?"

I shrugged. "You'll hit me?"

"I'd never hit you." He clenched his teeth and flexed the muscles along his jaw.

"How then? How would you hurt me?"

"Stop this."

"I'm not finished. So, emotionally, you'll—"

"You deserve better than what I am," he snapped.

There it was. The choice he'd taken from me. My decisions were mine. All of them. I wouldn't allow anyone to take that away from me.

"But do you want me?"

"I think you know the answer to that."

I pressed myself against his rigid body. I stroked the back of his neck and played with the ends of his hair. His body responded, his eyes burning and his arousal straining between us. His arms remained at his sides, but his hands were no longer in fists. He'd lowered his head during my attempted interrogation. His mouth was near mine.

"Elle, pushing me this way is reckless."

His rumbling voice, the gravel, it made me ache. I wanted to kiss him, wanted his hands on me, and I longed to touch his face, but I did nothing.

Instead, I reproached him in a soft manner, my lips close to his, "Reckless or not, here's the thing. I decide the level of emotional risk I'm willing to assume. You manage the physical risk for now. I've accepted that. But everything else is still mine."

I launched myself off his chest with both hands and walked away. "I decide what I deserve," I shouted over my shoulder, heading down the beach.

"That's far enough, goddamn it," he shouted at my back.

I looked behind me to see if he'd moved. He hadn't. An overwhelming urge to run from him rushed through me. I wanted to get away from Will, from the responsibility of caring for

Lissie, from my losses, my life. So, I did run. I raced along the beach, not caring if someone was waiting at the other end to kill me. I ran and freed myself from it all, if only for a few moments.

I never looked back. I just ran.

Will grabbed me from behind, lifting me from my feet mid-stride. "What the hell are you doing?"

"Let me go, Will, damn you!" I twisted to get out of his grip.

He held on tightly. "Give me your word that you won't run again."

"Go to hell!"

Without warning, he positioned me over his shoulder and headed for the beach house. He crossed an arm over my thighs to restrain my legs and gathered my wrists, holding them in one hand behind his neck. "Christ, Elle, you do have a temper."

I called him names and demanded he let me go, but he ignored my insults until we reached the house. I pounded on his back when he reached down to open the door.

"Stop this, or I'll smack your arse," he threatened, putting me down with a furious jolt, pinning my wrists to his chest. His body was cemented to mine, and he was aroused.

We were aroused.

"You said you wouldn't hit me."

"Quite right, but I'll smack your arse if you don't quit this tantrum."

I pushed harder. "Fuck you, Will."

Charged blue eyes—pale, white-hot—rested on my mouth for a minute.

"Maybe a good, hard fucking that you can't forget is exactly what you need."

God, his erection, the heat coming from his body.

"Let's go find out," I challenged, chewing on my bottom lip, matching him stare for stare.

"Go to your room, Elle." He released me abruptly, reminding

himself that a good, hard fucking was exactly what he wouldn't give me. "And do not leave this house."

Will walked away then, his stride graceful and primal, his confidence enough to convince us both that I would do as he'd commanded.

nine

Staring out at the moon, I pounded the side of my fist on the doorframe, recalling a conversation I'd had earlier with Will. He'd taken another hard-line position, insisting we'd have to skip Isobel and Gran's funeral. Not only had the Order taken our family from Lissie and me, but also, they'd stolen our opportunity to say good-bye.

They would be there, lurking in the shadows, waiting for an opportunity to get to me, he'd said.

I imagined Reverend Archer's prayer as he committed the bodies of my grandmother and my sister to the earth for rest and their souls to our Father in heaven. The vision failed to soothe me.

For whatever reason, no one was on guard outside my bedroom on the veranda, and I needed a connection, craved Will's comforting presence, though I was still angry with him. I went to the kitchen, but none of the men were there either.

Through the window, the intensity of the sea called out to me.

I answered, leaving the kitchen to make my way down the uneven path to the beach, seeking freedom from the endless, painful clutter in my head. I would stay for only a minute, I thought, stepping knee-deep into the water, where my lungs filled with ease again.

Brisk water struck my thighs.

"I'll just clear my head for a second," I whispered back at the sea. "He'll come and get me back inside anyway. He's probably coming out now. He never misses a thing."

I closed my eyes and inhaled, taking a deep breath through my nose, refocusing on the turbulent ocean. I extended the length of my arms backward and pulled in another breath.

A thick arm squeezed my neck, preventing an exhale, and a crude whisper told me not to move. Cold steel replaced the arm at my neck.

My body and my mind failed me. I couldn't move. I couldn't think.

An assassin was behind me, pressing a knife into my throat. He slogged through waves, dragging me into deeper water. His blade's sharp edge chilled the skin where it demanded the attention of my carotid artery.

Blood pulsed violently through my veins. Pain twisted inside my chest.

"You die tonight, and this will finally be over," he said as he gathered my hair in his other hand. "I don't even have to spill your blood out here." He had a British accent.

I still held my breath. Both lungs burned, pleading with me to use them. When I released the breath that I'd held hostage, my choking gasps were followed by a sharp inhale and a loud exhaled cry.

"Shut your fucking mouth. No noise." He yanked on my hair.

My blurred vision improved as oxygen reached my blood again. I heard the respiration of my lungs and the thumping of my heart inside my ears. It grew louder. I could no longer hear the crash of waves.

The executioner moved us out into deeper water. His voice was a distant echo inside my head. "You made this quite easy, coming out here alone while my men distracted yours. Stupid fucking girl."

A wall of waves rolled in, and I stumbled on a slimy rock, losing my balance. I fell, the force of the undertow pulling me down, yanking me from his grasp, dragging me several feet away from him.

He lumbered through the waves and jerked me upright by my hair. I gulped air and vomited seawater. The brine burned my sinuses as I choked on both.

"How 'bout some more of that?" he asked with a cruel laugh. He turned me then, toward the beach, my house, and wrenched my head back. "Take one more look. It'll be your last."

He planned to drown me.

It was my turn. I would follow my sister in death.

But he stopped with a sudden lurch and put the blade against my throat again.

I gasped. Salt blistered my lungs.

Before us, my defender stood. Will was there.

Clouds moved out, allowing me to see him well in the light of the moon. His posture was tall and erect, his stance wide, and his fists were clenched into weapons. The muscles in his jaw tensed, and his chin jutted. Veins bulged in his neck and in his arms. His eyes flashed with fury and the promise of death. He was a dangerous storm in his own right.

"Focus on me, Elle," he thundered above all other sound. "Look at only me."

As I locked on to his stare, terror fled from my soul, and those raging flashes of emotion in his eyes soothed me. Maybe I was sick for feeling that, or maybe my mind was completely broken. Either way, the fire in his eyes was my lifeline. His darkness was my salvation.

Cloud cover rolled back in, thicker this time, and Will became a dark silhouette against a blanket of haze. I felt the intensity of the assassin's rising desperation as he considered

Will's shadowed form. I searched the darkness until I found Will's eyes again. He nodded at me.

Strength climbed from my quivering stomach to my heart.

I elbowed the assassin twice.

He grunted and grabbed his gut in reflex, losing his grip on the knife. It fell away from my throat, into the water. I dislodged my lower body from his. He still held my hair in his other hand.

"I can snap your neck just as easily, bitch," he spat through his teeth, yanking my head back.

Before he secured my body against his again, a sharp pop and its echo rang out into the night. Then another. The second bullet hit the assassin's leg, causing him to jerk and contort.

"Hold, goddamn it," Will shouted over his shoulder to the beach.

The assassin steadied himself, using my shoulders, shielding his body with mine.

I couldn't breathe, couldn't draw breath or release it.

He was strangling me.

I lost Will's eyes. Terror reclaimed me.

Will charged, a bellow rupturing from his throat. His powerful arms ripped me away from my captor's hold and thrust me in the direction of the shore.

Freeing waves whisked me toward land, other people. I forced my exhausted body onto all fours and clawed my way through stones and rotting seaweed onto the beach, where I collapsed. My lungs purged seawater and filled with air at the same time. I lay there, gasping and choking, closer to death than I'd ever been, the side of my face pressed into wet sand.

Hands on me, someone touching me. Blankets.

My mind let it all go, giving way to darkness.

I REGAINED CONSCIOUSNESS INSIDE ON THE LIVING ROOM SOFA, where Ben was keeping a close watch over me, too close. He scrutinized my actions as if he were expecting something from me. I trembled with cold and shock but had nothing else to give.

My soul was numb.

Male voices rumbled, drawing my brain out of its fog.

"Where is she?" I heard Will ask.

"Stop. You'll scare her, man. You're covered in blood." John.

"Stay here, Ellie," Ben ordered, leaving me.

"I need to see her myself. Move your arse—now." Will.

I shoved the blankets covering me onto the floor and followed his voice.

Ben and John blocked the doorway into the kitchen with their broad shoulders, as if they were protecting me from him.

Will would never hurt me. That, if nothing else about him, I knew.

I needed to see that he was all right. "Let me through, please," I croaked, wincing at the burn.

In the small gap between Ben and John, I watched Will look down at his body, his hands. He removed his T-shirt and tossed it into the trash bin, then as he wrapped a towel around his fist, he said to the guys, "I won't say it more than once. She asked you for something. Do it now."

They stepped aside, and I exploded forward, racing to Will. He caught me and lifted me into his arms. His warm lips rested on my temple, a soft kiss, as he held me tightly against his bare chest. My heart raced, recognizing before I did that I was falling for the dangerous man who'd just killed another to save my life.

His rough whisper swept over my ear. "Are you all right, baby? Did he hurt you?"

"I'm fine." I swallowed against the pain, lying a little.

"Never do that to me again, Elle." He pressed his lips to my skin again, allowing another warm kiss to linger on the side of my face.

We didn't allow our eyes to connect. We knew better, what it would mean for us in the power of that moment. He lowered me to my feet, and the towel unraveled from his hand. His fist was a mess.

"Let me dress it properly for you, Will."

After a brief argument, he let me clean the wounds on his knuckles and wrap his hand with sterile gauze. He'd taken a life with those bare hands, and he didn't want me to touch them. He didn't want me close to the death he had caused. But what he'd done couldn't change how I wanted him.

And, God, I wanted him.

"Why is it that you're good at this, Elle? Have you practiced with someone else?"

Rather than respond to his possessive assertion, I pressed harder than necessary on the ice compress. "There. Leave it for ten or fifteen minutes. Repeat in an hour."

"Merciless woman." The corner of his mouth twitched until he let his lips curve, then he winked.

I smiled too. "I agree to go to England with you."

"Yeah?" He was surprised.

I couldn't see another path forward. I had nothing more to lose. Lissie had everything to lose.

We had no one else in Connecticut. If she was Ethan's daughter, she had a family. A father, a grandmother, uncles. What was more, I wanted retribution for our pain to help us heal. The yearning had taken me by surprise, burning slow somewhere deep within, and it continued to rise.

Going with Will meant I could sort through the mess at the source to get answers and find justice. I could also learn to protect myself. And there was Will himself, the man I'd craved since the notion of a painful love story rolled onto the street at that damn parade.

"Yeah. Our passports need to be picked up. I'm not going

back to that house, but I'll tell you where to find them. And I'd like you to grab a few things for me, if you don't mind."

Will nodded and checked his watch. "Whatever you need. The plane is set to leave in sixteen hours."

LATE THE NEXT AFTERNOON, AS I FINISHED PACKING, WILL rushed into my bedroom. "Police are headed this way."

I ran to the living room and peered out the window. Josh Mendes was getting out of his car. "It's Josh, and he won't bother coming to the front. I should meet him on the veranda before he gets to the back door."

"You're not going out there," he said, taking a protective stance, his hand on my arm. "We don't know what he wants from you, what he's planning to do."

"Will, listen. He won't hurt me. I'll convince him to let me leave."

His other hand gripped me, both now pulling me to his chest. "What makes you think he'll let you go? I sure as hell wouldn't."

"What? I'm not with him anymore, and *no one* owns me," I snapped.

He opened his fingers, releasing me, and stepped away.

Ben said, "You two need to get over this personal shit and get out there. Explain it to him. Your options are quite limited at this point. Good news is, he's alone."

I edged forward into Will's space again, until his breath warmed my face. His dark energy surrounded us. "Ben's right. We have to tell Josh. But promise me, Will, that you won't hurt him."

He tucked a lock of hair behind my ear and nodded. "For you, all right. But let me be clear. If he becomes aggressive with you, in any manner, I can't keep that promise."

I nodded, and we stepped out onto the veranda as Josh was climbing the steps.

"Why haven't you answered your goddamn phone?" Josh shouted. "State police are due tomorrow, and you haven't even been interviewed. What the fuck is wrong with you, Ellie? After all that's happened, I find you here, shacked up—"

Will moved in against Josh before I could get between them. "You'll watch your fucking mouth when you speak to her, cop."

"Go fuck yourself. I saw the two of you that night, standing outside at Nick's. I have questions for you as well," Josh said.

Will's chest vibrated.

"Josh, please. Give me a chance to tell you what happened."

Will interjected, "Listen to the hoarseness in her voice. She was almost killed last night. Assassins will come for her again. You're not calling the shots here, not with her."

Josh's gaze jumped over to me, fell to the bruises forming on my neck. His expression softened.

"Go inside, Will. Let me talk to Josh alone. I'll tell him what he needs to know."

Will agreed, but he didn't go far. As he spoke to his brother, the rumble of his voice passed through the wall that separated us and calmed me. I was safe, protected.

I sat on the deck of the veranda, and Josh lowered himself next to me. He watched the cotton-like clouds drift over the Atlantic and listened as I shared my story—a dreadful story that even I hadn't fully grasped. It was surreal. I'd fallen down a rabbit hole.

I told him everything.

"Jesus, you've had me so worried. I thought you were dead. Lissie's unharmed?"

"Yes, she's unhurt. I'm sorry to put you in this position since we're no longer—"

"Don't say it, Ellie. I know I've lost you. You don't need to remind me."

"All I can say is, I know I won't survive without him. If I stay here, the authorities won't believe me, and I'll lose, just as Isobel did."

He closed his eyes. "Go to England. No one will stop you if you leave tonight."

"Don't risk your career any further, Josh. Do what you need to do after I'm gone."

"I'll make my report in the morning. I can't offer more time than that. My superiors will attempt to force you back once you've been located."

"But doesn't the government need an indictment to extradite?"

"Yeah, but Connecticut could ask the State Department to revoke your passport during the investigation, potentially provoking deportation."

There wasn't much to be said after that, nothing that would provide comfort in any case. We sat, his arm around my shoulders, my head resting against his, not speaking. After some time passed, he pulled away and left without a word. He had warned me before. If not lovers, then we weren't friends either.

I'd lost everyone. And I was about to lose my home as well.

I stepped into the beach house, and Will was waiting for me, his eyes searching mine, searching as if he were inspecting my soul. He must have discovered the sorrow that flowed through me, the sadness that I'd hidden from the rest of the world, because compassion filled his eyes. He opened his strong arms and tucked me tightly inside them, cutting off the pain before it could take me down.

"We're free to leave tonight," I whispered against his chest.

ten

I WATCHED LISSIE RUN BACK AND FORTH, PAST THE WINDOWS inside the private jet Will had hired, exploring the cabin's luxurious interior with John. Will and I stood outside on the tarmac with Ben, waiting for him to sort through the customs documentation with the pilots.

Will's hand covered the small of my back. "Are you ready?"

"I'm ready." I bit my lip and avoided his eyes.

Flying was a nightmare for me, and I had failed to tell him how sick I might get if the meds didn't knock me out. I'd seen several doctors, and they'd all said the same thing. It was in my head, aviophobia compounded by panic disorder and the fact that my parents had died in a plane crash.

"What is it, Elle?"

I glanced at the plane again. "Nothing. It's fine." Anxiety slashed at my empty stomach.

After following my nervous glance with his own eyes, he faced me, taking away my personal space. "Why didn't you tell me? How bad is it?"

"I've taken something for it. With any luck, I'll sleep for most of the flight. If not, I'll just have to get through it. I should check on Lissie, and it looks like they're waiting for us." I flashed him an uneasy smile and nodded at the pilots.

"And they'll continue to wait. What can I do to make it easier for you?"

"I don't know that anything can be done."

"We're not leaving until I know what you need." The back of his fingers brushed over my cheek.

"Keep an eye on Lissie for me?"

"Of course." His soft touch moved to my battered throat, his fingertips and his eyes resting there.

I closed my eyes. "Will?"

"Yeah?"

You're what I need.

"Elle?"

"I'm sorry for the way that I've behaved."

"Don't be. And never apologize, not to me." He slipped his hand around to the back of my head, pulling me close, lowering his mouth to mine, and then he whispered against my lips, "Always knew you would challenge me."

Then, he kissed me.

When he released my lips, my soul mourned the loss. We stood motionless for a minute, like we had turned to stone, each of us locked on to the other's gaze. Will's eyes pleaded for forgiveness before he took my lips between his again. I touched his face and nodded, forgiving him for the way he'd hurt me with his refusals.

He threaded his fingers into my hair and slanted his mouth over mine, pushing past my lips with his tongue. The intense, unyielding way he kissed me made his intent clear—he was driven by his desire for me and nothing else. He was taking what he wanted. Something in him had shifted after I was attacked on the beach and again after Josh showed up.

As the sun's last ray dived below the horizon, Will and I tasted each other for the first time in a stormy but deliberate tangle of our tongues and our arms. We didn't stop kissing until we were all that existed. The world was gone, time was gone. We shared one breath.

His fist tightened in my hair as he pulled back and stared beyond my shoulder. His gaze returned to mine, and then he placed one more soft, lingering kiss on my mouth.

"Someone's here to see you off," he said, letting go, stepping back. Although his eyes remained on mine, the next words he spoke went to Ben, who appeared beside me. "Handle this for me."

Will walked away.

WE HAD BEEN OVER FOR MONTHS, BUT THE PAIN ON JOSH'S FACE was unmistakable. I had never intended to hurt him, never intended for him to witness the intense, passionate kiss that I shared with Will only minutes earlier.

"I'm sorry," Josh told me. "I couldn't leave things the way we did. I was an asshole to walk away from you at the beach house like that."

"It's okay. I'll never forget what you're doing for me tonight, Josh."

His brown eyes pleaded. "Please don't go, Ellie. Get in the car with me. Listen, I believe everything you've said. I'll convince the chief, and we'll provide you with police protection."

Ben's arm held Josh's car door shut as Josh attempted to open it. "Don't do it, cop. She's not getting in this car. Your fucking police failed. We must protect her now."

I put my hand on Josh's arm, hoping to keep the peace. "I'm going to England. Maybe they'll still get to me. But if it were to happen here, Lissie would have no one. I explained this to you."

"I don't know how to live without you here."

"You already do that." I put my arms around him. "Talk to Jess for me. I don't want to risk her life by reaching out to her right now. She's already leaving frantic messages."

"I'm begging you to let me help you the right way." He pulled me closely against his body.

"Ellie," Ben warned.

I didn't need an explanation to understand why his warning was serious. Will's refusal to see my interaction with Josh had spoken volumes.

I pressed my lips to Josh's cheek. Our last good-bye.

In the next moment, as I was about to step away from Josh, we were ripped apart.

Will pinned me against a nearby metal building and held me there with his body while his hands pushed through the long layers of my hair, gripping my head, the nape of my neck. He'd torn across the tarmac with unbelievable speed and force.

He asked me in a low, menacing tone, his mouth close to my ear, "Do you want him?" His erection hardened against my stomach. "Do you?" The muscles along his jawline contracted.

As I measured the jealousy that consumed his eyes, his scent messed with my head, encouraging my brain to interpret his fierce nature as the treatment for my restless soul. I was distantly aware of the other men arguing behind us.

"He's not hurting her," Ben told Josh.

The buckling of metal. A body slammed onto the hood of the car.

Will nipped at the rim of my ear, then kissed away the sting. "I'll kill him."

Panting, aroused, I dug my nails into his wrists. "You won't hurt him. I want you."

eleven

WILL BACKED AWAY FROM ME, OFFERING HIS HAND, AND I TOOK it without hesitation. He pressed my fingers to his lips before leading us across the tarmac. As soon as we reached the jet, he let go and busied himself with the luggage and the pilots. I couldn't take my eyes off of him.

Neither of us had said a word since he'd held me against the metal building.

He sensed my stare and stilled for a moment, his back to me, and then he turned and reconnected. His expression revealed penance. "Get settled for the flight, Elle." He tilted his head at the plane's entrance, sending me inside.

Through a window, I watched him search the pilots for weapons.

"You'll get used to it." John winked, a smirk tugging at his mouth, turning him into a miniature version of his brother.

I wondered if the girls fawned over him at school.

"He doesn't intimidate me." I tasted my lips. The rich flavor of Will's kisses still lingered there and on my tongue. The fury and the subsequent remorse I'd seen in his eyes filled my mind.

"Few people can say that. I'm quite glad you're one of them."

Lissie raced up the aisle again, wearing a backpack filled with stuffed animals, her activity pulling me out of my head. It was getting late, and she'd soon slow down. I hoped she would sleep through the flight as well.

"Come here, sweet girlie. Let's get your bed ready, so it's all set when you're sleepy."

The plane had a full galley and two separate cabin areas, both with luxurious white leather seating and walnut paneling. John helped me convert a reclining seat in front into a bed for Lissie. As we finished, Ben boarded, but he went straight into the cockpit by himself.

"What is he doing, John?"

"Preflight check, looking for anything suspicious. He was a pilot for the Royal Air Force."

Alarm began to race through me. The precautions Will had undertaken were serious and exposed the enormity of what we faced. I corralled Lissie and sat her on my lap, holding her to gain some sense of security.

John positioned himself in front of us as the pilots boarded, his protective stance obvious.

Will entered the cabin last. As he headed for the rear seating area, he stopped to pull me onto my feet and take me along with him.

Lissie slid down as I stood and followed, leaping between us after we sat on the plush leather pullout sofa. She was already at ease with Will. She'd found her very own superhero.

He pushed a wild lock of brown hair out of her face and gave her his undivided attention. "When you wake up, we'll be across the ocean. Your castle awaits, princess."

"Are we going to see a real castle?" She grasped his hand, her eyes and her mouth wide with excitement.

"Something like that. You'll enjoy Eastridge, but first, you sleep."

Their sweet moment caught me off guard. My heart lost a beat.

"Your toothbrush is there." I pointed to the lavatory. "Then to bed."

Lissie agreed to the bedtime plan but only after Will said "castle" again. She adored his accent.

He relaxed his back against the sofa, tucking me beneath his arm. "We'll take off when you're ready. I want you to be comfortable with the flight. Once she's settled, you'll sleep here."

Snuggling against his body was as natural as being home. I sensed it was the same for him. I burrowed deeper into the warmth of his side. "Good. Keep me close to the lavatory."

The muscles in his arms tensed. "How bad is it, Elle?"

"I don't know this time. I've never flown on anything like this. How long is the flight?"

"Not more than seven and a half hours." He captured my hand and kissed it.

It wasn't enough. I wanted to feel his lips on mine again.

But first, I had to get through the flight.

WILL CLOSED THE PRIVACY PANEL BETWEEN THE TWO CABIN areas, handed me a bottle of water, and poured more whisky for himself. "Tell me what I can do to help, Elle. Clearly, you're not able to sleep."

Drowsiness wasn't overwhelming me, as it should have been.

"Stay with me, on this bed. Let them take off."

He nodded once, a refined bow of his head.

After speaking into a phone on the wall to instruct the pilots, he settled on the sofa bed with me, stretching his legs over the length of it next to mine and extending his arm along the back as he drank from the glass. “Come closer to me. Maybe what you need is a good distraction.”

I looked up at his handsome face, his assuming smile, and moved closer. “Maybe.”

The aircraft began taxiing down the runway.

Will took my water, set his glass aside. He laced our fingers and stared at my mouth, then met my eyes. “You’re all right with the way I kissed you earlier.” It wasn’t a question, though his eyes searched mine for confirmation, consent.

“Yes.” I let go of the disobedient smile I’d been fighting. “Are you planning to do it again?”

He wrapped his arm around me and abruptly lowered us onto the mattress, repositioning himself so that his body, his lips hovered above mine. “You have no idea.”

My stomach flipped. Butterflies, not nausea.

Will trailed his fingers down my leg until he reached my toes. He hesitated for a moment before he closed his hand on my foot and dragged it up, bending my knee, spreading my legs apart. His hand slid to my thigh. He rotated his wrist, his long fingers extending around to my backside, gliding beneath the frayed hem of my denim shorts.

“You need to wear more clothing when you’re in close quarters with me.” The deep timbre in his voice grew more distinct.

I’d had it. I grabbed his face, drew his mouth close to mine, and breathed my words onto his lips. “I am fully clothed.”

“I have your bare arse cheek in my hand. It’s not enough to keep me out.”

“Then, don’t stay out.”

He shook his head, smirking, and then he kissed me, sucking on my lips until he chose to push his tongue into my mouth to explore mine. His kiss was like velvet, smooth and self-indulgent. It was luxurious and addictive. He was attentive and generous.

Will's diversion tactic was working. We were in the air, and I could think of one thing—being touched by him, everywhere.

"No more holding back," he said in my ear.

Heat blistered my skin as he kissed his way from there to the edge of my blouse, where he worked the buttons.

I admonished, "No more, Will."

"I'll give you what you want, Elle."

I reached for his hard length after he pushed it into the soft space between my legs. He caught my fingers and kissed them before confining my hand above my head.

I wanted him. "I—"

He shut my mouth with his. Need burned in his eyes when he pulled back. "You must think this through and be certain because once I've had you, it can't be undone. No other man will touch you again, not as long as I'm alive. You need to understand how it'll be with me. Remember who I am, what I've done, what I'll do."

His warning was clear. *I'm the bad guy, and you'll belong to me. You must be okay with that.*

And I was. "Will—"

"You'll hear me out." He pressed his lips to mine, then dragged his mouth over my cheek to my ear. "I want you. Bloody fucking hell, I can think of nothing else. Make a clear-headed decision, Elle, and be quite certain about what you want. Know what you're getting with me. If you choose me, if you fail to make a decision at all, I'll take what I want from you. If you decide otherwise, I'll protect you from a distance. I can't be this close and not have you. The choice is still yours at this point."

What he didn't realize was that I'd also fallen beyond reason. We were in the same place, and I wanted to ease his worry.

I ran my fingers along his jawline, my nails scratching through his slight beard. "I have thought about it. You know how you always win? Well, I always know what I want. It's you, Will."

He stared at me for a moment, into my eyes, seeking, approving, and then pushed the blouse off my shoulders, his eyes sweeping over me from head to toe. "You're quite beautiful."

"Kiss me again," I told him. "You're still in the red. I'll let you know when you're caught up."

He grinned and pressed my back deeper into the mattress with more of his weight. His fevered lips were on mine then as he opened the button on my shorts. Pausing at the zipper, he said, "I'm taking this off. I want to see more of you."

I nodded. I was his for the taking.

"Need to touch you. I've waited so long." He used his kiss to burn a path from my lips to my stomach as he pushed the shorts from my hips and down my legs.

I moaned and arched against the sensations. I needed him. Nothing else mattered. The taste of scotch on his tongue, his scent, the feel of his hot mouth on my skin—God, I was high.

When he returned to my mouth, I yanked at his shirt until he pulled it over his head. He slipped his hand down into my panties and pushed one, then two fingers inside me, drawing a sharp cry from my throat that he swallowed with his kiss.

"Christ, you're smaller than I expected. So tight, baby, and so wet," he murmured, circling higher with his thumb as he moved his fingers in and out of me.

He tested me. Watched me. Pushed me.

No words formed in my head as he increased the intensity of his touch. Pleading for release from the ache he'd caused, I pulled his face to mine and cried the one word my brain had retained. His name.

He smirked against my mouth.

I writhed beneath him and cried out again, this time climaxing—shattering into billions of tiny fragments of myself. He owned me with his kiss, thrusting deep with his tongue, swallowing every sound that I made.

"You're mine, Elle." He swept hair away from my face. "So

beautiful. I haven't even had you yet, but it's too late. Never let another man touch you again."

"Only you," I whispered, lost in his eyes.

He acknowledged our agreement with another of his slight nods and kissed me once more before he got up from the sofa bed.

"Leave it," he ordered when he saw me reach for my blouse.

I snuggled into the blanket and watched the muscles in his shoulders and back ripple as he stretched, the way a lion might when rising from his den.

twelve

WILL CAME BACK FROM THE FRONT CABIN AREA, WHERE HE'D gone to check on Lissie, and sat next to me on the sofa bed as he spoke into his phone, "Handle it, Ethan, before we land. I don't want any opportunities created by delays at Gatwick." He took my hand and kissed it while listening to his brother's response.

Panic rushed up my spine. Were they talking about me?

"Do you feel all right, Elle?" Will asked, disconnecting the call. "Your skin is on fire."

I shook my head, increasing the dizziness that had begun to buzz about my brain while he was gone. "Why does she want me dead? It's absurd for the Queen to believe I would move against her son." The thought was random, incoherent, or maybe it was right, I didn't know.

"The Queen has been known to get her hands dirty, but remember what I told you. These extremists are not supported by the Crown," he said.

A cold sweat consumed me. I prattled on like a child, "Why doesn't she make them stop?"

"We can talk about this later. You aren't so well, baby."

Beads of sweat formed above my top lip. I covered my ringing ears. "Medicine."

Will went for my handbag. The cabin spun, and I collapsed onto the pillows. His words, whatever he was saying, and the fumbling of his hands through my things sounded as if they'd come from the end of an echoing corridor. He placed an arm behind me and held a small pill on his palm.

I swallowed several times to get it down. My throat burned. My skin burned. "I'm so hot."

"Lie back. I'll get something cold." He placed me on the pillows again, and moments later, he reappeared from the lavatory with small towels soaked with cold water, pressing one to my forehead and the other to my neck. He backed away when I reached for him. "My body heat will increase your temperature."

Nausea hit me fast and hard, taking control of my body. I covered my mouth and clawed at the blankets in a desperate attempt to get to the lavatory. Will got it, and he carried me the few feet to the door, gently setting me inside on the floor. I fell to my knees, and he was on his behind me, holding up my hair and my convulsing body.

"Jesus, Elle. You haven't eaten enough. You're ripping apart your gut."

I was sicker than I'd ever been. It was stupid of me to not have eaten, to not have taken a larger dose of meds to knock me out. I dry-heaved for ten or fifteen minutes more before collapsing into Will's arms. The tempo of my heart was erratic, and my weak body was listless.

Will settled on the floor and held me, his big body half in and half out of the lavatory. He ran his fingers through my hair and soothed me with his protective whispers.

Violent tremors shook my body then. Disjointed thoughts overwhelmed me. I was frightened. My blood turned cold, so cold. A heavy blanket tightened around me, suffocating me. My mind rebelled against the attack, but my body had no fight left.

"Not yet. Please don't kill me," I whispered.

"Look at me, Elle. Focus on my eyes." The blanket was Will,

his warm arms and body wrapped around my frigid, trembling form. "Your mind isn't clear. We need to get fluids into you." I dug my fingers into his arm. "I won't let go, Elle. I promise." He pressed my face to his bare chest and kissed the top of my head.

Will grabbed his phone and called his younger brother in England. "Thomas, get a paramedic to the tarmac on standby, not some fucking ambulance driver. What? You're breaking up ..."

He lifted himself and me from the floor and put me back on the sofa bed, then headed for the front. He quickly returned with a bottle of cloudy water and took off his jeans to get beneath the blankets with me. His skin seared mine when he pulled me against his body and wrapped his scorching arms around me. The kisses he placed on my forehead and temple were like fire.

"Try some of this water," he said.

I shook my head.

"I'll give you a little more time, then you must."

My icy body melted further into Will's heat. Trembling slowed to shivering, and at some point, soothed by the thundering of his heartbeat against my face, I fell asleep. He woke me several times to make me drink the electrolyte-enriched water. I drank with success three or four times, but the last time, another wave of nausea rolled through my wasted body.

"Going to be sick," I croaked.

Will wrapped me in the blanket and lifted me, sitting us on the floor again near the toilet. He gathered my hair and waited patiently while I heaved up the water that I'd taken in. I fell against him and closed my eyes.

"Open your eyes, Elle," he ordered, lowering my head.

I tried but failed to focus on his eyes.

"Do not close them. Focus on mine. Understand?"

But I had nothing left to give. I allowed my lids to fall shut again, leaving my fate to him. Senseless, daunting thoughts ran wild inside my head, tormenting me, knowing I couldn't fight back. The lyrics were dark and eager, convincing me that I couldn't feel my heart, that someone was killing me.

I'd fallen sick on the plane, but that wasn't the worst of it. I'd also fallen apart.

My mind had broken.

thirteen

IN THE FOLLOWING DAYS, REPRESSED GRIEF AND FEAR CAME forward as a destructive cyclone of emotion. My mind fought back the one way it knew how, forcing a mental lockdown. But after four long, rainy days, the sunshine radiating through the windows drew me out of bed.

I counted them. Nineteen deer frolicked across the side lawn of the boundless estate, their spirits wild and free. One small doe stopped and fixed her eyes on my window. Through her, my soul looked back at me. It scorned and provoked and pushed me to let in the pain.

As if she were satisfied with the message that she'd delivered to me, the little female ran back to the herd and left me staring at my reflection in the pane of glass, leaving it clear there was one way to free myself from the darkness into which I'd fallen. I had to feel the pain. I needed to acknowledge it, so it would leave me. Before that moment, my broken mind had refused to embrace the idea.

Will wound his arms around me from behind and watched the deer play.

"Will, go on. Do something for yourself today." It was time

for me to get it together, and I had to be sure I mended with my own pieces, not his.

"I can stay. Try the medication."

He'd been staying in that room with me, protecting me from my grief and depression. He allowed me to absorb his strength and fuse with his soul. It was the only way for me to be free of the pain. From the moment we had arrived in England, he'd accepted the burden and carried it as his own. I'd never done anything more selfish than that.

"No," I said. "I need to feel it."

I sent him out before the first tears fell.

I shoved the numbness away and pulled the pain inward. Every splintered piece of my heart cut me deep, and those cuts bled heavily. My soul mourned Isobel. She had been so young, my sister's life ended too soon. And for Gran. Her death had been unintended. She'd been in the wrong place at the wrong time. My soul howled for the parents I'd never known, for those years of my life I'd had with my sister and my grandmother but still felt as though I were all alone.

I cried with the force of someone who was drowning. Snot and tears mixed together in my mouth, choking me. I screamed soundlessly and writhed as pain and loss ripped through my hemorrhaging spirit. Fear and anxiety were all that remained when I found the strength to pick myself up from the floor.

Stumbling into the bathroom, I whispered hoarsely, "Fear and anxiety can be managed."

Steam would provide relief for my sore throat and gritty, swollen eyes. I turned on the hot tap and stepped into the shower, allowing my mind to recall only as far back as our arrival.

Most of it had been a quiet blur for me after landing in England. The paramedic had administered intravenous fluids, and once my heart rate had stabilized, Will had carried me from the plane to his car. "I've got you, Elle. You can trust me," he had said, protecting me in his arms.

I remembered being comforted by the car ride, the smooth roar of the engine, the luxurious floating of the wheels over asphalt, the security of Will's embrace. I had curled around him on the back seat of his Jaguar—a strong, sexy car that suited him well—while his brother Thomas drove us through the lush green countryside to Hastings.

The ancient seaside town on England's southeast coast, which curiously had the same name as Will's family, was located about two hours and fifteen minutes south of London. The estate was situated on a ridge above the sandstone cliffs that overlooked the English Channel.

I understood during our drive that Will favored Thomas when it came to matters of security. Thomas's massive size and his disposition paralleled Will's the closest. They looked a lot alike, even with Thomas's contemporary contrast to Will's classic handsomeness.

I smiled, rinsing away the rose-scented soap, recalling how nice it had been, seeing the four brothers greet each other with such affection at the airport.

When I emerged from the bathroom almost an hour later, fresh linens covered the bed, and a silver tray filled with sandwiches, cheese, and fruit was on the table. Will had warned me about the efficiency of the household staff.

I slipped into my white silk robe, pulling the pins from my hair and letting it fall, my mind wandering back to Will. He would return soon. A tiny flutter tickled the walls of my stomach.

As if summoned by an intuitive force, he pushed through the door with a bottle of scotch in one hand and a bottle of red wine in the other. He poured without saying a word as he watched me, evaluating my mood, watching it brighten before his eyes.

What we'd shared in the prior days was intimate and beautiful, chaste even. His kisses had been tender and sweet, his arms a sanctuary. But that was all about to change. Neither of us could wait another moment to lose ourselves to that one incomparable connection we hadn't yet made.

A smile tugged at his lips as he stalked across the room and towered above me with a drink in each of his hands. He waited for me to meet his eyes. "When I said you were mine, I meant it. No one and nothing takes from me what is mine. So, Elle, you will come back from this. Back to me. I want us to do this properly." His voice was strong as it delivered his first command since we'd arrived.

"Drink." He put the wine into my hand.

As I measured the determination in his eyes, I sipped and waited for his next words.

"You'll eat with me tonight. Now or in an hour, but you will eat before this night is over." He nodded at my glass. "Another."

I took another sip and stared at the man who had threatened to smack my ass for poor behavior in the States, the man who had shattered me blissfully on the plane, using nothing more than his fingers. The man I wanted more than anything.

His brows flashed. Had he read my mind?

One of those long fingers guided the glass to my mouth before he went to refill his own. While at the table, he lifted the bottle of medication his physician had prescribed for me and examined the label. Then, he stared at me, pushing his gaze deep into my soul. Without moving his eyes from mine, he released the bottle of antidepressants into the wastebasket.

He shot his whisky and came back to me. "You haven't said a word, but your eyes tell me everything. Those beautiful green eyes." Will swept locks of my hair out of his way and threaded his fingers through the back layers. He pulled my mouth to his and sucked hard on my lips, murmuring against my mouth, "Goddamn it, Elle. I can't wait any longer to have you."

The wineglass slipped from my hand, splashing red at our feet. Neither of us cared. He opened my robe, and it slid from my shoulders, falling to the floor on top of the mess, revealing my bare body. I reached for him, my heart fluttering, but he stepped back.

"I want to look at you." The blue of his eyes was lost. "Christ, you're lovely." The same words he'd said when we met in Stonington on the pier, said with the same charged eyes.

My lips curved into the same nervous smile.

"You know what will happen if I don't leave this room."

I nodded.

"That's what you want. All of me." His tone suggested it was something I shouldn't want, something that should offend me.

"Yes, I want you, Will."

He erupted, became an explosion of fiery emotion. He tore his shirt over his head and dropped his jeans as he consumed the space between us. I gasped at the sight. He was enormous. His erection was enormous. My body quivered like a virgin who'd never seen a man before, but my desire for him countered the nervousness.

Will smirked.

Then, he lifted me into his arms and carried me to the bed. He pushed his tongue past my lips as he fell onto his elbows above me. Our kiss was a firestorm of pent-up emotional and physical desire. It boiled in our blood. It was bone deep. His skin burned into mine until I couldn't tell the difference between us.

Persistent banging on the bedroom door. We ignored it until he couldn't.

Will leaped from the bed like a starved animal having his meal taken from him and shoved into his jeans. "The fuck," he snapped out at his brother after nearly jerking the door off the hinges.

"Jesus." Ethan hesitated. "We're going to lose Stanbury if you don't speak to him now. He agreed to stay on if you get your arse back to work and handle his offshores. Otherwise, he's pulling everything. There's nothing more I can do."

Will pushed his fingers through his hair and looked over his shoulder at me as he spoke to Ethan, "Yes, all right. I'll take care of him." He closed the door and tugged on his shirt as he came back to me. "We were so close, baby." His rasping words swept over my ear before his lips rested at my temple.

"You weren't concerned about contraception or—"

"I saw your pills on the plane, and I was tested before I came to get you. I would never touch you without knowing it was safe for you."

"Oh." I suddenly felt shy. "What about me?"

"I had assumed you would be on top of that as well."

I nodded, and he grinned.

"Good," he added.

"Take care of your business, Will. I'll wait for you."

"Promise me you'll eat. I'll speak to Mrs. Bates about your green salads."

Before walking away, he plucked a raspberry from the silver tray and placed it inside my lips, then he put his mouth on mine, smashing the soft berry with his tongue, tasting it and me.

I fell against the pillows, beaming, remembering the incredulous look on his face when he'd realized a kale and avocado salad that I'd eaten at the beach house was my entire dinner.

As Will stepped through the doorway to leave, he glanced over his shoulder and found my smile.

He said softly, "There you are."

fourteen

Late the next morning, I lay in bed, still alone, thinking about the recent days that had passed.

Will had worked late into the night and then left for his office in London without waking me. It was easy to forget that his career was something other than fighting my personal death squad.

While staying at my side through those first several days, to keep me from falling deeper into the wicked depths that reached for me, he'd told me more about his family and his business. He'd gone to Oxford, earned his MBA, and cofounded a private equity firm with Ethan, where they maintained positions as active partners.

The lockdown in my head had kept me from responding, but I'd been right there with him as his captivating voice led me through his stories.

Will had described his company, how it functioned. He and Ethan focused on different aspects of the business, each with a management team that worked beneath him. Ethan conducted research and sourced investors and investments while Will negotiated contracts, closed deals, and monitored portfolios. Ethan mastered building their network, but Will was the closer, which made complete sense to me. Will was both commanding and charming when he wanted something.

The London financial community openly recognized Will and Ethan as the youngest founders of one of its most successful private equity firms.

Their father, Richard Hastings, an MI5 intelligence officer before his death, had trained his sons to be his private soldiers, but he'd also insisted on exceptional education. Ethan had completed his MBA at Oxford two years before Will. Thomas held a master's in mathematical finance and would soon join his brothers at Hastings Group.

Surprising me, Lissie slipped her angelic little face into the room and grinned like the devil. "Aunt Ellie! Will said you feel better now. You wanna come on my super-secret castle tour?"

She needed me, and I'd let her down, leaving her with Will's mother while cowering inside my own darkness.

"Definitely. Come in here, Lissie. Help me quickly choose something to wear."

She giggled as someone chased her away from my bedroom door.

Mrs. Bates then pushed into the room with a housemaid close on her heels. "Up with you, dear. It's almost twelve. You must be starving. William said you'd eat for us today." Her lilting Irish accent was hypnotic. She turned to the housemaid. "Lily, say hello to our young lady of the house."

"What? No, I'm not that. I'll come down to the kitchen after I dress. Well, if you'll tell me where to find it." I clutched the sheet beneath my chin. It smelled like Will.

"No need, Ms. James. I have a tray ready for you now." Lily's voice was small, and her English accent was quite different than Will's.

"Ellie," I corrected. What the hell? *William* was in big trouble.

"Don't blame him, dear. I do things my way round here." Mrs. Bates read my face. She muttered to herself then, "It's time one of them lads attached himself. Lord knows Mary could use a daughter."

I put my hand to my forehead. "Mrs. Bates, this is really all a bit too much."

She tossed my robe onto the bed and eyed the mess she found beneath it on the floor. My cheeks heated. She canted her head, and her eyes hit the bathroom door. "Don't mind us. Go on then."

The two ladies stepped out of the room, into the corridor, so I threw on the robe and hurried into the bathroom.

When I returned, the bed was made, and dozens of pretty white and blush-pink flowers were arranged around the room. A special variety of roses, I thought. Some were in crystal vases and some in vintage urns. I tugged at a large white flower, plucking it loose from a cluster. I held it under my nose and inhaled its rich fragrance, sighing as I waltzed across the room to soak up the sunshine.

Will hadn't bothered with a card.

"*English* roses, dear. The lad will give you nothing but the best," Mrs. Bates told me with a clever smile, pulling the door shut on her way out.

A satisfied smile claimed my own face as the image of Will's magnificent body filled my head. But it wasn't just his appearance. There was something about the way he moved, the way he said my name. These things changed me, took me to a carnal place within myself that I'd never known existed.

When he returned home from London, I would have all of him.

I FINISHED DRESSING WHILE EATING AND WAS PLANNING TO GO find Lissie when the text alert on my phone caught my attention. There were seven voice mail messages and three times as many text messages.

I'd contacted the carrier to extend my coverage to England before we left Connecticut, though Will had cautioned me not to take my friends' calls to keep them safe, to keep us all safe.

I didn't read the texts because it would reveal that I had opened them, but I didn't think anyone could tell if I had listened to the voice messages.

Jess: "Hey, it's me, and you're scaring the hell out of me, Ells. Josh said you're safe, but I need to hear it from you. Call me back, damn it."

Josh: "I did some digging. I know who he is, which means I know where you are. I never thought—well, at least his resources are immense, so he should be able to keep you safe. He'd fucking better."

Josh: "Keep your eyes and ears open. You're considered a suspect in the investigation now. I'll do what I can to lead them in another direction, but you left me with nothing useful. Ask him if he can do something about that. Stay safe."

Josh: "I miss you. Do you love him? Come home, Ellie. Just come back, and we'll fix this." He'd been drinking.

Jess: "I know you would tell me to trust Josh. He says this is for the best, you being gone, that I should let go. That's bullshit. You're my best friend, my family. I can't pretend you were never here. Damn you, Ells. Damn *him.*"

I didn't listen to the remaining messages. I couldn't bear to hear more of the pain I'd caused them, caused Jess. In order to live, I had to hurt her.

To live, I had to let them call me a suspect in the murder investigation of my own family.

Feel the pain, I reminded myself.

Tears spilled down my face. My stomach twisted into knots.

Fear. Anxiety. The feeling of being trapped in a cold place. Then anger.

I threw my phone at the wall, and it damaged the floral damask wallpaper.

fifteen

I STARED AT AN OLD PAINTING, *WILLIAM THE CONQUEROR AT THE Battle of Hastings,* hanging above the bar in the billiard room. I couldn't tell who had painted it but planned to research that when there was time. Strange how well it suited the moment, as I waited for my own William to return.

That was what Will had done. He'd swooped in to save me and conquered my world.

"You're late," I whispered behind my glass of Dom Pérignon.

I'd tuned out the music and the conversations happening around me.

Earlier, after Will had called and said he was driving back from London for the night, Thomas had convinced me to dress for dinner and have a drink with his friends while I waited for Will.

I'd been occupying myself with the exploration of Eastridge with Lissie while Will was gone. God, I'd missed her. Will had shown her around the house and encouraged her to claim it as her castle. He'd given her free rein of the entire estate.

Eastridge was a stately eighteenth-century Georgian country house, built of native stone. It had been renovated for modern comfort in recent years, though the old charm of the soaring, ornate plastered ceilings, original oak floors, and Baroque-style wall panels had been preserved with care. Stunning original fireplaces graced most rooms, as did ancestral portraits and other timeworn paintings.

The grand cantilevered staircase had been restored to its original splendor. It seemed to float high above the central great hall, and at the top, it split the first-floor corridor into north and south bedroom wings. Balusters, newels, treads, the substantial but graceful winding handrail were all made from Scottish oak and detailed with simple but elegant carvings.

On the ground level, a huge modern kitchen with an informal dining space and a comfortable family lounge area extended across the back of the house.

The drawing room and a formal dining room were on the right side of the great hall while a library and the billiard room with a full custom bar occupied the left side of the hall. The basement had been converted into a training center, which included a gym that was the size of a professional basketball court.

Something unspoken about Eastridge lured Lissie and me in, making us fall for it. Sometimes, when the house was quiet, an odd breeze, slight and cold, would touch my skin, as if to let me know the silence was intended, that it was a presence, and all was fine.

But the only presence I sensed now was Will's. He was home. I turned in his direction, pitching a slow, flirtatious smile.

He stood with his hands in his trouser pockets, one shoulder leaning against the casing of the billiard room doorway. He wore a dark blue tailored three-piece suit with fine plaid detail and a crisp white shirt, unbuttoned at the neck. His thick mane was pushed back instead of swept to the side. His charged eyes scorched a path into my soul.

The whole room became *him.*

One of the girls with Thomas's friends whimpered. She was right. Will was sexy as hell. I only just suppressed the sounds of my own pleasure.

Will was the kind of man who enjoyed the chase as much as he did his prize's submission, and I had no desire to deprive him of either. Though I wanted to run to him, I leaned against the bar, where I'd been scribbling on a napkin, and took a sip from my glass. I watched the smile dangle from the corner of his lips as he crossed the room.

I'd dressed for him in the way that I would have for a first date under normal circumstances.

Gran used to call me Miss Fancy because I loved wearing dresses. It was silly. My grandmother had been one of the most fashionable women that I'd known, and she'd been my influence.

"Style choices should be conservative, to please the women around you. It takes only one small thing to satisfy a man's imagination," she'd once told Isobel and me as she peered over the rim of her red-framed readers with a tight smile.

My red sleeveless dress was a fitted sheath that hit below the knee, except where the front slit bared my right thigh. My nude Louboutin sandals were the perfect complement.

Will left very little space between us. He took the drink from my hand and finished it himself. The most handsome man I'd ever seen leaned in close to my ear and sent a chill along my spine. "Elle, it's late, but I'll make it up to you." His lips brushed along my cheek to the corner of my mouth before he straightened his back.

"You'd better." I placed a kiss on the underside of his bearded jaw. "Have you eaten?"

He shook his head and pushed his hot gaze down into mine. His masculine scent overwhelmed me. My knees threatened to give.

He lifted my hand and pressed his warm lips there. "You're beautiful."

"Thank y—"

"If you two are quite finished, where's Ethan?" Thomas interrupted, startling me.

Will turned to him with a raised brow.

"Ah, right." Thomas filled my glass and poured whisky for himself and Will.

"I need to fight before I head back to the city. Meet me on the mats at six," Will said.

They threw back the scotch and pounded their glasses on the wooden bar. That was it. I was finished sharing him until morning. I tugged on Will's hand and led him toward the kitchen. Mrs. Bates had left a plate warming for him, and she'd shown me where to find it. But once we were in the hall, he backed me against the doors beneath the staircase and kissed me.

His lips were at the base of my throat, his words vibrating against my skin as he spoke, "I'm taking you to my room tonight."

I ran my fingers through his hair. "That's poor behavior for a proper Englishman."

Will's hot gaze moved down the front of my dress as he played along. "You can worry about my virtue later. I need to be inside you, baby. I will have you, and I'd rather not wake the house." He dragged his eyes back to mine and pushed his arousal against my body.

A little breathy, I pushed back. "Dinner for you first. You'll need your strength, with your impending fight and all."

He grinned. "You wore this for me."

His hand glided up the slit, over my thigh. A soft moan escaped me.

The back of his fingers brushed the edge of my panties. "I'll take that as a yes."

Remembering where we were, I moved his hand away and

then stumbled on my words. I didn't know why. It had made him happy, and that was the point, wasn't it? "I haven't been myself since—well, I do prefer dresses, and, yes, of course, I did wear it for you."

He tucked his forefinger under my chin and caressed my lips with his thumb. "Good. I'm going to buy you quite a lot more."

As he lowered his head to kiss me again, Thomas called out his name.

Will snapped at his brother but kept his head lowered, his eyes on my mouth, "Better be important, goddamn it."

"I just received that text. They're all here now. She needs to see them," Thomas insisted.

"Yeah, all right, let's get this done." He put a soft kiss on my mouth, let go of my chin, and pulled out his phone to send a text message.

Six to the hall now.

I gripped his arm. "What is it, Will? Tell me what's happening."

"There's no need to panic, Elle. I'll have you meet the security team while I'm home."

As the words left his mouth, he moved us aside, and three men came through the basement door. Another came from the front entrance, and two others from the billiard room.

It was the Six, as he called them, Will's private army. Six former soldiers of the British armed forces, skilled marksmen and combat fighters who were now training at Eastridge. To the public, it was a security team for the estate and the family's other properties, but these men understood their real purpose. Will employed them for my protection, to help keep me alive.

The soldiers surrounded Will and me in a tight circle, their broad backs forming an impenetrable barrier. Each held a weapon in a low, tactical position until Will commanded them to disband.

I could do nothing more than stare with my mouth hanging wide open.

"This is Ellie James," Will said to the men. He gave a clipped nod, and a man stepped forward, closer. Will turned back to me. "This team is for your protection. In the future, when things are sorted out, Joe Turner will be your lead personal protection officer."

The man who had stepped in front of us shifted the rifle onto his shoulder and greeted me with a callous hand. "It will be my honor," Joe Turner said.

sixteen

THOMAS AND THE SIX HAD GONE, LEAVING US ALONE IN THE kitchen.

Will wiped his mouth on the dinner napkin and then kissed my neck. “Elle, come with me to bed now. Tell me you will.”

“I will. As soon as you tell me what I want to know.” I gave him a smile, batting my lashes a little, something he often responded to. “Please.”

He swept me into his arms and headed for the staircase, passing through the hall. “On the way. Ask quickly.”

“Why six? And why military-trained soldiers?”

“I would have nothing less.” To connect the dots for me, he outlined the level of violence the Order had undertaken in the past.

I kissed his neck as he climbed the stairs. “Go on.”

“You must understand, there is a sickness in men like these. They’re no different than the vile extremists of the early religious crusades.”

I nodded. There was one more thing I needed to know. “You have daggers.” I had noticed when he packed his black duffel before our flight. “Why?” I whispered.

He ignored my question.

I touched the corner of his mouth with mine. "I want to know."

"A bullet is merciful. Those who try to hurt you will suffer." A dangerous energy vibrated through him as he said the words, and God help me, I was enthralled by it. "No more talk like this," he added as we entered his bedroom.

Then, he pinned me against the bedroom door he'd just locked and took my mouth with his. I'd never been kissed by a man so fierce, never known passion so raw and powerful could be expressed in a kiss. I wanted his power, wanted to breathe it in. I needed to feel it inside me.

He tossed his jacket and waistcoat, and I quickly unbuttoned his shirt, tugged it from his shoulders, and dragged my lips over his magnificent chest. He fisted my hair, twisting it through his fingers, and drew me back to his mouth.

"I need to be inside you, Elle. I'm mad for you." His deep voice was rough, and the sensual way he'd said my name unmade me. It was like an imperious purr.

Oh God.

I spun and lifted my hair, so he could unzip me. Goose bumps trailed behind his velvet kisses as his mouth followed the descent of my zipper. He grasped my shoulders and turned me back to face him, causing my dress to hit the floor and pool at my feet.

I stood before him, weak with anticipation, wearing the red lace bra and panties I'd chosen for the dress, for him. He stared. His eyes lingered, sliding up and down without care. A blush warmed my cheeks. He purred my name again, and blood rushed to my core.

I was out of my mind for his touch. I wanted to feel his skin on mine. More than that, it was a need, something I had begun to ache for while he was away in London. I stepped out of my shoes and fallen dress, anchored my arms around his long neck, and melted into his body as I inhaled the warm scent on that sensual spot at the base of his throat. His full bottom lip caught my eye. I lifted onto my tiptoes and nipped it.

"Ten fucking years—that's how long I've wanted this, wanted you. I swear you're a witch."

"Maybe I am," I teased with a wicked smile.

He moved our bodies with speed and grace, as though we were one, like a predator stealing its prey. My back was pressed against the wall, and he was against me. A guttural vibration moved upward until catching at the back of his throat. Capturing both of my roaming hands and holding them in one of his above my head, he dragged his other hand from my lips down to my thigh and kissed me hard.

I moaned against his mouth.

A framed picture loosened from the wall. Will instinctively batted it away before it hit me and sent it crashing to the wooden floor.

I locked my legs around him when he lifted me into his arms and carried me to his bed. He sat down at the edge and pulled me tightly against his erection, and as I straddled his lap, he filled his hands with my hair again and kissed me until we shared a single, ragged breath.

I bit his neck, and he tossed me onto the bed, prowling up and onto my body. He was so far gone that he didn't realize he was crushing me with his weight. I pushed hard against his chest and dug my nails into his flesh. He lifted and effortlessly supported himself.

His lips slid down my neck to my breast and sucked and pulled on my nipple through the lace. He came back to my mouth and claimed it as he dragged his fingers down the front of my body. He stopped when he reached my panties. With one powerful tug, he snapped the delicate lace and tore it off.

I cried out when he pushed his fingers inside me.

"So fucking tight, Elle," he said against my mouth.

He pleasured me with his thumb, as he had on the plane. His

fingers moved in and out, and he pushed me higher as he increased the intensity. Another cry parted my lips and swept against his as I came.

"I need you." His words were desperate but controlled. His body stilled, and he waited with burning eyes for my response. The growl lying in wait at the back of his throat vibrated.

"I'm yours. Take all of me." It was a whisper, but inside my head, the words screamed. Because he made me feel. Because my soul was no longer empty.

I reached between our bodies to help get his trousers out of the way. As soon as his erection was free, I wound my fingers around him, sliding my hand up and down his length.

He groaned, a throaty sound of torment and pleasure. The band of my bra abruptly contracted as he unfastened it, and then he captured my hands and confined them above my head once more. He released them when he took control of the rest of my body, anchoring me tightly in one arm and yanking the lace from my chest with his other hand. His knee pushed my legs open wide. Cool air hit my wet core, driving my need for him higher.

My body responded to every touch, arching closer as his mouth lightly teased my skin. I moaned, pleaded with him, begged. But instead of pushing himself inside me, he slid his hand between my thighs and pushed his fingers into me again.

"Will, please. I need you now."

He shut my mouth with his, kissing me again.

"You're small. I don't want to hurt you, baby." His voice was all gravel.

Will was huge. He was power, and by comparison, I was small and delicate. But I didn't care. If he hurt me at first, it would be good pain.

"Please, Will," I begged.

He smirked, pleased with my desperation for him, and then he kissed his way down the front of my body. More heat surged through my blood. He gripped on to my hips and drew me to his mouth. He buried his face between my thighs.

"Oh God," I cried out, panting, pulling his hair. Each time he intensified the pleasure, I pulled harder. I cried his name as my body shattered, fragmenting into billions of pieces of myself against his mouth.

When he finally shoved inside me with one fierce thrust, his mouth owned mine, and he swallowed my scream. He buried his face in my hair as his body shuddered with need, forcing himself to be still, cursing against my neck as he kissed me there while still deep inside me. He filled me completely. I could feel him throbbing—he was a second heartbeat within my body.

His white-hot eyes burned into my soul when he lifted his head to find mine.

Will's embrace tightened as he lowered his face to my neck again. "*Christ.* You're so tight," he mumbled while battling hard to find the strength to calm himself, clearly wrestling with his self-control.

I clung to him with all that I had when finally, he moved inside me. I cried out as he stretched me. Though he'd commanded my surrender, he held back. I could feel the restrained power surging within him. Before my brain could stop me, I arched up against his heavy thrusts and writhed beneath his dominance, pushing him to let go of more.

"I want all of you, Will," I demanded.

And with that, he gave me what I desired. He covered my mouth with his, the kiss as intense as all the others but different. It was a claiming kiss. Our teeth banged. My bottom lip split and bled from the force. His chest vibrated.

"All that I have is yours." His voice was raw as he sank deeper inside me. He drove hard and fast, filling me over and over until everything we were burned away.

We became something else, something we'd never before been separately.

We were remade.

Another unexpected orgasm ripped through me. I screamed his name against his lips, my body and soul shattering a third time.

Every muscle in his body tensed. He lifted his head and threw it back. The growl once lodged at the back of his throat broke loose, morphing into a roar as he came. His breath was heavy as he dropped and burrowed into my hair again. When the shuddering of his body settled, he turned his face and kissed my neck, kissed my butterfly.

"I'll never let you go, Elle. Never."

I was breathless. Thunderstruck by his storm.

Will rolled onto his back and pulled me to his chest, and while I was in his arms, he owned my body and possessed my soul with strength and tenderness.

seventeen

WILL WAS ALREADY DOWNSTAIRS IN THE GYM BY THE TIME I woke.

I'd slept in his arms without dreaming through the entire night. There'd been no nightmares—no knives, no distorted faces, no deaths. There had been only Will.

He planned to leave for London after he trained with Thomas, and I couldn't bear the thought of not kissing him once more before he left. I leaped out of bed and found my dress where he'd draped it neatly over the back of a chair and hurried down the corridor to my room.

"G'morning, dearest. Lily will get on with breakfast soon," Mrs. Bates lilted as she misted the roses with water, doting on them with the affection of a proud parent.

"Mrs. Bates, really, I don't mind having breakfast in the kitchen."

"Neither you nor dear Mary will be subjected to breaking your fast with the lads or the children," she harrumphed. "Ladies of this house will be afforded the respect of privacy in the morning hours. I'll see to it."

I'd picked the same fight with her over several mornings,

battling an antiquated custom that she adored for some reason, and every morning, she refused to yield. I could demand it from Will, but I'd decided instead to make an effort to accept the traditions of his family home while I was there.

"Okay, you win." I flashed a smile and headed for the shower, though I rolled my eyes at the thought when I stepped under the spray of warm water.

After a quick shower, I headed down the staircase just as John climbed up. His sweat mixed with the trickle of blood from a small cut above his eye and ran down the side of his face.

I stopped short. "You're hurt?"

He dabbed the laceration with a fingertip and grinned. "That's nothing. It happens."

I lifted a brow. "Which one?" Will and Thomas were massive by comparison.

"Thom. Did you see how the rain cleared out again? The weather is perfect."

"Don't tease me, John. Where is Will now?"

"Going at it with Thomas still, repaying him on my behalf maybe."

As John resumed his climb three stairs at a time, sunlight burst in from the foyer.

Eastridge was a fantastic house, but I craved more, felt trapped. I needed the sunshine touching me, warming me, needed to walk along the edge of the sea and feel its energy. South East England was known for its verdant landscapes, quaint villages, and charming coastline, and I wanted to see it for myself.

I slid my phone into my back pocket and hit the foyer, hoping for one or two breaths of fresh air.

"I can't let you out, Ms. James," one of Will's soldiers said as he stepped in front of me. His expression was sober, but his eyes were kind. He smelled of evergreen and new leather.

"Are you serious?"

"Sorry. You'll need to speak to Will. His orders. Shall I take you to him?"

It wasn't his fault, but I snapped anyway, "Count on it. Yes, take me to him."

We headed for the double doors beneath the staircase in the central hall. At the bottom of the stairs was a corridor full of closed doors. The first three were solid wood with no visible handles. Electronic pads were mounted on the right side of each. Farther down the corridor, two sets of steel doors led into the gymnasium. The soldier pushed one open and waited for me to pass through, following as I made a beeline for Will.

Will stood with Ben and Thomas at the far end of the gym, toweling sweat from his face and neck. He saw us and sprinted across the pale wooden floor. "What happened? What's wrong?"

"This happened." I pointed at his sentry.

He dismissed the guy with a slice of his chin. "Why are you upset? You know what we're up against. There will be a guard at the door from now on. He's doing his job."

I hooked my hands on my hips. "I only wanted some fresh air. I wasn't going to leave."

Will closed the gap between us and forced me to meet his eyes. "I'll do whatever is necessary to keep you safe, and you will cooperate."

I narrowed my eyes. "I'm not your prisoner."

"Goddamn it, Elle." His jaw clenched, and his eyes flashed, warning me that he was prepared to fight and win. "We've been over this."

"You—" I halted my argument. I wouldn't fight with him. I couldn't bear the idea that we'd be distant in both the physical and emotional sense while he was away. Instead, I placed my hands on his forearms. As I traced the veins there, my thoughts changed course again, and I made a gentle demand. "Take me to the beach, Will."

His face relaxed, and he exhaled. A bead of sweat fell from

his forehead and landed on my cheek. He was thoughtful for a minute before nodding. “After I finish here and make some calls. I’ll drive back to London later.” He wiped the drop of sweat from my face with his thumb.

“Really?”

He lowered his head and pressed his salty lips to mine. “I’ll deny you nothing.” Then, he grabbed the phone from my pocket and shouted for Thomas.

“Oh. I listened to the messages.” I looked at the floor. “I’m a suspect now. Josh wants to know if you could ...” I didn’t know how to finish the sentence.

“I know. He called me in London at my office. It’s all right.” He pulled my chin up. “US police demand that you be interviewed. My lawyers will make certain it’s conducted by the London Met Police Commissioner. He’s an appointee of the Queen, and we know she doesn’t want an investigation from abroad any more than we do. If we grant the request, they’ll quite likely drop the matter.”

“What do I say?”

“The lawyers will prepare and manage the interview.”

“What if they don’t believe me?” I tried not to panic, my body vibrating with the need.

“You didn’t do anything wrong, Elle. You’re an innocent victim, not a criminal. I’ll get the cop anything else he needs privately. He and I agreed to clean it up, and we will. I promise.” He handed my phone to Thomas. “Get rid of the account. Scrape everything online and remove as much as you can.”

Thomas was a genius with devices, the internet, and computer systems. I had heard that he and one of his close friends from Oxford could hack anything. He would break through the firewalls of the phone company and the social media sites to remove the traces of my history.

Vanished, just like that. Gone like the rest of my family.

Thomas quickly swiped through my apps. “I’ll get you another phone this afternoon. You can still follow Jessica, but wait for me to set it up, so I know it’s secure.”

eighteen

Mary and Lissie traded a quiet, warm smile as we finished our art project, perhaps reminding each other about a secret they shared, or maybe remembering something special from their morning walk.

I was shocked at first, but also completely thankful for the way Lissie spoke to Mary with such ease. Grannie, she called her.

Mary Hastings was a gentle, caring woman. I couldn't imagine any child rejecting her love. It must have been difficult for her to hold back with her sons. I had no doubt that she'd still imparted pieces of herself. The tenderness Will drew from his fierce depths was proof of his mother's influence.

It weighed heavily on my heart how unprepared I was to raise a seven-year-old. I'd ruin Lissie on my own. Her growing relationship with Mary relieved me of the pressure and afforded me time to search for the best path forward for Lissie and me, if one existed. My role in her life might change a lot with Ethan in the picture as her father. He would be her legal guardian.

I inspected Lissie's hands after she scrubbed the purple paint from them. "Good job, girlie. The paint's all gone."

She smiled at me with Ethan's eyes.

"Your turn, Chelsea." I lifted Ben's three-year-old daughter up to the sink and washed her hands. "There. All good?"

"Good!" she squealed, clapping her hands under the running water.

"You're getting Auntie all wet, silly girl."

"Me too!" Lissie shrieked.

The three of us giggled as I shifted Chelsea to one hip and reached for the faucet.

Will caught my hand and pulled it back. He kissed my fingers and shut off the water himself. "Let's get on to the beach, Elle." His grip was firm. He eliminated the space between us.

Chelsea twisted, uncomfortable with the closeness of the giant looming above her.

"Get changed," the giant said before he bent and placed a kiss on my lips.

I stared up into his magnetic smile, stunned by his display of possessive affection.

Mary stood at the center island, slicing bread and cheese for the girls. She narrowed her eyes and scolded her son, "You know better, William. Go on and wait for Ellie in the hall."

Will scowled at his mother, but as he left the kitchen, he mumbled an apology to her.

A giggle escaped my lips. I covered my mouth before another slipped out.

"It's all right, dear. That one," she said, gesturing with a knife in her hand in the direction he'd gone, "has always been a handful. Stubborn like his father and equally lionhearted." She smiled then and stared at nothing with distant eyes. Her unfocused face was beautiful. It was clear she was caught in a memory of her late husband.

I gave her another moment. "Does he look like Richard?"

"Quite like Richard. In fact, he's the spitting image. His walk, even his voice. All four of my boys have their father's eyes."

My gaze shifted to Lissie. I wasn't sure if Ethan had discussed it with anyone other than Will, so I self-corrected and hoped she hadn't noticed. It wasn't my place to tell her.

"Hastings eyes are hard to miss," she added. "There's a fiery element. Only it's—"

"White," I finished.

"Yes, white. Like lightning. You know, dear, when he came back from America the first time, the clarity in his eyes was unmistakable. We knew then if conflict with the Order ever resumed, it would be Will's war, not Ethan's. We didn't know how it would unravel, just that it was so. I suppose Richard knew in his heart long before that. He'd always been much harder on Will."

"Will's a good man with a good heart despite the cards he's been dealt, the game he's been forced to play. His tenderness with me is unmatched. You know that, right?"

She smiled wide, and a twinkle bounced around inside her honey-brown eyes. "I do. Get on, Ellie. He's done his time."

The back staircase was perfect for my escape from the kitchen. In my room, I stepped into faded denim boyfriend shorts with split side seams, a sleeveless white blouse, and strappy heels. I tossed lipstick and sunglasses into my black leather shoulder bag before dashing out the door.

Will waited in the great hall, as his mother had instructed. He met me at the bottom of the stairs, wearing one of his confident smiles. His brows flashed, and he rubbed his chin. "Christ, Elle. Your legs are a mile long. Maybe we should just go upstairs. We can go out another day."

"Oh, I think we'll do both." I flipped several strands of hair over my shoulder and treated him to a slow, mischievous smile. "Beach first."

"Not until you kiss me." He lifted me from the last step.

"If I do that, you'll not want to leave. Swear we'll still go."

He nodded.

I hooked my legs around his hips and cradled his face in my hands, then slanted my mouth over his, tickling his lips with my tongue. He opened and thrust his tongue impatiently against mine. When he was satisfied with his victory, he put me down but didn't loosen his grip on my waist.

"Is it still the beach you want?" he teased.

I thought about it, shaking my head as though the image of us tangled up in bedsheets could ever be erased from my mind. A cocky grin slid across his face.

"Yes." I pulled back and dragged my eyes to the bulge that would push above the waistband of his jeans if he didn't cool it. "And if you're a good boy, maybe we'll use that later."

"Count on it."

He caressed my ass as we walked out the front door.

I WAS OUTSIDE EASTRIDGE FOR THE FIRST TIME SINCE ARRIVING in England. It was seventy-eight degrees Fahrenheit, and not a cloud floated in the sky. The glorious sun caressed my skin the minute we stepped through the doorway. I took in the flourishing landscape and decided to paint it someday. An airy bouquet of earthiness after a long rain, freshly clipped grass, and lavender wove through my senses. I inhaled deeply, noting a faint, salty nip of the sea, and smiled.

Thomas pulled up in a black Range Rover with dark tinted windows. Ben rode shotgun. John sprinted out of the house behind us and yanked open the car door before we reached it. I cuffed him on the shoulder and winked, receiving a grin and a countered wink in return. Will and I climbed into the back. He locked his arm around my waist and slid me closer to him after John piled in on the other side.

"Weapons?"

"Secured. You don't want any of the Six?" Thomas looked at Will in the rearview mirror.

"Not this time. Let's roll."

Anxiety made its move. I squeezed Will's thigh and chewed on my lip. "Is it safe?"

He tightened his arm around me. "The locals aren't aware you're here. There might be some initial confusion, but these people aren't the enemy. They'll support you, even protect you once they're used to the idea. There's nothing indicating assassins are here, but it won't be long before they arrive. I want you to experience Old Town before that happens."

I took a deep breath and forgot to release it.

"Breathe, baby. I won't let anyone hurt you. Someday, you'll walk the streets of London with me." He winked and kissed my forehead.

I exhaled and nodded. I trusted him. If he said it was okay, then it was.

"I'm going to show you how to use a handgun properly. I bought one for you. You'll handle it only when I give it to you."

"What?"

"I'd be a fool not to teach you."

A gun wouldn't be much use for me, not in the UK, where firearms possession was broadly prohibited. Will's family was well connected, and he knew how to find policy loopholes, but his methods wouldn't work for a foreigner like me. But I understood his goal. I would be exposed to guns, and I needed to know what to do should one fall into my hands.

"I should learn to fight."

"No," he snapped.

"But—"

"I said, no." His back stiffened. "I won't see you beaten and bruised."

I leaned over his lap and gawked at the passing scenery. Wild forget-me-nots bloomed along the edge of the forest, and bumblebees buzzed about the blossoms. Several deer loped throughout the trees.

"We'll see," I said.

Thomas drove down the ridge until the estate ended near the old main route, then headed into the heart of Hastings, which was the area they referred to as Old Town. It could have been the model for Stonington, though it had a much edgier feel. It was like the ancient town dangled from a precipice but worked hard to hoist itself up as it evolved alongside a younger, hipper generation.

The streets were filled with people and celebrations. There were vendors selling drinks, food, fresh-caught fish, and crafts. Local artists painted portraits for those who posed. Solo musicians and traditional marching bands dueled for attention. A carnival queen and her court paraded through the cobblestoned streets.

Parking was limited, and many streets were closed for the town's annual weeklong late summer festival. We pulled into a small, gated lot behind a charming pub with a crown sculpture mounted above its front entrance.

Will caught my unasked question. "It's one of Ethan's investments. His partner runs it."

A cute girl with short blond hair stepped out of another car and approached Thomas. She was fashion-model thin and six feet tall with her heels. He took hold of her hand.

"Ellie, this is my friend Kirsty."

She presented me with a timid smile and a nod. "Quite nice to meet you."

I returned the smile but saved my American-accented words for later when she was more comfortable.

We all walked down a quaint alleyway with stacked Tudor-style buildings on both sides until it ended at the fishermen's beach—or the Stade, as it was called. Not far to the west was the historic pier, reaching proudly into the English Channel, even as it endured the workmen and machinery of a substantial renovation. The remains of William the Conqueror's castle sat high upon the west ridge beyond the pier.

"No sand?" I stopped to slip off my sinking heels after seeing Kirsty do the same.

"There's some close to the water." Will canted his head toward the channel.

I looked down at the pebbles digging into the bottom of my feet. "Is this pebble beach part of the ecosystem, or was it placed intentionally?"

"Shingle beach. It's natural." One corner of his mouth curved with amusement just before he swooped me into his arms and headed toward the water. When he put me down, my feet hit soft sand.

It frustrated me when he wore his dark aviators. I counted on reading his expressive eyes. "Take them off, Will."

He hooked the sunglasses on his T-shirt and his hands on my bottom. "Better?"

I locked into his gaze and nodded.

"This sweet, plump arse fills my hands perfectly," he teased, squeezing to demonstrate.

"Plump?"

"It's perfect. *Christ.* You're beautiful."

I pulled his face down until his lips burned near mine, and he took my mouth with his.

"I can't get enough of you, baby," he said once he broke our kiss, his warm breath still touching my lips.

It took me a moment to recover. "So, you won't be leaving tonight?"

An eye-crinkling smile ate up his face. "Well, if it's an order."

"Not at all." I kissed his cheek, then tugged on his arm. "Let's walk. I want to see more."

It wasn't an order or a demand. It was a suggestion.

Suggestions left him an out when he needed one. I recognized how serious things had been getting between us. From the moment he'd made his decision to take what he wanted on the tarmac in Connecticut, he'd been all in.

I suffered when he wasn't there at night. Missed his raspy whispers in my ear, telling me everything was okay, the fire in his eyes when he looked at me, his equal measures of tough guy and tenderness, and the security of his arms. And I battled nightmares without him. But I wouldn't use these excuses to hold on to him. I needed to be certain he was making choices, not fulfilling obligations.

Will grabbed my hand and gestured east. "I want to show you something there."

We headed away from the activity, soon coming upon a quiet expanse of shoreline beneath the ridge. The English Channel's passionate disposition had carved striking eroded walls into the sandstone cliffs. It was gorgeous. We dropped our things, and he led me into the water.

Will pointed above the cliffs. "See to the right of the Wellingtonias on top of the ridge?"

I stepped back. The tide swept over my knees. Beyond the cluster of trees, the house's second story and chimneys came into view. I stepped back again, and there was Eastridge, perched high above where we stood. She was an elegant stone fortress, standing tall and proud, announcing her presence to all who dared to look her way.

"How beautiful," I breathed, mesmerized.

He tugged me closer to the beach and kissed me as an aggressive tide swept in.

A burst of cool sea air washed over my flesh and left behind a blanket of goose bumps. It carried a whispered message, as it had on the coast of Connecticut. I arched my back and let go, trusting Will to hold me while I closed my eyes to send a silent reply, acknowledging that it had found me. My hair floated behind me with the next hard-driving breeze.

In that moment, something peaceful, something so honest that it almost hurt, staked a claim in my unguarded heart.

Will pulled me back into his arms fully and pressed his forehead to mine. "You were never lost, Elle. I knew where you were all along. I've been waiting, giving you time."

nineteen

THE RESTROOMS AT ETHAN'S PUB WERE SET IN A WOOD-PANELED alcove for privacy. I opened the ladies' room door after freshening up and found Will waiting with the handsome, possessive smile that had awakened my soul and changed me.

From our table, I explored the pub's artful, hipster charm. In addition to tables with board games painted on them, there were snugs with casual leather seating. The generous bar had been handcrafted from reclaimed wood. Original fireplaces anchored each end of the pub. Local artists' works for sale filled the walls, and daily newspapers and books were scattered about.

I thought of Nick's and the similarities. I thought of the old Victorian house where I had grown up and the beach house at Lords Point. The art gallery, the grade school children I'd taught. The stars over the open waters of the Atlantic. I thought of everything I had cherished in Connecticut. But truth be told, I didn't miss it. Not really. I was too busy falling in love with England, a place where reminders of abandonment and heartbreak had grown distant.

I snuggled deeper into Will's side for reassurance.

He leaned in and kissed the tip of my nose. "You're reflecting quite a lot today."

"I'm … well, I think I'm happy here. It feels right."

A gratified smile had his face before a seriousness chased it away. "So, I can stop worrying over the idea that I might need to chase you round the globe?"

"Yes."

"And you'll let me know if that changes?" He brushed his lips over mine.

"Yes."

With tenderness and discretion, he kissed his way down my neck. "Let's go home."

I twisted to see his eyes. "You need to start for London soon?"

"I'm not going. Can't sleep apart from you tonight."

His gaze jumped to a yellow envelope that a server placed in front of him. "What the hell is this?"

"I don't know, sir. A man paid me fifty pounds to put it in front of you."

"Show me," Will commanded of her.

"I can't. He left out the back door when I came over to your table."

Ben flew to the back and burst through the door. He returned inside seconds later and shook his head. It was too late. The man was gone, camouflaged within the festival crowd.

Will opened the envelope and took out two large photos. Both had been snapped from an elevated position and showed him carrying me from the plane. Thomas, Ethan, John, and Ben flanked him. An obvious protection detail. The Cross of Saint George was stamped on the front of each in red ink.

He tossed the photos onto the table, pushed back against his chair, and stretched. "War it is, motherfuckers."

Thomas came in from walking Kirsty to her car just then and grabbed the photos. "I guess it's on then, brother."

They knew where I was. Assassins had watched Will carry me onto British soil.

I swallowed and battled anxiety and fear as they worked to overwhelm me. They lurked in tandem, courting my mind, waiting for an opportunity to steal the kiss that would seal the deal. I shook them from my head, refusing to hide, choosing to fight. I corrected my posture and took a deep breath and released it. Despite my best effort, one traitorous tear found freedom and rolled down my cheek.

"You're safe. I promise." Will caught the tear before it dropped from my chin. "No one will get past me to you." He rested his lips along my temple. "I swear it, Elle. Please trust me."

I sniffled and then smiled. His commitment to me was unreal. It was beyond comprehension.

"I trust you, Will. Take me home now."

After Ben inspected the car, he pulled up to the entrance, and the rest of us climbed in. He hit the lock button and met Will's eyes in the rearview mirror. "Left side of the street, dark sedan, two men. Drive or fight?"

Will's attention shifted to the sedan. "Drive out of town first." He tucked me into both arms tightly. The muscles in his arms tensed. "Open up the cache, John."

Ben pulled away from the curb and headed out of town. The dark car followed.

John lifted the mat and a panel beneath his feet and retrieved two pistols, inserted a preloaded magazine into each gun, and handed them to his brothers without a word.

Will cuffed Thomas's shoulder, and Thomas gave him a quick nod.

I stared straight ahead, choking back the fear that swam in my blood. Illuminated clouds hung low in the magenta-and-blue twilight sky, the sun having dipped below the horizon only moments before.

Will strengthened his embrace. "Thomas and I are going to get out. You will stay in the car, Elle. John will restrain you if you try to get out." His tone was hawkish. He lifted my chin and stared hard into my eyes, seeking obedience.

"Okay," I breathed, my heart banging against my sternum.

Will's arms tightened more, creating an impenetrable cocoon. "Prepare yourself, John. Keep her in this car, by force if necessary," he told his brother. Then, he lowered his head and planted a soft, haunting kiss on my mouth.

Ben accelerated. So did the car behind us. He hit the brakes. Both cars skidded, tires screeching as rubber smoked and burned. Metal crunched, and glass shattered as the sedan plowed into the back of us.

Will's body absorbed the impact I should have felt.

Ben threw the Rover into reverse and accelerated again, pushing the sedan until it dislodged from our bumper and lurched sideways, sliding it into the gravel at the edge of the road.

Will and Thomas were out of the car at once. In the time it took me to twist and track them through the broken rear window, they'd torn the two men out of the dark car and held them at gunpoint.

Ben remained behind the wheel with the Rover still running. "Shit!" He slammed the gearshift into park. As he leaped out, he shouted at John and me to stay in the car.

John held my hand, the sweat of our palms mingling. "Shit," he echoed. "Look up ahead."

I turned and saw a police car approaching from the opposite direction. It sped up and abruptly engaged its vibrant emergency lights. Wine rebelled in my clenched stomach. I fought a wave of nausea with measured breaths.

Ben jumped back into the car and handed the guns to John. "Pull the mags and get them back into the floor." He put the windows down. A blast of crisp air slapped my face. "Ellie, sit up straight and don't give us away with panic. Will can fix this. This was an unfortunate car accident and nothing more."

twenty

MY STRENGTH HAD CRUMBLED AFTER WE MADE IT BACK TO Eastridge. I cried, and Will soothed me, promising me things I wasn't sure anyone could ever deliver.

Before Will let go of my hand outside the bathroom door, he placed a tender kiss on my palm. "I need to touch base with Ethan and reach out to some clients. No more worrying, Elle. It's been handled."

A hot bath with the essential oils Mary had given me then helped to ease me more.

Will was sitting on the armchair, talking into his phone when I came out of the bathroom. His voice was low as he spoke to Ethan, "They were unarmed messengers. Their information is on the police report now. In any case, I was clear—further involvement will cost them their lives."

I hadn't taken anything into the bathroom with me other than a clean bra and panties. I shrugged to myself, assuming he was busy anyway, and headed for the closet. I didn't make it that far.

Will said my name and summoned me with his long fingers. "Turn round," he commanded when I stood in front of him.

I obliged, giving him the "plump" view he desired.

He continued his conversation with Ethan as he stared at my

ass. After he filled his eyes, he filled his lap with me, making sure my backside was fit snugly against his erection. "I'll ring you back later. Something just came up." He disconnected and tossed his phone onto the table.

"Really? Something just came up?" I teased.

"You've been tormenting me with this pretty arse all day." He gripped my hips and ground himself against my lace-covered cheeks, his words warm against my hair. "Give me what's mine."

"Take it, savage."

A primitive grunt came from his chest as he moved us across the room. The back of my legs hit the mattress, and I fell onto the bed.

He pulled himself into check as he stripped. "You're good, baby?" His fierce eyes burned with intensity, but they were also softer than the night before. "Last night, I mean. You'll tell me if I hurt you."

Will climbed onto the bed and supported the weight of his body above mine, inhaling against the skin between my breasts.

He had hurt me with his first thrusts, but I wouldn't concede to it. He was significantly bigger than I was, but once he stretched me, it was amazing. And more than that, it'd connected us on an emotional level never before equaled for me. I needed that from him.

"Do it again, Will. Make me feel."

We didn't bother with a slow burn. We shared the same urgent sense of desperation. I needed him inside me, and he needed to be there. My fierce defender gathered my wrists above my head in one of his hands and brushed his lips over mine.

"When I'm inside you, you'll surrender to me completely. Every time, Elle." Then, he eased into me one rock-hard inch at a time.

I panted and moaned, insane from the intense desire he stirred in me.

His possessive whispers brought me to tears.

"You're an angel, my beautiful angel. I'm never letting go."

When he finally pushed in deep, he swallowed his name as I sobbed it, and then he kissed the tears that had slipped away from me. "Let go. Give yourself to me," he commanded.

And as I gave up everything he'd claimed, we burned to ashes and became one breathless, sated existence. He maintained mind-blowing control, covering my mouth with his to absorb my cries and quelling his own when he came.

I fell asleep on his chest, but when I woke, he was in the chair again with his laptop, stuffing half a sandwich into his mouth. Documents and newspapers were spread over the floor and hung from the chair arm.

"I kept you from your work."

"Stay beneath that blanket until I'm finished here." He looked up over the screen and winked.

I wrapped the sheet around myself and went to the bathroom. My stomach rumbled before I could get the damn door closed.

"You'll eat, woman," he called through the door.

I was starving and gladly ate the sandwich Will had brought up for me while watching him harness his intense physical energy and apply it to his intellect. He was as intelligent as he was strong.

After a client call, during which he'd spoken only French—and my God, was that sexy—then another to Ethan, he stood and stretched. The movements were graceful and majestic. He was a magnificent lion.

"I have something for you." He grabbed some old books and set them on the bed.

"What's this?"

"Look through them. See if anything stands out. Don't push me for an explanation unless you've done that." He countered his firm words with a soft kiss. "I need to go down to the gym and run."

The books were heavy and quite old. One was a colossal tome covered in worn brown leather with black straps that buckled to hold its contents within. There was a golden three-budded cross, made of tarnished metal, fastened to the cover by rivets. The same metal was used for decorative corner pieces.

The other book was smaller and less ornate. It was covered in black leather that was dappled with shades of gray, caused by time and wear. Aged red satin ribbons dangled from several pages. I opened to the first ribbon-marked page. The print was small, imperfect, faded. I skimmed at first, reading the last few paragraphs with more care.

> *The rightful young Plantagenet king, Edward V, and his brother, Prince Richard, Duke of York, were held captive in the Tower of London by their uncle Richard, Duke of Gloucester, after the death of their father, King Edward IV. It is known that the boy king met his death in the Tower by natural causes, whilst the prince was removed in secret a fortnight thereafter.*
>
> *Prince Richard remained in exile in the South of France, under the protection of French kings, where the prince's own royal lineage continued. He took a wife of noble blood, and she bore him three sons and one daughter.*

Will had already explained it to me. He didn't need to provide proof. He'd given me his word, and I believed him. But there it was in black-and-white, journalized centuries ago.

I picked up the giant tome and unfastened its buckles. It was full of genealogical charts, some with pages of explanation, some without. I leafed through until I landed on the page of King Edward IV and delicately slid my finger over the decomposing page to Prince Richard's name. Somehow, I still expected his chart to end there.

Prince Richard, Duke of York, my ancestral grandfather, had his own page.

My mind wandered as I allowed my eyes to follow the fading, blotted columns of names down the page until reaching the bottom, where the last generations were more legible. I sucked in a sharp breath but shouldn't have been surprised by what I found there.

My great-grandfather had dropped his surname and changed our family name to James when he and my great-grandmother settled in Connecticut in 1898. He'd been born *John James Plantagenet.*

Just as overwhelming was the sight of the final names on my family tree—the names of my dead parents, Edward and Elisabeth James. There was a footnote ascribed to my father's entry.

> *Edward James was the last-born male heir of the successive patrilineal descent of King Edward IV and his son, Prince Richard. Edward James's grandchildren, male or female, will not be known as heirs of the throne unless his daughter acquires it as rightful Queen.*

Tears threatened, but I pushed them back and summoned anger in their place. I dragged my finger, indelicately this time, from the top of the page to the bottom. They were all gone.

The pain caused by my sister's death returned and ripped through me. I compelled myself to allow the pain its due, binding myself to the anger.

My throat tightened, and I clenched my jaw. My mind swam. I cursed. If it wasn't for that damn footnote, Isobel would be alive, and assassins wouldn't be looking for me. There had to be another living bloodline stronger than mine. There must be someone else.

I flipped back to King Edward's page. Richard had been his only surviving son. I wondered though, about the king's brothers.

Of course, there were two, which I should have recalled from my studies. Edward's youngest, Richard III, had had several children, but none who were legitimate had survived. And there was George Plantagenet, the Duke of Clarence. George had had one son and one daughter, but they'd been deprived of their legacies after George's treason. Both had been executed as adults by a Tudor king.

The Tudor kings had suffered paranoia, which was the only cause for the executions. That paranoia was Prince Richard's fault. Richard hadn't had the courage to fight for his birthright as his father had done. Instead, he bribed imposters to antagonize the Tudors while he hid among the French like a coward. Richard had allowed the burden to fall to his sons, who had later bound themselves to a line of warriors named Hastings.

I thought about George's grandchildren. Curiosity gripped me.

George's daughter, shown as Countess Margaret Pole, had been executed at the age of sixty-eight, and she'd had surviving sons and daughters. It was a fully matrilineal line, so her family was never targeted by the Order's reformations.

I dragged my finger along the descending names on the countess's page. Only two generations beneath her, there was something I hadn't foreseen. I swallowed and whispered the surname, the word sweeping over my lips but making no sound.

At the bottom of that page, I found his name. Will's name.

William Richard Hastings.

I tossed the old tome as if it had burned my fingers.

twenty-one

WILL'S BODY FILLED THE DOORWAY. "ARE YOU ALL RIGHT, baby?" His sensual, masculine scent drifted into the room and confused my thoughts.

"These books are legitimate?" I looked at them, lying near the foot of the bed.

He responded only with a nod, still not coming beyond the threshold.

I pulled my knees to my chest and rested my chin there.

"You said you wanted me, Elle. You might reconsider now that you know who we are."

"I won't," I snapped, whipping around to find his eyes. "I want you."

He stalked into the room, pinned me to the bed, and kissed me like tomorrow would never come. "Your life is going to be harder with me in it, not easier."

He was driving at something, but I wasn't able to piece it together. There was too much banging around inside my skull. And then that kiss.

"It's too late. I warned you." He sat up on the mattress with his legs crossed and pulled me onto his lap, facing him. I locked my legs around his waist, and he pushed my hair away from my face. "It's too fucking late, Elle."

"I don't understand. What are you saying?" I rocked my pelvis.

"Don't do that." His hands gripped my hips, making me stop, and then his expression softened. "We'll clear this up first."

"What are you trying to tell me?" I asked.

"It could all be yours, truth be told. The timing is right with the nation's growing unrest. But you must know that I will never give you up."

"What?"

"I'll find a way to secure your claim, Elle, if it's what you want."

"That's crazy, Will. I just want them all to leave me alone."

"Being with me, you become a greater threat. I'm quite certain the Order will perceive the combining of our lines as a strengthening of your position."

"I don't care what they think."

"I'll fight for you either way, whatever you want, because I won't live without you, but you need to tell me which endgame you desire." He wasn't going to let up, not unless I showed intelligent consideration.

I nodded. "I understand. Do I have all the information now?"

"Yes, you have what I know. I'll never lie to you, Elle."

I believed him. He was not a liar. Will was loyal to the point of obsession.

I held his face in my hands. "Why not tell me sooner that you carried the same bloodline?"

"It's not quite the same. More to the point of your question, Ethan leads the family. We're still a little old school here. I respect his position, even when I don't agree with his decisions. He believes you'll grow paranoid, like your sister." He stared into me with those beautiful blue eyes.

I winced at both the softness in his eyes and the thought of

Isobel. It was an accurate description of her behavior. I'd thought it was the pregnancy that had changed her, but it was London. Whatever she'd experienced with Ethan had altered her.

"What do you believe, Will?"

"I believe you're strong. It's a quiet strength, but it's absolute, and it fuels mine. It's the loveliest thing I've ever seen. In time, you and I will end this madness."

I was stunned by his words and the confidence behind them. I couldn't move my gaze from his. I'd never seen myself through someone else's eyes. Will showed me a woman with fire and determination, who was forgiving and capable. No damsel in distress stared back at me.

But the truth was, I'd stolen glimpses into the most vulnerable part of his soul. What I'd found there powered my strength, emboldened me.

I lay my head on his broad shoulder. "I want a life with you. Nothing more, nothing less. Fight for that, Will."

His response was delivered in an unyielding, breathless kiss. He pulled me tightly into our tantric position, his erection wedged between us, and together, we intensified our kiss. My hands were in his hair, and his were in mine.

"Elle, never leave me. Say it," he commanded.

I whispered close to his ear, "I'll never leave you."

He put my back against the mattress, and a growl vibrated in his throat as he removed the silk nightshirt from my body. "I'm going to taste all of you, every beautiful piece of you."

Arching my back, I pushed closer to him, so close. It was never enough. I was desperate for him.

And I would never leave him.

Will lifted and rolled onto his side, his eyes filling with white heat as he burned a path down to my breasts. His gaze slid over the curve of my hips and caressed the length of my legs. "You're so beautiful," he said before dropping his head to place a sweet kiss low on my abdomen. "I know that I hurt you each time, that you don't tell me."

"It's only for a second, Will, until you're fully inside, then you feel incredible. It will stop with more practice. I promise."

I grinned and drew one from him.

His mouth covered mine, and two of his long fingers pushed inside me and then another, working to stretch me, luring a soft cry from my throat. "You're always wet when I touch you, baby."

"Because I always want you." I reached for his heavy arousal, and he captured my hand as quickly and kissed it.

"Don't push me. I can't maintain control when you do."

"Then, don't. I need you."

"My control is determined by yours, and even then, it hangs by a thread. Let me love you my way, Elle. Submit to me."

Will's body was more than strong. The power that coursed through him had to be managed and his need for dominance controlled. My pushing was a show of impatience, not an objection to that need. Because once he kissed me, touched me, there was nothing that could keep me from surrendering to him. There was no help for it.

I nodded. "Do it now. Touch me now. Please."

I would plead. I would beg. Whatever it took. The craving for him was deeply rooted in my gut, and it never diminished, it only grew. He had planted the seed when he kissed my hand on that pier.

The sheets rustled, tangling as his body covered mine. He kissed me with a smirk on his lips and then dragged his mouth along my skin until he reached his destination. His hands gripped my thighs and pushed them open wide, and he continued with his original plan, to taste all of me.

As I shattered in ecstasy, he shot up my body with his. He captured my mouth with his and shoved deep inside me with a savage groan before the contractions of my orgasm finished.

He cursed against my neck, his trembling body forced still. "*Christ.* I'll never get over that."

I arched against him, wanting more, using my hips to meet his as he moved in and out of me. Arching, grinding, my nails in his flesh.

He slowed and ordered my surrender. "Let go, Elle. Move with me, but do not push me." His authoritative words resonated, forcing me to see what he needed.

When I gave him the control, he could rein himself in and take us to a beautiful place neither of us had ever been without the other.

Will filled me over and over while creating erogenous friction in all the right places. I squeezed him with my knees and cried out against his lips. He was like a god, the only man I'd ever had who could shatter me that way. He soon followed me over the edge, my name on his lips resembling a benediction and a curse.

The roof might have fallen in, or the world outside could have ended. But not ours. When Will pulled me to his chest and held me the way only he could, he made it clear that our world would survive, no matter the odds or the cost.

DREAMS PLAGUED ME THROUGH THE NIGHT, BUT IT WASN'T THE usual murderous faces pursuing me. The old leather tome became a living, breathing demon that night, and its contents haunted me.

A scream burst from my lungs. I threw myself to the edge of the bed and sent a lamp crashing to the floor. I kicked and writhed until reality gripped me.

It was Will who reached for me, not one of his fifteenth-century ancestors.

"Come to me, Elle," he ordered, his expression worried.

“I’m sorry,” I told him as he pulled me back into the safety of his arms.

He caressed my cheek with the back of his fingers.

“It’s only a nightmare. No one can get to you. I won’t let that happen.” Then, his tone shifted. “I’ll kill them all first.”

twenty-two

Bad Company shouted from the speakers, and fifteen billiard balls broke with a sharp crack as Will and I entered the room the following afternoon. Ethan was home from London. It was the first time I'd seen him myself since the airport.

Ethan tossed his cue on top of the table and pointed behind the bar, where Thomas lowered the volume on the sound system. "Hello, darlin'," Ethan drawled before taking my hand and moving his gape from head to toe, landing at last on my eyes. "Christ."

Will tensed as he measured his brother's bad form. I slid my hand up his arm and gave his biceps a light squeeze. Ethan was testing him. We both knew it.

Ethan crossed his arms over his muscular chest and grinned. He was broad like his brothers, but unlike them, he stood no more than six feet tall. His hair was light brown, and he had a notable bump on the bridge of his nose, as if it had been broken a few times. Ethan's eyes and his handsome grin were indistinguishable from Will's.

My God, Lissie looked so much like him.

"I'm so glad you're home, Ethan," I said. "I'll leave you to your business with Will, but at some point, I'd really like to talk about Lissie."

Ethan nodded, and I released Will's arm and curled up on the sofa, content to be alone with my thoughts and sketchpad. I could feel them both watching me as they discussed China's tumbling stocks and its impact on the European market. A nervous client worried it would affect his leveraged buyout.

It was Lissie's pretty face on the paper when I lifted my pencil.

Will dropped onto the chesterfield next to me. "Your talent is remarkable, Elle." He studied my drawing, wearing a smile that was handsome as hell. "Tell me what you need to start painting again."

"Late mornings filled with natural light from the northern sky."

Ethan sat on the sofa across from ours. "Set your easel up in this room." He nodded at the windows. "Listen, next week will be quite busy for us in London. I need my brother to focus and close some business. I'm hoping you'll help me with that, darlin'."

I turned to Will. "Take me with you."

"I'll be tied up with new investors," he said, shaking his head.

"I don't want to be so far away from you all week."

"You'll stay here."

I narrowed my eyes, but since he wasn't leaving for a few days, I let it drop. I'd hit him with it again later when we didn't have an audience.

My brain shifted gears. My mouth opened, closed, opened. Unbidden words finally escaped. "Lissie looks like you, Ethan."

Ethan jerked his eyes to the floor.

"Is she yours?"

He shrugged.

"But it's likely?"

He made eye contact. "Yes."

"Do you plan to tell her and raise her? Do you have a plan?"

"When I confirm she's a Hastings, I'd like your help with that and telling her."

I withered beneath Will's arm. Ethan's response should have pleased me. I wanted Lissie to have a family, her father. But his willingness sliced into my heart, carving out another piece of wreckage. It was yet another loss for me.

"I won't take her from you, Ellie. She needs you. I know that."

"You really didn't know?"

"I'll figure this out. Blood is blood, always to be protected, no matter the circumstances."

Even though he'd said all the right things, anger whispered in my mind, reminding me how horribly the loss of my sister's life hurt, and I snapped, "Why weren't you there for Isobel?"

Compassion filled his eyes, and he dismissed my aggression. "I'm sorry. I should have been."

My throat started to close. Tears were next, so I changed the subject. "Have you instructed Will to keep anything else from me? I mean, your family tree doesn't make a difference to me. And I don't give a damn if others see it differently. So, if there's more, I'd like to know. Tell me now."

Ethan looked at Will, a wide grin spreading from his mouth to his eyes. "There isn't anything else, Ellie."

They both grinned, compelling me to narrow my eyes in warning.

"Stop it, both of you."

"There's nothing more," Will said low in my ear as he wound his arms around me.

Ethan winked and then strode back to the pool table. He and Thomas became dark silhouettes against the gray afternoon light that flooded in through the bank of windows.

Will leaned in and sealed his mouth over mine. The tenderness of his kiss was intoxicating. He lingered at my lips and didn't care at all that his brothers watched. Maybe that was the point.

A dreamy sigh slipped out of me as I gave his face a gentle push away from mine. "I promised to spend time with the girls. Lissie will be waiting for me."

"Take them out for a walk. Stay in the east and south gardens."

"I can go outside?"

"I need to get some work done, make some calls, but yeah. I'll send out someone else."

"You'll be watching the security monitors when you should be working," I teased.

My defender, my brilliant lover, conceded with a nod, and I placed a kiss on his cheek.

Leaving the room, I heard Ethan say to Will, "Christ, now, I see why you've gone mad."

"You fuck, don't rile him," Thomas snapped.

I rolled my eyes.

THE EXTERIOR OF THE WEAPONS ROOM WAS DECEIVING. IT hadn't occurred to me that there was anything other than a storage room there. Will placed his hand on the electronic pad, and the door slid open with a slight burst of air. We stepped into a deep, cavernous room. The door closed on its own.

It was time for my first shooting lesson.

"You're quite sure you want to do this," Will said more to himself than to me.

"You're not really asking, but yes, I'm ready."

The first area where we stood was the weapons vault. Rifles, handguns, and daggers hung on the walls and rested on shelves.

He pointed out the licensed weapons. The pistols he planned for us to shoot were illegal in England, as were most of the weapons.

Nothing he showed me in that room, nothing he did or said registered in my mind as a deal-breaker or scared me. My feelings for Will were absolute. Not even his sins could change that. I'd considered the idea of being sick and broken once before. Or maybe it was love. I'd never been in love before, but I'd heard it was blinding that way.

We walked beyond the heavy worktables with metal stools that ran along the north and south walls to the four steps that led down into the shooting pit. There was one large worktable in the pit as well as targets that were positioned at different distances and angles.

I watched Will as he picked up a magazine from the table and began to fill it, the slight clicks echoing through the pit. Neither of us spoke as he filled more and finally inserted one into the small Glock he'd bought for me.

He released the slide. "Look at me, Elle."

I met his eyes.

"There isn't a manual safety on this pistol."

"Oh. Well, how safe is that?" I bit my lip and fidgeted.

"Quite safe. It won't fire unless you pull the trigger. You'll keep your finger off the trigger unless you mean to pull it, baby." He pointed to the parts of the gun and explained.

"Got it," I said, taking mental notes.

"Christ. This is fucking mad."

"You don't trust me?"

"I do. This just isn't what I wanted for you." He stared at me. "Watch me first."

He picked up his larger Glock and positioned himself in front of a target. His feet were spread the width of his broad shoulders, and his arms were extended and strong. His T-shirt clung to him as he moved and flexed, defining the sheets of hard muscle beneath it. The jeans he wore hugged his tight, round ass and his muscular thighs.

I studied his body, taking pleasure in every detail.

He looked over his shoulder and shook his head at my flirty smile.

I winked.

The corners of his mouth twitched, and then he turned and fired a dozen or more times, creating one jagged hole in the center of the target.

Will then positioned me and stood against my backside to guide me. He adjusted the earmuffs he'd put on my head and placed my finger outside the guard, keeping his on top for control. "Pull once." His finger moved mine to the trigger.

I pulled. And flinched. I might have closed my eyes.

He slid his hands back and rested them on my shoulders. "Don't close your eyes. Use the sight. Do it again."

I fired again. The second time wasn't as intimidating. I fired three times without hesitation.

His hands moved down to my hips, and he briefly pressed his lips to my neck. "Empty it."

I pulled the trigger five more times.

Will reached around my body to remove the empty magazine and insert another into my gun. He kissed my neck again and pointed to a different target. When his hands were back on my hips, I aimed and fired the ten rounds.

After our fourth repetition, he pulled the pistol from my hands.

My head was light. I was high.

He caught me as I jumped into his arms and smashed my mouth to his, demanding his kiss. He set me on the table, pushed my legs open as he leaned in, and pulled me tightly against the growing bulge in his jeans.

I kissed his throat, growing more intoxicated as his pulse leaped beneath my lips.

"I need you, Elle," Will said, using my hair to pull me back to his mouth.

Ethan cleared his throat.

Will dropped his head and splayed his hands against the table, one on each side of me. His cheek brushed mine, the friction of his scruffy beard sending a shock of pleasure through me.

"What do you want, Ethan?" he snapped.

"The door has a lock," Ethan said. "Next time, you might use it. Dan Jones requested a dinner meeting this evening, so I'm leaving in ten. Decide what the week looks like, so plans can be made. I'll be back in the morning for a chat with Mum."

Will glared over my shoulder at his brother. "You know what it looks like."

"I don't think I do."

"Stop talking about me as if I'm not here," I said.

Will straightened his back and pulled me off the table. He stared at me through narrowed eyes. "My answer hasn't changed."

"I still want to go with you. Thomas and Ben can take me shopping while you're at work." I volunteered them only because I knew if Will were to come around, that was how it would go down anyway.

The door opened and shut, but neither of us looked in that direction.

"I'll hire you a personal shopper."

"I'll do my own shopping. And the nightmares will come."

"You still have them when I'm here."

Of course, he was right. I shrugged.

"I can't accomplish shit when I'm distracted with worry over you. Billions move through the firm, and I need to see to that properly. Christ, Elle, you're asking me to leave you alone in a public house, to turn you out onto the streets of London. I'm not going to do that."

"Thomas and Ben already protect me when you work. Here or there, what difference does it make?"

He planted his feet wide and crossed his arms over his chest. His tone became sharp and measured. "I can control this fucking environment—that's the difference, woman. I said, no."

I walked away, and he let me. When I glanced back, he was cleaning the guns.

We were at an impasse, and one of us needed to give in. But it didn't become clear which of us it would be until he came to bed that evening.

Will slipped in behind me. He pulled me close and wrapped his bare body around mine. "Don't be angry with me," he said near my ear after pushing my hair aside. "I watched a man almost take your life. I relive it every day, and I can't handle the thought of another getting that close. I won't lose you, Elle." His words were as tender as the warm kiss he placed on my neck.

A tear fell onto my pillow. To hold back the rest, I squeezed my eyes shut tightly and swallowed. I understood where he was coming from. I allowed my rigid body to relax into his heat and slipped my hand into his, lacing our fingers.

It hit me then, as he stroked my hand with his thumb, that his mother's reprimand the day before in the kitchen had been intended as a lesson for me as well. She'd said tacitly,

"He'll get what he wants because that's who he is, but you must be strong enough to make him work for it, so he never takes you for granted."

Only a woman who had loved deeply and lived as fully as Mary had could guide another like that. Lissie's face flashed through my mind. She would need that too.

I quelled my desire to turn to Will and give him his win. He'd get his victory in the morning.

He kissed my shoulder, and we drifted to sleep, our bodies resting in a contented tangle.

twenty-three

I HAD PLANNED TO CATCH WILL BEFORE HE WENT DOWN TO THE gym, but when I woke, Mrs. Bates was there instead. “I’d rather have breakfast with the girls this morning,” I told her.

She stared at me with her hands on her hips. “With the children, you say?”

The large Irish woman was as stubborn as she was traditional, and she didn’t accept back talk from anyone. So perfect for Will and his brothers, not so much for me.

Her eyes softened, surprising me. “Well, go on then, dearest. The lads should be cleared out by this time.”

I dressed and rushed down to the kitchen, where Lissie, Chelsea, and I finished every pancake put before us after making smiley faces on them with fruit and pats of butter.

Eastridge’s kitchen was warm and inviting, the largest I’d ever seen, and it was the one gathering space that made the mansion feel like home for Lissie and me.

More than ready to see Will, I kissed each girl on the head and hurried from the table, bouncing off his chest as I pushed through the door leading into the central hall.

“Oh, Will, I was—”

He grabbed my bottom and jerked me up into his arms.

Desire surged through his body, and the fire in his eyes burned into mine. I held on to him, my arms clinging to his neck, my legs around his waist, as he swept us into the privacy of the drawing room. In a flash, my back was against the wall, and his mouth covered mine. Will took the kiss we'd both wanted the night before.

I surrendered, falling deep into his fierce affection.

"You're avoiding me," he said against my skin, where he'd just kissed my butterfly.

I panted, laboring to catch my breath. "I was just looking for you."

"We should talk about it."

Our bodies were connected, his erection the only thing between us.

"Yes, but I can't think like this. Put me down."

He hesitated, then allowed me to slide down his front. I ducked beneath his arm and moved across the room to stand in front of the windows. As I savored the morning sunshine, I touched my swollen lips, wanting more of his brutal kisses.

Will stared at my mouth, watching me touch it, before going to the chesterfield with his stack of newspapers. "You'll do as you're told if you go to London with me." His tone was sharp, layered with resolve. He was giving in, though it displeased him.

I was still high and pleasantly surprised but also annoyed. He would read everything on my face, so I turned and searched over the lush landscape for my favorite little doe.

A newspaper made a thumping sound as it hit the table, and his scent reached out to me. He was coming closer. "Elle, you must agree."

Irritated by his shift from desirous to stern, I faced him. "Maybe you should define 'do as you're told' for me."

"Of course. When I tell you to do something, obey me."

"I think what you mean is, I should trust your direction if exposed to danger."

"When, not if. The threat is substantial, though you want to deny it."

I wasn't in denial, not after all that had happened. I shook my head and whispered, "I don't."

We stood, unmoving. Our stares locked into an even match. We did that sometimes—allowed our eyes to beat into each other. In those moments, words meant nothing to us. They didn't exist.

Through my eyes, he dived beneath the surface of his fear and mine and found something that neither of us could live with. My death at the hands of our enemy terrified us, yes, but beneath that lurked something else with the ability to hurt us. Confinement would alter me, cause me to suffer a slow, emotional death. I'd become an empty shell if we couldn't find a way for me to live freely. We'd never make it as a couple that way. I'd never make it that way.

We stayed that way, staring, without words, together understanding what we hadn't been able to reconcile as individuals. Living was more than assuring breath. We knew what we were up against. The risk of future encounters with assassins was unavoidable.

We chose to live.

"All right, baby," he said, breaking the silence. "I'll do whatever it takes to provide you with as much freedom as possible." It was a rare gift—his ability to decode the messages hidden on my pages. The vulnerability of it was unsettling, but it was also one of the things I loved most about him. He could reach me where no one ever had.

I closed the gap between us and wound my arms tightly around his neck. "Thank you, Will." My words and tears choked me. I buried my face in his shirt and waited for the thundering of his heart to reset me.

He protected my exposed soul inside his strong arms and waited with me, his words softer than usual. "The thought of someone hurting you again drives me to a very dark place, Elle. I need you."

I lifted my face and kissed his lips. "I need you too. We'll keep each other out of that darkness."

He nodded and smiled.

"Who won?" Ethan asked, poking his head into the drawing room.

"Fuck off, Ethan," Will told him while still smiling at me.

They would discuss security detail for London and then move on to business. I didn't want any part of it, so I kissed Will on the neck, smiled at Ethan, and headed to my bedroom.

"How does she do that?" I heard Ethan ask.

"We compromised."

"So, the intractable king learns to compromise. I quite like it."

"Don't press me, brother. You won't be afforded the same."

"Ah, but we both know it's more than that, little brother. Seeing you with her, well, you have my full support. Do whatever you must." Ethan hesitated. I heard the rustle of newspaper. "Christ, those fucking eyes."

"You'd better never touch her, Ethan."

"I think we're all quite clear on that point."

I ran up the staircase, away from the sound of their fraternal pissing match. All four of the Hastings brothers were aggressive males. It was sometimes like living with a pack of wolves. Ethan yielded to his brothers more than I imagined Will might. When it came down to it though, sibling rivalries and egos were set aside, and the eldest male was given his due.

Will texted me not long after I settled on the small sofa in my room.

Bond Street.

Two words, but I knew what they meant. I entered Bond

Street into the search bar on my web browser and smiled at the results, realizing he was setting us up in the heart of an upscale shopping district. Jimmy Choo appeared as one of the listed retailers, and I giggled. Shoes and me, we had a thing.

When we'd left the States, I had brought with me everything I had at the beach house as well as the clothing and shoes Will had picked up with our passports, but it wasn't much compared to my well-stocked closet back home.

"I'll buy you whatever you want in London," he'd promised on the way to the airport. It was a sincere gesture of pure intent.

I had no doubt even then that he would give me the moon, capturing it with his bare hands, if that was what I wanted.

"Thank you. Your protection is more than enough. I'll take care of myself otherwise," I had said.

The spark in his eyes had warned me that it wouldn't be the last time we would speak about it. It'd also stirred something in me on a deeper level, reminding me that I was falling for a ruthless man with an obscure past, a man driven by the desire to win.

twenty-four

Lissie shouted good-bye and waved with both hands from the first-floor gallery landing, as if she were suspended magically above the great hall. I couldn't help but laugh at the princess in her tower.

The group Will and Ethan had pulled together was gathered for final details as we prepared to leave for London in four separate cars.

A handsome smile lifted one side of Will's mouth higher than the other. "We'll drive to the city in my car, Elle, just you and me. My brothers will manage the security logistics when we arrive at the hotel. You and I will have dinner."

I bit into my bottom lip for a second to keep from squealing. "Is this … have you planned, like, a date?"

"Yes." His cocky wink made my stomach flutter. "I'll need to run through some numbers tonight with Ethan, but I want time with you first, baby." He pushed a kiss onto my lips at the same time he picked up our bags, and then he went out to bring the car around.

Will had vowed to give me something close to normal, and that was exactly what he was doing. He tucked me into the passenger side of his sleek black Jaguar like a gentleman, wasting no time as he jumped in and sped down the ridge.

The scent of heaven's woodlands drifted across the car. Tracing my lips with my tongue, I thought about how well he kissed them. His eyes burned into the side of my face, and mine fled from the fast-moving English countryside to him. God, he looked amazing behind the wheel. He drove just as he did everything else—fully in command.

Through my stare, I willed him to me.

He leaned over and kissed me, murmuring something about the color red.

"What?" I breathed against his lips before he moved to refocus on the road.

"When you go shopping, be sure to get another red dress."

"Favorite color?"

"When it's on your body. And, as you know, that now belongs to me."

I smiled. I wanted to belong to him. "You're quite full of yourself this afternoon."

A big, easy smile covered his face, although he kept his eyes on the road. He reached for my hand as he settled deeper into the leather seat and accelerated.

WE PULLED UP IN FRONT OF AN ELEGANT BOUTIQUE HOTEL located a few blocks southeast of London's Manchester Square. Will opened the door and took my hand, hesitating for a minute after I stepped out, allowing me some time to take in the streets of London.

A west-pointing street sign caught my attention. "Wallace," I whispered, dazzled.

The Wallace Collection was a significant assemblage of art that included originals by the Old Masters and also an exhibit of eighteenth-century French works. An artist's dream. One of my dreams.

The satisfied grin on his face gave him away. He'd anticipated the moment. "If everything goes well this week, I'll take you through."

I touched his cheek and rewarded him with an affectionate smile. He pulled my fingers to his lips. Several unexpected camera flashes went off from the opposite side of the street. Will wasn't bothered by the intrusion in the least, so I dismissed it as well.

The hotel doorman approached. "Mr. Hastings?"

Will nodded. "The three cars behind me as well."

"Shall we park the cars for you?"

"Not this time. We'll park and manage the bags. Thank you."

The young doorman bowed his head and opened the hotel entrance door.

Joe Turner sprinted over from one of the other cars. "I'll park your car, so you can get her off the street. We'll set up and see you later."

Will placed his hand on my lower back and ushered me between stately white columns into the grand Victorian building made of red brick. As we passed through the door, he put cash in the doorman's hand. Not for service, but for silence. He guided me across the polished floor of the quaint lobby to a lounge styled in rich woods and earth tones and gestured toward a sofa in a semi-private space reminiscent of an old English snug.

"You've been here?" I asked.

"Yes. This place belongs to one of our clients. It does quite well, so I want one of us with you at all times. No wandering. You must be accompanied, even on our floors." He pulled out his phone and read a text message as we sat.

"What do you mean, our floors?"

"Ethan cleared the fourth and fifth floors. Sleeping rooms are on four, and five is one large suite that we'll use as a private lounge."

"Is all that necessary?"

He leaned close and inhaled against my hair, and my breath quickened in response.

His voice dripped with the same deep gravel he used in bed. "Yes, it's necessary. Don't be con—"

He stopped mid-sentence and turned to the bar server, who had coughed to draw his attention. "Get her a glass of Chateauneuf-du-Pape. Macallan for me if it's stocked, Laphroaig otherwise," Will said, his pronunciations flawless. "And do not clear your throat for my attention again," he added.

His focus jerked back to me. "I wouldn't bring you otherwise. Don't be concerned about the indulgence when I'm not. I make quite a lot of money, and I spend quite a lot. Get used to it."

"Occasionally, your arrogance is off-putting, you know."

"Yeah." His ego was too great for even him to dismiss.

The server returned to Will's side with our drinks.

Will retrieved my glass of wine and handed it to me. "Taste," he ordered, and as he studied my face with a raised brow, I did taste it.

The wine was delicious, though the alcohol content was higher than I was used to, but he had known that when he chose it.

"Very nice, thank you. Where are your brothers and the other men?"

His face lit with satisfaction. He grabbed his scotch and sent the server away with a food order. "Inspecting the rooms and setting up shop in the security office. One of ours will monitor the surveillance cameras inside and out at all times, and another will patrol the property on foot."

"And you'd rather see to my intoxication than check things out for yourself?"

"I'll do that after I carry you to bed." He smirked.

That masterful little smile unmade me, sending shivers along my spine. My unruly body prepared for his, heat building between my legs. I slid my hand to his inner thigh.

His hand captured mine and squeezed it. "You need to be careful when you're out tomorrow, Elle. You'd better make damn sure you come back to me, unharmed."

"You've covered the bases. And that's part of the plan, right? You said you wanted to expose me to the public, to gain allies."

"Introduce, not expose you. Christ, it's not the same thing. I don't like that it won't be me out there with you, protecting you. You pushed me, baby, hard."

"If you really don't want me to go without you, I won't do it, Will."

He kissed my forehead and then pulled me against the sofa beneath his arm. "We'll do this. It's time for me to bring Thomas on board, place my trust in him."

"You trust Ben."

"In a different way. As close as we are, there's no guarantee he'll assume the same kind of risk as my brothers. Nor should he. Enough of that shit. No spoiling our date."

We laughed together out loud. Though I feared what we knew was out there, biding time, my spirit was light, and my heart was filled with something I'd never known, never expected.

"I'm so happy it's you, Will. I can't imagine getting through this with anyone else."

He pressed his lips to mine. "I won't let you down."

"I know."

"I'll be tied up tomorrow and most of the following day. We'll see how the rest of the week goes. Thomas will take you shopping. Ben and some of the Six will go. You must do as you're told, Elle. Promise me. I have business matters to handle, and I'll need to know you're okay."

"What will you promise me?"

"Anything you want." He swallowed what was left of his whisky and held up the glass in his surly way to call for another. "Give me your word."

I sipped on my wine and considered him.

"Give me your fucking word, Elle."

The server was back with two more drinks, again holding the tray near Will.

Will jerked his chin toward the cocktail table. "No more wine. Keep the whisky coming." When he didn't get anything from me, he took my glass from me and set it on the table. "You must promise. You understand what we're up against. I've left Ethan to run the company for months, and I need to take care of some clients this week. I can't accommodate avoidable distractions."

What crossed my mind next took me by surprise. I looked up at him from beneath my lashes. "Stay with me every night. Even if you get back late. You don't have to wake me if you don't want to. But be there. With me."

He nodded. "That's it?"

"No other women, Will." The bitter taste of regret abruptly filled my mouth. Jealousy had never been something that possessed me. But there it was.

Women looked at Will like they wanted to devour him.

He was mine.

"What?"

"Ethan sleeps around when he's here. I do understand that."

He grinned. "So, that's what you're worried about."

"Well, yes."

"And you assume I do the same." That wicked grin remained on his face.

I snapped at him, "I won't have it, Will. It's a deal-breaker for me." There. I'd discovered one.

He pulled me against his body, filled a hand with my hair,

and kissed me hard. He thrust his tongue into my mouth, tasting me, possessing me. My heart thumped wildly as I fell into his impassioned kiss. When we broke, he pressed his lips to mine several times, sucking, gently sucking, before he loosened his grip on my hair and rested his forehead against mine. We stayed in that position for God knew how long, wrapped up in each other.

There was nothing else.

A thought entered my mind but was lost before I could make sense of it. Anything outside of the space we shared became pointless. His hand still owned the back of my head, preserving the contact between us. It was an incredible, intimate moment.

"There is only you. I swear," he breathed, caressing my lips with his thumb, placing a soft kiss there.

We laced our fingers and rested our combined hands on his thigh.

A woman with long silver hair arranged two elegant place settings and platters of food on the cocktail table. She untied a decorative cord from around one of the napkins and placed it on top of our combined hands, gesturing in a way I didn't understand. "Carry on, loves," she said with a warm smile.

twenty-five

ETHAN APPROACHED US AS THOUGH HE'D COME FROM NOWHERE. His words destroyed the peace Will and I had found after the passionate kisses we shared only moments before that. It was becoming a habit—his inconvenient interruptions.

"Pop over to the security office and see that everything is to your satisfaction. Thom and I will stay here with Ellie until you get back."

Will nodded at Ethan and then kissed the back of my hand. "I won't be long, Elle. Eat something while it's warm."

Ethan and Thomas moved leather club chairs closer to the sofa. Ethan pulled out his phone and scrolled through his email, cursing about the volume of new messages.

"So, we're going shopping," Thomas said with a wink.

The four of them had the same eyes and used that wink often. I loved that about these brothers—how they chose to show rather than subdue their affection. I wondered if their father had done the same.

"Sorry. You'd probably prefer to do something else. But I insist on shopping, and he insists it must be you in charge of my security. Did you stop to get Kirsty?"

"Will and I talked earlier, and he's right. Until things settle down, it must be either him or me. I did stop for her, but I can't have my attention divided, so she'll stay here while I'm out with you."

I smiled. "Can you keep up?"

He shrugged one shoulder and winked again. "You'll tire long before I do, Ellie."

"What is this, and how do I eat it?"

"Yorkshire puddings. The smaller ones are sweet," Thomas said, pointing to one of the platters. "What are you drinking?" He scooped a pudding from another platter, cut it into small pieces, soaked them in gravy, and handed me the plate.

Mary Hastings might not have had much to do with training her sons, but she'd taught them other things. Her boys opened doors, sent flowers, kissed hands, and prepared Yorkshire puddings.

"Chateauneuf." I took a bite and moaned, stuffing another into my mouth right away. "This is delicious. Roast beef and what, watercress?"

Thomas nodded. "It's a great pairing, but it'll make a small woman like you sleepy."

"He plans to work late tonight," I muttered through a mouthful.

"Maybe not after the snogging we just walked up on."

"Thomas!" I felt my cheeks burning and diverted my attention back to the plate. I'd never heard the term before, but the meaning was clear.

Will appeared at that moment and stared down at me with his handsome smile before returning to his seat on the sofa. He canted his head toward the bar to send his brothers away, determined to finish what we'd started. My date grabbed one of the sweet puddings and held it up to my mouth. I took a bite, and he shoved the rest into his mouth and watched for my reaction.

It was a little bite of heaven, a soufflé-like treat filled with toasted coconut and warm, melted chocolate. "That is so good.

You'll make me fat with your English food, Will." The dribble of chocolate on his mouth was utterly kissable. I dabbed at it with my napkin.

Will leaned in and sucked chocolate off my bottom lip. "Next time, do it like this." He demonstrated again. Sensing my undeniable arousal and after adjusting his own, he smirked. "Drizzling some on your lovely, naked body in my bed would be quite good as well."

Sweat dotted the nape of my neck. I wanted the chocolate, the nakedness, his bed.

The rest of our party began to drift into the lounge, chasing away our intimate mood. Drinks flowed, and the guys carried on in a raucous manner. The camaraderie was remarkable. It might have been a blend of brothers by blood and brothers-in-arms, but it was a band of brothers nonetheless.

I thought of the tattoo on Will's shoulder. His father had inked the same shield on each of his sons when they turned eighteen. It was a traditional rite of passage for a Hastings, and once accepted, it committed them to the pact meant to keep me alive.

Feeling drowsy, as Thomas had predicted, I snuggled into Will's side with my head on his chest, gripping his shirt loosely in my fingers. His heartbeat and his voice relaxed me, both rich and strong.

He kissed the top of my head. "You're tired. Let's go up to the room."

I said good night to the guys, and then Will and I entwined our hands as we headed for the elevator. The moment the doors closed, he swept me off my feet.

"Will, what are you doing?"

"I told you I'd carry you to bed. I'm a man of my word, if nothing else."

I laughed from my belly.

"I haven't seen you laugh as much since—"

"Don't say the words," I said, my voice and my heart dropping.

"It's all right for you to be afraid."

"I'm not." My need for him displaced fear and logic most of the time, but the words resting on my lips in that moment were a lie.

"All right, baby." Will pushed through the door of our suite, into the bedroom, and kicked the base of the bed to see that it was solid before he lay me on it. He removed my heels, tossing them onto a chair, and dragged his fingers along the arches of my feet. "Christ, even this turns me on."

Our eyes connected as his body covered mine.

God, I wanted our clothes gone. "How long before Ethan shows up again?"

"Not long." He pushed his hard arousal against my stomach and kissed me, owning me with a single kiss. "Goddamn it," he grumbled, lifting himself first onto his palms, then getting to his feet. "You'll be the cause of my ruin, woman. In my absence, he's fucked up quite a lot."

"You'll fix it."

He winked. "Yes. Sleep, Elle. I'll be on the other side of the door."

After he closed the door, I went into the bathroom to get ready for bed. I could already hear their voices from the sitting room, the deep thunder of Will's, the smooth roll of Ethan's.

Their meeting didn't keep me from falling asleep. In fact, it lulled me into it.

But as soothed as I might have been, another nightmare breached the darkest recesses of my mind. This time, I couldn't wake up. I couldn't cry out. I'd fallen into a state of sleep paralysis. I didn't know how much time had passed before my body caught up to my brain. Finally, I jerked myself upright and cried into my hands for a moment before calling out for Will.

Will rushed into the bedroom and pulled my trembling body

into his arms. "It's a nightmare. No one is here. No one can hurt you, Elle."

"Please make it stop," I whispered.

"I'll stop them," he promised.

"We'll get them," Ethan said. He patted Will's shoulder and slipped out of the room.

twenty-six

I STARED INTO THE BATHROOM MIRROR AND RAN MY FINGERS through my long brunette layers. It was the perfect time to make a change. I was coming to terms with the real me … or the new me—I wasn't sure which it was. But it didn't matter. The important thing was that I understood the evolution strengthening and defining me.

Will had been gone for hours, and I had no idea at what time I'd see him next.

The hotel concierge rang back and confirmed an immediate appointment at one of London's premier salons. No waiting. The Hastings name turned heads and moved mountains throughout South East England. London was no exception.

My phone chimed with a text message from Thomas.

Don't open the door until I'm on the other side. Hit me back when you're ready.

I replied immediately.

Ready now.

He was at my door within a minute.

"I should check in at the salon within thirty minutes." I forgot myself and pushed through the center of my four-man protection detail, heading for the elevator.

"Hold on, Ellie. Do not walk off like that. You'll behave with me as you do with Will."

I turned on Thomas, a hand on my hip.

"You know what I mean," he said. "And when did a salon become part of the plan?"

"Just now. The concierge helped me."

"Christ, you're not going to make this easy."

I handed Thomas a piece of paper with the salon's information and a list of the shops that I wanted to hit. "I printed it for you because I wasn't sure if you had time to see my email."

He skimmed over it. "I read the email before you added this appointment. Let's get on with it." He pressed the elevator button and held out his arm, confining me behind his big body as the doors opened.

"We'll be done by tea tomorrow," I promised.

As we left through the lobby entrance, Thomas picked up a newspaper on the way out and cursed. An intimate photo of Will and me from the night before was on the front page. The caption and the write-up speculated about the Hastings Group CEO's return to London and how his absence had been connected to the mystery woman in the photo.

"Will set it up himself. I'm quite sure about that," Ben said.

Thomas tossed out the paper. "Yeah, quite right. I thought it might take another day to circulate."

We walked several blocks, doing our best to blend into the pedestrian traffic. As we arrived at the salon, Thomas and I were greeted by the owner and delivered to a posh lounge, where we were offered mimosas and breakfast quiche. Ben and the two other men waited for us at the coffee shop next door.

When I finally pulled my eyes from the mirror and stepped

out of the luxurious chair, Thomas loomed in an overprotective manner, but he wasn't saying anything. I'd been aware that he hadn't allowed me out of his line of vision at all.

"Well?" I asked. "What do you think?"

A renowned colorist had transformed my boring brown tresses into bouncing waves painted with shades of swirling caramel and flaxen. From a distance, I might have been mistaken for a blonde.

Thomas extended his hand. "I think you're lovely and my brother's a lucky man."

I gave him my hand and a smile, allowing him to lead me across the salon, but stopped when we reached the door. "I need to check out."

"I've done that. Let's get to the shopping."

"Wait, what?"

He pulled me outside into the sunshine.

"Thomas—"

"No."

I refused to move.

"We don't want a paper trail with your name on it, so your credit cards can't be used. Anyway, do you think Will's ego would allow for it even if security issues didn't exist? You're with him now. Get over the money thing, Ellie."

"But—"

"Move, or I'll carry you," he teased.

As we walked, I pouted a little.

"Listen, I know things are different in America, independence being the theme of every-fucking-thing. Remember where you are. I suppose it's paradoxical, but it's the way of England's old blood. We're progressive and traditionalists. Some things never change, and some do quite a lot. When it comes to our women, we lean traditionally. So, my brother won't allow you to spend your own money. And you shouldn't trouble him over it. It would be the same with me."

"You buy Kirsty's things?"

"Our relationship isn't the same as yours. If she were the woman for me, then I would."

"Is she going to be?"

"I'm happy with her in the present. I don't see her as my future."

"Ugh."

"What?"

"She's in love with you, Thomas." I'd noticed that look in her eyes whenever he touched her the day we all went to the beach.

He cursed under his breath, reminding me of Will.

After a late lunch, we left Jimmy Choo and the shops of New Bond Street for the dress boutiques of Old Bond Street. Thomas and Ben might never walk into a designer dress shop again, I thought. I'd asked to go into nearly every boutique and tried on loads of dresses before settling on what I wanted.

After exiting another dressing room, not feeling quite right, I reached for Thomas's arm. "Would you take me back to the hotel? I'm feeling a little light-headed."

"Of course." He winked to remind me that he'd won, that he'd outlasted me, and then he placed his hand on my back to guide me out. "I've arranged for your packages to be delivered to the hotel."

Ben stepped in front of us. "Hang on, mate. We've got company. Let me have another look."

Thomas peered out one of the shop's side windows. "Clearly, they know something. There's too many, too quickly. I'll take her back in a taxi. Get me a car, then meet us at the hotel entrance for cover."

The moment we stepped out the door, we were overwhelmed

by the camera flashes and shouts of the notorious London paparazzi. Anxiety hummed in my ears, pulsed in my blood.

"Ellie James, pose for us, love," someone shouted.

"It's her ... the proper heiress!"

"Are you here to claim your place in line for the throne?"

Paparazzi surrounded the four men protecting me. I was secured inside an impenetrable security formation within that circle of photographers.

"Back the fuck up," Thomas said, stiff-arming an aggressive individual. "You all know you're going to get your story, so cut the bullshit and give us some space."

A man pushed a mic mounted on a long pole into my face. "There're photos of you with Will Hastings circulating. Are the two of you a couple? Why are you with his brother now? Have you come to the UK to claim your inheritance?"

My chest constricted.

Thomas batted the mic down. "Ellie and my brother are together. I'm assisting Will with her security detail. No other comments will be made today."

"Let her speak, Hastings," someone else shouted.

Others from the street joined the melee. People shoved and yelled. The noise moved through my head like echoes in an empty tunnel. Panic consumed me, and I clutched Thomas's shirt, my knuckles turning white.

He locked me inside his arms and shouted at Ben, "Get the car, damn it."

Paparazzi reinforcements arrived. Some punches were thrown.

Thomas pushed me into a brick alcove and pressed my back to the wall, using his body to shield mine. "I'll move you from here to the car as soon as I believe it's safe. You can hold on to me, Ellie."

Gripping his shoulders, I locked on to his eyes, finding comfort there, and focused on slowing my breaths.

Ben appeared behind Thomas's back. "Follow me. I'll clear the way. The car is ready. This won't stop until she's completely inaccessible."

Thomas nodded over his shoulder at Ben, then said to me, "You're going to feel me touching you." He looped his arm around my waist to demonstrate. "You must not get separated from me. I want you to stay right on Ben's heels. No gap. Understand me?"

I nodded and wiped angrily at the tears running down my face.

"Quite right. No more crying. This is nothing," he told me, smiling.

It was past three a.m. when Will slipped into bed and pulled me into his embrace. We were face-to-face, and our bodies were pressed together with our arms and legs woven together like the threads of a well-made tapestry. I buried my face at the base of his neck.

He picked up locks of my hair and inspected the color, twisting strands around his finger. "There's a beautiful blonde in my bed." Exhaustion was apparent in his voice. "Mine."

I pressed a secret smile against his warm skin. "How did you know it was me?"

He cupped my chin and pushed my head back to inhale against my throat. "As beautiful as you are, I can identify you by your scent alone."

"That's creepy, Will."

He inhaled again and moaned.

I dragged my fingers along his jawline through his beard. He hadn't trimmed it for a while, so it was longer than his usual scruff. "You're tired."

He let out a slight grunt, and we joined our lips in mutual tenderness and closed our eyes.

"Baby, I was lost before you came home, so destructive," he said in a vulnerable whisper before relaxing into sleep.

But he was gone again only a few hours later.

Rain pounded against the windows, waking me.

Lightning streaked across the London sky.

Thunder cracked.

I sat up with a start and choked on nothing.

My dreams had been pleasant and lucid instead of horrifying. I'd been in and out of consciousness, aware that I was dreaming. At one point, it seemed as if my father had been standing next to our bed. He hadn't said anything, although he never did whenever I dreamed of him.

It was difficult to sort through the reality of those hours.

Will's words. Had he said them, or had I been dreaming at the time?

"Baby, I was lost ... so destructive."

My heart insisted there had been more.

"I love you."

Looking over at Will's side of our king bed, I found the long-stemmed red rose he'd left there for me. I lifted it to my face and inhaled while considering my unreasonable mind.

There had been times in my life when I feared something that was about to happen, and when it came to pass, my brain had locked down and blocked it out.

"Shit. Oh God." I'd done it again.

twenty-seven

THOMAS STOOD OUTSIDE THE HOTEL ROOM DOOR WITH COFFEE IN each of his hands, eager to wrap up my list of errands for the day. "We'll take my car, two men, and use the owner's private entrance," he said.

He'd planned it to go without a single hiccup. After we collected my dresses from the boutiques, those that had been fitted overnight but not yet delivered, we made a few more stops, including a second run to Jimmy Choo, and then finished with afternoon tea, as I had promised.

The hotel lounge's opulence was just as it had been in the evenings.

Ethan joined us as we were seated. "Hello, darlin'. You're looking quite well."

I was delighted to see him, truth be told. It meant Will wouldn't be far behind.

He summoned the hotel manager, insisting she sit at our table.

I sipped on my tea and sampled fancies and scones while listening to Ethan's plans to have a lavish spread and a well-stocked bar put out in the private fifth-floor lounge. He and Will were hosting a cocktail party for some new clients in the evening.

"House wines, champagne?" the manager asked.

"I don't want to see house wines." Ethan turned to me. "Would you like Dom Pérignon?"

"That sounds nice. Oh. You mean, it's all right for me to be there?"

He nodded at the hotel manager to dismiss her. "Yes, of course. Everyone is looking forward to meeting Will's sweetheart."

"What?"

"Yeah, sharing a few personal details is important in this business. Potential investors and buyers like to hear that we have lives outside of the firm."

"Which one of you did the sharing?"

"I couldn't have stopped him from going on about you even if I'd tried."

I smiled at the thought, missing Will.

Ethan stood and offered me his hand. "Come, darlin'. You and I have a meeting with the commissioner."

"Commissioner? But where is Will?"

"Do you think either of you would benefit from his inability to control himself? His drive to protect you can't be restrained, not even with the authorities."

Tears stung the back of my lids. I wasn't sure how to get through the interview without him.

"I ordered this, Ellie, and that he not discuss it with you in advance. He isn't able to say no to you. I won't have my brother investigated."

Ethan was right. I had to push back at the fear, at the anxiety rushing through my cooling blood, and trust him. Allowing Will to participate would be an absolute gamble. I slipped my hand into Ethan's and nodded, barely breathing, and he led me to a private meeting room. He never let go of my hand.

The interrogation began and ended in a gentle manner. Typical procedural questions, one of the lawyers had pointed out. Two were present to guide the interview, as Will had promised.

Commissioner Brown was kind, offering sympathetic smiles as he laid out his questions. I'd liked him from the moment he entered the room. He had a stocky build and comforting blue eyes. It was clear there was some level of friendship and respect between him and Ethan.

"So, again, for the record, you arrived at your home at approximately ten minutes before eleven p.m., and at that time, when you found your sister and grandmother lying in the foyer, there was no one else in the house."

"Other than Lissie, that's right," I said.

"These questions have already been asked and answered. We're done. Send my personal regards to Stonington's captain," Ethan interjected.

The commissioner nodded to Ethan in solidarity before turning back to me.

"Thank you, Ms. James. I'm deeply sorry for your losses. I am offended by the insistence of the American police that we should put you through this." He bowed his head, and then Commissioner Brown left the hotel with his two detectives.

"Have a nice hot soak and get dressed," Ethan told me as we arrived at my suite. "You did well. Will should be here soon."

He kissed my hand, and I closed the door, grateful for time alone to settle my thoughts before Will returned.

THE HOT BATH HAD BEEN RELAXING AND ALSO REINVIGORATING. I finished dressing and gazed into the full-length mirror while waiting for Will. I couldn't wait to see him. The green of my irises popped against the smoky eye makeup on my lids, dramatic shades of charcoal gray and deep plum painted onto my skin.

After hesitating, I'd put on the black cocktail dress that hugged my figure and complemented it with strappy platinum stilettos, choosing to save the new red dress for an intimate evening with Will.

I'd never done anything as expressive with my hair. Making that change, as small as it was, liberated me in some bizarre way. A mischievous smile marked my lips, and my reflection nodded with approval.

There was abrupt knocking on the door, then Ben's voice came through it. "Ellie, open up."

I jerked it open. "Where's Will?"

"He said he couldn't reach you. Is everything okay?"

"Fine. Oh, I left my phone in Thomas's car. He said he'd bring it up. Where is he?"

"Ethan wanted to see him."

"Will should be here by now," I complained.

"He said he's in a contract negotiation and to meet him upstairs."

"Is he angry with Thomas? Is that why Ethan wanted to see Thomas?"

"He doesn't seem angry with anyone, only the situation. He won't allow it to go down that way again. Anyway, he's better equipped to deal with the press than the rest of us. I need a drink. Come on. Let's go up."

"So, he knew about everything yesterday."

"Yes. Grab your bag."

I tossed my lipstick into my clutch and grabbed my sketch portfolio.

THE VIEW FROM THE ROOFTOP TERRACE WAS AMAZING. The warm sun was only just setting over Manchester Square. I was sketching the northern London skyline, where the graceful steeple of a prominent historic church reached for the clouds. The steeple's Gothic style made it look as if it had been plucked right from the tip of one of Westminster Abbey's towers.

I knew the moment Will arrived. I could feel the weight of his stare, his desire, as he watched me examine my work. I stole a side-glance at him, and it was impossible not to smile.

He wore an elegant gray suit, tailored perfectly to his body, and that fiery gaze. I wanted to run to him, but I managed to wait it out, allowing him to come to me. When he stepped out onto the terrace, my protection detail moved inside.

Will's body heat and his irresistible scent closed in on me from behind, and then his strong arms were around me. He inhaled through my hair and fingered some of the blonde tips before he pushed it out of his way to trace the butterfly on my neck with a fingertip. My skin prickled with goose bumps.

I let my head fall back against his shoulder. "I've missed you, Will."

"Kiss me, baby," he said, and my heart flipped.

I turned and searched his eyes. I was stuck there, lost in my desire for him.

Unwilling to wait for my kiss, his mouth covered mine, and he kissed the breath from my lungs. He took everything from me with that kiss, owned every piece of me.

"You're so much more than beautiful. You're my beautiful angel." He pulled back, and his gaze moved up and down my body.

He drew me to him again, pushing his erection against me, and slipped his tongue past my lips for more. One hand applied pressure to my nape, so I couldn't escape his kiss, and the other moved up my thigh, sliding beneath the hem of my dress.

"I need you," he purred. "Need to be inside you."

His fingers brushed over my panties.

"Me too," I breathed against his lips.

The terrace spun. I was flying.

Someone cleared his throat. Probably Ethan. Maybe Thomas.

Will ignored it and pushed another kiss deeper, drove it beyond a kiss, his fingers now caressing me under the lace, flesh on flesh. I broke the kiss, moaning against his mouth, and moved his hand.

He smirked as he caught his breath. I punched his shoulder. He'd almost made me come.

"Ethan said the interview went well."

I nodded, still catching my own breath.

"I'm taking you home tonight. I'll bring you again, but for now, I want you home at Eastridge. I'll shut down Hertford for an evening and give it to you when things are clear."

Hertford was the mansion in Manchester Square that housed the Wallace Collection. I peeked around his shoulder at the square and smiled. The lush gardens and the mansion were silhouetted against the glowing amber backdrop.

"I know."

He would. He'd stop time for me if he could.

He pressed his smiling lips against my forehead.

"But what's going on? Tell me, Will."

"The questions the paparazzi asked, knowing who you are—the press didn't have that information yet. I hadn't provided that. It was fed to them by someone else."

"You mean, the Order?"

"I'm quite sure it was a warning. So, we're leaving after this cocktail party."

A cold rush of anxiety slid through my body. "They're getting closer," I whispered.

"Make no mistake, Elle, they are coming." He strengthened his embrace as if he'd felt the panic rush through me. "You'll be safe at Eastridge."

"Are you coming back to London?"

"James is coming along well. He can handle most things on my behalf, but clients expect to see me. Investors expect to deal directly with me. And I need to look into questionable transactions Ethan conducted while I was away. The stakes are high in this business, Elle. Our success depends upon aggressive leadership."

"I understand. Who is James?"

"I'll introduce you. He's inside along with others waiting to meet you."

"I'd love to see your office sometime."

"I don't think the boss will mind." His smug wink made me ache for more of him, and he knew it. His hands slid down to my ass. "I won't come back until I've had a full night with you in my bed, Elle."

Then, he led me inside, where inquiring minds waited.

twenty-eight

WILL AND I PASSED THROUGH THE CENTER OF THE ROOM AND headed straight for the bar, where he placed a glass of champagne into my hand without letting go of the other. I shifted my weight and squeezed his fingers to ground myself.

"Ease into it, Elle. They'll adore you."

"Why must they stare?" God, I was nervous.

"Who wouldn't? Christ, you're amazing."

"Will," I complained. I needed more than an expression of ego-driven pride.

"Perhaps it's a rude society in comparison to your politically correct upbringing. You'll get used to it." He took a drink from his whisky glass. "They're curious. You've nothing to worry over." His gaze moved over my shoulder, and he nodded as he pulled me to his side.

James Jackson gestured for my hand with a knowing smile. "There she is, the lovely one I'm dying to thank for my job security." He squeezed my presented hand with affection. "It's my honor to meet you. Welcome to England."

"Thank you, James. It's so nice to meet you too."

He was tall and elegant with light-brown skin, warm brown

eyes, and a showy grin. His head was shaved bald and his facial hair tightly groomed. His presence was similar to Will's. Intelligence and authoritative charm whirled around him, though his immediate disposition was a little warmer.

Will flashed his marvelous grin. "She might as well sign your checks."

There was obvious trust and respect and even friendship between the two. James was a principal at the firm, Will's right arm. He directed the staff and operations under Will's areas of responsibility and researched ideas for investments and acquisitions. And then some.

Will called out to a client, "David, come have a drink with us."

The two men shook hands in a manner that exceeded the boundaries of a cordial business greeting. Their professional relationship was new, but they had attended Oxford University together. They had partied and chased women together, I thought.

"This is my wife, Caroline."

She offered her hand to Will. "It's quite nice to finally meet you. David talks about you nonstop."

Will held her hand for a moment. "Does he? I'd like you both to meet Ellie James."

Caroline turned to me. "You're so lovely, Ellie. Shall we go chat while these men have their boring business conversations?"

Thanks to my gran, I could play the elite-class social game as well as anyone. After a quick check of my nerves, I reinforced my posture and set my glass on the bar, and in the same fashion she'd done to Will, I offered Caroline my hand.

"Champagne?" I asked.

Stunned by my reciprocated presumptuousness and then delighted, she grasped my fingers and smiled without uttering a word.

Will squeezed my other hand to express approval as well as amusement and then kissed it before allowing me to pull away.

I led Caroline to one of the sofas, calling over my shoulder to Will with a playful smile, "Will, send over a bottle, please."

He dragged his stare from my ass and winked, sending the bartender over to deliver our bottle with a jerk of his chin.

Pretty, pretentious Caroline was a stay-at-home mom, full of small talk about her girlfriends, great shoes—I gave her bonus points for that—and her three young children. She pushed hard for a story about Will and me, admitting she had seen the tabloids and known who I was. Still, I offered nothing more than the timeworn story of destined lovers.

Those moments of shallow exchanges with Caroline rekindled my longing for Jess's company. I missed her so much.

"Come on, darling. Give me something. Each of your families has rejected your God-given right to nobility. Others would kill for it. There must be more to the story."

She had no idea how true her statement was. Others had killed for it. Many had died for it.

Will carried on across the room with a group of men, leading a spirited conversation about a historic referendum that the British had recently voted on. I caught his sensual, hungry stare and thought about how mind-blowing he would be later in bed.

Can't wait, I shot back at him through my own stare as I chewed on my lip.

"Show me to the toilet, Ellie," Caroline said, interrupting my silent conversation with Will.

Kirsty had joined us on the sofa a few minutes earlier and volunteered to go in my place, so I used the opportunity to gain a minute alone with Will. I summoned him with my curled finger.

He excused himself and came right to me. "Elle, I'm mad for you," he said close to my ear as he tugged on his collar.

I ran my hands up his arms. "Well, if that's true, you should take me to bed." I removed the knot from his tie and slipped it loose from his neck.

His throat rumbled as he forced back my idea.

"You're sweating. Why are you still in your jacket? Give it to me."

He did, and then I unfastened the top buttons of his shirt while he worked at his cuff links. I held out my hand before he could put them into his pocket.

He raised a brow but dropped the black diamond cuff links into my hand.

"I'll put them into your pocket myself." I smiled from beneath my lashes while discreetly sliding my whole hand into the front of his trousers. He was growing hard.

"You don't play fair, witch."

I shrugged and rolled up each of his sleeves into neat folds and then dragged my fingers along the inside of his forearms. "Better now?"

He stared down at me, his eyes burning white-hot with desire.

"Everyone is watching, you know, waiting to see what you'll do next."

"It doesn't matter." He lowered his head and brushed his lips over mine. I shivered. "Give me ten minutes to wrap up, and we'll get out of here."

I was tired of hearing Caroline recount her nights out with the housewives, so I wandered into the fresh air near the open terrace door with Thomas. I was only half-listening to his conversation, my mind unfolding all the things Will had said about the Order, and for some reason, I was comparing his words to the last nightmare I'd had.

Jarring me from my thoughts, Will appeared between Thomas and me and smacked a newspaper against his brother's chest. "What the fuck?"

Ethan was quickly between the two of them. He grabbed the

newspaper. "Where did this one come from? Christ," he said, arching up into Thomas's face to say something else that only the two of them could hear.

Thomas snapped something back, then made his way across the room. He kept one eye pinned on Will.

"Let me see." I pried the paper from Ethan's fingers.

I'd seen most of the tabloids earlier that day but not this one. It featured a close-up of Thomas and me. I knew the exact moment it had been snapped, after he pushed me into the alcove to shield me with his body. The deceiving headline about our alleged passionate embrace was ignorant at best.

I turned to Will and placed my hands on his chest. His eyes revealed jealousy.

"You know what happened, Will. You know it's another tabloid lie. It's nothing."

He took hold of my wrists. "It's fucking inexcusable. Don't expect me to accept it for anything less than that. Go sit."

Ethan interrupted before I could respond, "Ellie, go on. Let me talk to him for a minute."

I pulled my wrists free, backed away from Will, and trusted Ethan to manage the situation. I watched Will follow Ethan to the bar as he glared over his shoulder at me and then across the room at Thomas. Ben joined them, and the two worked without success to ease Will's thoughts.

I grabbed my sketchpad and doodled nonsense, anything to keep from looking at him.

Ethan startled me when he sat and offered me a glass of champagne. "I need your help."

"How can I handle him if you're not able to?" I shook my head at the glass.

"You own more influence than you understand. You must learn to tap into that when he needs it. But don't test him unless you're prepared to see him go after someone."

"*Test* him?"

Ethan picked up his drink. "The public viewing a photo that might be misinterpreted stings the ego all the same. Treat his reaction the same as if he were assuming an affair, which he is not."

"I see." As poor as the timing was, something else tore at my heart. "Did you love her, Ethan?"

I yearned for another connection to my sister.

He paused with his whisky at his lips, frowned, and then swallowed what was left in the glass. "We were different. You and Will can have what you both clearly desire. It was complicated for us."

I narrowed my eyes. "You didn't answer the question."

"Yes." Ethan gave me the one word I'd needed to hear. "I know how much you miss her. She loved you more than you know. She talked about you quite a lot." He paused. "I should have been there for her. I am sorry."

A single tear rolled down my cheek.

"Stop it, Ellie. Save your tears for Will."

I wiped it away and swallowed the knot in my throat. He was right. Will had been gentle and comforting, caring for me with a profound tenderness while I worked through my grief and depression, and he still protected me from the anxiety. He was everything to me. It was Will's shoulder I wanted to cry on. Only his.

"We'll talk more about her soon. And Lissie. You have my word. You're family now, and anything I can do to ease your pain, I will. But right now, I need you to go over there and reassure him. Men like my brother ... well, let's just say, there's a bit of self-doubt that comes with the notoriety he possesses. Go on," Ethan ordered. "I need this settled between my brothers."

I pushed down the hem of my dress and headed toward Will. He drained his glass and watched me approach. Indignation dripped from him. Even so, I couldn't help touching him, sliding my hands over his bared forearms.

"What are you doing, Will?"

His hardened eyes challenged mine.

I slid my fingertips beneath his folded sleeves and pushed him for a response. "What are you doing to us?"

His eyes dropped to my hands, to the floor. "Elle, if I hurt you—"

I snapped at him, interrupting, "I'm not a dog. I do not *sit.*"

Will jerked his gaze back to mine. Self-reproach joined the emotional mess in his eyes. "Forgive me," he ordered, pushing hair away from my face. "I'll never speak to you in that way again."

"No, you won't. Because—" I halted my words, surprised by my own thoughts.

I could imagine no scenario where an ultimatum turned out well. Will was the type of man who walked away. His harsh words had stung, yes, but it wasn't enough for me to push him away. It wasn't a deal-breaker.

He leaned in and pressed his lips to my temple, his words soft against my skin. "It won't happen again, baby. Come out to the corridor with me."

I stared at him as Ethan's words about my influence danced on my brain, realizing that while Will's emotions might become volatile, he would never walk away from me. His hand locked around mine, and we exited the lounge.

"Elle, I need to be sure you understand me. Look at me," he commanded.

I met his eyes with mine.

He softened his harsh words. "I will destroy any man who touches you or threatens to take you from me, and you must never forget that. I cannot accept even the appearance of it. That's what I've become with you, and there's no way back from it."

I'd had no idea at the time, but I had taken great pleasure in drawing out a baser instinct from his soul, an instinct that behaved like a feral beast, one that he could never eliminate or oppress again.

The beast would need to be reminded from time to time that Will was the one and only man for me. And Will needed to know that there was no longer a point of return for me either.

I was madly in love with him.

He reached out for me with his eyes. “Say something.”

I didn’t know why, but I didn’t say a word. I couldn’t stop from pushing him further.

Will ran his fingers through his hair, paced the floor, cursed. When he found his resolve, he came back to me and tucked a finger under my chin, luring my eyes to his. “Do I need to get down on my knees and beg for you to love me back? Is that what you need from me, Elle? Tell me what you need, and it’s yours.”

I gasped and then whispered, “You did say it.”

The muscles in his face relaxed, and his eyes softened. “I love you. I’ve loved you from the moment you first looked at me with those beautiful eyes.”

I knew as soon as he said the words, they were the reason I always pushed him. I needed him to love me. More than that, I needed him to love me beyond just love.

Tears rolled down my cheeks one at a time, as though life were stuck in slow motion. I’d never traded a confession of love with another human being, and I didn’t know how to give that to Will, to put it into words outside of my thoughts. I was held captive by silence.

He jerked me into his arms.

Our mouths collided.

I wound my arms tightly around his neck and encouraged him with my tongue to deepen our kiss, to leave me breathless, to love me with all that he had, and to feel how much I loved him without hearing the words.

In the next moment, my back hit the floor, a sharp pain driving along my spine.

Will was on top of me.

"Don't move," he shouted into my ringing ears as he covered my body with his.

An explosion had forced us from our feet.

twenty-nine

ANOTHER VOLATILE, RUMBLING SHOCK WAVE RIPPED THROUGH the fifth floor of the hotel, followed by the sounds of more splintering glass and wood. The lounge door blasted from its hinges and flew more than fifty feet beyond where we lay.

Will remained on top of me. "Don't move, Elle," he repeated, though neither of us could hear much aside from the ringing aftermath of the explosions. He locked his gaze deep into mine and held it steady. "I've got you, baby. Breathe out."

My lungs expelled a shuddering exhale. I was mindless, frozen.

"In. Out again," Will instructed. "Are you hurt?"

I shook my head.

Ethan, Thomas, and the others burst into the corridor. Some of them had visible lacerations, caused by flying objects and glass. No one appeared to have life-threatening injuries.

Ethan's phone was pressed to his ear. He shouted information as he received it from the security command center. "Four is secure. Hotel is locked down. Get her down to the room. No elevator. Use the stairs. Go now."

Will brought us to our feet, and we raced to the stairwell exit. Ben flew in front of us and kicked open the steel door, exiting first. The stairwell echoed with pounding feet as everyone else followed.

When we arrived at the entry to the fourth floor, Will shouted back at Ethan, "I won't take her in there without searching first, goddamn it."

"Thomas and I will do it. The rest of you stay here," Ethan ordered.

Drops of blood fell onto my arm. It wasn't mine.

"You're hurt. Let go, Will. Let me see!"

He released his tight grip, complaining as I inspected his body, searching for the source of the blood. A piece of the door had hit him on the back of his neck, but it was a superficial laceration.

"Thank God," I breathed, wiping at the blood with the palm of my hand.

Thomas came back and held open the door. "All clear. Come on. Let's go."

Everyone huddled in the center of the corridor on the fourth floor, where there was no obvious impact or damage.

Ethan was on his phone again, but he disconnected within a few seconds. "No one can get in or out of the hotel. All guests have been ordered to their rooms. I've delayed contacting police, but it won't be long before neighboring establishments do. Two explosive devices were detonated on the roof. The second one made it to the terrace. There are no serious injuries, and it will stay that way. We don't have much time to act independently."

Ethan shifted his eyes to Will, and the two shared a dark, knowing look. Ben and Thomas closed in at my sides when Ethan jerked his head at Will to pull him aside for a separate conversation. I heard only parts of their exchange when their voices were raised.

"Fucking cowards, terrorizing an innocent woman because they're afraid of her DNA." Ethan palmed Will's shoulder. "We need to move now."

"You know me, Ethan. I'll find a way. Motherfuckers are dead."

The reality of what had happened and what was to come began to sink into my horrified, confused mind. I cried out for Will, and he immediately secured me in his arms.

"You can't fall apart on me, Elle. I need your strength now. I swear they'll not get to you. No one will take you from me."

I felt it then, the vibration deep within him. His calm before the storm.

I nodded with my face against his chest. We'd chosen this path together. And I trusted him, trusted the raging emotion in him that had become my lifeline.

I am strong, I chanted in my head.

"How many?" he asked Ethan.

"Five that we could see. Our team caught it on camera and locked down before they could get inside. You must trust Thomas or Ben to protect her. She'll be safe if you and I drive them away from here."

Will held on to me tighter. He'd stay if I pleaded. He would choose me.

The truth was sometimes hard to see, but Will's truth was always clear for me. Every piece of his life was an all-or-nothing decision he'd made. There was no gray, no space in between all or nothing, and his resolve never faltered. That was why I knew he'd choose me. That was how I knew he'd destroy the moon for me. I was one of his alls.

But I also understood that he had to be in the fight. He needed to be the one who made it safe for me. And I needed his brothers to keep him safe. So, I lifted my face from his chest and found his eyes. The unfailing strength there powered my own.

"Ben," I told him. "I'll stay with Ben."

The corner of his mouth twitched as he pushed a lock of hair behind my ear again. He understood every thought I'd just had.

His expression became stern. “You must do exactly as he says. If you do that for me, then we’ll all be safe. Say you will.”

“Yes, I will,” I promised.

Will went into our room and quickly came back out, dressed in jeans. He held two weapons—items I’d had no idea he’d carried along from Eastridge—one of his daggers and a handgun.

I wondered how he and his brothers would conceal their weapons and how the whole thing would play out with law enforcement. Were officers from Scotland Yard on the way? What would be written in tomorrow’s newspapers? What would be reported on the broadcast news?

Will jolted me out of my head with a hard kiss. “I do love you, Elle.”

I touched his face. “Tell me again when you come back. Show me when you come back, Will.”

“Okay,” he breathed onto my skin, allowing his hands to drop from my waist. He gripped Ben’s shoulder for a second before joining Ethan and Thomas near the exit.

I steadied myself on Ben’s arm. My shaking body fell into a cold sweat as I stared through a fog muddled with horror and panic and awe. Three fierce brothers stood before me, shoulder to shoulder. Three men committed to saving my life. Three boys trained to kill by their own father.

My heart was beating too fast, and vomit rose to the back of my throat.

Will looked back at me over his shoulder one more time.

I corrected my posture and met his eyes with forced confidence.

“Let’s do this,” Ethan said, his smooth voice filled with determination.

Then, the Hastings brothers hit the streets of London.

thirty

THAT HAD BEEN THE NIGHT WILL'S WORLD SPUN ENTIRELY OUT of his control for the first time. The night he allowed rage to seep into his soul. The same night he set into motion the aggressive strategy he'd been pulling together since his first visit to Stonington ten years earlier.

A few hours after Will had left the hotel with his brothers, he'd instructed Ben to move me from London back to the estate in Hastings.

We waited at Eastridge through the early morning hours for word from London while journalists on television delivered breaking news of a domestic terrorist strike. The reports indicated that the terror group remained unidentified and at large. My heart knew it would stay that way for the public—an unresolved act of violence, the truth hidden, another dark lie.

In the drawing room, my phone and Ben's rang at the same time. His weary eyes met my nervous stare as he answered his, and I answered mine. He mouthed Thomas's name.

"Elle."

I almost wept, so thankful to finally hear his voice. "Will."

He hesitated. His breath was irregular. "I lost him. Ethan is gone."

"He's gone?"

"He's dead, Elle. My brother is dead."

I choked on his words, on the sound of his suffering.

Mary's perceptive eyes targeted me as she waited to interpret the words I would return into the phone, but my breath refused to push anything out.

"Wait for me there, baby. Stay inside and follow Ben's instructions."

"Yes, of course," I whispered. "I'm sorry, Will ... I'm so sorry."

"Talk to my mother for me. I can't do it, not like this."

"I'll take care of her." I watched Mary's watery eyes fill with pain.

"I know you will. I'll see you in a few hours, Elle." He abruptly disconnected our call.

I reached out my hand for Mary, not really knowing how to comfort her. She came into my arms and wept in a reserved manner, then pulled me along with her to the south-facing windows, where gentle rain tapped a melancholy tune against the panes of glass.

"Do you remember what I told you, Ellie? This is it, how it unravels and becomes Will's war." She was disconnecting from the world around us as she gazed outside to the weather-darkened sky.

"Yes, I remember. I'm so sorry, Mary. So sorry for everything, all that you've lost."

"Quiet, dear. You have no fault in this. You, my sons, you're doing what you must to survive in someone else's cruel game. Walk me to my room now. I want to have a lie-down."

John had been quietly watching, pacing around the drawing room and the great hall, waiting for his brothers to return from London.

I stopped him and cradled his face in my palms, noting again how much he looked like Will. "I'll be just upstairs, settling your mom and checking in on the girls. If you need me, you come up and find me."

He nodded, his eyes diving to the floor.

I helped Mary to her room and then settled myself in Lissie's room to pass the time, hoping for a distraction from the anxiety that threatened to rip through me. I couldn't allow it to pull me under. Will needed me strong while he grieved the loss of his brother, and nothing could keep me from being there for him.

Hours later, Ben opened the door, startling me. "Will's downstairs, asking for you."

I leaped up from the floor, tripping on the box for Lissie's board game. "What? How long has he been home? Were they hurt?"

Ben kissed the top of Chelsea's head and angled his head toward the open door. We stepped out of the bedroom.

"They weren't injured. But, Ellie, he's not himself. He hasn't stopped drinking since they came in about thirty minutes ago. He hasn't said much other than to tell me not to get you and then to send me for you. Thomas has gone to be with Mary in her room."

"Damn it, Ben. You shouldn't have waited. Can you stay up here until the nanny comes back? Tell her we might need her to stay over, to discuss that with Mrs. Bates, and not a word to Lissie."

I didn't wait for his response. I sprinted along the corridor and down the stairs.

Will was in the drawing room. He sat on the chesterfield and drank whisky as he stared across the room with unfocused eyes. The bottle on the table beside him was almost empty.

I pried the glass from his hand and gave it to Mrs. Bates. "Bring water and coffee, please. We'll need sandwiches or whatever your staff has available. I'm sure he and Thomas haven't eaten today."

She dropped her somber eyes. "Don't worry, dear. I'll see to it."

Will never said anything, but when he finally lifted his face, his grief-stricken eyes came to mine, revealing the depth of his broken heart. My own heart splintered at the sight of his pain. I choked back a sob. I wanted to take it away, take his suffering into myself and bear it for him.

He reached for my hand.

God, he was too quiet. I wanted to cry out for him.

I wanted to shout up at the dark clouds that I'd take more, to give the pain to me instead.

Will pulled me onto his lap, hugging my waist tightly as he pressed his face into my chest. Something unintelligible rumbled from his lips. He squeezed me harder, turning his face only enough to breathe.

I wrapped him in my arms with courage and strength and held him while he swam through his emotions. He worked hard to hold it all inside, to keep everything he was feeling from breaching the surface. My heart was tough enough to protect us both in that moment. The realization took me by surprise, though his vulnerable actions made me believe he'd expected it.

It was a dreadful moment, and it was a wonderful moment. His heart was broken, and mine was full. Because I'd finally learned how to love someone.

John came in and sat on the sofa with us, his nervousness finally submissive after his hours of pacing. Heartbreak and fear haunted his eyes. He needed Will. His brother was the closest thing to a father he'd had since Richard Hastings had died nine years earlier.

I reached out to John and offered him my hand. He took it and slid closer, and after meeting my eyes for reassurance, he rested his cheek on his brother's shoulder.

The acceleration of Will's breath against my skin was telling. He was affected by John's suffering. He shifted his position, pulling his brother beneath his arm and me deeper into his lap so that we were face-to-face.

"Elle, I—"

"Shh, I know. We can talk later." I placed a tender kiss on his lips.

The muscles in his face and his shoulders relaxed, and he brushed my cheek with the back of his fingers.

Mrs. Bates returned with a cart. She placed it near the old mahogany serpentine sideboard and filled a plate with roast beef sandwiches for Will. Her warm hand touched my arm after she set the dish on the table beside us.

"Thanks. Mary and Thomas have something upstairs as well?"

She nodded before bustling back to the kitchen.

Ben came in and immediately caught my silent plea for help with John. "Come on, mate. You'll have a sandwich with me," he said to John.

John was beside himself and without guidance, so he did whatever he was told. The two of them ate in silence near one of the fireplaces while waiting for Will to come around. It was easy to see he was everything to them both, just as he was to me.

"You must eat too, Will." I kissed his cheek. "You have nothing other than the whisky in your stomach."

He nodded and planted a lingering kiss on my neck.

I handed him the plate. "I'll just run upstairs quickly and check on the girls."

"You'll stay with me," he commanded sharply, setting his plate on the chesterfield, shifting so my bottom dropped into the small space between his and the sofa arm.

He slid an arm behind me and grabbed a sandwich with his other hand. I wasn't going anywhere.

Mrs. Bates came back and handed me a bowl of fruit and yogurt. "Nanny Sue will help with the children until bedtime, dearest. You'll be more at ease if I manage them overnight myself."

"Very much so. Thank you, Mrs. Bates."

I finished my dish while Will ate his sandwiches and drank coffee. Every time I looked over at John, my heart sank deeper. He was really attached to Will. He loved Ethan without question, but most of the pain he expressed seemed to be for Will's loss. I had an urge to cross the room and hold John to make him feel safe and loved, but I didn't. Will's emotion simmered just beneath the surface, and anything might set him off. He'd been clear. He wanted me at his side.

The best way to help was to continue combining my strength with Will's, to give him whatever he needed, so he could find his way back and provide his family with the support they urgently needed.

Will shifted his weight and settled deeper into the leather cushions. His fatigue was obvious. He hadn't slept more than six hours in those past four nights.

"You should get some rest," I told him, suggesting we go upstairs.

He wove his fingers through my hair and pulled me to his mouth for a sweet kiss. "Not sure if I can sleep, but I need to hold you."

WHEN I CAME OUT OF MY BATHROOM, AFTER GRABBING SOME things to keep in Will's room, he hadn't moved. He was still leaning against the frame in the open doorway. I slipped my hand into his, and we walked down the corridor to his small suite.

Although he was quiet, I sensed the storm that threatened to burst from his soul.

"It's just us now, Will. You can say anything, whatever you need to say."

"I don't know what to say. Don't know what to do," he said hoarsely.

He wasn't ready to talk about Ethan or what had happened out on those streets, and I wouldn't push him. He might never tell me in detail how Ethan had been killed, and if that was what he needed to get through his pain—to not say the words out loud to me—then I was all right with it.

"That's okay. Whatever it is you need, whatever you need to do, it'll come to you when you're ready." I put my arms around his neck and lowered my forehead to his chest. A swell of emotions overwhelmed me. I lifted my teary eyes to his and pleaded. "For now, tell me you'll always come back to me. If anything were to happen to you—" I shook my head, the tears falling now. "I love you, Will. Swear to me that you'll always come home."

His beautiful blue eyes came alive, the dull haze clearing. "I swear to you, I will."

Suddenly, he grabbed fistfuls of my hair, applying pressure to the back of my head as he forced his mouth against mine. I whimpered, and he gentled some but remained fiercely driven by strong emotions. Pulling back, he caressed my lips with his thumb, staring at them as he dragged my bottom lip down ever so slightly.

"Christ, how I love you." He pulled the shirt over my head, leaving his velvet kisses on my shoulders. "I swear I'll come home to you, Elle."

His greedy mouth came back to mine, reasserting his claim. We stripped away each other's clothing slowly, and then we went to the place where no one and nothing else existed. Everything he was, all that he had, went into making love to me. We burned away everything, burned away his silent grief, and we became one again.

Will followed my climax with his, a feral sounding, snarling release, then buried his face in my neck until his shuddering body was calm again. He was still inside me as he lifted our bodies and sat back on his heels, unwilling to separate our physical intimacy from our emotional connection. His forehead rested against mine.

"I can't do this without you, baby."

My arms were locked around his neck and my legs around his hips. "You don't have to do it alone, Will. I'm here."

He fell into a deep sleep then and rested that way over the next few hours, his body motionless, except for the slow, cadenced rise and fall of his chest. I drifted in and out of sleep while watching him.

Just after closing my eyes again, I heard a soft knocking on the door.

"Please let me in." It was John, his words slurring together.

I opened the door, and he fell into my arms, the smell of whisky on his breath, his clothes.

"Where's my brother?"

"Quiet. I don't want to wake him. John, what have you done?"

His eyes widened, and then he covered his mouth.

"Here, turn and lean on my shoulder." I helped him into the bathroom, where he crouched in front of the toilet and clung to the bowl as he vomited. I kneeled beside him, gently rubbing his back and wiping his face with a wet washcloth.

"Sorry. I'm s-so sorry, Ellie."

"You don't need to apologize to me. I do understand. But you'll have to answer to your brother when he finds out what's going on. I don't think he'll like this."

Will then appeared inside the bathroom doorway, towering above us with his massive size. I arched my neck back and raised my chin to examine his expression. No anger, only empathy.

John thumped against the wall with unfocused eyes, as if he could let go now that his brother was present. He slid to the floor, passing out on the cool marble tile.

“Come on, baby. Get up. You’ve done enough.” Will took my hands and helped me up from the floor. “I’ll get him to bed.”

Will carried John out to the sofa and covered him with an extra quilt from the bed, tucking him in the way a father might swaddle his young child. But it was the protective, loving kiss that Will placed on John’s forehead that hit me in the heart. It was unexpected, so beautiful.

My eyes welled up.

Will turned to me and caught my watery smile, the back of his fingers caressing my cheek. Lost in complete reverence, I slid my hands up his arms and whispered his name. His lips parted as if he were going to say something, but instead, he lowered his head and kissed my lips with tenderness.

“Go see your mother and Thomas. They need you, Will.”

A weighted exhale. He nodded. “I won’t be long.”

I didn’t open my eyes when he climbed back into bed later. I cuddled into his side and lay my head on his chest. Our limbs instinctively tangled, and we slept.

thirty-one

SUNLIGHT AND WILL WOKE ME. A SLIVER OF SUNSHINE breaking through the draperies warmed the skin on my shoulder, and he kissed it.

John groaned from the sofa in the small, open sitting room.

"Goddamn it," Will snapped.

"He doesn't know what to do. Show him," I gently urged, tracing Will's jawline with my fingertips, dragging my nails through his scruff.

"He's softer than we were at that age."

"Does it matter?"

"Yes, it matters. He's a Hastings."

"Do you plan to give him the same kind of life you were given?"

The moment Ethan had died, Will had become the family patriarch by default. The Hastings family had remained constant in aristocratic tradition, so not only would Will be the estate's primary source of support, but also, his decisions would determine a great deal about how they would all live.

He shut down inside his thoughts for a minute. "He'll have more choices. Still, he must be a man of strength." A strand of hair fell onto my cheek, and he swept it away, his tone softening.

"See? Can't do it without you. Everything about you is so lovely, and it encourages me to find something better in myself."

"That's beautiful, Will."

"That's you, baby."

Losing him still weighed on my mind. Without him, I'd have nothing. "Do you believe there's an afterlife, that our souls are eternal and go on, still knowing and feeling? Do you think Ethan will find Isobel?"

"Elle."

"He loved her."

We would never know their story, only that he loved her.

"Seems he did. He never made other commitments."

"When we're gone, are we going to find each other? Will there be more time for us?"

"I don't want to disappoint you because in truth, I don't know what I believe, but understand that I don't subscribe to the idea of heaven and hell. Christ, if there were such a thing, we certainly wouldn't be together." He lifted my chin with his finger. "Neither of us is going anywhere. No one can take you from me, and I'll always come back to you. Rather than wading into philosophical reflection, I need you to trust in that, trust me."

"I trust you." I had from the moment he pulled me out of that bloodstained foyer in Stonington.

But it was hard to not worry, to not become insecure. He was forced to fight assassins, to kill or be killed. Because they wanted to take my life. It wasn't your run-of-the-mill relationship hurdle. It would never be as easy as that for us.

"Relationships scare you. I see it in your eyes. In time, you'll trust ours and feel safe with it." He crushed his mouth to mine, pressing a brutal kiss onto my lips. Then, he got up from the bed and called out to his brother as he headed for the bathroom, "John, move your arse. Hydrate and meet me in the gym."

Will's mood was shifting, his grief evolving.

John and I understood he was about to be punished for the whisky binge. I slipped a robe over my pajamas and poured him a glass of water, and he pulled himself upright, grumbling, miserable.

"Will," Thomas called out through the door.

"Come in, Thomas," I told him.

Lissie slid down from his back and raced inside, onto the sofa cushion by John. I sat with her, and she hugged my neck.

"This one has been roaming about, looking for you." Thomas looked at his younger brother and shook his head. "Jesus. Don't do that shit again. Did he order you to the gym as well?"

John bobbed his head and held out his water glass for his brother to refill.

"How is Mary this morning?" I asked.

The woody scent of Tom Ford soap rushed out from the bathroom when Will opened the door. I could see enough of him through the arched opening to know that he was wearing only a towel around his hips.

"Are you fucking kidding me?"

"Will." I covered Lissie's ears in case he complained more about the growing audience in his room.

Will went into his closet to get dressed, and when he came out to the sitting area, he stood there for a moment, staring at the four of us. I watched him, and I also looked at Lissie and his brothers. He sat next to me then, pulling me beneath his arm. Our eyes met, and his shoulders relaxed. I touched his cheek.

We'd just shared a glance at our future.

"We need to tell her, Elle."

I had hoped the next serious conversation with Lissie would be one in which we introduced her to Ethan as her father, but instead, she would learn Uncle Ethan was gone. I couldn't imagine a better time to tell her than while she was enveloped in the strength of the three uncles she'd already grown to love.

"Lissie," I started …

She hid her tear-stricken face, as she often did with sad news, and refused to see the world. Death was hard enough for an adult to understand and accept. She was just seven, and she'd already lost far more than she deserved. Ethan hadn't spent much time with her, but she still felt the loss because of its harsh impact on her new family.

I held her and stroked her long, messy brown hair and waited for her to come back to us.

Will's eyes were filled with pain again, which caused my own to fill with tears. He kissed my temple and rubbed Lissie's back. She surprised us both when she reached for him. Will pulled her onto his lap and placed a kiss on top of her head.

"Mum," Thomas said, rising.

I looked up and marveled at the strength I found in Mary's eyes.

She stood in the open doorway with both hands over her heart as she admired the gentle compassion of her three remaining sons. She gazed at me and smiled before grief reclaimed her and washed away the joy.

"Come down soon, Ellie, and break your fast with Mrs. Bates and me in the drawing room."

She turned and floated down the corridor, the flowing train of her black silk robe stretching out behind her.

THE MEN WERE STILL IN THE GYM WHEN I FOUND THEM THREE hours later. Will was training with both of his brothers at once. His strength was inconceivable. I'd never seen such power flow from one man.

"What's going on?" I asked Ben.

"He's teaching his brothers to respect his command, establishing boundaries."

I flinched when Thomas suffered a punishing hit to his gut.

As big and as strong as he was, he still couldn't beat Will. It wasn't the fighting that shook me. It was how they went after each other with the same determination as if an enemy were there before them.

Ben noticed my reaction. "You must learn to accept things for what they are here. I don't mean here, in England, I mean here, with Will. We were raised to … well, you know who we are."

I released the breath I had been holding. "I understand, and I'll get there. So, how has he been this morning?"

"His entire life changed the minute Ethan died. He has quite a lot to come to terms with. He'll be the best leader and provider his family has had. But I warn you, Ellie, he'll behave like an arse until things settle down. Don't let him get away with it. And when you take him on, be certain it's from a position of strength."

Ben and Will had been together from the age of twelve, trained side by side by their fathers, both intelligence agents for the government. The only time they'd spent apart was when Ben served in Her Majesty's Royal Air Force and Will studied at Oxford University.

Will hit John, and his body flew several feet before he landed flat on his back. "You will stay out of my whisky, boy. When you are man enough to handle it, you'll drink with me, not behind my fucking back."

I ran to John and kneeled on the mat beside him. He'd lost the color in his face, and he was hardly breathing. The combination of Will's hard blow and his back slamming against the mat had thrust the air from his lungs.

John dug his heels in and launched himself away from me, shaking his head. His thrashes to drive me away were confusing, but then I got it. I was making it worse for him. Will wouldn't tolerate one of his brothers accepting help like that, being soft.

As painful as it was to leave John as he fought to regain his breath, I moved away.

"You will not coddle him," Will shouted, a menacing storm headed my way.

God, he was magnificent. And different. His sorrow had transformed to anger. I hooked my hands on my hips and narrowed my eyes as he advanced on me. He left no space between us, though he kept his hands at his sides.

"The only thing you'll find, meddling down here, woman, is a smacked arse."

I rose onto my tiptoes, still not even close to his eye-level. "Shall we step out and see?" I looked at the doors, back to his eyes.

His gaze followed mine. He became aroused, his erection pushing against my stomach.

"Get out of my gym, witch."

Will's words often sounded insensitive to those who didn't know him. But *witch* wasn't the same as *bitch* to him, not with me. *You own me. Everything I have, everything I am, it's all yours*. That was what it meant in our case.

I offered him a compassionate smile. He didn't need another sparring partner. He needed me to understand his pain, time to work through losing Ethan.

Regret, sadness filled his eyes. He bent his neck to kiss my lips. Before moving his mouth away from mine, he told me that he loved me.

I whispered back against his, "I know. Me too."

"Do you need me, baby?"

"I was just checking in." I kissed his cheek. "Work through this however you need to, Will. Feel the anger. Be furious. But come back to me at the end of each day."

He gripped my waist and kissed me again, a sweet, warm kiss. As he turned to go, the softness in his eyes receded, and anger consumed them again.

Crossing the length of the pale wooden floor, I licked my lips, tasting the salt he'd left behind.

A grunt and a thud shot up through the rafters. Another thump, softer. I counted to three before looking back over my shoulder. Thomas and John were getting up. Will was toweling sweat from his neck, his gaze following the movement of my hips as he watched me leaving the gym.

I swore his eyes were glowing.

It was from that moment on that Will distanced himself from me, spending his time in the gym and on the phone with his lawyers.

We didn't make love when he came to my bed that night.

It didn't matter how hard I pushed him, he didn't give in.

He threatened to leave the room.

It wasn't about me or us, I realized, after he locked me in his arms, kissing me tenderly along my temple, as he'd done the night I was attacked. His rejection was triggered by his protective instinct. He was managing the strength that surged through his body by physically exhausting himself and denying sexual intimacy between us. He was searching for a way to purge the anger that burned him from the inside out.

But it was more than anger.

It was rage.

thirty-two

WILL HAD BEEN QUIET AT THE FUNERAL. THE WORDS HE SPOKE to guests after we returned to Eastridge for the luncheon were brief and cold. He didn't eat or sit. He chose to lurk in a dark corner, where he could keep an eye on me while he worked on a bottle of whisky.

When he'd had enough, he jerked his head toward the staircase and waited for me to walk in front of him, guiding me to my room with his hand on the small of my back. "Stay here until you're told the estate is clear." The kiss he placed on my mouth was distant and cold.

Before he managed to slip away from me, I grabbed his face between my hands. Tears burned my eyelids. His behavior had become so dark, and it scared me.

"Let me help you," I whispered.

He pulled away. "Go inside, Elle. Leave me alone."

I shook my head. "No, I won't."

I followed him around the corner and through a door that led up another flight of stairs. The space hadn't been renovated like the three lower levels of the house. Oak floor planks were unfinished and worn and creaked beneath our weight. The walls in some places exposed roughly sawed lath with plaster so thick that it was like stone and held dimly lit sconces that cast unsettling shadows. Battered wooden doors with small metal brackets lined up along the corridor like soldiers at attention. I imagined the little cards with handwritten names on them that had been displayed in those brackets—names of servants from a time long ago, I thought.

Will knew I was behind him, of course, but he continued anyway. We walked in silence. The first window appeared, light rain drumming against it. Shadowy clouds circled around the moon. He stopped walking at that point, and I plowed into his back.

"Elle, it's not a good time for you to be near me. Go down to your room."

I was determined not to leave him alone in the state he was in. He'd been there for me, taking care of me, carrying the weight of my burdens. I wasn't going to remain passive as he fell deeper into his own darkness or allow him to bear his grief alone. I loved him. His pain was my pain.

Watching his broad shoulders rise and fall, his breath flowing in and out of his body, I waited for his next move. We stayed that way for several long moments. Silent and on edge.

I reached out and touched his back with my fingertips.

His breath stilled. Everything stopped moving. His shoulders, time. When he turned to me, warning was written in his wild eyes. The beautiful pale blue had been eclipsed by black.

I straightened my back. Whether he was a beast or not, I wasn't leaving him. "You need me."

He closed his eyes, nodded. His scent filled the surrounding space. It seemed as if an eternity had passed before he opened his eyes, but when he did, he drove his gaze into mine, and he bared everything. Pain, fear, guilt, and the anger that had given way to rage.

I winced.

As he stepped closer, looming over me, hunger joined the

chaos in his eyes, and his hot breath touched my face with his words. "Good. You should be frightened."

Will had never intimidated me.

"You know I'm not afraid of you. I'm afraid you're not working through those emotions. I won't lose you, Will. I'll fight for you if you won't do it."

He erupted, the calm before his storm coming to an end. He filled his hands with my hair and pulled my head back to cover my mouth with his, pushing his tongue past my lips. His kiss was unyielding and savage.

I pressed against his body, his sheets of hard muscle, fusing myself to him. I wanted to ease his torment, chase away his heartbreak. I would give him anything. I would give up everything.

The force of his kiss split my lip. He came down from his ruthless high when the metallic tang hit his tongue but only for a moment to inspect and then tenderly kiss my broken lip. The storm returned. His hand moved from my hair down the front of my body and lingered on my thigh for just a moment before he slid it under my skirt, into my panties.

I melted into his hand.

"I'll take you right here if you don't walk away from me now," he snarled in my ear.

"I'm not leaving you."

"Then, you'll scream for me, Elle. You'll scream my fucking name." He pushed two fingers inside me, and with the third, he earned his name, cried out loud.

Will's mastery of my body was undeniable. I came fast after he moved those long fingers in and out, twisting them, while using his thumb to drive me over the edge. As I cried his name again, he covered my mouth with his and thrust his tongue against mine, and when he was satisfied with the depth of our frenzied kiss, he found another fleeting moment of tenderness and placed a soft one on my swollen lips.

He moved our bodies then, as if they were one, positioning us against the wall. He held me so tightly that nothing else that wasn't us could survive in between.

The same fingers he'd had inside me went into his mouth, and a growl started in his chest, moving up to the back of his throat, where it waited impatiently. After tearing off my panties with a skilled yank, he lifted my skirt and pressed himself against me with even more force.

I tried to push him back to unbutton his shirt, but my strength was no match for his madness. So, I did the only thing I could to bare his chest. I clawed at the buttons and ripped them from their tiny threads. He eased back with a smirk then, just enough to give me access. His smooth, sculpted chest was my home, and he knew it.

My hands and mouth covered his skin. I pinched one of the cords in his neck. Hard. With my teeth. He grunted and grabbed fistfuls of my hair again, reclaiming my mouth with his. His erection strained and jerked between us.

I fumbled frantically with the fastenings on his trousers, and when he was free, I took his heavy arousal into my hand and stroked it. Another guttural sound escaped him as I squeezed, making it clear that he was beyond any point of return. He would take what he wanted from me with abandon and without regret.

Will jerked me off my feet, into his arms, and backed me against the wall. I wound myself around him, and when he shoved inside me with one severe thrust, I screamed his name again. He yelled mine. But then he forced his vibrating body still and burrowed into my hair. I didn't know how long we held each other that way, both panting and fevered, before he lifted his head and searched my eyes.

I dragged my fingers through his hair. "I love you, Will. Don't stop."

"Jesus, Elle." His voice was hoarse, not like his, like a feral animal's. He pushed harder against my body to stop my rocking hips. "You know how mad it is—the way I love you, need you. You don't know what you're asking me for right now. You can still leave." He brushed my ear with his sweltering lips.

"I won't leave."

The strength of his arms intensified as he began to move inside me. Then, he threw his chaotic mix of his emotions into our fire, and he let it burn. The thrusting of his hips deepened beyond the force he'd ever allowed himself to use with me. He lost himself to rage. Rage was the one demon that grew when tossed into fire. The flames reached higher as he thrust into me. It was as if fuel had been poured on top of the mess that he was, engulfing him in a fiery hell.

Deeper. Harder. It was approaching too much.

I raked my nails along his back, drawing beads of blood, and I screamed.

The roar of his climax reverberated through the corridor at the same time.

I collapsed onto his chest and shoulders, seared and drained, making him support the weight of my limp body as we worked to catch our breath.

His arms, lungs, and voice trembled. "I was too rough with you." He kissed my neck with remorseful tenderness.

"You were lost."

Will steadied me on my feet but held me in his arms. He lowered his head and pressed his face against mine. "Say you'll forgive me." Then, he dropped onto his knees, his face against my stomach. "Baby, forgive me. Say the words."

His plea shocked me as it slapped me across the face with his pain and exposed his one true vulnerability—hurting me. It was the one thing that could put him on his knees, and watching it play out horrified me.

He hadn't hurt me, but the intensity of his strength in those last moments was becoming unbearable. Had he pushed me any harder, I would have stopped him. As far gone as he had been, it might have taken a harsh slap, but I had no doubt that he would've stopped.

"Elle, I won't allow you to move away from me until you say something."

"Come back to me," I demanded, knowing he understood.

He stood and lowered his eyes to mine.

"Will, you didn't hurt me, but you could have. You can never lose yourself that way again."

He shook his head. "Never. I swear. I'll never hurt you."

He took a step back but maintained our eye contact as he pulled down my skirt and fastened his trousers. His lips soothed mine with sweet kisses as he pulled me into a protective embrace.

A sudden sting caused me to arch when he rested his hand on my back.

"What's wrong—you're hurt?"

I stalled. "It's been a long day. Neither of us has slept much. Come to bed with me."

"Tell me, goddamn it. Did I hurt you, Elle?"

"It's nothing. It's just … I think it's just from the wall."

Will spun me and lifted my blouse. "I did hurt you."

The friction from the old wall boards had torn through the fabric and abraded my skin.

I tugged down my blouse and slipped into my heels.

"I'm sure it's nothing." I looked around for my tattered panties. He'd stuck them in his pocket.

He stared at me with wide eyes like I'd committed an egregious crime. "Don't dismiss what I did to you."

"It's from the wall, not by your hand. Honestly, Will, you should see your own back."

My words made him angrier. "Not by my hand, but still my fault. I'm the last man who should ever leave a mark on you." He raked his hair and paced, cursing at himself and at the God he wasn't convinced existed.

"Stop it, Will. Please. We have more important things to deal with."

His fury escalated. "There is *nothing* more important to me than you. I've been clear about that. Still, you test me."

I reached for him.

"You deserve much better than this, than me." He backed away from me until he bumped into a door. He turned and punched it. The old wooden door broke from its hinges and crashed to the floor. He kicked it, sent it flying several feet beyond the doorway. But that hadn't been enough to satisfy his anger. He picked up the wrecked door and threw it, smashing it against the wall. It splintered into raining pieces.

I ran over to him, but he pulled away.

"Will, stop this. Please!"

He blew out slow, heavy breaths, though it wasn't from exertion. It was hard to tell if he was winding up more or calming himself.

"Ellie, step away from him," Thomas said behind me.

"This doesn't concern you. Get the fuck out of here," Will snapped, stalking toward his brother.

"Quite right. You come at me, not her. What are you doing, brother?" Thomas snarled through his teeth, something I hadn't witnessed before. "You want to hurt her?"

Will stopped. He looked from Thomas to me, his eyes softening. "I love her. I'll never hurt her."

"You're losing it, and she's too fucking stubborn to leave you to it. She will get hurt."

Will stared at me for a moment before reaching out to me with his hand. When I accepted it, he pulled me to his chest and held me securely against his heaving body. "I'm going to London for a while, Elle." He lifted my chin and forced me to meet his eyes. "You will stay with Thomas."

"No, I won't. You can't—"

"Please. You will," he commanded softly.

Hot tears stung my cheeks. "For how long?"

He shook his head and then kissed my lips. "I'll come home soon."

I clutched his shirt tightly in my fists and buried my face there. "You can't leave me. I won't let you leave me." My breath stuttered as I sobbed the words. I choked when I heard them replaying in my head, the same words I'd shouted at my dying sister.

"I'm not leaving you, baby. I need to take care of some things. And I must fix this. I swear to you, I'll make it all right." His long fingers wiped at my cheeks, and his warm lips kissed mine. We both tasted my tears. "Go on. My brother will keep you safe." He pried my clenched fingers from his shirt and eased me into Thomas's arms. "Restrain her if you must and keep the Six close at all times. She is their only purpose. And now, yours."

Thomas held me from behind.

I twisted and pulled.

I panicked, my heart refusing to accept what Will had just said, telling my brain that he was leaving me, just as everyone else in my life had done.

I pulled and struggled.

Thomas had no choice but to use his strength to secure me in his arms.

Will ducked into another room and came out with a metal box.

He looked at me once more, resolve in his eyes, then he walked away.

"Please don't leave me," I whispered at his back.

thirty-three

No one ever told you that love hurt. They told you it healed your soul and gave you hope. You would hear all the lovely stories, the fairy tales, the descriptions of euphoria, but the story about the pain would go untold.

Gran used to tell me that love was equal parts risk and reward, but she had never elaborated on either one. Of course she hadn't. She was English, raised to be indifferent in the face of love.

Will loved me. He'd said it several times since London. And he'd told Thomas. I saw it in his eyes when they burned into mine, felt it in his fevered skin when he touched me. He loved me beyond obsession, killed for me. I believed him when he said he'd never stop. Still, when he'd left, it hurt.

He was struggling with Ethan's death and the resulting responsibilities. And when he'd said he would make it right, he meant make himself right. My heart splintered each time the words echoed inside my head. He was broken. Even so, when he'd left without me, it hurt.

Thomas and I were on the little floral sofa in my room. He sat on the edge, leaning forward, and I sat with my legs tucked beneath me, one side of my face pressed to the back. Two armed men were guarding my door while we waited to hear from Ben that the estate was secure.

"He didn't leave you, Ellie."

I snapped at him, "Stop saying that."

"Stop thinking it."

"I'm here, and he's gone. He didn't say why he was going or when he would be back. So, you tell me, Thomas, what should I think?" I used the back of my hand to wipe at another tear blackened by my mascara.

He reached for my hand, thumbed away the dark drop, and then held my hand between his. "You're missing information that will help you better understand." His eyes remained on the floor. "When our father was murdered, there was retribution. Will needs that now, for Ethan. It's what we know, what our father taught us."

"What are you saying?"

"The assassin who killed Ethan walked away. Will won't have peace until he avenges our brother's death. He'll grow angrier as the guilt rides him harder. He knows the cost if he allows it to continue driving him. Everything. You."

"So, he's gone to find the man who murdered Ethan. Why couldn't he tell me?"

I understood. I could relate to the desire for vengeance. It still burned within me, though I'd been forced to admit that the magnitude of my enemy was beyond the scope of my own ability. I'd been naïve to think that I had that kind of power, to punish. But Will did. And he would.

"Come on. You know he'll move mountains to spare you. Listen, you must understand we're at war here. It might not be a grand war of countrymen defending the kingdom, but it is war. Forget the romanticized stories found in history books. No matter the size of the conflict, it's never gallant, never easy. And he worries about your nightmares. I hear it's quite awful."

I shrank away from his eyes. They were too much like Will's. "Ethan told you?"

"I can't stay in here with you, but if you choose to sleep downstairs in one of the open rooms, I can keep close."

The idea of anyone other than Will near me when I slept was uncomfortable. Thomas would always be my defender in Will's absence, the next Hastings in line who wore the inked shield on his arm. I needed to get used to it. Will had inherited more responsibility than most were challenged with in a lifetime, and I had to be supportive, but my formidable desire to be with him caused me to battle with myself over and again.

"I'll be fine up here, but thank you, Thomas."

He nodded. His half-smile was hopeful, but his bouncing leg and wrinkled brow revealed something else. He knew that I was lying.

THOMAS STOPPED ME IN THE CORRIDOR LATE THE NEXT MORNING. "Have breakfast with me," he said. "Coffee and two bites of toast in your room aren't enough."

I shrugged. "I'm not a breakfast person. And you know Mrs. Bates will take a switch to us both if she finds me in the kitchen with you and the men."

"Fuck that. Let's go." He pointed to the staircase.

I rolled my eyes and went down to the kitchen with him.

John was delivering a heated explanation to a table of men in their military-style training clothes. "I'm telling you, man, the earls of Arundel and Sussex were the same. The names were interchangeable for centuries."

"Kid's right," Thomas said. He handed me a plate and started to fill it for me.

"That's too much. Take the sausage back. I won't eat that."

He glared at me as he moved the sausage to his own plate.

“American women don’t eat the way English women do,” John teased.

“She’s highborn English. Try to remember that, little brother, before Will beats your arse again.”

Will hated it when others referred to me as American or *the* American. He’d encouraged me to embrace my heritage. “Your blood is the purest that exists,” he often reminded me.

“She sounds like one,” John said, using his best American accent.

“That’ll change in time.”

“All right, guys. Many American women eat sausage. It’s just not for me. Anyway, what’s all this about earls?”

Thomas looked up from his plate and stared at me. “You don’t know?”

“Know what?”

“Christ, maybe there’s a reason he hasn’t told you. Wait for Will to tell you.”

“Or maybe it just hasn’t come up yet with all that’s happened. He swore there’d be no more secrets, so spill it, Thomas.”

“Will is the earl of Sussex. I mean, if he chooses it. Our father had a disagreement with the Crown and renounced the title when our grandfather died, and as a matter of respect, Ethan honored that decision.”

“What?” The bombshells never seemed to end.

The Hastings men had descended not only from George Plantagenet, but also from an ancient line of fierce warriors rewarded for their victories by kings and queens many times over. One of those spoils of war was a prominent position among the peerage, the Earldom of Sussex.

“He’ll see the Queen’s ministers and inform them of his intent this week.”

“So, he’s no longer avoiding other people?”

“I didn’t say that, Ellie.”

"Yes, of course you did. Maybe I should go to London."

"You're not going anywhere."

"You do realize I'm a grown woman?" I snapped.

"Yes," was all that he could say.

I WENT TO BED EARLY THAT EVENING, RIGHT AFTER LISSIE, AND as I'd expected, I tossed and turned for hours. So, when my phone rang at three in the morning, I was still awake. Stumbling through the darkness, I banged into the table with my hip and fumbled to find the ring's source. I switched on the lamp and picked up my phone with caution.

It had morphed into a ticking bomb.

"That's your own heart drumming," I whispered stupidly to myself, lowering my bottom to the floor. I stared at the phone, at Will's name, without answering.

What if he wasn't coming back?

It rang a second time, again with Will's name and the photo of us that John had snapped the day we went to the beach. The same day Will supported me in his arms as I reached out to the sea and reclaimed myself. The day my head and my heart had finally connected as one.

I swiped to take his call. There wasn't enough air in my lungs to push out the sound of my voice.

"Elle," he breathed into the phone.

I managed his name. "Will."

"Forgive me."

Tears welled, flooding my vision. The sob clinging to the back of my throat prevented words. One would release its hold and break me. I listened to him breathe instead.

"I didn't mean to wake you. I'll be home today. Don't leave the house. Wait for me."

Thomas had told him that I'd mouthed off about going to

London. Anger burned away the tears. I didn't know why, but I couldn't resolve the unbidden pain that his leaving had caused.

"You heard. I threatened to leave, and now you're coming back to do your job."

"Jesus fucking Christ. That's not—" He stopped and softened his words. "I'm coming home to you because I never left you. There were matters to be handled, none of which could challenge my desire for you. And I won't allow you to leave because I can't live without you. I hurt you. I swear I'll make it up to you. I fucked up, Elle. Say you'll forgive me."

His words dripped with sincerity and they broke me. There was no holding back. I choked on the ambush of emotion.

"Goddamn it, Elle. Don't do that. Don't cry." He cursed to himself. "You'll wait. You will not leave the house without me." And then he hung up.

I blew my nose and dried my eyes, smiling as my heart recognized that it had been *my* Will on the phone, commanding me, refusing to live without me.

He'd slain his demons.

My phone rang a third time.

"You're not a job. You never have been. Believe me when I say that I love you, baby."

"Tell me when you get home."

thirty-four

John corrected my position before he demonstrated the proper technique for powering through with the left shoulder to throw a right cross. “Your reaction time has been great. Let’s try it again. You duck, I throw this time. Let me know when you’re ready.”

“I’ve played a lot of tennis. That helps.” I shifted into a defensive position. “I’m ready.”

I’d started training on the mats with him the day after Will left. Will had refused to teach me, insisting it was his job to fight, not mine. I came up with another plan, and when he’d left, I was pissed off enough to implement it.

John could fight. Like his three brothers before him, John had begun training when he was twelve, but unlike his brothers, he had been easier to convince that I should know how to defend myself. But I wasn’t so naive as to believe I’d manipulated a Hastings male into beating me with his fists. I knew he’d been given permission and instructions and only because he was much smaller than the others and he had no experience outside the gym.

I had approached Thomas first, but he’d given me a lecture similar to Will’s. “There’s quite a lot of pain that comes with hand-to-hand training. I won't allow you to suffer that way. You can't imagine the physical strength involved. When we fight, it takes over, and we become something else. It has to be that way, or we die out there. Don't ask me again."

But I could imagine. I'd seen it the day Will fought both of his brothers at once and experienced it the night he took me hard against that wall. It was unbridled strength, like nothing I'd ever witnessed.

"Forget about it, Ellie. Anything you've seen is nothing more than a scratch to the surface," Thomas had said after he read the thoughts written on my face.

"Get out of your head," John said, drawing my focus back to him. "You're dodging now. Let's go."

Will appeared beyond John's shoulder just as John swung his fist.

It was an immediate distraction, and I missed my cue to evade the hit, taking a blow to the face. The force knocked me onto my ass. I hadn't lost consciousness, but it took a minute before I regained my vision, black slowly giving way to light.

The thump and Will's snarl registered in my ears before my rattled brain could grasp what was happening. He'd slammed John against the wall.

"You'll take care not to hit her again if you want to see another fucking day."

After Will released him, John crouched forward and placed his hands on his knees. He raised his head and stared at me as he worked to catch his breath.

I'm fine. Sorry, I mouthed.

Will turned to me, his eyes diving into mine as he moved closer. He pulled me to my feet, towering above. "Are you hurt, baby?" His warm scent saturated my senses.

I shook my head.

My heart banged around in my chest, wanting him with

desperation, hesitating. I hadn't yet found resolve from the pain I was never entitled to in the first place.

I had no right to be angry with him. Not only had he been grieving and broken when he left, but he'd always been the broken one. It was through no fault of his own. His father and I, we'd broken him. Richard Hastings had raised his son to be a soldier, a killer, forcing him to take lives. To save mine.

Still, anger circumvented reason, and I hit him. Tears erupted as I pounded on his chest with the sides of my fists. I shouted at him, "Never do that to me again!"

He grabbed my wrists and pulled me tightly against his chest, forcing me to reconnect with his eyes before he pushed his way into my mouth. His kiss was a storm of emotions. It was passionate and fierce, tender and apologetic. It was perfect.

But I fought him, anyway. I twisted and pulled back.

His beautiful eyes burned into mine with determination while his fingers opened and released my wrists. "Tell me what you want me to do. Tell me what you need."

The gravel in his voice drove shivers through me.

I wanted him to kiss me again. I needed him to hold me.

I slapped his face.

He accepted the harsh slap without a word, nodding to assure me that he had. Then, he took my wrists back and pulled me against his body again.

"Get the fuck out," Will said to our audience, his voice booming, rumbling through the rafters. John and the other guys scurried into the locker room.

He slanted his mouth over mine and claimed it, allowing his emotions to drive him. There was no anger. There was no rage. Only love. Possessive, all-consuming love. The only thing that could have completed me more than that kiss would have been having him inside me.

"Forgive me." No longer a plea, it was a stern command.

There would be no compromise. William Hastings, my conqueror, would get what he had come for.

I was locked onto his stare and wanted him with a madness that couldn't be explained. I wound my arms around his neck and breathed against his lips one word, giving him the one thing he planned to take from me if it wasn't offered, "Forgiven."

He lifted me into his arms and held me with ease, like a comfortable extension of his own body. I lost my breath when he took my mouth and slipped his tongue past my lips again. We kissed with unrestrained, fierce, breathless desire.

I'd once read you needed only to breathe when you were not whole. I'd scoffed, called it rosy poetry. But the moment I forgave him, forgave myself, our combined strength became our breath, and I got it.

"You are everything, Elle. You're the purest part of me, the one piece that's good, the piece that holds the rest together. You are mine, and I'll never leave you. Don't doubt me again."

I was high. My own words escaped me.

"The world round us will change, baby. But how I love you will not."

We pressed our mouths together again, and then pulling back, I confessed, "I can't find myself when you're away."

"Look harder. You'll find us both. I promise." He kissed my forehead, my temple, my lips.

As individuals, we were broken and lost. But as a couple, we were whole. I cemented his pieces together, and he anchored me to the place where I belonged.

I smiled at the thought of how well we fit together. "Come shower with me, Will."

His chest rumbled, and his warm mouth found my butterfly. "And then to bed."

I wiggled my fingers through his shorter hair. I had loved his hair before, loved watching him rake it back when he was frustrated, but the textured, disheveled style he came back with was quite suitable to his handsome face.

John banged through the door. "Uncle Robert is here, and he insists on a family meeting."

"Goddamn it, John," Will said without moving his eyes from mine. He grinned. "Bunch of cock blockers round this house."

I laughed.

"I told him you are the only one who can call a meeting, but he carried on until I couldn't stand it any longer. He's waiting with Mum at the table."

"Christ. All right. We'll be there soon. Go on, wait upstairs for me." He hesitated while his brother left the gym. "First, there's something I want you to see, baby. If I don't get this thing off my arm, it'll drive me mad."

I hadn't noticed that his left arm, from elbow to wrist, was wrapped in a thin layer of gauze. "You've been injured?" I slid down the front of his body.

One brow lifted, and then the corners of his mouth twitched as he unraveled the gauze.

I sucked in a sharp breath and gaped.

"It's not finished. When I called, heard you crying, I couldn't get out of that chair fast enough."

I swept my fingers over his inflamed skin, unable to pull my eyes away from the tattoo that swallowed up the mass of his left inner forearm.

It was a masterfully detailed dagger, draped in an elegant vining rose. The artist used feminine details like butterflies and swirling patterns to design the dagger's masculine hilt. Along the length of the blade was my name, spelled as he said it—Elle. The letters had been crafted so artfully that they looked as if they were engraved into an actual blade. The overall detail was extraordinary, in black and varying shades of gray. There were two splashes of color. Crimson drops of blood dripped from the tip of the blade onto his wrist and a brilliant green gem adorned the center of the hilt.

He'd said it wasn't finished, but I couldn't imagine what he intended to add.

I raised my eyes to his. "It's so beautiful, Will."

"You are more beautiful."

I couldn't stop touching it, circling the gem with my fingertip until it hit me, and I recognized the icy shade of green. "Is that—"

"The color of your eyes."

My skin tingled. My breath caught. I shook my head. "I don't know what to say."

"Say you love me, Elle. There's nothing more I'll ever need."

I shoved my hands into the back pockets on his jeans and met his eyes from beneath my lashes, flashing the secret smile that belonged to only him. "I love you, Will. I'll love you always."

A tiny flutter tickled the walls of my empty stomach when he smiled from his eyes for the first time since Ethan's death. He lowered his head, and we joined our lips.

Then, hand in hand, we left the gym to slay the next demon in our path together.

thirty-five

WILL STOPPED IN FRONT OF A DOOR OBSCURED WITHIN A SMALL alcove inside the billiard room. I had never noticed anyone using it before, and it hadn't been on Lissie's secret castle tour, so I'd assumed it led to an unfinished room or storage.

"Never mind my uncle, Elle."

I nodded. "Whatever it is, I can handle it."

He agreed. "Yes, you can. You'll learn things in this room, but it doesn't change anything. None of it makes you less safe." He pressed his palm to the electronic pad, and the door slid open, revealing a high-tech conference room.

It was more like a situation room. A war room, I thought.

There were maps and photos pinned to the walls. Some were old, some new. The security monitors I'd heard him reference consumed most of the space on the large far wall. A carved wooden table and twelve high-back leather chairs occupied the center. Two sophisticated computer stations were present as well.

Will placed his hand on the small of my back and guided me into his war room.

Robert Moore stood, cleared his throat, and rubbed his pointed, gray-stubbled chin as he stared at me. Honey brown eyes like Mary's twinkled beneath his drooping lids. His wide mouth curved upward. Then, he moved his gaze from me to Will. "Come, William. Take your place at the head of the table. Bring the little rose along to keep you in line."

Will ignored his uncle and pulled me to the other side of the room, where his mother waited.

Mary hugged her son before positioning me in the chair on his left, instructing me with tact and discretion. She sat on my left and held my hand for a moment, her smiling eyes drifting to Will's tattooed arm before lifting to meet mine. Her warm eyes crinkled more, though the curve of her lips remained subtle. She squeezed my hand with approval before letting go.

I smiled to assure her that Will's enthusiasm was reciprocated.

"Let's get on with it," Will said. "What news do you have then, Uncle Robert?"

"I found the leader inciting the Order. Jack Lewis is the name, and he seems to have aligned with someone within the community for information, but I've yet to hear any local names. Proceed with caution at tonight's dinner. Certainly, that informant could be someone invited to Eastridge."

Will gripped his brother's shoulder. "Find Lewis quickly, Thomas." He turned his attention back to Robert. "Thank you. I appreciate the help."

"Your mum and I have questions about your time away that we'd like answered."

"I suppose you do, and I'll provide what's appropriate. But know that you'll not press me the way you did my brother."

Leader, informants, a dinner. Anxiety knocked hard at my mind's door. I reminded myself not to open it. To defeat it, I needed to face it, but only through a locked window. I had what I needed to win, the one thing strong enough to keep me away from that door. I reached out to him, clutching his thigh beneath the table, and the bitter, metallic taste in my mouth dissolved.

Will's hand found mine. He leaned in. "All right, baby?"

I pasted on a smile and inhaled the warmth of his breath. "Yes."

He raised his voice, anger and menace seeping into it. "The Order will soon learn with whom it is they're fucking. I'm neither my brother nor my father. I'm the one without mercy. I've planned for this day. But there's something more important that should be understood. This is no longer about an old pact for me. It's personal. I will not tolerate threats against Ellie on any level, and anyone who challenges this will pay."

"I'm with you, brother," Thomas said. "Zero tolerance."

Ben nodded. "I'm with you too, my brother."

"So am I," Joe Turner added.

After accepting the allegiances with a modest bow of his head, Will leaned forward and addressed Mary, "What questions do you have for me, Mother?"

She smiled, pride gleaming in her eyes. "Did you meet with the ministers this week, dear?"

"Yes. The prince attended the meeting as well, though his only genuine interest was to discuss his investments. My terms were made clear. The Crown either eliminates the Order or uses its prerogative to allow me to do so without penalty or prosecution."

"But what leverage do you have to make a demand so great?" Robert asked.

"The Queen and her son will aid me, or I'll break them financially. I can take the resulting hit. My wealth is now greater. Ethan and I worked hard to pull their private assets into our firm, not because we needed their fortunes, but because I knew this day would come."

Thomas leaned back in his chair. "And so, how do we come away from the attack in London?"

"The Crown exercised its influence with Scotland Yard and the National Crime Agency. To preempt speculation and avoid additional public rumor—because now the public knows Ellie's home—the ministers pressured the director general to keep the case out of the National Counter Terrorism Security Office. It's been buried." He paused, looked at his mother, and softened his tone again. "What else, Mum?"

"They're all right with the fact that she's here? They might never truly be happy about it, but they're settled with it?" Mary protectively placed her hand on my arm.

Will nodded and exchanged a perceptive smile with his mother. Their exchange, his hand holding mine, and hers on my arm, caused my heart to flip.

Uncle Robert shifted in his seat. "What about her claim to the throne?"

"Ceded. No revocation."

Robert frowned. "And the earldom?"

"I haven't yet decided."

My head was spinning. I couldn't have imagined the depth of the situation. Will had expected it. His knowledge and his steadfast readiness were staggering.

Robert pushed his luck. "You're rather terse with your answers."

"I've shared what's appropriate. Anything else is our personal business. And as for your disapproval, move past it. Elle and I will decide what we want and how we'll live." Will looked at his watch as he stood and then offered me his hand. "Thomas, find me in a few hours."

"Are the two of you joining us for lunch?" Mary asked.

"No," we said at the same time.

"Have something sent up," Will added, winking at his mother.

Disarmed by her son's charisma, she blushed. And with that, I fell deeper in love with him.

We stopped near the bar in the billiard room, where he discussed the Six's schedule and estate security with Ben, and I sorted through my thoughts, trying to wrap my mind around everything. He'd done as I had asked. He'd ceded my antagonistic claim. It didn't matter if he reclaimed his family title or denied it, I would support him without question. I would follow Will anywhere, give up everything to have him. Wasn't that what I'd already done?

"Elle," Will said, drawing me out of my head.

"I'm sorry, what?"

"Come on, baby. I'm mad for you." He eased me against the bar and kissed my neck. "Come upstairs with me, or I'll have you right here." His mouth roamed in a playful frenzy.

I shrieked, delighted with his relaxed behavior. "I'm getting into the shower first."

"You have ten minutes while I get my things from the car. Then, you're all mine, and I don't care where I find you. *Mine.*"

thirty-six

My room was filled with brand-new arrangements of fragrant English roses.

Lily followed me in with a tray of food. “Most people are afraid of him but not me. I see how lovely he is with you. Oh, to be so lucky in love!” She was fun when Mrs. Bates wasn’t around, made me smile.

“You’ll find love too, but first, you’ll need to get out of this house a little more,” I teased. “Do you mind taking that to his room? He’ll be up soon.”

She left with the tray, and I raced into the bathroom. I showered and slipped into my cropped jeans and a T-shirt, then plucked the pins from my upswept hair. Will’s voice resounded in the corridor. His presence was as considerable as the estate itself, and neither thrived without the other. I grinned and opened the door.

God, I’d missed him.

He’d been intercepted by the kids. Lissie clung piggyback-style to her superhero while John made a case for an afternoon at the beach with his friends. I watched him interact like the father of two children who had lost theirs and wanted him even more.

“Go on, John, but remember what I said about tonight.” He

swung Lissie around to his chest, kissed the top of her head, and nudged her in Nanny Sue's direction. Then, with scorching eyes and impatient hands, he pulled me into his embrace. "I've already waited years for you, woman. And still, you keep me waiting."

"Well, you know what's said about those who wait. Now, take me to bed, Will."

He swooped me into his arms with a grin and carried me to his room, locking the door behind us. The same delicate fragrance from my room crashed into me. I stared at his bed. It was turned down and covered with a blanket of white rose petals.

"Elle." He pulled the shirt over my head and unfastened my bra. His tongue stroked mine, and then his kiss moved down to my breasts. "So beautiful," he said as he caressed me there, lowering his head to take one then the other into his mouth.

I moaned and twisted my fingers through his hair.

He was fierce and gentle as he tugged down my jeans and panties in one swift move. "Show me your back, Elle."

I stepped out of my clothes and turned around.

Will gathered my hair and hooked it over one shoulder. Taking my hips into his hands, he stared at my back for a minute before kissing the tender pink blemishes there. He'd worked through his anger, but his heart still struggled with his having been so lost that he'd allowed the rough wall to abrade my skin.

"It'll never happen again, baby."

"I know," I said, shivering as another of his velvet kisses caressed my skin.

I faced him and placed a kiss at the base of his throat, gripping the hem of his shirt. I pushed upward until he yanked it over his head and tossed it. His chest was beautifully sculpted, so broad, so smooth, and bore those scars. I kissed it, kissed the scars and the shield inked on his shoulder.

He pulled me tightly against his body with his powerful arms, their fine, golden hair making me aware of the sexy trail that began at his navel and led into his jeans. I pulled back. He watched as I unzipped him. His fingers tangled in my hair, and he made sure my mouth couldn't escape his when he bent to kiss me. I slipped my hands beneath his waistband and pushed his jeans down over his hips.

I dropped to my knees and kissed my way down that golden path.

"You don't have to—"

He lost the words when I took him into my mouth. I'd never given a blowjob to anyone before Will—never had the desire—but with him, it was something I couldn't imagine either of us doing without.

With a savage grunt, he fought to control his thrusts, wrapping fistfuls of my hair around his hands, resisting the urge to push deeper into my throat. His eyes glowed when I looked up to meet them. "Christ, Elle, you're killing me." He jerked me up from the floor, into his arms, and carried me to bed, where we fell into a deep kiss that I prayed would never end.

"Open," he commanded, positioning my legs where he wanted them.

He pushed his fingers inside me.

I cried out. And even before I did, I knew he'd cover my mouth with his and swallow it. It wasn't something meant to keep me quiet. He needed to control the sound, so he could feel its vibration. When he saw or heard my reactions, it wasn't enough. He needed to feel it in his soul. It was who he was. There was nothing violent or threatening about his desire for control in bed, so I gave it to him. There wasn't much I wouldn't give up for him. Still, I clawed at his shoulders, desperate for release.

A knowing smile claimed his face as he gathered my wrists. "You've a long way to go, baby." He raised my hands above my head. "Hold on to the pillow and don't release it. You'll want to let go, but do not."

I clung to the pillow, and he continued to wear that smirk while I pleaded with him.

"Will, please. I need more."

He shut me up with a fiery kiss. A kiss that wasn't destined to stay in one place. He used it to devour my body as he took it lower and harder. He buried his face between my thighs.

I screamed his name sooner than I wanted to. He drove me insane with his tongue while curling his fingers inside me, making me to shatter with such intensity that a billion stars danced throughout the galaxy in celebration.

Our eyes connected, and a sense of urgency gripped him. He shot up and slammed into me with one fierce thrust, swallowing the sharp cry it tore from my lips. He immediately restrained his body and locked his gaze onto mine. "I can't live without you," he told me softly.

Will kissed me and ground his hips before subduing himself again. Nothing less than full control would do. Even as his muscles strained, as his breath quickened and his eyes burned, he made deliberate, measured moves. He was proving to us both that he'd never again lose himself to rage or volatility when he made love to me.

I acknowledged his controlled behavior with a calculating smile. And then I pushed him to the one place he couldn't control. I demanded through our burning stare that he say more, do more, prove more.

He nodded, preparing to grant my silent request. Will never denied me when I demanded something of him. He understood my certifiable need to challenge him, as I understood how reckless it was to push a man like him.

"I love you beyond words. Kill for you without shame or regret. Never doubt me, Elle." He crushed his lips to mine and teased with his hips again. "You will marry me. Say it."

Lost in his eyes, my soul fell deeper into his, and there, I found all that I'd waited for. "I will marry you," I said in a breathy whisper.

My hands slipped down, driven by the intense emotion stirring in my chest. He captured them, pinning them to the bed, his fingers entwining with mine.

"Again." Another sharp command.

"I'll marry you, Will."

He bowed his head and locked in our commitment. Then, enraptured by my submission, he finally let go, loving me hard on a soft bed of roses.

AFTER MAKING LOVE, WE FINISHED OUR LUNCH AND LAY ON THE bed again, my head resting on Will's chest. "What would you have me do?" he asked me.

I traced his inked dagger and watched goose bumps run up his arm. "I won't tell you what to do, and you know that. Are you leaning in one direction?"

"If I accept reinstatement of the title, it will strengthen us."

"How? I mean, what would it represent?"

"Well, in the present, titles are a mark of prestige and status, a fascination by those without, and not much more. The status doesn't hold the political or financial weight of times past," he explained. "That makes no difference to me. I already have more financial influence than most. I think the real benefit would be the drawing of allies to us. People will support us to be associated with the title."

"How would it affect the Sussex counties?"

"It wouldn't really. It would give people something new to cheer about, obsess over. Some lands my father lost might come back with the title, but it's not a great deal. Properties generally aren't acquired this way anymore."

I yawned. "Would you be willing to redirect any attached

income back into the community? For instance, provide support for a more sophisticated pier renovation."

"I'll deploy funding to whatever venture you desire." He yawned.

"That's crazy, Will. You know I don't have a lick of business sense." I rubbed my chin against the golden stubble on his jaw and kissed his neck.

He chuckled. "My lovely little artist. I wouldn't change a thing. Just paint me a picture, baby. I'll execute the plan."

"You mean, James Jackson will execute."

"James, my arse." He tickled me, a good-humored reprimand for offending his ego, and I giggled like a little schoolgirl.

"You're right though. I need to do something."

"Work with me, Elle. Run one of my businesses."

"We've established that's not my thing."

"I want you close to me."

We dropped it there and fell asleep in a tangled mess of sheets, arms, and legs.

When I woke, it was to the restrained thunder of his voice as he spoke to Thomas. I lay there, feigning sleep while they had their meeting in his sitting area. It made no difference to me what their business was about. I was unwilling to be roused physically or emotionally from my divine bliss.

"She'll rest as long as my voice is present. Just keep it down. How was she?" I heard Will ask.

"Angry at first, irritable. I had to tell her, brother. She's aware that you hunted Ethan's murderer. I didn't want to fight with her. She was upset as it was. Then, this rubbish with the hand-to-hand bouts. That, I don't want any part of it. She shouldn't be doing it."

"If she continues training, we'll need to ride John, so he doesn't slip up and hit her again." Will released a heavy breath. "She suffered, and that's on me. I appreciate how well you cared for her."

"I wear the shield, same as you." Thomas hesitated, allowing his tone to relax. "You know I'll always protect her."

"Yeah. Any new leads on Jack Lewis?"

"I'm working on it. Do we need to deal with immigration? I can put together a rootkit and access their system after a few test runs."

"Leave the Home Office alone. Her heritage is too strong for them to deny citizenship. I'm going to marry her, so it doesn't matter anyway."

"Not hard to figure out your plan after seeing that fresh ink on your arm."

"It's not part of a plan," Will snapped. "I love her."

I smiled.

"Why do I feel like you've held something back?" Thomas asked.

Will didn't respond, not audibly anyway.

"Ah, additional leverage then. Why didn't they use MI5?"

"The target was with MI5. Enough said."

"Before I let you get back to your nap, any concerns about this evening?"

"Uncle Robert seems sure there's someone local providing intel. Circulate but stay close. Once the community leaders meet her, they'll be supportive."

"They'd better be. We've put quite a lot in—money, protection. If they don't support her, we cut them off."

"If only it were that easy, Thomas. After we shore up support here, we'll look to London for the same. You need to get on with joining the firm. I need you there."

"Give me a few weeks to wrap up some other projects. By the way, I took care of some scumbag from Westfield for old Mr. Miller last week. I did not take Miller's payment."

"Good. No more pay for protection. And no more paid hits. Now that Ellie and Lissie are with us, it's time for this family to move in a different direction. For our mother's sake as well.

Look into that flower shop Mum has her eye on. And find me Lewis."

After the door closed, Will returned to our warm nest of twisted sheets and rose petals and pulled me back onto his chest. My awareness faded into a sound, dreamless sleep.

thirty-seven

John waited outside my bedroom door as I ran my cold hands along my hips and reassured myself that the sapphire dress that I wore was appropriate.

I'd been careful to choose something that covered my back well enough to spare Will the discomfort of seeing the blemishes exposed. It was a fitted, sleeveless gown with a conservatively draped V-neckline and ruched side seaming. The color reminded me of the moonlit sky over the Atlantic, the shimmering metallic threads mimicking twinkling stars. My pretty Choos peeked from beneath the fluted, floor-length hem as I walked.

"Ellie, let's go. Will said you'd be ready." John.

Will was delayed with business, so he'd sent John for me. It had come as no surprise that he had chosen his seventeen-year-old brother as his replacement. His ego wouldn't allow for me to make this entrance on the arm of another grown man.

I gave my formal but messy updo another once-over in the mirror, twisting a loose wisp around my finger to curl it, and then opened the door. "Okay, okay. Cut a girl some slack."

Dressed in a tailored suit, John stood with perfect posture. He flashed a wide grin and winked, offering me his arm. "I'll be your date until Will gets here."

When I failed to interlock our arms, he took my hand into his. He was becoming more and more like his bold brothers every day.

I put on a smile and fought the nervousness in my stomach. When we stepped into the corridor, the savory aroma of roast beef hit me, and the air was already buzzing with conversations, clinking glasses, and the clanging of silverware on china. John ushered me down the staircase like the young aristocrat he was born to be, hesitating at the bottom as he searched the two-story great hall for Thomas, as he'd been instructed.

The hall was filled with long wooden tables covered in fine white linens. Tall cocktail tables along two walls were covered in the same fabric. The carpets had been removed, and the wooden floor had been buffed to a shine. Lit candles flickered while chandelier crystals sparkled and cast rainbows about. Floral arrangements with creamy white roses adorned the tabletops, the sweetness of the subtle fragrance gently blended with myrrh. Sideboards were filled with savory hors d'oeuvres and decadent desserts.

The billiard room had been transformed into a full-service bar. I longed to slip in behind the bar to pour drinks and chat casually about nothing important. I missed Nick's. No, maybe not Nick's, but Jess and me together at Nick's. Images of her singing and the two of us bumping hips as we served drinks during a full house on a Saturday evening filled my head. I needed to hear her voice. After Will finished his cleanup project in Stonington, clearing my name, I'd be allowed to call her. Until then, I could only follow her tweets incognito.

"You look amazing. It'll drive him mad, you know."

John's compliment and his affectionate insight surprised me, yanking me out of my head and back to Eastridge.

I squeezed his hand and smiled. "I'm lucky to be at your side right now, handsome."

Fifty or more people mingled, drinking, snacking, making

small talk. Several more came through the foyer and brought a breath of fresh, cool night air with them.

Thomas stood near the center of the hall, and I decided shelter in his company was my best bet until Will turned up. I tugged on John's arm and headed for Thomas. He looked up from his conversation with a young couple and strode toward me, welcoming me with a warm smile.

Thomas possessed the same desirable traits as Will. He was fiercely protective, his charm was woven with arrogance, and he was generous and loyal, but somehow, his presentation of those same qualities was different, lighter. Someday one lucky woman would win his heart, and he'd make her as happy as Will made me.

Thomas placed a thoughtful kiss on my hand and whisked me into the drawing room. "I don't want you in the center of the hall until Will's here."

Two guards followed and stood inside the door. The large room was reserved for family. Thomas poured me a glass of champagne and scotch for himself and guided me to the closest of the two fireplaces.

With each minute that passed in a house full of strangers and no sign of Will, I grew more anxious. I bit my lip. I fidgeted. I drank.

Thomas leaned against the mantel. "You're safe, Ellie. Security measures are in place." He opened his jacket to show me that he was armed. "Slow down, or you'll get pissed."

I gulped what was left in my glass and shrugged. I extended my arm for a refill.

He lifted a brow and confiscated the glass. "You're too lovely for that."

Will's warm scent hit me from behind then, followed by the feel of his hands on my waist. "Elle." His breath washed over my neck, and his lips brushed my ear. "You look exquisite."

Thomas and John headed out to the hall. My guards moved to stand outside the door.

The tension in my body melted as I fell back against Will's. I dragged my fingertips along his tight beard and smiled. "Finally."

He made no excuses, nor did he offer an explanation for being late. His lips brushed across my shoulder. I didn't know where he'd been or what he'd been doing, and I didn't care. He was there, pressing his arousal against my backside, and that was all that mattered.

"Your arse looks so good in this gown."

"You're a very naughty Englishman."

"And you quite like that, don't you, baby?" There was no mistaking the conceit and satisfaction, the sensuality layered in Will's words.

"Yes," I whispered.

He was the bad boy all the girls at college had swooned over. The billionaire bad boy in the movies and in romance novels women absorbed like they were their only source of oxygen. The badass man I'd never thought I would want, not until *he* rolled into town and pressed his lips to my hand.

"Turn. Let me see the rest of you."

When I faced him, he wore the sexy grin that would never be enough. His charged eyes lingered without care as they burned me from head to toe, inspecting every inch of me.

My body screamed mindlessly for him. It begged me to spread my legs and demand him to take me right there. I needed his touch like I needed air. I contracted my thigh muscles and reminded myself where we were. God, how insane—what was wrong with me?

His grin stretched wider.

"You've been up to something, Will."

"Still working on my return to your favor."

Since he was in a lighthearted mood, I decided to play along, smiling from under my lashes. "Maybe you should work a little harder."

"Let's see if this advances my position." He fished a bracelet from the inside breast pocket of his jacket and fastened it onto my wrist before I even realized what he was doing.

I stared at three sophisticated strands of perfectly aligned, alternating cushion cut, marquise, and round brilliant diamonds and lost my breath for a moment. White light, similar to that in his eyes, reflected through the diamonds, making them twinkle with brilliance. There had to be thirty carats.

Then, I stared at him. "What did you do?"

Someone in the hall called his name.

"Will, why would you do this?"

"Because I wanted to. We've been over this." He moved his gaze to the doorway and snapped, "Just a fucking minute," then returned to our conversation. "We're not going to keep doing this, baby." He laid it out for me again. "I have quite a lot of money. I make quite a lot of money. It's only money, and I like to spend it. I'll buy you many things, and you will accept that. Shall we go upstairs and fight over it?"

It was a fight I wouldn't win. I narrowed my eyes, anyway. "Well, could you at least give me the many things you insist on buying when we're alone, so I can kiss you?"

He grabbed my waist and drew me against his body. "You can kiss me now."

"But—"

Will shut my mouth with his tongue. His amazing, wicked tongue. When he broke our kiss, he touched one of my blushing cheeks with the back of his fingers and smirked. "Let's get this done, Elle."

We entered the great hall, holding hands.

Uncle Robert, who'd assumed the role of master of ceremonies, delivered an announcement that surprised me. "Ladies and gentlemen, the eleventh Earl of Sussex and the Lady Eleanor of His Majesty King Edward the Fourth's house."

I squeezed Will's hand and gave him a dirty look.

"It wasn't me." He glared in turn at Robert.

Panic stirred in my blood. "It will upset the Queen."

"That's who you are, Elle. I'm surprised he didn't say Her Royal Highness. Old supporters of the blood will never change. They'll talk about it until their deaths and whisper the same from their graves. You'll always be their last White Rose."

And there it was. The reality I needed to face in order to be free.

I thought of the herd of frolicking deer that continued to leap and play within view of my bedroom window. The little doe. How she taunted me with her freedom, showing me what could be mine. All I had to do was accept the truth. I'd done that to some degree, but I needed to be fully committed. No in-betweens, no gray areas. I was no longer the hidden girl across the sea, no longer living a lie.

Will kissed my hand.

My lips needed no instruction from my brain to smile in adoration at the one person who'd been honest with me. Will had shown me who I was, revealed who I could be, and I was madly in love with him.

"So, you made your decision."

His mouth twitched with a controlled smile. "You asked me to fight for us. I chose to strengthen our position." Then, he shook hands with the first guest in the queue that had formed before us.

thirty-eight

What the hell? Robert Moore was at it again.

He raised his glass and clanked it with silverware. "Friends, it's time for dinner. Please take your seats." He waved to Will and me. "They're quite wonderful. Lord Sussex is the youngest to ascend to the title in decades. He blessed England when he brought home her last daughter of the purest blood, certainly the loveliest ever to grace our presence. And—"

"Sit down, Robert," Will interrupted. His voice boomed through the hall as he stood. "Unlike my father and my brother, I've claimed my station as a peer of the realm." Grief washed over his face but vanished after a moment. "It would please me to not be addressed as Earl or Lord Sussex. I'll remain William Hastings by name in most cases."

Champagne and whisky glasses clinked.

Men and women shouted, "Hear, hear, mate!"

He nodded at the waiting catering staff. Floorboards creaked, uniforms rustled, and their shadows dashed about as the waitstaff delivered steaming dinner dishes to the tables.

"Anyone positioned on the few properties returned to me in the Sussex counties won't be affected. You have my word. Business continues as usual. Thomas and I are available to you all.

Anyone hurting needs only to reach out to us. We're here to help. Spread the word."

Will extended his hand to me with a small touch of dramatic flair.

My stomach rolled with nerves, but still, I needed to focus and stay out of his way, allowing him to carry out his plan. I found his eyes, slipped my hand into his, and stood at his side.

"It would please me most for you to welcome Ellie into your communities. She is the incontestable heiress of her house, and the Crown has offered to confer nationality by descent."

"But only if she gives up her God-given birthright," someone shouted.

"True enough, mate," Will agreed.

"Make her your countess," another called out.

He teased guests with one of his magnificent wide grins. "Do you all think a woman of such grace would have me?"

There were hoots and howls of laughter.

"Long live the White Rose," one table chanted.

Will took the opportunity to become serious. "There have been attempts on her life, and there will be more. Protect her." His last two words resonated above all sound.

Once more, guests hailed, "Hear, hear!"

An adrenaline flush tingled through me. I was stunned. Will commanded the room, captivating everyone in the hall with his unassailable charm. These people *wanted* him to stand among them as a leader.

Will made a show of placing a protective kiss on my forehead and winked. "Let's eat," he said, repositioning my chair.

Chairs scuffed wood, plates and silverware clanged, and the hall hummed with conversations again. Savory and sweet scents combined and created one delicious aroma. My empty stomach rumbled.

Someone called out Will's name.

"Go on," he called back, searching the room as he stuffed another piece of roast beef into his mouth and chewed.

A hunched, white-haired man raised a shaky hand to identify himself. "My wife and I wish to thank you, sir. Your family saved our store. Our cash and stolen items were returned." It was Mr. Miller, the man Thomas had helped.

His son stood. "You have our support, sir."

"God save the White Rose," the older Mr. Miller added.

Will graciously bowed his head at the two men.

I squeezed Will's thigh as I smiled at the Millers through the heat of another blush, receiving in return a devoted bend at the waist from each man. Will captured my hand and raised it to his lips. The extravagant bracelet sparkled. As stunning as it was, it was no match for the scintillating light in his eyes in that moment.

"Now, that's a fucking piece of jewelry," Thomas said. He flashed a complicit grin.

Mary narrowed her eyes and shook her head. "Must you boys always curse?" She patted my arm, and I caught a twinkle in her eye. "It's quite perfect, dear. My son has flawless taste."

All three of her sons leaned forward and eyed their mother as though she'd lost her mind. Swearing was part of who they were, a mannerism imparted by their father, I thought. I rarely used that word, but it never offended me when it came from their mouths. She dismissed their incredulity with a delicate flick of her wrist.

Will stood, swallowed his whisky in one mouthful, and pounded his glass onto the table. "Something on your mind, Mr. Green?" His voice rumbled through the hall. He'd sussed out dissent among the ranks, though the rest of us had missed it.

My heart accelerated, the hammering dropping into my stomach. My gut lurched in nervous rebellion then, recognizing that something dreadful was about to happen.

Thomas knew his brother well and understood Will's

outburst. He jumped onto his feet, positioning himself behind me, receiving a curt nod of approval from Will.

"I won't ask again." Will removed his jacket and dropped his arms. His hands clenched into fists. "Is there something on your fucking mind, Green?"

"Your reputation is indeed earned, I see," Charles Green barked from a crowded table. "It's quite clear you're the seductive, barbarous hellion they say you are." He pulled long from his glass, rising to his feet.

"Maybe. Yet here you stand in my house. You drink my whisky and seek whatever advantage you can gain. Go ahead, insult me. But know that you straddle an important line of demarcation. Fall on the wrong side by threatening what's mine, and you'll find out how barbarous this hellion can be."

Chairs screeched across wood planks as Green's three brothers got onto their feet. The Six moved around the perimeter of the hall. It grew quiet, and the air became still, laced with menace, contempt, and fear.

I held my breath, anxiety consuming me.

"Look at you. Uncompromising and sanctimonious. You'll never maintain peace with the Crown. My family will no longer support your pact. One woman—" Charles Green pointed at me, slurring his words. "For the sake of many, let them have the last one. Find another for your pleasure."

Will soon had the man's throat in his hands. "You're threatening her?" he asked in the collected manner I recognized as the unnatural calm before he lost control.

Green's face turned red as Will applied more pressure to his throat.

"Since you're familiar with my reputation, you must know I won't hesitate to retaliate when threatened." Will's nostrils flared, and the muscles in his face and jaw grew tighter.

I stared at Will. Intense pale eyes were overcome with rage.

The storm was about to hit. He lifted Green from the floor, and the breathless man's feet kicked at air.

The sight, those flailing limbs, forced my brain from its lock-down, and I shouted at Thomas, "Do something. Stop him!"

When Thomas and Ben sprang into action, crashing through tables and people to reach Will, so did Charles Green's three brothers.

Other men shouted. Someone screamed. People ran for the door.

I cried out for Will, but he couldn't hear me.

Thomas and Ben were unable to convince him to release the dangling man, whose face was now blue. Finally, Thomas wrapped his arms around Will's throat from behind and dragged him backward.

My cries for Will only drew undesirable notice. Green's brothers crept through the chaos and surrounded me.

The youngest held a revolver at his side. His words rattled close to my ear. "You can't be worth all this."

If he pointed that gun at me, if he touched me, he was a dead man. I knew that. Fear climbed up the back of my throat. I swallowed it. No one would die if I could talk him down.

"Walk away now," I urged. "You know this won't end well. Just walk away now while there's still time."

Another Green slithered closer, his stinking breath drifting into my face. "You're right, it won't. Not unless you make it so. Seems you have his number. He can't stop himself from falling all over you." His deep-set eyes moved up and down my body. "Can't say I blame him."

All three closed in tightly around me.

"Please. Let me go to him before he looks this way. If he—"

My name blasted from Will's mouth. It was too late. He was already moving across the hall, throwing things out of his way. Plates and glasses shattered. A chair sailed through the air. His eyes were locked on Seth Green, the man stupid enough to come near me with a gun.

I stepped in front of Seth, shielding him for a moment from his certain death. It was senseless.

He wrapped his arm around my waist, pressed the revolver between my shoulder blades, and shouted, “Back off, Hastings, or I’ll end this. I’ll kill her.”

Time slowed to a crawl.

As Will cleared the distance between us, I locked onto his eyes. I was powerless but sickly comforted by the rage and violence burning in them. The rage and violence represented my life, and as long as it burned in Will, I knew I’d live.

“Six,” Thomas shouted. The single word that commanded the six soldiers to me.

“Come to me, Elle,” Will shouted at the same time. His feet left the ground as he dived toward me.

Ben was on his heels, making a dive of his own.

Will’s heavy body took mine to the floor, twisting to keep from crushing me. The air still slammed violently from my lungs.

Ben’s arms wrapped around Seth, his considerable weight taking them both down, causing the wooden boards beneath Will and me to kick back as they hit the floor next to us.

They wrestled for the gun.

The gunshot exploded in my ears, and my body jerked.

thirty-nine

CRYSTALS FROM A CHANDELIER TINKLED AS THEY SPLIT INTO shards and rained down over us. The strength of Will's arms increased, enveloping me tighter, increasing the depth of the security he provided.

From beneath Will's arm, I watched Ben and Seth Green fight. Ben gripped the man's chin and the top of his head. Seth was thrashing, fumbling for the gun. Ben wrenched the man's head at an angle and snapped his neck, the sight of it horrifying, sickening.

I freaked out. I pushed my face into Will's neck, clutching frantically at his shirt and his skin, and sobbed. I choked on the metallic tang filling my mouth.

"I've got you, Elle. I won't let go. I'll never let you go, baby," Will said, purring the words to soothe me.

He maintained our position on the floor until Thomas and the Six surrounded us with their weapons drawn. He still held me tightly in his arms as he brought us to our feet.

"Where is my mother?" Thomas shouted at someone.

"With Robert," I said against Will's chest. Robert had rushed Mary out, thank God.

As he'd promised, Will didn't let go. He held me as he made

decisions and directed his team. "John, upstairs. Keep Mum and the girls in one room with you. You protect them. Stay until you're told it's clear." He sent one of the armed guards with John.

I buried my face at the base of his throat and cried again.

He kissed the top of my head. "It's a precaution. They're safe. You're safe. I promise."

"I can take Ellie upstairs to your mum," someone offered.

A soldier, Joe Turner, blocked the man's way. "Step away from her, sir."

Once they were commanded to me as they had been, no one other than Will, Thomas, or John could touch me or get between their bodies and mine.

"She stays with me," Will said and then barked at someone else. "Get that fucking thing out of my house. Put it outside, so the police can pick it up."

That fucking thing was the body of Seth Green. No way would anyone walk into Eastridge, making threats with a gun and live to tell the story.

Will and I stood there for several more minutes. I soaked his white shirt with my tears and the blood from my broken lip, and he commanded his men as he protected me in his arms. "Get the rest of these people out of here. Shut down all entrances and secure the estate. Lock up those three Greens, but don't touch them. You know where to hold them, Thomas. Then everyone get to the war room."

I had to get it together, so I didn't impede Will's ability to sort this out. This was what my life had become and there was no alternative. It was time for me to toughen up and deal with my reality. "I'm sorry," I whispered, though I still clung to him with my face buried.

I could do better than that. I was stronger than that. I lifted my eyes to his.

He cradled my face in his hands. "Never apologize to me,

Elle. You're not to blame. No one could be more innocent in this fucking mess than you. What happened here tonight is my fault."

Will always blamed himself, although none of it was his fault. He'd never chosen this life. His fate had been no different than mine, a predestined circumstance into which we'd been born. Our fathers had bound us to the same legacy, but he'd been given the greater burden. I only had to live. He had to wage war to keep me alive. I thanked God every day for Will, for his promises to me.

"No, Will." I steeled myself against the fear, the pain, and pressed my red-stained lips to his. A wave of cold resentment rushed though me. "Our families, their legacies, their damn lies are to blame."

He nodded, his expression reflecting my own resolve. "You're right."

We exchanged smiles.

Will secured his arm around my waist and led me to his war room.

It was on.

WILL SCRUTINIZED EVERY CORNER OF THE ESTATE, EYEING THE security monitors on the wall while we waited for the others to complete their tasks and make their way to the war room. Strategic thoughts flashed in his eyes. His determination was a force unto itself.

That evening was the first time I saw his entire team assembled. Thomas and John were loyal because it was in their blood, and because they loved him. The other men were loyal of their own free will. Those were the faces I explored now. The hardened expressions of Ben Scott and Joe Turner. I studied the lines and creases on the foreheads and around the eyes of Andrew, Colin, Daniel, Henry, and Eric, the other soldiers who'd once carried the weight of Britain's protection on their backs. I would pay more attention to these men in the future. They followed Will to protect me. I owed them more respect than I'd given.

Uncle Robert came in with the last man. "Can I be of some assistance?"

"Not here. Mum is still grieving. Spend your time at Eastridge with her." I'd gathered from conversations with John that Robert and Richard Hastings had had a rocky relationship, which might have been the reason for Will's detachment when it came to his uncle.

Watching Robert leave, I wondered if I was also in Will's way. He always attempted to shield me from the details of the violence. Would my presence in his war room hinder the conversations he needed to have with the men? He needed to deal with the three remaining Green brothers and the police, not to mention strategize and plan his next moves against our enemy.

Truth be told, I didn't want to be fully informed. I liked knowing that Will handled things and not knowing how he did it. It spared him the worry that I might see him differently. I wouldn't, of course. But it was one of the few things that I could give him, to ease him, so I did. God knew the scales of our relationship tipped significantly in his favor when it came to giving and sacrifice. He never asked for anything other than for me to say that I loved him.

I folded back his sleeves. "Take me upstairs, Will. I want to see the girls and Mary. I'll wait for you in your room."

Satisfaction flickered in his eyes, and his shoulders relaxed. "Get started with a detailed rundown. Cover every meter of this estate. Every corner must be secure. No mistakes," he told his team. "Put one of your drones in the air and have a look, Thomas. I'll be right back."

His strong, tattooed arm snaked around my waist again, and we headed upstairs.

"You've recovered remarkably tonight," he said as we reached Lissie's door.

He was right. I had fallen apart. But I'd found the strength to pull it together, recognizing it was time to accept what I couldn't change. My connection to him revealed my strength. It revealed *me*. I smiled and pulled his forehead to mine. "You deserve the credit. Go plan your war, Will."

Our lips connected and lingered for a minute. The depth of his tenderness made me high.

Watching him go, I whispered, "William, my conqueror."

WILL RUBBED THE BACK OF HIS NECK AND CURSED UNDER HIS breath when he came into the bedroom later that night. I sat up. His voice was strained. He was exhausted. "I didn't mean to wake you, baby."

"You didn't. What is it?"

He sat on the edge of the bed and dropped his head. "It's not going to be easy for you, this goddamn life with me. The things I must do."

I lifted onto my knees behind him and kneaded the muscles in his shoulders and neck. "We know this. Our life together will never be simple."

He reached up and found one of my hands and pulled it to his lips. "You deserve more than some fucking mercenary."

He didn't know that I'd listened to his earlier conversation with Thomas. "You're no longer that. You make the rules now. No more paid hits."

"If you want something else—"

"Don't, Will." He meant *someone*, not something else. We both knew the something could never be changed. "Don't you do that to me."

"Goddamn it. You have the right to choose. Think about who I am, all that I've done."

I climbed into his lap, facing him. "I've made my choice. I know who you are, that your past haunts you. I also know that the lives you've taken since we met on the pier were necessary—to save mine. You are my defender."

"Yes." He put his arms around me. He still stared at the floor.

"More than that, you are my love."

His eyes came to mine.

"Don't destroy us. We're not Ethan and Isobel. We'll live and find our way through this. Take my freedom from them and give it back to me. Take it, Will. Because *that's* who you are."

"Jesus, Elle," he whispered. His embrace strengthened as he pulled me snugly against his body. He buried his face in my neck and inhaled. "There're no words. I can only hope you're able to feel my need for you, my love for you."

My heartbeat was steady and strong. I wanted him to hear it before anxiety and fear robbed me of it once again. I wound my arms around his head and pulled his ear to my chest. "I do. I know."

We were face-to-face when I woke up a few hours later. Will's eyes were open, and he was staring at me. They were clear, beautiful. The dark circles beneath were almost gone, and the muscles in his face had relaxed.

"Why aren't you in the gym?"

He plucked rose petals from my hair. "You slept so peacefully."

"You should wake me when you don't go downstairs."

"I'll never do that." He placed a hand on the back of my head and pulled me to his lips. "Promise me you'll have something more than coffee for breakfast."

"Yes, okay. What will you do today?"

"Spend some time in the gym. Make some calls. The sun's

shining, and it's quite warm. We'll go down to the beach and then have a casual dinner out."

A warm, ethereal feeling flowed through me. I smiled and touched his face.

"I know you miss it, baby." His eyes charged. "I'll take what belongs to us. I swear."

He kissed me hard and then climbed out of bed and stretched like the lion king he was. I watched as he strutted toward the bathroom. He was, without a doubt, aware of my contented stare at his tight, round ass.

Mrs. Bates's lilt drifted along the corridor and stopped outside the door. I rolled my eyes and sighed as I padded across the soft wool rug and slipped into my robe before she opened the door and called out for me.

forty

Will and I were alone in his car at the front of our small army as we headed into Old Town. There were fifteen of us, and five more young men, friends of Thomas and John, joining us at the pub. Girlfriends of the Six had been invited, adding three more to our crew. It was time we'd considered the personal lives of the men who fought for us, the honored lives belonging to those faces I'd studied the night before. If we were going to step out of the shadows, we would eliminate as many restrictions as possible.

After we filled the private car park, we walked down the busy cobblestone streets to the beach and spent a quiet afternoon in the sunshine. The cool, salty breeze caressed our skin. The tide was high, the undercurrent strong, and the water cold, but it was still comforting to be there. Waves clapped like thunder as they slapped the shoreline.

I couldn't have been happier.

Will playfully tossed me onto the blanket and lowered himself over me after chasing me through the edge of the water. He hovered above my lips with his. "What do you hear?"

"Nothing. I hear only you." My whispering messenger was silent that day. My soul was full. As much as I loved the sea, I finally understood that it had never been my home. It had been the beacon tasked with getting me home.

As if reading my mind, Will said, "You're home, baby." Then, he slanted his mouth over mine and claimed me with a devoted, relentless kiss.

"Let's go," Thomas shouted along the beach at everyone as he and Kirsty walked east along the shoreline, approaching Will and me in our favorite spot beneath Eastridge. "Christ, I'm starving. Let's get on, you two."

Will softly kissed my lips, and then without looking away, he asked his brother, "Why is it you all have such shitty timing?"

"It's not that at all. You can't keep your greedy fucking hands off her is the matter. Time to move. Information has been circulated."

The street was filled with patrons dining and shopping and merchants selling their goods. The energy of the community was intoxicating. Locals, government officials, business owners, photographers flocked to the restaurant as we arrived. People behaved with respect and approached in a thoughtful manner, excited to see their new earl and curious about me. I recognized several city councilors from the night before at Eastridge as well as some other faces. They were oddly blithe, as if the chaos from the night before had been erased from their minds.

Will bought every bottle of a local winery's VIP reserve from the restaurant. He shared that and the chef's best hors d'oeuvres with everyone who stopped at the front patio while we waited for our dinner table. The chef appeared twice and offered a private dining room, but Will declined both invitations.

Will and Thomas flaunted our presence but remained cautious. Security detail was maintained around me. A message had not only been sent, but also had been hand-delivered. Will wanted the town of Hastings, wanted it for the benefit of my freedom, and he was taking it. It was, after all, his namesake.

The food and drink demand of our party filled the charming

seafood house with complete chaos. I'd never seen as much food on a restaurant table before.

"Give Jessica a ring tomorrow," Will said.

"Really?"

"Yes, of course."

"Is everything okay? In Stonington, I mean?"

"The cop got all that he needed, and we satisfied his captain with the commissioner's interview. The case is closed."

I kissed his cheek. "Thank you, Will. You don't know how much it means to me, the way you take care of everything, the way you give me what I need most."

Satisfaction danced in his eyes. He knew.

The director of the local art museum approached our table then, asking to speak with me. Will was unfriendly for the first time that day. He grumbled in disapproval as I invited her to take the seat next to me, moving John over one.

I whispered at his ear, "I'm sure her purpose is harmless."

The director was sincere, touching my arm as she spoke. Her kind smile reminded me of my beloved professor of nineteenth-century art history. She stayed only long enough for a few sips of wine, closing with a predictable request for my support of the museum association.

Will threw his napkin onto the table and drank another shot of whisky. He leaned back against his chair and pulled me into his side. "You look quite happy. You're so beautiful." He brushed his warm mouth against my shoulder. "Let's go home."

"It's been a lovely day. Thanks." I swept my fingers along his inked forearm and extorted a smile from him. "You don't plan to cover this when you're out?"

"Why would I do that." He grabbed my hand and kissed it. "Thom, go up front and settle this bill, so we can leave." Then to John, gesturing at his own chair as he stood, "Move over here." Will watched his brothers do as he'd ordered, then he headed for the restroom.

Three men appeared from another part of the restaurant and stepped in front of Will.

The Green brothers.

Ben flashed to Will's side in an instant. Wood scraped wood as the other guys in our party rose from their seats. A few moved that way until Will jerked his chin and issued the single-worded command, sending the Six to surround John and me in that impenetrable circle of protection. Thomas sprinted from the front to Will's side.

The thrashing of my heart reached my stomach and pitched back up to my throat.

John held my hand beneath the table. "I bet they're trying to wring more money from him. He's paying for the funeral. Shouldn't even do that. The bastard came into our house with a gun and threatened you. He deserved death. Looks like the rest want it too."

He went on to tell me that the Greens had agreed, after some persuading, to bury their dead brother quietly. Each had claimed they didn't know their youngest brother carried the gun to Eastridge and apologized after Will reminded them that he had tracked and punished the man who beat and raped their sister three years earlier.

The expressions and the body language of the Green brothers troubled me. Those men were not on board with the plan. Will's fisted hands, his clenched jaw, and the deliberate way he moved told me I was right.

The circle of men around John and me parted as Will came through the center. "Let's go, Elle." He took my hand, took me home.

Later that night, Will and Thomas went back into town alone.

They hunted the Greens.

forty-one

MY PHONE CHIMED WITH A NEW MESSAGE, BUT IT WASN'T FROM Will. It was past noon, and he wasn't home yet. Torment and unease overwhelmed me. I tapped on his name and called him again while wearily descending the stairs, halting when I heard his ringtone somewhere back up on the first floor.

He was in the house, but he hadn't bothered to let me know that he'd returned.

I turned and darted upstairs, following the sound of Will's ringtone. Thomas and Ben stood near a guest bedroom, their expressions like deer caught in the headlights of a car. Thomas held Will's phone in his hand.

"Why aren't you with Will? And why do you have his phone?"

Thomas stared at me with his mouth open, saying nothing. Then, "He asked me to bring it to him."

My chest tightened. "Where is he, Thomas?"

"It's not a good time, Ellie."

"Where is he, and what happened last night?"

"Listen—"

"What happened, damn it?" Images of Will, lying lifeless

assaulted my heart, sending a shock wave of pain through my body. I hugged my abdomen as if it would hold me together.

"He's going to be fine; I promise." Thomas placed his hand on my back to comfort me while snapping at Ben, "Fuck this. He's too deep into his head. He doesn't realize what he's doing to her."

Ben tried to reason. "Will's resting inside, getting himself together. His shoulder will be all right."

God, he was hurt. "Was he shot?" I whispered.

Thomas interjected. "He was cut. A physician minded the wound this morning. It's not quite as bad as it might seem."

Avoiding me wasn't about the injury. Will refused to see me for some reason.

Ben's warning from one of our talks in the gym knocked around inside my head.

Don't let him get away with it.

I dropped my arms and straightened my back. "Let me in, Thomas."

"Do you want me to go in with you?" he asked.

"No, we'll be all right."

Thomas held my gaze for a minute, and I could see in his eyes that he'd noted my confidence. He nodded and walked away. Ben followed.

I stepped into the guest room with Will. He lay, propped against a stack of pillows, drinking from a lowball tumbler. One shoulder was bandaged, but otherwise, he was physically whole. He turned his face away from me to search outside the window for something to hold his eyes.

Tears welled in my eyes, and a broken sob stuck in my throat. Relief had to wait. We needed to settle a matter between us first. I drew breath through my nose and straightened my shoulders. Will had underestimated me. There was no way I would allow such behavior. Because like him, I would fight to protect what was mine.

I snatched the whisky glass from his hand. "I won't be replaced by this."

"You shouldn't be in here." He fought to keep his eyes trained outside.

"You don't belong in here either."

"Leave."

"You know that I won't." I touched his bandaged shoulder. "Tell me what happened, Will."

"Leave me, Elle."

Anger consumed me. I wouldn't let him do that, wouldn't allow him to shut me out. I threw the glass at the fireplace, and it shattered against the surround. "I will never do that to you, Will."

His eyes met mine. He grabbed me, pulling me down on top of him. He held my wrists so tightly that it stung. The muscles in his shoulders and his arms quivered.

I searched his eyes and found anger, among other things, but rage wasn't lurking there. That anger was the beast that reared its head when he believed something had hurt me. Knowing this, the reason behind his torment, I straddled his hips, even more determined not to back down.

When I turned my wrists to relieve the stinging sensation, he quickly opened his fingers to release me. "Don't push, Elle." Dark eyes. He was wrecked.

The situation with the Greens caused him to question himself, to retreat emotionally.

I cradled his face in my hands. "Why are you shutting me out? You took a hit, but that changes nothing between us. It's nothing we can't manage."

He pointed to his shoulder. "*This* is nothing. That's right." Then, he pulled my hands away from his face and locked on to my wrists again. "But what I've done, that's something. That's the fucking nightmare you should be concerned about."

"Now, we're getting somewhere. Tell me, Will. What could

be worse than what I already live with or see each night in my dreams?"

But he didn't need to say anything more. I understood what messed with his head. He blamed himself for the Green brothers' change of heart, believed their rebellion was his creation. He worried others would do the same.

"You are persuasive and successful, a powerful man. But the decision they made to come after us? You don't get credit for that."

"I'll fix it," he snapped, his anger still present but diminishing.

"Remember, whatever happens, whatever we must fix, neither of us is whole without the other." I untied the string at the waist of his sweatpants. "Shall I remind you?"

He grabbed my hair and drew me to his mouth. His strength was overwhelming. "I need you. Christ, how I need you."

Will needed his pieces cemented together. Something I could fix.

I pressed on his injured shoulder. It was the only way to take the advantage from him. He jerked and lost his grip. I pulled my mouth from his and kissed my way down his neck, his chest, dragging my mouth over his skin until I reached his trail of fine hair, and then I tugged like a savage at his sweatpants.

"Never shut me out again, Will."

"Never." The rhythm of his rising and falling chest intensified. "I'll never," he repeated as he tried to roll me onto my back.

But I pushed on his shoulder again.

He fell flat onto his back, and his voice crashed against the floral-papered walls. "Goddamn it, Elle!"

I stared at him, at his handsome face, his sculpted body, his enormous erection. "Fucking magnificent," I whispered.

Will's mood shifted fast, as it often did, and he smirked. "Did you just say fu—"

I locked my mouth around his wide crown.

His chest rumbled, and a primal grunt came from his throat as his hips bucked. He threaded his fingers through my hair and used it to leverage his grip, to control his thrusts into my mouth. His wild eyes met mine, burning with white fire.

The muscles in his chest rippled when he chose to overthrow my rule and flung me onto my back across the width of the bed. "Be careful with that, woman. You're pushing me close to madness," he panted against my lips. He kissed me and then dragged that kiss down my quivering body, sliding off my jeans. Smooth kisses teased as he trailed them over my thighs.

When he at last gave me what I wanted, I pulled his hair and arched, pressing hard against his mouth. A growl vibrated in his throat.

He had, from the very first time he'd touched me, mastered the precise rhythm and intensity that would take me over the edge. He could take me there within seconds or draw it out as long as he wanted. He'd also mastered knowing the exact moment my orgasms would begin, so he could do with them as he pleased. He was the master of my soul.

With his tongue flattened and pressing hard again, I shattered, screaming his name.

Satisfied, he shot up and drove himself inside me with a sharp thrust, swallowing my cry. He stopped moving for a minute to gather his control. Against my neck he said, "I don't want distance between us. I only meant to spare you my dark mood. I'm sorry."

That caused my anger to resurface. I used his injury again, squeezing his shoulder, so he would roll onto his back and I could reclaim my position on top. I made sure he stayed inside me.

"Goddamn it, Elle. I said I'm sorry."

I dropped my head, saying nothing.

"Don't be angry. Look at me." His hands gripped my hips.

I lifted my chin, meeting his eyes. "Give me all of you. Everything," I demanded.

A sudden wave of anxiety flowed through me, and I collapsed onto his chest.

He moved our bodies, reversing our positions until he hovered above me, and pressed his mouth to mine with tenderness. "I love you." Another gentle kiss on my lips. "I'll give you everything, my angel, always. But this, we'll do my way when you're no longer angry with me. And willing to yield."

We stared into each other. Tears ran down the sides of my face, wetting my temples and sliding into my hair. He'd been stabbed. I could have lost him.

"You scared me, Will."

"I'm an arsehole."

I nodded with enthusiasm. That was even better than an apology.

He grinned. "You're schooling me, baby. I used to be much worse."

"I know." My heart smiled first before it spread to my face.

The chuckles we shared against each other's mouths became a passionate kiss, and then he moved inside me, filling me over and over, loving me his way. Will was back in control, as he needed to be, and as I needed him to be. Giving myself over to him, yielding to his dominance when he was inside me, eased my soul, took me home.

Will controlled what went on in our bed and in our life together, but he gave me something in return that was more valuable. His key. It unlocked a power that was all mine, the power to push him until he was no longer an arrogant business executive or a cold-blooded mercenary or the warrior born to protect me.

I could turn that key and strip him down to the man behind it all. The man with a tender soul who loved me hard, no matter the cost.

forty-two

Several days later, Will hauled his favorite worn leather sofa across the billiard room and placed it close to the bank of windows where I'd begun to paint again. The room wasn't ideal with the bar and its traffic, and I disliked being exposed on the ground level, but it had the most accessible north-facing windows in the house.

We were focused on the rehab of Will's shoulder and connecting the pieces of our life. We'd agreed it was one life and talked about how to move forward together. Will and I might never be free of the legacy of our ancestors, but we would change that for the following generations. We were committed to ending an ancient war that had somehow made its way into the twenty-first century. We would close the rabbit hole.

Apart from my distinct American accent, living in England felt like a natural fit. Eastridge was my home. Will was my home.

"Where's John in his education?" I had no clue about the education system in England.

Will answered without looking up from *The Wall Street Journal.* "He's indulging in a gap year before university. It's common here, though I'm not certain it was right for John. I'm worried his enthusiasm will be lost. He doesn't show interest in anything other than football as it is. Lissie needs to be enrolled in primary school. Mum can deal with it."

"I probably don't need to ask, but is he good? In the game, I mean."

"He is, of course."

Newspapers rustled as he continued to work through the regular stack. The smell of fresh ink mingled with the spike lavender I used with my oils. I imagined it was how any home we shared would always smell. I loved that he preferred the paper medium to digital. Black-and-white, no shades of gray, no vibrant distractions.

"Maybe that's his way out of this mess."

"We'll see."

"Do you think the community—damn it!"

"What's the matter, baby?"

"Oh, I'm just trying to oil out *Neptune*, but she's not cooperating."

"The community will settle down."

I peeked around the canvas. "Your mother said you'll need to check your ego first."

He winked, took a drink of his coffee, and opened *The Times*. "*Neptune*?"

"The old fishing boat in Stonington."

"And you've painted it from memory." His newspaper dropped onto the sofa, and he came around the canvas to watch me fine-tune my work. "Christ, it's quite perfect. Are you attached to it?"

"I'm almost done, which means I'll probably never look at it again."

"I'll have it framed, and we'll gift it to the seafood house where we had dinner. Don't sign it yet. That'll be done ceremonially when they hang it."

I looked away from the canvas to see a plan burning in Will's eyes. He planned to polish the loveliest gems that gave me joy, to take them away from our enemy or anyone who challenged him and give them to me. Those gems, places like that seafood house, would be the safe houses of my freedom.

He put a sweet kiss on my lips and made my heart race before going back to the chesterfield to open another daily.

"When will Thomas start at Hastings Group?"

"Soon, Elle. He's preparing now."

"I'll hunt you down, William Hastings. I won't be left alone while you spend all your time in London."

"You would, I believe that. There will be quite a lot of back and forth, but we'll figure it out. You are my priority. Lissie too."

We'd decided to officially get Lissie's paternity, using his DNA, because he and Ethan shared many common markers used in the testing. I'd searched for Ethan's toothbrush, but the household staff had disposed of it.

"What if she's not?"

"You have nothing to worry over." When he didn't get a response, he moved his eyes from the black-and-white print to my face. "Look at her. Watch how Mum looks at her."

"Your mother knows?"

"She suspects. It's rather hard to miss. How do you feel about adoption?"

"Adoption? You mean, you would adopt her as your own?"

"We. Ours. Mum can help. And the nanny stays. I don't want us to manage raising a child round the clock. I need you with me." My possessive lover stared at me, waiting for an obedient response, one that I wasn't providing. "Don't fuck with me, Elle."

I was obsessed too, though. I nodded. Tension drained from his handsome face. "I know you love her. But we do need time, and that must be our priority. You first, Will."

He exhaled, his broad shoulders relaxing.

"Lissie should have your name. She's your family. No one

outside this house needs to know she's my niece. I know she's safe, that it ends with me, that I'm all the Order wants now. I still can't help worrying for her."

Will was next to me in a flash, angered by my choice of words. Words chosen to test him. He pulled me to my feet. "You'll stop talking this way. *You* are my family. *You* are safe. And it ends with *us.*" He secured me in his arms and protected me with his fierce affection. "Say the word, Elle. Us."

No matter how many steps forward we took, one of us always seemed to lose our footing, forcing the other to right us again. I pressed my ear to his chest. As a child, strange as it was, I had been soothed by severe coastal thunderstorms in the night while tucked safely in my bed. That was what it was like to hear his heartbeat when he held me.

"Us," I repeated.

"Lock down on it. It's the only thing to keep us from stumbling." He pulled my chin up to kiss me. A soft kiss, meant for reassurance, that quickly bloomed with desire. He pushed his hard length against my stomach and left me breathless. "I have something to show you." One corner of his mouth twitched before a striking grin consumed his face.

I pushed back against his arousal. "I've seen that before, you know."

His throat rumbled, and he owned me again with his kiss.

My body absorbed the feel of his touch, absorbed his taste, his scent, even the sound of his voice. It infused my blood with it, producing the high that I'd become so desperate for, every day and night. I was a damn junkie.

Will led me through the great hall and we kissed as we climbed the staircase. When we arrived at his bedroom, he pulled me past the door.

I tugged on his arm. "Take me to bed, Will." I needed my fix.

He grinned and swept me into his arms. I was about to complain, but he shut my mouth with his, an effective tactic he used often. At the end of the corridor, he stopped in front of a set of doors. He set his palm to the electronic pad on the wall. A lock clicked, and the door on the right side opened.

He kicked the door open wider. "Welcome home, baby."

I squished my brows together. "What?"

"Our separate rooms are too small. And separate. We need more space." He stepped inside. "I won't have lath and plaster between us any longer."

"But—"

"Elle, you'll give me this," he commanded, setting me on my feet. He narrowed his eyes and stared into mine.

I shook my head as if that would clear it and give me good sense. God, it was stupid to wonder why he hadn't asked me to move in with him. So stupid to fear living with him. We already lived together.

Living in Will's house hadn't been my long-term plan when I'd decided to run to England. It had been because of my resolve to bide time and seek information and vengeance, but more importantly, it was for Lissie's sake. But more truth slapped me in the face as I stared up at him now.

I'd fallen in love with him before England, and I had come here to be with him. As clichéd as it was, he'd had me at hello. That rumbling, accented hello on the pier had unsettled the silence of my lost soul and changed me.

I studied his pale blue eyes, so beautiful. No fire, only love. And determination. His enormous, unchecked ego wasn't going to be denied. I swallowed hard, overwhelmed by a surge of emotion. I'd been over it in my head more than once—my love for him was insane, irrevocable.

The thought put a smile on my lips. I dragged my fingertips over his unshaven jawline. "You're right, this makes sense for us. I want to share this suite with you."

Will smiled, took my hand, and kissed my fingers, then he led me through our master suite.

Inside the entrance was a living room that included a plush gray sectional and a beautiful wood dining table. The original fireplace was preserved, though it had been converted to gas and surrounded with sleek, built-in shelving. A generous wet bar was in one corner, its elegant cabinets with etched glass doors displayed shining crystal barware. A stocked wine cooler was tucked in on one side of the sink and a dishwasher on the other side. Will's favorite whisky and a multifunction espresso machine sat on top of the white marble counter.

He led me into an incredibly opulent bedroom that had sweeping blue draperies framing two ornate oriel windows that faced east, overlooking the English Channel. I might see the lights of Boulogne-sur-Mer on a clear night, I thought. There was a masculine wooden desk on one side of the room for Will. Our huge four-poster bed had a grand headboard made of rich mahogany, and it was covered in layers of luxurious white and blue linens. Gorgeous silk Persian rugs covered parts of the wood floor.

I stared with a gaping mouth, looking around our romantic boudoir.

Inside the bedroom were three doors. The first led to our master bath, finished in white-and-gray marble. The second was Will's walk-in closet, already filled with his clothing and weapons. One oversize rack displayed his tailored Italian suits.

I lifted a brow in question. I hated the thought of him leaving me for London.

"Soon." He kissed my forehead. "We'll figure it out."

Beaming with satisfaction over what he was about to reveal behind door number three, he opened it up and nudged me inside. I turned and turned. I stood inside a posh custom dressing room so large that it might take decades to fill. It was an entire room, with its own fireplace, an antique settee, white fur rugs, and a crystal chandelier.

When he saw me eyeing the glass box displaying Pearl, he

put his arms around me. "It's a lovely family heirloom, baby, meant to be treasured, not fired."

The old gun didn't mean much to me, but what he'd done with it meant everything. My eyes stung with unshed tears.

"Will, my God. This dressing room is everything. It's magical."

"You'll fill it in time." His face lit with pride.

"So, that's the trick. You build your woman an irresistible dressing room and hold her captive by virtue of the temptation to fill it." I lifted onto my tiptoes and nipped his earlobe.

He caressed my ass. "Whatever it takes to tie you down. There's one more room for you to see." Holding both my hands, he pulled me through the living room to a set of French doors.

Natural light flooded the space on the other side, the north wall of the room all windows. A stunning vintage easel displayed a waiting canvas, and a tall project table with built-in shelving had painting and sketching supplies.

Will stood with his body pressed against my backside. He held me, resting his chin on top of my head. "What do you think? This is the lighting you wanted."

I stared at those windows, stunned. Tears welled in my eyes. The thought he'd put into creating a wonderful little art studio for me blew my mind.

"We'll change anything that doesn't suit you. Quite a lot of traffic moves through this house. I want you to be comfortable."

I whirled around to meet his eyes. "Will," I squeaked. Finding my voice, I told him, "Everything is perfect as it is. God, it's suitable for the duke and his queen. The thought you put into these spaces for me is amazing and generous, and I'm grateful. I'm so happy at Eastridge with you." I kissed his lips and hugged his neck.

"For an earl and his countess," he corrected in a half-whisper near my ear.

I pulled back. “You were meant to protect me, *defensor mea,* not give me the world.”

A warm smile played at his lips as he swept a strand of hair away my face. “I plan to do both.” His lips touched my forehead. I shivered. He drew deeper from his reserve of tenderness.

The back of his fingers brushed my cheek. “You did say you’ll marry me.”

I’d meant it when I said the words to him. But I was unprepared for more conversation about it outside of bed. He hadn’t mentioned it since, and it hadn’t occurred to me that he might want to get married soon.

I hit him with what must have been a stupid expression. “It’s too soon.” Nervousness cut into my stomach. “It’s too soon for us to get married.”

“No, baby, it’s not.” His lips grazed mine one, twice. “I’ve loved you for a decade. You know that. I need this, need you to be mine.”

“I’m already yours. A marriage certificate doesn’t make or break that. We do.”

“I want the vows, need to know you’re not going anywhere.”

“Will, it’s just that—” I could hardly breathe.

He wasn’t interested in my opposition. Before I said another word, he gripped the back of my head and kissed me hard. “You and me … there’s nothing else to it. My life, all that I have, is worth nothing without you.”

He took my mouth again but with tenderness and devotion this time. His lips were intoxicating, like velvet, and when he kissed me that way, when he spoke in that soft tone, it was easy to forget my senses and to forgive his offenses. I lost myself, moaning against his mouth as he growled into mine.

Then, he reached into his pocket and pulled out the most beautiful ring I’d ever seen and held it to his chest between us.

forty-three

The engagement ring was sophisticated, timeless. Pavé diamonds on the face and on the sides of a platinum band led to a diamond halo of fourteen brilliant solitaires that surrounded a fiery ruby. The ruby was a huge cushion cut gemstone, and the light that flashed from its crown reminded me of Will's passion when he made love to me.

William Hastings didn't get down on his knee or recite a practiced speech. He remained true to form, which was one of the many things I loved about him, exhaling a sharp command. "Marry me."

My pulse raced. Fear, driven by the unknown, was the worst fear of all, and in my twenty-seven years, a marriage never existed in my home. Marriage was my unknown. I opened and then closed my mouth.

For me, there had never been any husband-and-wife role models, no leading examples. I'd lost my parents when I was two years old, and my grandfather had passed before that. Isobel's husband, David, had left town after three short months of their marriage. I held my sister night after night when she could no longer bear the pain on her own. She cursed the institution and blamed it for his abandonment. She and David, who had been her college sweetheart, had married soon after they learned she was pregnant, but they'd never moved into the same home.

I wondered if he had learned or suspected that Lissie wasn't his child.

What if marriage changed Will and me? What if it ruined us? I couldn't lose Will to a piece of paper. I couldn't live without him.

I lowered my eyes to the floor.

From the moment we'd come together, Will had excelled at recognizing my internal battles. This time was no different, yet it was. It was the first time one of my emotional struggles hurt him. We both wiped at the tears streaking down my face.

I wanted to tell him that I was scared. Tell him that I loved him, that I couldn't live without him, there would never be anyone for me but him, there was never anyone before him. But fear wouldn't allow my heart to say the words.

I should have looked at him, let him see into my heart, but that damn fear kept me from meeting his eyes, and I hurt him more.

He placed the ring on the mantel and said, "You'll wear this when you're ready." Then, he left me alone in our suite without another word.

I leaned against the door, listening to his footsteps fade away. When they were gone, my gut wrenched, and emotion hurled itself out from my soul. I fell to my knees and cried. The memory of the pain I'd experienced when I found Gran and Isobel lying on the floor came back to me. The pain I suffered now was different. It was worse.

According to my heart, hurting Will was a mortal sin. It writhed in my chest and ripped itself to pieces to punish me. I wound my arms around myself in a foolish attempt to minimize the damage.

Lissie called out to me from the other side of the door. "Aunt Ellie? Thomas sent me. Can I come in?"

I couldn't let her in. I reasoned that she now had the love and support of a strong family, so it was okay if I pretended not to hear her. Thomas or Mary would comfort her and keep her away from Will if necessary.

"Uncle Will looks really mad. He's punching the bags hard. Is he mad at you?"

Damn it. She'd been down in the gym. I pulled myself up from the floor and opened the door. Lissie rushed in to hug my waist.

"He's fine," I lied. "Everything is fine. You know how hard the men here train. Will has a lot on his mind right now, that's all."

She regarded me with perceptive Hastings eyes. "Then why were you crying?"

Caught in my own web, I wiped my face on my sleeve and tugged her out the door. "Come on, girlie. Let's go find something to do in this castle of yours." We walked hand in hand along the corridor. One more ragged breath stung inside my chest. I released it. "Let's stop in the kitchen and ask Mrs. Bates if we can have pizza for dinner."

"Yay!" she squealed, skipping along beside me.

MRS. BATES CREATED A CLEVER TABLE IN THE DINING ROOM FOR the kids that was set with handmade pizzas and iced wine chillers, filled with bottles of different flavored sodas. Housekeeper or not, the overbearing Irish woman was part of the family, and she loved making everyone happy.

Mary and I watched Lissie and John teach Chelsea how to properly enjoy pizza. Their laughter floated through the air like a beautiful melody. It was impossible not to laugh with them.

Will had avoided me through the afternoon, keeping to the lower levels of the house while I'd stayed upstairs with Lissie.

He appeared outside the dining room now, caught up in a serious conversation with Thomas and Ben, the expressions on their faces severe.

I knew Will's look. Assassins were getting closer, coming for me. We were running out of time.

"Hold up a minute," Thomas said, startling me out of my thoughts. He popped in and grabbed a warm pizza from the buffet, playfully reproaching his mother, adding a kiss on her cheek, "Where was all the fun when I was growing up, Mum?"

Mary's twinkling eyes gave her away. She was charmed by her son's affection. "Things have changed, yes, but I've always loved you boys the same, Thomas."

Will's hot stare burned into me from the hall. I uncrossed one leg and crossed the other and drew circles on my plate with a fork. I was afraid to look at him, afraid to see what I'd done to him.

Thomas sat down at the table across from me and made a low whistling sound to catch my attention. With his mouth full of pizza, he encouraged me to go to Will with the tilt of his head. After he swallowed and smiled, he whispered, "Go on."

I slid my chair from the table and went into the hall with Will.

He offered me his hand. His forearm tattoo lurched forward and caused my heart to twist and punish me again. Even after what I'd done, he was reaching out for me, still wanted me. The dagger bearing my name called out. I placed my hand there, instead of on his palm. Using his other hand, he gripped my waist and pulled us away from the dining room.

My eyes remained on the floor. I felt like an ungrateful child who deserved a spanking.

Will lifted my chin and studied my eyes. "Christ, you've been crying."

I closed them. I couldn't bear the contact.

He pressed a gentle kiss to my forehead, then moved it to my lips. "Don't do that, baby. Don't cry. I can't take it when you do."

I wanted more. More of him would make everything right again. I opened my eyes and met his stare, prepared to accept responsibility for my behavior. I searched for his pain but couldn't find it. I searched for anger but didn't find that either. His eyes were flawless, invincible.

"You should go enjoy your family," I whispered like a coward.

He shook his head, frowning as though I'd said something absurd. "I'll see you upstairs soon. Carry only what you need for the night. I'll move the rest of your things to our suite in the morning." He kissed me softly again, released my chin, and headed toward his war room.

I TWISTED MY HAIR INTO A MESSY BUN AND STEPPED INTO THE shower after grabbing a few things from my old room. The rich fragrance of the soap reminded me of the fresh English roses Will had asked Mrs. Bates to place in our new bedroom.

Steaming hot water sluiced down my front when he slipped in behind me and pressed his hard body against mine. Breath rushed from my lungs, and my head dropped back against his shoulder. We would make love, and everything else would fade away.

My skin tingled in the wake of his stirring kisses, behind my ear, on my neck, over my shoulder. His hands caressed my curves. He pressed his rigid length along my spine, and my blood heated.

"I need you," he breathed against the back of my neck before pulling my mouth around to his.

Every touch was deliberate and gentle, every kiss the same.

I turned in his arms and locked onto his eyes. As hot water

rained over our bodies, a small voice whispered inside my head, encouraging me to give him what he needed, to marry him.

"Time is yours. I won't push you, Elle."

"What do you mean?"

"Does my word mean anything to you? I've said, I'll deny you nothing." He paused for a moment, his eyes dropped, and his words softened again. "Tell me your hesitation isn't because you doubt me, and I'll wait as long as you want."

My heart thrashed, punishing me yet again for Will's pain and confusion, forcing me to face the truth. I wanted to wear his ring. It took a moment for me to overcome the thickness in my throat.

"Will, I love you. There's no one I trust more than you or believe in more. You're it for me. Always."

He stared into my eyes, searching my truth. When he was satisfied, he leaned in and smiled against my lips. "I know you're scared. That's all right. I understand you need to confront matters and challenge me. That's all right as well. You do drive me mad, woman." He sucked gently on my bottom lip as he turned off the water.

I pulled the pins from my hair and released the long layers, then wound my arms around his neck. "You wouldn't be happy with a woman who didn't challenge you once in a while."

Will swept me into his arms. "You're it for me, baby."

I kissed the bandage on his injured shoulder as he carried me from the shower to our bed. Our wet bodies fell onto the mattress as one. His kiss was fierce but gentle, his passion bursting yet reserved.

When I reached between our bodies to touch him, he captured my wrists. "Don't push me tonight." Then, he buried his face in my neck and kissed my butterfly. "Not tonight."

From that moment until we slept, everything he did was slower than usual and filled with intense emotion. His white-hot eyes were softened with devotion as they locked onto mine and lingered on my body. It seemed as if he were trying to capture and preserve our time, creating photographs in his mind.

As we made love, he filled me, stretched me, changed me.

Everything from that day burned to ashes, and we became whole once more.

The love we shared was an obsession for each of us. It had no equal, and it was greater than my fear. I would wear his ring. I would marry him soon. Before either of us left our bed, I would tell him so.

Will wrapped me in his strength and made love to me again before we drifted to sleep.

Three hours later. Pounding. A voice.

Our arms and our legs blissfully tangled, my hair fanned out over Will's chest.

More pounding. Shouting.

I was awake. It wasn't a nightmare.

Thomas was shouting for his brother.

He beat on the door with his fist. "Will, goddamn it, get up now! Armed intruders are on the property."

forty-four

BEFORE I COULD SORT OUT IN MY SLEEPY BRAIN WHAT WAS happening, Will had already shoved into his jeans, sprinted to the door, and let Thomas into our suite. "Sitrep," I heard Will say.

Thomas followed him into his closet. I stayed just outside the door. "Eight men, all armed, sitting low near the north border. They're not yet aware we've spotted them. Protocol was implemented. Those here are in the weapons room. The others should roll in soon. We have one out on foot for cover while ours come up the ridge."

"*Fuck.* Prepare one of your drones. Put John on the monitors and comms. Arm him and lock him in. Go," Will commanded as he strapped a double chest holster across the width of his broad back and inserted two daggers. Before he turned to me, he holstered his Glock on his hip.

I stood behind him, trembling. I wore the sheet from our bed.

"Elle, you must quickly get dressed and get your phone, so I can take you downstairs." He pocketed his phone and reached for another gun.

I couldn't move. My body was cold with fear, frozen.

"You must go, Elle."

The time had arrived. We were under siege.

My mind refused to move forward, even as my feet carried me to my dressing room. I pulled on panties, jeans, a bra.

Will came to me within minutes. "If the power is lost, a secure generator will support the essential functions necessary. You will be safe." He pulled a sweater over my head and helped me slip into my shoes.

We didn't have time for questions, or time for me to make sense of what was happening. I recognized the life-and-death urgency in his tone. I knew he was going outside to fight assassins.

All that mattered was that he came back.

After I grabbed my phone and a few other items, Will guided me down to the basement training center. We entered the weapons room, where the security team was gathered, then he pushed through a wall panel that led into an alcove housing a steel door. With his palm on the electronic pad, a mechanical gear turned and clicked like he'd unlocked a bank vault. The door hummed as it opened. He locked an arm around my waist and used the other to hold the door while looking inside.

Mrs. Bates held Chelsea on her lap. The little one slept inside a bundle of blankets. Mary sat with her arms around Lissie, who was quiet but very alert. Mary looked at Will, pleading with her eyes, saying her youngest son's name.

"I need John's help with communications, Mum. He'll be locked inside the war room. No harm will come to him. I'll send him down as soon as I can," Will told her. He pulled the door shut, pressed my back to the wall, and kissed me.

Ben extended his arm into the alcove and handed my pistol to Will.

Will kept me pinned to the wall with his body as he ejected, inspected, and reinserted the magazine. "You won't need it, but I won't leave you unarmed in this situation. Remember. Ten rounds. Chamber each by racking the slide. Finger off the trigger unless you intend to pull it."

I nodded. "I remember."

My heart thumped so quickly that I thought it might burst from my chest. Anxiety wrecked my stomach. Silent, terrified screams banged around in my head.

"No one leaves this room. You'll allow no one other than a Hastings to enter. There's a monitor beside the door. If you can't see who it is, do not open the door."

Outside the alcove, magazines clicked into weapons. Slides screeched over metal. Red laser beams hit the walls. Voices of soldiers preparing for battle rumbled.

"Will?" I whispered.

"Do you understand me, Elle?"

"Yes, but—"

He became an intense storm. "You must do exactly as I've said, goddamn it!"

"Okay," I snapped.

"Nothing else matters right now." He placed the gun in my hand.

He was wrong. One thing mattered. And in that moment, to me, because he was heading out into what I could only imagine was like a war zone, it mattered more than anything. There was no way I would allow him to fight before I could tell him what he needed to know, that I wanted to marry him.

I pulled the engagement ring out of my pocket and pressed it into his palm.

"Put it on my finger," I demanded.

His eyes locked onto mine, and everything else fell away. "You're sure?"

"My answer is yes, I'll marry you. Yes, sooner than later. I want to wear your ring."

"When did you know this, Elle?"

"When you were inside me. I needed us to burn away my fear together, and we did."

Will shook his head and smiled. "Christ, you're a handful sometimes." Then, he slipped the sparkling ruby onto my finger and kissed it. "You are everything to me," he breathed against my lips. He pressed his mouth against mine as he pressed his hand against the electronic pad on the wall.

Before I could respond, tell him that I loved him, he launched me into the safe room and pulled the door shut, locking me inside. I stumbled from the force and caught myself on a chair.

Lissie raced to me. She threw herself against my body with enough energy to knock me off-balance again. We fell back against the door. I wrapped one arm around her and raised the other for Mary to take the gun from my hand.

Lissie had been quiet until the moment she'd collided with me. While I held her, I wondered if she remembered her time in the secret room in Stonington, the day we'd lost Isobel and Gran. I wondered if she thought about our former life in Connecticut.

She'd fallen quickly and hard for our new life and new family. She loved Will and his brothers, and they loved her. He was the closest thing to a father she'd ever had. Mary was already her grannie, and the connection they shared was remarkable. Though we had no legal proof she was Ethan's, it was hard to believe otherwise. Her turbulent Hastings eyes were undeniable, and she'd inherited not only his eyes, but also Ethan's warmth and sense of adventure. To have this family ripped away from her would devastate her still-healing soul.

I kissed the top of Lissie's head and held her tightly while she hid her crying face in my sweater. "Your uncles will be back. I promise."

We finally moved from the door after she pulled my hands to her chest and found the ring on my finger.

She lifted her face and hit me with those eyes. "It's the prettiest color ever. Are you getting married to Uncle Will?"

"Yes, I am." I tucked a finger under her chin and caressed her tiny dimple beneath my thumb.

Her eyes sparkled.

"See? He must come back soon."

ANXIETY WON. ONCE LISSIE SETTLED ON THE SOFA WITH MARY again, I settled in the bathroom and vomited.

We saw nothing. We heard nothing. We knew nothing until John came to the safe room two hours later. I ran to the door and crashed into him as he came through it.

He held on to my arm, keeping me steady. "It's okay, everyone is safe. The estate is secure." Then he looked directly at Mary. "Thomas is inside, Mum. He's fine. Everyone is fine. No injuries."

I pulled away. "Where's Will?"

John gave his mother a slight nod and avoided my question.

"John?" I snapped.

"He's fine, like I said, Ellie. I watched on the monitors. They fought nine men, but two got away."

Seven more dead, a fast-growing burden for Will to carry. But there was something else going on.

"What are you not saying? Two got a—" I gasped. "Did he go after them?"

John lowered his eyes and nodded.

I tore out of the room and ran up the stairs, taking two at a time until I reached the ground level. I shouted for Will. Eight men were in the great hall, removing weapons from their bodies and toweling sweat and weather from their faces.

Will was not one of them.

I clutched onto Thomas's rain- and blood-soaked shirt. "Thomas, go after him. Please!"

Thomas handed his gun to Ben and pushed me backward. "Someone give me a clean shirt." He tugged the one he wore over his head while pushing me back again.

"Find him. Go with him," I pleaded, still grabbing at Thomas, my fingers digging into his flesh.

"Stop it, Ellie," he ordered low in my ear, giving me an opportunity to pull myself together. But I didn't. He wrapped his arms around me and hauled me into the war room, turning me loose once the door closed behind us. He quickly pulled on someone else's T-shirt. It was too small, his massive size second only to Will's.

"Where is he?" I shouted. Thomas retreated, and I pursued him step for step around the conference table. "Tell me!"

He placed his palms against my shoulders to keep me at arm's length, but that wasn't what caused me to stop in my tracks. It was how he stared at me with Will's eyes. John and Lissie had the same eyes, too, as had Ethan. But there was something about Thomas that made his even more like Will's, and it frightened me on a level that I didn't understand.

I crumbled onto the table and sobbed. He gave me a moment before gathering my boneless body to lock me in his arms for comfort. "Is he hurt?"

"Jesus, Ellie, you have a fucking temper."

"Thomas," I warned, my wet face buried in his shoulder.

"No, not a scratch. He went after the two we lost. He'll track them and kill them, and he's not coming back until it's done. I need you to stop crying."

"Why is he alone?"

"He ordered everyone to stay here with you."

It was my fault Will was out there alone. I broke again, clutching Thomas harder. Sobs overwhelmed me and caused my body and my breath to shudder. I was a mess.

Cursing beneath his breath, Thomas pressed me harder against his chest and waited for me to finish my ugly crying. He stroked my hair and pressed his cheek against my head.

"Thomas, you must find him. He's all alone. *Please*," I cried.

There was no way to stop Will once he made a decision. The only thing I could do was get someone out there with him.

"I can't leave you," he said softly. "If he's not here, then I must be. You know that. You'll never be without one of us again. You'll never be alone again, Ellie."

Those words, the promise.

I nodded against his chest, fighting fear, summoning strength. I lifted my head, but I wasn't ready to meet his eyes.

"Tell me what's going on. I need to know."

He pulled back and paused, gathering his thoughts, then handed me a towel. "The Greens fell in with Jack Lewis. They were the informants Uncle Robert was tracking. We dealt with two of the three brothers. Charles ran, leaving his brothers to die. Yesterday, we received intel indicating that he and Lewis were planning to draw you out. Will believes what he's doing is the best way to keep you safe."

I wiped my nose on the towel. "He was planning to leave?"

"He's been torn up over this, Ellie. He allowed them into our home, gave them money."

Hot tears pooled in my eyes again.

"Will hasn't left you. He's on a mission, and you must learn to think of it that way." Thomas grabbed my hand and stared at the ring. The ruby and diamonds twinkled beneath the lighting. "You know who he is and what he must do."

Thomas was right. No one was stronger or more intelligent and determined than Will.

"I'm sorry. I had no right to—"

He cut me off. "No apologies. We take care of ours round here."

I sniffled and wiped away the last tear. "You sound like your brother."

"Yeah." He opened the door and waited for me to pass through, but before I did, he grasped onto my shoulder and stopped me. "There's something I've been meaning to say. He's never apologized to anyone until you. That's a big fucking leap for my brother."

forty-five

WILL DIDN'T ANSWER HIS PHONE AGAIN WHEN I CALLED FOR THE tenth time, and I didn't leave a message again. Voice mail messages were useless. He didn't listen to them. I'd decided to rest, but without Will, not knowing where he was or when he was coming home, I couldn't sleep. His scent still clung to the sheets, so I would lie on our bed if for no other reason.

I put my phone on top of his pillow and stared at it, compulsively pushing the home button. The ruby on my finger and its bright halo caught my attention and sent me back to the moment I'd decided to wear the ring. I was in Will's arms, protected from the world by his power. He was moving inside me, filling me with his body while his possessive whispers filled my soul.

"You're mine, my angel, and I'll love you until my last breath," he'd said.

I flopped onto my back, raising my arm to break a ray of sunlight with my hand. I admired my heavy engagement ring, twisting it from side to side, watching it sparkle. The band was loose, so I slipped it off my finger and looked inside the band to see where the jeweler might cut it for sizing.

My heart stopped. There was an inscription.

Until my last breath. W

The script was elegant and poetic, flowing with grace, its romance transforming the *W* into butterfly wings. My fingers fell to my neck. I remembered what he had said about my birthmark before he placed his first sweet kiss on my lips. His eyes had shown him a *W*, not a butterfly. I slipped the ring back on and covered my heart with both hands, locking that memory safely inside me.

An aching lump grew in the back of my throat.

Those four words—*until my last breath*—were more proof of Will's unbelievable commitment to me. And they reminded me to be more decisive, to be stronger. I would never be his equal in physical strength, but I could be his partner in other ways.

Will hadn't left me. I'd abandoned him, leaving him alone in our fight. He didn't need my complacency, he needed a partnership with a little breathing room. Same as me. I could stay out of his war room if that eased his conscience, but I would no longer add to his burden by remaining ignorant.

"Never again," I told the ruby. "I'll never do that to him again."

I swallowed the fat lump in my throat and got my ass out of bed.

On my way downstairs after a shower, I bumped into Mary in the corridor. She reached for my hand as we walked toward the staircase. "I spoke with Thomas."

I tried to think of something to derail the conversation but came up short.

"Who we are and where life with a Hastings takes us, well, it never gets easier. There's nothing we can do to stop the madness when it comes round. But there're a few things I know for certain, dear. William has the strongest mind and heart this family has seen in generations. He will fight for you and come back to you. Nothing will stand in his way."

I smiled. "He will. I believe that too."

"Richard would have taken such delight in how you handle his son. You're very forgiving, Ellie. You soften him and you challenge him." She pulled me to a stop, her honey eyes glistening. "Even as a boy, he would make something worse before turning it into something better. It's the way of a lionhearted man. He'll endure more, but he'll accomplish a great deal more. His brother was the opposite. If something wasn't laid out perfectly before Ethan, he'd give it up."

The way he'd given up Isobel, I thought.

"I miss Ethan terribly. But he and your sister did leave us something quite special."

"You know about Lissie?"

"I do," she admitted. "Come with me."

We went to her room at the end of the south corridor wing, where she removed a sealed envelope from a safe in the wall and handed it to me.

"Open it, Ellie."

"Are you sure?"

"The solicitor wouldn't have given it to me if it were unwelcome news. I imagine there's an unopened copy of the same lying around William's business office. Go on, open it."

I opened the envelope and found the results of a paternity test. Ethan's signature appeared on the consent form. He'd initiated the test when we were in London. I skimmed the pages explaining method and settled on the analysis conclusion.

It was a bittersweet moment, a win and a loss at once. Ethan had died before knowing beyond any doubt that Lissie was his daughter.

Mary reached for my hand. "When shall we tell her?"

"Will should be here. I'd like him close when she learns that Ethan was her father."

Lissie would need Will. He could give her the kind of strength and love she deserved. He would ease her broken heart with his tenderness and show her it could be mended again. Her heart would have so many stitches before she turned eight years old.

"How long have the two of you known, dear?"

"Will thought so from the moment he first saw her. Ethan agreed and planned to tell her. He wanted to be her father. She's never had that, and now..." I steeled myself against a wave of sorrow.

"I promise you, he would have loved her well. But now, it's our job."

I nodded. "I've already made mistakes."

She patted my arm and smiled. "As I have with my children. Whatever you need, Ellie. Nothing would make me happier than to help raise my granddaughter. I can take on as much as you'll allow."

I nodded again, my heart reinflating.

"Before we go down, there's one more thing." Mary pulled a wooden box out from the safe and opened it, displaying a treasure nestled in blue velvet lining. "This is an authentic piece from your line. Richard's mother came upon it somehow."

It was a beautiful wedding tiara, encrusted with shimmering diamonds and sapphires. Knowing that it was something my ancestral grandmothers had worn made me speechless. I ran my fingertips along the silver curves to be sure it was real.

"Most heirlooms were left behind, for fear they might lead to your family's identity. When it's safe, we'll hunt down more. Wear this one when you become my daughter." She locked her kind eyes onto mine, and as only a mother could do, she threw my words back at me. "See? He must come back soon."

Mary Hastings put her arm around my shoulders and walked me to the door, and just before she released me, she whispered near my ear, "I sent him. I knew he loved you, and it was time for you to save him from what he was becoming."

forty-six

He came at me again, and I threw him to the floor.

John and I had been working hard on different takedown techniques every day after Will left but without much luck. The seventh lesson and the turning technique did the trick. I finally got it.

I enjoyed the time John and I spent together on the mats, and the youngest Hastings was more than happy to prove his mad skills. Will now required supervision during my sessions, so Ben helped us out.

John jumped up from the mat. "Well done, Ellie. That's the one, then. You're too delicate for the other takedowns."

I threw him down again. "Don't call me delicate, damn it."

"Well done indeed." Ben pulled John to his feet and then gestured for me to show him my hands. He unraveled and rewrapped one. "This must remain snug to prevent damage. And he's right. You are delicate. You're supposed to be, and that's quite all right."

That was as close as Ben came to affection. He rarely smiled at anyone other than Chelsea. I'd heard him laugh a time or two, but only after he and Will finished a few bottles of whisky.

"It's not. What if I'm attacked again?"

He rolled his eyes. “You’ll never be without protection again, and you know it. Christ, he’s created a small army for you.”

“Have either of you heard from him today?” I asked everyone the same question every day. Will had instructed them to keep their mouths shut around me, and they did, even when my temper spiked.

Ben and John told me no at the same time.

“Where is Thomas?”

“Looking at the monitors,” John said.

Ben narrowed his dark eyes, warning me. “Don’t push him, Ellie.”

“I just need to talk to Will. You all act like I can reach through the phone and drag him back by his ear.”

“Can’t you?”

I squared my shoulders. “Yes, Ben, you’re right. I want him to come home.”

“Exactly. He’ll say no once, maybe twice. You’ll plead with him, and he’ll give you what you want because no never means no when he says it to you. If he comes back before he finishes, you’ll be at greater risk, and he’ll be distracted. One of you will die. So, let him do what he needs to do, for fuck’s sake.” He walked away from me, his gait smooth and confident.

I should have told him. I should have shouted it at his back. I wanted to be an extension of Will’s strength, not a distraction.

Thomas would understand and trust me to help if he knew that was what I wanted to do. I headed to the war room to find him. The door was open, and Thomas stood with his back to me.

He stared at the monitors and spoke into his phone. “It’s not helping matters, believe me. Fix this, brother.” He paused, listening. “We agree then. And you’ll do it today.”

I covered my gaping mouth. It was Will. “Give me the phone, Thomas,” I said, putting out my hand to steady myself on the wall. What if he refused to talk to me?

Thomas shook his head. "Don't you do it, Ellie. Christ. Yes, she's about to—"

Will's interjecting curses were loud enough for me to hear.

Thomas handed me the phone.

"Elle." The sound of Will's voice crashed into me. I closed my eyes and clung to the way he'd said my name. "Don't cry, baby."

I wiped away one tear. "I won't. God, I miss you," I breathed. "Say you're coming home."

"I'm not finished but soon."

"If you can't come home, let me come to you."

"You will stay there."

"I can't bear another day."

"You can, and you will."

I needed to get someone out there with him. "Send for Ben. Let him do this with you."

"I want him there to protect you."

"I have Thomas and the Six. I don't need them all."

"Elle, listen carefully—"

"You send for him, Will. I need to know you're not alone. You must give this to me. I'll accept nothing less."

He was quiet, thoughtful. I could hear his breath, and I ached to feel it against my skin.

"You swore you would never shut me out again," I added.

"I'll send for him. Promise me you'll settle down and wait for me to come home."

"Promise me you'll come home."

"Yes, always to you."

"You must send for him at once. And call me every night."

"You're becoming quite the little negotiator." There was a smile in his voice. "Thomas will give you another phone, and when I can, I'll ring you on that one."

"Okay," I breathed into the phone. "Okay, yes. How is your shoulder?"

"It's fine. No more worrying, Elle. This will be over soon, and I'll be home, in our bed with you."

He hung up, and I hugged the phone to my heart.

"All right?" Thomas asked softly.

"Fine. You heard?"

"I did." He smiled, holding out his hand for the phone.

Will always kept his word. He'd promised to call for Ben, and he would make it happen. I wanted to be there when Ben received Will's instructions, so I tugged on Thomas's arm, and we headed down to the training center. The guys would be secretive about location and details, but I would have the satisfaction of knowing Will was no longer out there alone, wherever he was.

When we found Ben, he'd already ended the call. He unmasked a rare smile and bowed his head. "Well done, Ellie. Well done."

I leaped at him with a hug. "Bring him home to me, Ben."

They walked toward the weapons room with their heads together and their voices low. Thomas glanced over his shoulder and smiled at me before the door slid shut behind them. He was as relieved as I was. Ben left within the hour.

I fell asleep early that night, staring at the burner phone Thomas had given me. I had pleasant dreams about seeing Will again as I slept for five consecutive hours in our big bed, wrapped up in sheets that still smelled like him. I might have slept longer if I hadn't received a frantic call from Jess at two in the morning.

JESS SHOUTED INTO THE PHONE. "ELLIE? ARE YOU OKAY?" Panic increased the pitch of her words. Conversations and loud music echoed in the background. She was at Nick's.

"Jess, what's wrong?"

"Where are you? Wait, I'm going to step outside. Just hold on—"

"What happened?" I asked. "Talk to me."

"Are you still in England?"

"I'm at Eastridge, yes, and I'm fine. What's going on?"

"I don't really know, but something's not right. I can't explain, but it just doesn't feel right."

"Everything was fine when we talked the other day, but now, you're starting to scare me."

"Listen," she ordered. "Detective Parker is here. He never comes in. He showed me your picture and asked me if I knew where to find you. He's definitely searching for you, but Josh told me the police closed the case, so it doesn't make sense for them to be questioning people again."

"That makes no sense at all. Will spoke with Josh not long ago. I've been cleared."

"I went heavy on Parker's drinks, but he still wouldn't give up anything. Maybe they found something else, some new evidence." She hesitated and lowered her voice to a whisper. "And there's more."

"What is it?"

"Hold on a minute. Parker's leaving."

"Do not hang up, Jess."

"Okay, he's gone. The guys from McFarland's year-round fishing crew were in earlier. That's what they do when there's no work, they come here and drink all day. Anyway, they were talking about Will. I asked why, you know, since he's been gone for a while. Ellie, they told me he's here. Said they've seen him twice. Tell me he's there with you."

Every muscle in my body locked down on her words. *They've seen him.*

"You okay, Ells?"

"He's not here."

"What's going on?"

"I'm coming back, Jess. I'll get a flight and call you with the info as soon as I get to the airport. Don't say anything to anyone. Do not tell anyone you talked to me or that I'm on my way. Promise me."

"Tell me what's happening!"

"I will, but I need your help first. I'll explain when I call back."

"I'm here for you." Her voice broke. "I promise. Be careful."

"Go straight home. I'll call you back soon."

Leaping out of bed, I ran to my dressing room. I grabbed a light sweater from the shelf and pulled it over my head, jammed my legs into jeans, and threw some more things into an overnight bag.

forty-seven

GOING BACK TO STONINGTON FELT LIKE THE MEANS TO END MY horrific nightmare. I couldn't discern what or how it might come about, but I sensed retribution. I wanted closure. Will would understand that. He would be angry with me, but he would understand and forgive me.

As consoling as that might be, to have justice for my pain, I needed Will more. I needed to see him and feel him, and I would do anything to get to him. He was the reason I was going back.

My chest tightened. Anxiety ripped through my blood and my bones.

Calm down and focus, I told myself.

I paced around the suite and hugged my abdomen, fear knotted in the pit of my stomach. I had to get out of the house without security noticing me on the monitors. Thomas wouldn't allow me to leave. He would lock me up and call Will. I had to be on a plane to the United States before he realized I was gone.

I dug through my Stella bag for a credit card and used it to reserve a seat to Hartford. If everything went well, I would arrive in Stonington in twelve to fourteen hours. Will's methods were much more convenient, I thought. There was one more thing to do before leaving the house. I quickly penned an apology to Thomas.

The old floorboards in the corridor creaked as I tiptoed through the shadows to Thomas's room.

I slid the note under the door. Just as I spun on my toes to go, his feet hit the floor. I froze in place, closed my eyes.

Could he hear the hammering of my heart?

His bathroom door banged into the wall, and I ran down the corridor, not stopping or looking back until I reached the master suite. I waited quietly for several minutes, praying that he'd gone back to bed without stumbling upon my note.

Thomas didn't pursue me, so I grabbed my things and headed downstairs. The taxi would arrive soon, and I had to make it out to the road before anyone noticed.

One of the soldiers was on guard in the foyer, near the front door. When he turned his back, I slipped out of my shoes and crept through the darkness, staying as close to the walls as I could.

I made it through the great hall. I would leave through the service entrance in the kitchen.

The kitchen was also dark. But damn it, Mrs. Bates was up.

I put my back against the wall.

The back hem of her flowery housecoat disappeared into one of the pantries as the light inside clicked on. A minute later, the light clicked off, and her slippered feet shuffled up the rear staircase. I released my breath. She hadn't sensed my presence.

Once outside, I avoided lit areas by ducking into the shadows and crawling behind trees and shrubs. The ground was wet, the chilly night air having layered everything with a blanket of dew.

A branch whipped against my thigh, slashing through my jeans and tearing my flesh. I covered my mouth and muffled a sharp cry.

When the lights of the house were no longer visible, I straightened and stumbled over the terrain. The scurrying of nocturnal creatures and the rustling of tree leaves set my nerves on edge. I startled and lost my footing several times, sliding on the softness of the downward-sloping ridge.

Intense burning traveled from the fatigued muscles in my legs to my chest, where my heart alternated between hesitation and wild fluttering. Finally, the road appeared.

The driver was waiting for me, as expected, when I emerged from the dark landscape.

DEBILITATING ANXIETY AND THE UNRELENTING ACHE IN MY SOUL for Will competed until I passed out from the medication and slept through the flight to the United States.

The flight attendant's soft fingers gripped my arm. "*Mademoiselle, c'est l'heure. Les roues sont en baisse*. The wheels are down." She smiled and handed me a bottle of water.

"*Merci.*"

The captain announced our arrival into Hartford. I turned on my phone and stood. My head spun, my knees weakened. I pulled in a deep breath through my nose, gripping the seat in front of me. Another deep inhale, exhale. I was too close to Will to let go now.

I looked at the screen. So many missed calls. Thomas. Jess. A blocked number, which must have been one of Will's. I tapped on Jess's name first, praying for her to answer right away.

"Ells, thank God. Where are you?"

"I just landed in Hartford. Are you close to the airport?"

"Yes, I'm here. I'll meet you at the gate. I'm warning you now, they're all looking for you, including Will."

"You spoke to him?"

"No, I haven't taken any of their calls. But I was getting worried after so many—"

"Jess, you know I'm fine. Don't take the calls. Have you learned anything new?"

"Ben said in his message that he's with Will. I'm to tell you that, so you don't do anything else stupid. Oh, and Detective Parker was at your house this morning."

"We're deplaning now. I'll see you in a minute."

I'd made a mess of things, and I wasn't sure if there was anything I could do to clean it up. Everyone would be angry with me, but at some point, they needed to realize I'd had no choice. I had to touch Will, had to feel him touching me to know I hadn't lost him. It was a desperate desire, a compulsive behavior.

I called Thomas next.

"Where the hell are you?" he shouted into the phone.

"Everything is fine. You found my note?"

"Fuck your note. Do you understand what you've done? Not only have you put yourself in danger, running off without protection, but you've also put me in an unbelievably bad position with my brother. He'll kill me for this, and he should. If anything happens to you—"

"I'm so sorry. There's nothing I can say to make you understand."

"Give me your location, and I'll come to you."

"There's no need, Thomas. I'll be with him soon."

"Christ, you found him. Why didn't you just tell me? I would have taken you."

"You mean, you didn't know he was in Connecticut?"

"No, I didn't. He was quite sure you'd get it out of me."

"I'm sorry, Thomas. I just landed here. I'll call you again soon." I hung up.

Jess was waiting at the security entrance. She caught me when I crumbled, shouldering my weight as we walked from the terminal to her car. As she merged onto the southbound highway for Stonington, I dropped my face between my legs and began to vomit with an exhausting intensity.

Jess rubbed my back as she drove. "We're going to figure this out. We'll get you feeling better, and then we'll find him."

Forty minutes later, I leaned back against the seat and took a sip of water. I kept my eyes closed as Jess pulled over on the side of the road. She took away the bucket and put a clean one on my lap.

"You still have your guns, right, Jess?"

I let go without her answer, fading into nothingness.

BEN STOOD OVER THE BED AND WATCHED ME WIPE THE sleepiness from my eyes. "Welcome back, sleeping beauty."

The sickness was subsiding. My body was slow to fire, but my brain was beginning to function as it should. "How long have I been out?"

"She said it's been seven hours." He tapped a message into his phone.

"Are you texting Will? Why isn't he here?"

"He wanted to know the moment you woke up. Why do you think he's not here?"

"What is he doing?"

"What do you think he's doing, Ellie?"

"Damn it, Ben. Stop answering my questions with questions."

"Just tell her what's going on," Jess said. "Do you guys know her at all? Tell her, or I will."

Ben glared at me. "Jesus Christ, Ellie. You should be in England. Do you understand how your irresponsible actions have affected the outcome of this operation?"

I rubbed my temples. "Save the lecture. I'll answer to only one man. Where is he? You're supposed to be with him, so that he's not alone."

"That's fucking rich, coming from you. You flew across the Atlantic—alone."

"Yes, I screwed up. Now, let's move on. Tell me what's happening."

Jess cleared her throat in warning.

"Jack Lewis and Charles Green are here," Ben said, glaring at Jess before addressing me. "They're looking to draw you out. Searching public records, looking for connections to something or someone. They came over as part of a faction of eight to start with. Will picked off several before I arrived. He's watching them now, waiting for the right opportunity to present itself."

"Go back to him, Ben. I don't want him fighting alone."

"He ordered me here with you."

"When will I see him?"

"He's quite busy right now. Tracking assassins and all, you know?" His shifting demeanor between anger and insolence was aggravating. And it was unlike him.

"You don't have to be unkind. I'm worried about him." Tears wet the rim of my lower eyelids. But I was stronger. I wouldn't let them spill over. "I love him. Put yourself in my position for a minute."

He spent a minute examining the carpet before moving his eyes back to mine. "I'm sorry. You don't deserve that. This isn't your fault. I'm worried too. He's certifiably mad when it comes to you, but that's not your fault either. He doesn't want to lead them to you and that's the reason he's maintaining distance from you."

I accepted his apology with a nod. "Give me a few minutes, and I'll come downstairs."

Rounding the corner into the kitchen, after throwing on clean clothes and pulling my hair into a ponytail, I was determined to take charge. It was time I partnered with Will and took control when it was necessary. Will managing me was one thing, but I wouldn't allow his men to order me around, not even Ben. If my directives were sound, the security team needed to respect my wishes. Will's safety was as important as mine. I would assert my position of strength.

I made a beeline for Ben. "No one knows Will better or how to anticipate the movement of these assassins like you do. Get back to him now, Ben. Jess will cover me."

Ben straightened his back and raised his brows.

"Jess, show him your collection of guns. Tell him about your skill. Will needs him out in the field, not here." I grabbed a bottle of water and headed back to the stairs. "Tell him I'm safe, Ben, and that I love him. I won't take no for an answer. Go back to Will."

I didn't wait for their responses or look back, though a smile hit my lips when I heard their footsteps moving toward her father's hunting room. My best friend teased Will's best friend as she unlocked the door, "He might be an earl, but in theory, she outranks him."

Jessica Johnson knew how to handle a weapon. To gain her father's attention, she had learned to share his enthusiasm for shooting and hunting. Two of the five pairs of mounted antlers on the wall belonged to her.

I found her alone in the hunting room after I showered. "Ben's gone?"

"Yes. Let's see what happens. He was concerned Will would send him back." She continued loading a compact pistol and a revolver. "He was out of line. I'm glad you set him straight. Will might give you a tough time, but no one else should."

"Jess, Will doesn't speak to me that way." I didn't want her to have the wrong idea about my relationship with him. "If I ask him for something, he gives it to me. Don't get me wrong. Yes, he's moody, and he can be a prick. He works it out in the gym."

One of her robust laughs burst from her gut. “Are you saying the Hulk is pussy-whipped?”

I laughed at her laugh. “It’s not that. God, no woman likes *that.* It’s more of a mutual thing. You’ll just have to wait and see.”

“So” —she cocked her head and lifted a brow— “he taught you to shoot.”

“Don’t be upset with me. I need to know how to use a gun now. You know I didn’t have the same need when you offered.”

“I get it. Everything has changed.”

“Yes, everything has changed.”

“Ben said you have a Glock 26 Gen4. That’s illegal over there.”

“I know. I don’t carry it. He keeps it under lock and key in the weapons room.”

“I can’t believe what I’m hearing, but I like it. Here, try my Ruger. See how it feels.” She handed me the pistol. “It has a manual safety, right here, unlike yours.”

It was about the same size as mine. I tested the sight. “How’s the recoil?”

“Not bad, but a little more than your baby Glock.”

“Jess, listen, this whole thing, it’s worse than you think.”

She frowned. “Whatever you’re holding back, say it.”

“Okay,” I breathed. “I need you to understand how dangerous these men are. They will kill me.” I drew a shaky breath. What would she think of Will? Would she see him differently, think of him as a cold-blooded murderer? “All men involved have killed others. All the men, on both sides.”

Jess nodded slowly. “Some just kill, some must kill. If the alternative is losing you, I’ll do it myself.”

forty-eight

I STARED OUT THE WINDOW INTO THE DARKNESS. "DAMN YOU, Will."

He was out there somewhere. I could feel him. He hadn't called or texted me. Nothing relevant had been broadcast over the Stonington police scanner or on television. Relevant articles were lacking in the newspaper as well. Jess and I had listened to the county's live emergency audio feed, hearing nothing of consequence reported. She even called her supervisor at the hospital for reports on knife and gunshot wound victims. There had been nothing in the past forty-eight hours.

I'd had enough. Jess holstered her revolver at her hip, and we headed out into the evening to find him. I was unarmed. We had argued about me carrying one of her guns without a license, and she'd won.

Stonington's night, with its waxing gibbous moon, was ominous and quiet. It didn't feel quaint and safe like it had in years past.

Everything *had* changed.

Jess drove past my abandoned house, but we didn't stop. I would never step foot inside it again. It wasn't about cowardice to me. It was about moving forward with my new life and leaving the pain of the past behind.

"Good-bye," I whispered as she hit the gas.

"You're sure?"

"Quite."

"You're beginning to sound like the British."

I smiled. The comment would have pleased Will.

"That's a huge rock you're wearing. You're sure about that too?"

"I've never been more certain about anything. He's everything, Jess. We're connected on a level I'm not sure others can see, and there are no words to describe it."

"It hasn't been long."

"I know. Time has become extraneous. It feels like we've already shared a lifetime."

"You've been through a lot together."

"I belong with him."

She nodded but kept her eyes focused on the street.

My heart twisted. I hated how she breathlessly waited for the perfect connection to develop over time whenever she dated someone new. She deserved more. I wanted her to find the wonderful, obsessive explosion of bliss that I'd found with Will. I wanted her to see that it was instant and unexpected.

"You're staring," she said, circling back to Water Street.

We drove down the boulevard again, making one last pass through the center of town, then headed for the town dock.

"Lissie misses you, Jess. And watching superhero movies with you."

"I miss her too. Will I see her again?"

"Come back with me, and you will. She loves England. She's quickly picking up the dialect and the accent from her uncles."

"Uncles? So, it's true. You've confirmed it?"

"It's true. I read the paternity results myself."

"It sucks that Ethan's gone. It would've been nice for her to finally have a father."

"His death has been hard on the family. We haven't told Lissie yet. I'm so thankful she has Will. You should see how she loves him, loves them all. They adore her. It was the right call, Jess. She has much more than I could have given her on my own."

"What would Will say if I came back with you?"

"Actual words, probably none. But he'll be supportive in his own way. He understands that apart from him and Lissie, you're all I have."

Jess pulled into the first lit area of the empty visitors' lot at the pier. We stood there, searching through the night for movement and sound.

Stonington's pier stretched along a peninsula of land covered in asphalt, often referred to as the town dock. Boats and cold-storage units and seafood-processing warehouses filled the area for as far as you could see. A cultural center used for the arts, meetings, and celebrations greeted guests at base of the peninsula.

"There're lights out there. Crew must still be here. Maybe someone has seen him," I said, longing to walk the pier one more time.

"Are you sure about the exposure?"

"You've got my back, so I'm good. If you thought it would be dangerous, you should have let me carry the gun."

Jess narrowed her blue eyes at me.

"Do you remember what Will looks like?"

"He's hard to forget. I won't shoot him or Ben. But if you're threatened, I will put a bullet in someone's head."

"God, now you sound like Will."

"This is serious shit, Ells. I won't risk having someone take you away from me."

I righted myself after stumbling on a warped plank. “Now, you *really* sound like him.”

“Then, I like him already,” she teased.

As we reached *Neptune*’s dock, I dragged my fingertips along the port side of her faded emerald-green hull. I’d missed her.

Generations of fishermen still shared their stories around town about the lost souls of these old boats. Maybe that was why I loved *Neptune* so much. Because we had both been lost souls, and we had comforted each other.

“You’re still quite beautiful,” I whispered to her.

“Shh, listen.” Jess’s flaming hair billowed behind her. “Did you hear that?” She wrapped both hands around the grip of her revolver and held it low.

I listened but heard nothing. Then, my body tensed as it released adrenaline into my bloodstream. There it was. The subtle cadence of boots on asphalt. Someone was following us. A sudden grating screech. One of the rusty sliding doors on a metal warehouse opening. Light poured out, shadowing everything in its path.

I prompted myself to breathe in, breathe out.

“Keep your back against the boat.” Jess’s tone was strong, resolute. “It’s too late to turn back.”

A creeping shadow crossed the small lot in front of the warehouse, and cold blood rushed through me, its frightened song humming in my ears.

“Freeze, asshole!” Jess aimed her gun at the shadow. “Hands over your head.”

“I’m unarmed,” the shadow called out, continuing in our direction.

“Liar. Stop walking and get on your knees. Do it, now.” She raised her gun higher, and the stout shadow fell to his knees with his hands in the air above his head. “I’m going to approach you.

If you move a muscle, you're dead." Jess then lowered her voice. "Stay there with your back to the boat, Ells."

"I told you, I'm unarmed. I lost my piece back there." The silhouette of his head jerked toward the other warehouses. The voice was familiar, but I couldn't place it.

"What's your name, why are you out here, and who are you with? And if you move, I'll blow your head off without your answers."

"There's some bad shit going on in this town. You should go home, red."

Jess moved closer to our shadowed detainee, one slow step at a time. "Parker? Why are you out here like this? You're a cop, for Christ's sake."

My heart crashed against my rib cage. My lungs quivered. Detective Parker, with a murderous hunting knife, had haunted my dreams many times. There were others, but it was his face I saw most often in those nightmares. Each time, he laughed and taunted, touched me in ways too awful for words, and then finally slit my throat.

I moved closer. I needed to see his face.

The disguised pieces that had drifted through my subconscious came together and finally made sense. How stupid that it had taken so long. The facts had been there. Parker had been posing as a police officer to help the Order get close to me.

"He's not a cop, Jess. Don't release him!"

Parker grinned. "Ellie James. So, you're back," he said with the British accent he'd been effectively concealing. "My mates are going to love this. You should've stayed in England, you dumb bitch."

Jess looked over her shoulder at me. "Get back against the boat, damn it, Ell—"

Parker was on his feet in a split second and nailed her in the face with his fist. Her gun flew from her hands and slid along the old wooden planks of the pier as she landed on her back. He climbed on top of her and put a knife to her throat.

He was going to take her away from me.

I screamed her name.

Adrenaline flooded through my body again, and something I'd never experienced overwhelmed me. Fight conquered fear. It overrode the usual lockdown that my brain bid. There was someone in my head. But she didn't sound like me.

Save her.

I obeyed, picking up the gun, aiming it at Parker.

"You will not take her from me."

He redirected his attention, his crude eyes meeting mine. "Oh, but I will. Just like I took the young female guardian from you by putting a bullet through her heart. She wasn't your sister, you know. She was meant to be a decoy and, as it turned out, another ineffective layer of protection. It worked for a while, until the Order grew suspicious and tested her DNA."

Words from the old tome Will had given me bashed into my skull ... *unless his daughter acquires the throne as rightful Queen.*

It didn't say one of his daughters, just *his daughter.* There had only ever been one.

So many lies. Fury and hatred blasted through me, and my blood boiled with it.

"She and your grannie were collateral damage," Parker added. "You're the one they want, the one I want. Joining them was my way to get to you, to hurt him. They destroyed my family. He—"

His shocking revelations hit me with the force of a hurricane, and my mind screamed for vengeance. I closed the gap between us, pushing the gun into his temple, cutting off his words.

"Drop the knife," I snarled.

He let the knife fall from his hand onto the planks. "If you live, ask him what they did to my family, ask about my sister."

"I won't ask. Get back on your knees."

Parker returned to his knees as I pushed the revolver's short barrel deeper into his temple.

"Pick up the knife, Jess."

She steadied herself and grabbed the knife. "Step back, Ellie. You're too close."

"He's mine."

"This isn't you. I won't let you do this. Step back."

Parker taunted me. "Don't worry yourself, red. She can't do it."

I stepped back, but my mind, the stranger in my head, focused on Parker. I lowered the gun to his chest.

"More, Ells. Please. Back up more."

The thought that guided me and its desire to deliver Parker's punishment didn't waver. My fingers absorbed the comforting feel of the revolver's grip, and I smiled at the sensation.

Parker was a dead man.

Will appeared before me then, and he stepped in front of my fucking gun.

forty-nine

WILL HANDED HIS GUN TO JESS AND JERKED HIS CHIN TOWARD Parker. His eyes burned into mine, unyielding blue challenging vengeful green. "Elle, I'm here."

I gasped at the way he'd said my name.

"You have a choice now. You can shoot him and become someone different or choose my hand, baby." He cautiously reached for me.

I didn't move, didn't reach for him, or surrender my weapon. I stared into his eyes and measured his words.

The stranger in my head continued her provocation.

Without breaking our connection, blue and green indivisible, Will stepped aside and allowed the sight of my gun to lock on to Parker's chest again. He knew better than anyone the battle raging inside me.

Boots pounded on asphalt and halted somewhere near me, behind me. A magazine clicked, and the slide of a pistol scraped metal as a round was chambered. Will didn't move. It had to be Ben.

Will's eyes delved deeper into mine. "I promise you justice. You must choose between that and vengeance. Either way, this man will never again see the light of day." His words were deliberate and powerful.

I blinked up at Will. I looked at Parker. He was sweating, his eyes shifting behind me to Ben's gun, then back to mine.

Ben's voice. He said something sharp to Jess, pulling my stare around to his scarred face. He'd placed himself in front of her, shielding her, though his eyes and gun were fully trained on Parker.

The energy that drew me to Will reached out and led my eyes back to his. There, in his intense, pleading eyes, I saw my future —our future, our life together in England. Visions flooded my head. I saw him slip a ring on my finger as I married him in a gown of white lace. I saw the white fire in his eyes as he made love to me. My lips smiling down at him as he kneeled and kissed my pregnant stomach.

"Elle, give me the gun," Will said, moving his hand closer.

My head cleared at the sound of his voice—the only voice to truly command me. I knew in that moment that if I made the wrong decision, it wouldn't be me who would create those beautiful memories with him. It would be a hardened, fallen version of myself living my life, stealing everything from me that I wanted with Will. A sinful, murderous pretender taking from him the woman he wanted to love until his last breath—his angel.

I lowered the gun and put my hand in his. "You're here," I whispered.

Will shoved the revolver into his pocket and caught me as I collapsed into his arms. "I'll always be here for you," he said, his words raw with regret. He pulled my ear to his thundering chest. "I'm here, baby. Right here."

Parker lashed out again. He was already a dead man with nothing more to lose. "Your reunion is touching. Enjoy the time you have. She won't last another six months."

A vicious snarl tore itself from the dark place where Will's beast dwelled, but before he could mete out punishment, vengeance reared her head one last time, and I beat him to it. Without thought, without granting my body permission, I pivoted into a swift side kick, releasing my anger, my sorrow, my pain as I launched my heel into Parker's face. Bone crunched, and blood flew from his nose, and then his back slammed against the asphalt.

I panted, the sound of it hissing through my ears. I was insane and numb at once.

Will anchored me tightly in his arms and moved us close to *Neptune*. He crushed me against his body and claimed me with a spiraling, fiery kiss that revived my senses. I countered with the same fire, grasping his bearded face. He pushed his fingers through my hair and drew me harder against his mouth. No separate breaths existed, no broken or lost pieces. Our souls reconnected, and we were whole again.

"Elle, how I love you," he breathed. He kissed me again, murmuring against my lips, "It's beyond madness." He pulled back abruptly and cradled my face in his hands, inspecting me with wild eyes. "Are you all right? Are you hurt?"

I lowered my eyes. "I'm not hurt. You must be so angry with me. I'm sorry, Will."

"Look at me," he commanded, and when I did, he shook his head. "I'm not angry."

"I can't bear to be apart from you." My voice broke on a sob.

"I'll never let it happen again." He wiped at the tears on my face with his thumbs. "I'll find another way. I will never separate us again." He pulled me to his chest, to my home, and I soaked in the heat of his body.

My breath, words stuttered. "I l-love you."

"You're tearing my heart out, baby."

I hid my face at the base of his neck and nodded, letting him know I would stop crying.

Seconds later, a gunshot blast rang out, and the world around me blurred.

I gasped for breath. My back slammed flat against *Neptune*'s wooden deck. A thick, bruising chain dug into my spine. Will had launched me over the side of the boat.

Then, Jess was on her knees next to me. She pulled me onto mine, and we scurried to the little cabin and shut ourselves inside as another gunshot reverberated and struck the boat's steel hull.

I heard a scream echo through my head and then realized it was my own.

I cried out for Will, shoving at Jess, shouting at her, as I clung to the cabin's rusted window frame. "I have to see him!" Jess gave up the fight to push me down to the floor and pressed herself against my back. She wrapped her arms around my vibrating body as I imploded with fear.

"Oh God, no. Will!" I pounded on the glass with the side of my fist.

Will and Ben had their guns sighted on three assassins and Parker. The hit men had their weapons sighted on Will and Ben at the same time. A red laser beam danced on Will's chest.

"He came," Jess whispered.

Josh Mendes appeared behind the assassins.

The glowing red dot disappeared from Will's chest as one assassin spun toward Josh and fired. The assassin missed Josh, and Josh put a bullet in him, killing him.

Although my stomach rebelled at the sight, I couldn't look away. I couldn't turn away from Will. I fumbled wildly with the latch on the window frame until the cloudy pane of glass slid open.

"Christ, it took you too fucking long to get here, cop," I heard Will say.

"Stand down, Hastings," Josh ordered. He'd lunged and locked his sight on to the remaining hit men, providing cover for Will and Ben. "I've witnessed no crime by your hand here today. Let's keep it that way."

"You'll give me that one," Will commanded, his menacing stare hooked on Parker. "I promised her justice."

Parker lurched, diving for the weapon of the dead assassin.

Will and Josh reacted instinctively, but it was Josh's bullet that pierced Parker's chest.

"Now, do your fucking job, Hastings, and get her out of here."

"You motherfucker," Will snarled.

The last two hit men took advantage of the pissing match and fired. A bullet grazed Josh's leg, and another ricocheted off the boat.

Josh fired multiple rounds, taking down both assassins.

"Get her off that boat and leave now," Josh urged as he called into the police department.

Will boarded *Neptune*, and I leaped into his arms. He lifted me, holding me against his warm body, putting a soft kiss on my lips. "We need to go before the other police officers arrive."

He vaulted over the side of the boat and held his arms out for me to fall into, and the moment my feet hit those familiar old planks, I knew I would never step foot on that pier again.

Josh gave a slight nod when our eyes met, then looked away. I had hurt him. But he'd still risked his life to save mine. Somehow, he'd buried his pain to collaborate with Will. I didn't know when their relationship had begun or even what it was. I knew only that they had worked together to clear my name in the case and now to stop the assassins.

I would never forget Josh Mendes. He was a good man.

As we passed by him, the two men clasped hands for a firm shake.

"Don't leave the country yet, Hastings. I'll be in touch."

Will nodded.

Through the darkness, we jogged hand in hand, following behind Ben and Jess until we reached the car. The four of us were bone-weary, eager to vanish quietly into the night, to be forgotten for just a little while.

"PULL OVER," WILL SAID A FEW MINUTES INTO THE DRIVE. There was a desperate sense of urgency in his tone. Before the car was at a full stop, he pushed out the door, rolling off the seat to his feet. Crouched on the side of the highway, he vomited. He stayed low with elbows resting on his thighs and wiped his mouth on the back of his hand.

I lifted his chin and stared into his disoriented eyes. "You're burning up. What's going on, Will?"

Violence and death rarely affected him that way. They had become part of his fabric.

It was something else.

As he straightened to his full height, his breath accelerated, and sweat ran down his face. He shifted his weight once, twice, again. "I need to sit, baby."

I called out for Ben. "Something's wrong! He's going to—"

Ben was quickly out of the car, supporting Will's weight.

"Right side. It passed through," Will said to him. "Get me to a bed, my brother."

"Oh God, you've been shot—and you knew it?" I yanked at Will's shirt and found the entry wound under his arm.

He'd taken the hit meant for me when he threw me onto *Neptune*'s deck.

The bullet had torn through his muscled flesh near the top of his rib cage. I glanced at my own body, where I'd been pressed against him. He'd bled on me, though neither of us had realized it at the time.

I threw his jacket to the ground while Ben held him and raised his arm, so I could pivot beneath to look for the exit wound.

Jess leaned over my shoulder and inspected the wounds. "The bullet cleanly passed through serratus anterior. Neither the lateral thoracic artery nor his lung took a direct hit since he kept going. We need something clean to press to the wounds to stop the bleeding."

We didn't have anything. We were on a stretch of highway with nothing in sight. I yanked off my jacket and pulled my long-sleeved cotton top over my head and pressed it strategically to both wounds.

"Hold it there," I demanded of Jess.

I grabbed my scarf from the ground and tied it around Will to hold the makeshift dressing in place.

Jess tugged on the scarf to make it tighter. "Good. Now, keep pressure on both wounds. Push as hard as you can. We need to get medical help immediately."

Will grew weaker from the blood loss and could no longer stand on his own. "Cover her up," he ordered, directing his slurring words to Ben after we put him in the back of the car. "Get us to the beach house."

Ben grabbed my jacket from the ground and held it for me with his head turned, and I slid my trembling arms into the leather sleeves and zipped up to cover my bra. My body was in shock, but I wouldn't let it break me.

I climbed into the back with Will and applied pressure to the wounds again. His face was pale, his breathing labored. Fear gripped me. I closed my mouth and commanded breath in and out through my nose, forcing it to steady, knowing my erratic heart would follow.

"Hospital," Jess said. "He needs proper medical attention. We can't risk further blood loss and infection." She looked from me to Ben, ignoring Will's beach house edict.

"You know how this works, Ben. I said, go to the beach." His nostrils flared, and his breathing sped up.

"Be calm, Will. Please." I kissed his cold lips. "We'll go, as you say, but then you'll defer to me, and I'll do whatever it takes. Do not fight me on this."

I had a plan.

He nodded and closed his eyes.

We couldn't risk the involvement of law enforcement. The bullets Josh fired from his police-issued weapon were defensible, but we couldn't allow ourselves to be connected to the deaths that had occurred prior to that. There was no way to know whether the authority assumed by British Parliament would prevail in the US, and if not, Will could go to prison in Connecticut for life.

Ben pulled back onto the highway and headed for Lords Point.

"Jess, help me. I can't lose him. I know that you can save his life. It's what you do."

I was asking for more than I deserved, pulling her further into our world, where she would never live the same life as she had before. It was wrong, but I needed her. Will was my everything, the one person I couldn't live without, and I would do anything to save him. *Anything.*

"I'm begging you, Jess. Please."

She stared, measuring the commitment in my eyes. The side of her face was red. Small beads of blood dotted a cut beneath her eye.

Locked on to my gaze, she said to Ben, "Hit the next exit and take a right. I know where to find the medical supplies we need."

fifty

Jess balanced over the console between the two front seats and injected Will with penicillin and morphine. She yanked the scarf and my shirt away from the wounds and treated them with a chemical hemostatic agent to aid the clotting process, then pressed sterile gauze against them.

"Hold here and press hard. I'll start the drip. He's lost a lot of blood, and not only that, but the fluids will also combat the toxic effects of myoglobin resulting from the muscle breakdown. I don't want to wait any longer."

I replaced her hands with mine. "Do it."

She had done everything she could for Will by the time we arrived at the beach house. The rest was up to him.

We dosed him with enough morphine to make him sleep, so he couldn't fight us as we cared for him. When he realized what was going on, he made me promise I wouldn't allow anyone else to touch him, and Ben and Jess both pledged to stay armed while he was out. Just in case.

Jess walked me through the proper cleaning and dressing of the wounds, and then I stripped him of his clothes, washed the blood and sweat from his body, and tucked him into bed.

His massive body burned through the morphine, and he

drifted in and out of consciousness. He moved from the bed only when he needed to use the toilet, insisting he would do that on his own. Each time we dosed him with another round, he kissed my lips and mumbled how he loved me before drifting back into a deep sleep and then sweating through it again.

I knew his body and mind were strong. He proved that as he tried hard to come out on the other side. Still, every second felt like a minute, and every minute felt like an hour. I wept when he was out, desperate for him to wake. I stayed in bed with him, leaving only when my bruised back ached. My body was something Will would fight for, so I curled into his and maintained contact with his fevered skin.

When I wasn't staring at him, I sketched. One image continued to fix itself in my mind, demanding to be released onto paper. It was the wedding gown I'd seen in the vision at the pier. It took almost no time to pencil its chic likeness.

Jess placed another box along the wall. "Here's one more." She'd gone to my house in town to gather some things.

"You didn't have to do that."

"It's no big deal. I grabbed a few irreplaceable items. Birth certificates, photos, fabulous shoes. You know, those sorts of things. It's late, so try to get some sleep."

"That's more than a few. I'm so lucky to have you. I couldn't have done this without you. I love you, Jess."

She stopped and nailed me with her wide blue stare. "You've never said that before."

"I didn't know how."

She smiled, glancing at Will, her eyes growing watery. "Love you too, Ells."

After Jess left the bedroom, I snuggled close to Will, but I couldn't sleep, so I dragged a box of photos close to the bed and started to trip down memory lane.

"My God, Isobel," I whispered.

She'd hidden her affair with Ethan so well, though I finally stared at the truth. I touched a photo of the two of them in a small album she'd never shared. Ethan his arms around my sister, and they looked happy. They'd been in love. It was a beautiful photo, one I would save for Lissie.

I traced the lines of her face. I couldn't recall Isobel ever looking that way.

My heart knew in that moment that what Parker had said was true. She wasn't my sister, not by blood. I was furious with her for the lies, and I ached for her, missing everything about her.

I flipped the page and found another photo of Isobel and Ethan. But in this one, they were with another person.

The third person was a man, his deceitful expression familiar.

All three smiled and held drinks high, as if celebrating something, and the hand of my sister's murderer rested on Ethan's shoulder.

I choked on my breath and slammed the album shut.

My mind spun with details I'd never questioned but should have. I swallowed hard and forced myself to see the truth. It had been staring me in the face for so long—Isobel's fascination with guns, the way she had known how to use them and carried one in her handbag; how she would meet me at Nick's, walking me home whenever she could; the paranoia and the overbearing behavior...

She'd known the truth, and she had been protecting me.

And there was her secret involvement with Ethan. She'd fed information about me, about the security of our situation to the Hastings patriarch—to Ethan. How else could they have known if danger lurked on this side of the Atlantic? Ethan hadn't found it necessary to track Isobel, to protect her the way Will protected me.

Ethan had known all along.

They both knew she wasn't my biological sister. She'd been planted in my life.

Will stirred and grumbled something unintelligible. Did he know? He'd sworn he had no secrets, that he'd never lie to me, and I believed him. No. Ethan had lied to him too.

I closed my eyes and held my hand against my forehead as if that would make it all disappear. I struggled to erase the unwanted image from my brain, that photo of Ethan and Isobel with Parker.

Reaching out to Will, I whispered, "I'm here, my love."

It was in that moment that I decided to keep the photo from Will. Although the meaning of it was unclear, my heart understood that it would cause him more pain. Had my sister and Will's brother betrayed us? One thing was very clear to me. When the truth came to light, it would affect us profoundly.

My mind spun further out of control.

What had Ethan and Will done to Parker's family, and what had happened to his sister?

IT WAS BEFORE SUNRISE ON THE THIRD MORNING AFTER THE shooting, and I was stuck in the same loop, berating myself for my selfish, reckless behavior.

Hindsight was a powerful and useless tool. I couldn't see it then, couldn't see past my determination to get to Will. I'd gambled with my life the day I left Eastridge, the life Will worked so hard to protect. That I'd made it through an international flight before falling ill—and worse, that no one had followed and murdered me—was nothing more than luck.

Worse still, my imprudence had nearly cost us *his* life.

"I'm sorry. I'll never do it again," I whispered.

Will pulled my back tightly against his chest and cupped my breasts. "It's all right, baby. No more apologies." His velvet lips brushed over my neck and then my shoulder, and his erection pressed against my backside.

I turned in his arms and dragged my fingers over his jaw, smoothing his unruly beard. Even in the dark, the natural color of his face was unmistakable. The fever had gone.

"Will, you're back."

Determined and finished with bed rest, he yanked the intravenous catheter from his arm. His strength surged, increasing with each breath. "My woman needs me."

"I do. I've missed you so much."

He winced from the pain as he moved above me and claimed my mouth. Balancing his weight, he held me and opened my legs with his knee. "I need you too, Elle," he said near my ear before coming back to my lips and thrusting his tongue around mine.

Rousing tingles raced along my spine and washed over my skin as my body anticipated the reconnection to his.

"I need to be inside you. Christ, these past few days, I've dreamed about it over and over." His voice was nothing but gravel.

"I'm yours. All of me is yours."

Will shoved into me with ravenous force and drew a sharp cry from my lips. Grasping for sanity and tenderness, he stopped moving and buried his face in my hair. "I'm sorry. I didn't mean to hurt you. I should have prepared you." His apology was about more than that harsh thrust. "I keep fucking up. Help me stop. Show me how, Elle."

I stroked his cheek with my fingertips. "Everything's going to be okay. I love you, Will."

Despite his best effort and the tormenting pain of his gunshot wounds, he couldn't calm himself for long. Our time apart had been more than either of us could bear, with too many emotions forced aside. He held me tightly, so tightly, in his trembling arms, and he drove into me hard.

I pushed against his chest with my palms. "You're crushing me, Will. Kiss me."

When he kissed me, the tension in his muscles eased, his

embrace relaxed, and he slowed down.

"I love you, baby," he whispered. "My angel."

Soothed by his bared soul, I lay my hands on the pillow above my head and surrendered mine to him. He settled into the position and rhythm that would shatter us both. His mouth covering mine, he swallowed his name when I cried it, then roared through his own climax.

Once he caught his breath, Will lifted us until we were sitting in our favorite position. He was still inside me, his powerful arms holding me close. Our gazes locked, and our breathing slowed. We were heart to heart and soul to soul, and I could feel the transcending depth of both. I ran my fingers through his hair and gently rocked my hips.

"Such grace and beauty. I don't deserve you, Elle."

His reluctance to be with me in the beginning had never been about what he believed I deserved. It went deeper than that. He judged himself unworthy of love. It had been a self-inflicted punishment for his sins.

I took his face into my hands. "Being with someone isn't a matter of what we've earned. Love isn't something we can deny for the sake of atonement. All that matters is how well we love the person we're with, and no other man could love me as well as you do. I need you, Will. Only you."

He kissed my lips before resting his forehead against mine. "Christ, saying that I love you doesn't feel like enough. The words aren't enough."

I held on to him, and there was nothing else. He was right. There were no words for our insane, obsessive love. It was exquisite, unconditional.

We eased back down to the mattress, and he collapsed onto the pillows with a grimace and an agonized groan. I snuggled against his body and lay my head on his chest, finding the heart-beat that was my lullaby. We closed our eyes.

All the lies would keep for a few more hours.

fifty-one

WE NAPPED UNTIL THE SUNSHINE WOKE US. I ROLLED OFF WILL'S chest and stretched in a lazy manner, absorbing the sunshine that beamed across the bed. The sun worked hard at dazzling me with its warm, golden rays as they pierced the panes of glass. I'd missed it, but the brilliant East Coast sunrise over the Atlantic could no longer hold me as it once had.

"I want to go home, Will. Can you travel?"

"Yes, we'll leave tonight." He lifted my hand and admired the engagement ring he'd put on my finger. He turned it and watched the light shimmer across the gemstones.

I swore the ruby had been carved from his heart. "I won't ever wear another ring," I told him. No other could bear as much love and sentiment as the one he was studying, the one inscribed with the words that meant the world to me.

He kissed the stone with a smile on his lips. "All right, baby."

I smiled, too, and scooted to the edge of the bed to get my phone from the table, handing it to him. "Thomas needs to hear your voice. Oh, but wait. We need to talk about him first."

"What about him?"

Guilt eclipsed my bliss. “Don’t punish him, Will. What I did, it’s not his fault.”

He was thoughtful before he responded, his silence wrecking my nerves. Finally, resolve filled his eyes. “I don’t blame my brother. And I don’t blame you. What happened was my fault. Forgive me, Elle. I should have learned the first time that I left you behind.”

“Don’t do that. I won’t let you do that. You can’t accept responsibility for every foolish thing that I do. I’ve never been good at following orders or directions. But I know I must do better, and I will try.”

“The day you stop challenging me, my rebellious little angel, I’ll wonder if you’ve stopped loving me. I want you just as you are—defiance and all.” Both corners of his mouth twitched, and his eyes flashed.

I found myself smiling once again. “Let’s call this one a draw.”

“There’ll be many—I’m quite sure of it.” With a full grin, he lifted the phone to his ear and waited for Thomas to answer.

My mind continued to drift while he and Thomas discussed arrangements for a plane to get us back to England, complete with an onboard medic this time. It was the first time anyone else had heard his voice since I had tucked him into that bed.

God, I had almost lost him.

“Tonight, goddamn it,” Will said into the phone as I closed the bathroom door. When I came out, he was rummaging through his duffel bag. He complained and scratched at his bearded cheeks. “Jesus, I need a shower.”

“Yep, you do.” I snickered beneath my breath for a moment, then straightened my face. “But more importantly, you need to eat.”

“Shower first,” he grumbled on the way to the bathroom. He stole a kiss as he strutted past me in all his naked glory.

Jess and Ben were making breakfast, and my stomach rumbled as the smell of bacon and coffee drifted beneath the bedroom door. I tied my robe and headed for the kitchen.

"Good morning," Jess exclaimed in a singsong.

They were sitting at the counter, side by side, with pistols tucked into their waistbands. She chewed on bacon and made some kind of list while he read the newspaper and drank coffee. They looked like an old married couple but with guns.

Jess teased me in her usual unabashed style. "We heard the two of you. We figured he should eat. Breakfast is still warm."

My emotions were too drained to manage a blush. I shrugged instead.

"We're to assume from the vigorous activity that he's regained his strength?"

Ben's tight mouth curved in response to her question.

My gaping mouth wouldn't shut, so I covered it with my hand. This time, my cheeks heated.

Ben cleared his throat.

"Stronger by the minute," I said. "Thomas arranged our flight home for tonight."

"Tonight? He's ready?" Ben asked.

"I think so. You should go talk to him. I'm sure you have a lot to discuss. But first, did either of you hear from Josh?"

"The cop visited twice. The case was reported as an unanticipated run-in with drug dealers. He said he'll call Will next week. We can leave."

"What do you mean, drug dealers?"

As Ben hit the hallway to find Will, he said, "Don't dig, Ellie. I've said more than enough."

"Will did what he had to do, Ells. It was the only way to protect Josh. And it did eliminate a good amount of heroin from the streets."

I shook my head in disbelief. What else didn't I know?

I'd wondered if I would see Josh before we left and if he was okay. Ben's words had revealed that answer. Josh would continue to communicate with Will as needed, but I would never hear from him again. I chewed on a slice of bacon and let the silence ride as I gathered my thoughts.

"You're leaving me again," my best friend blurted out.

"I can't stay here, Jess. You know that."

Her eyes dropped to her hands. "Yes."

"Come with me."

I'd turned her life upside down, and I was motivated by selfishness to shake it up even more. I wanted her with me, needed her support. She was as much my sister as Isobel had been.

"You were serious? Don't mess with me."

"Yes, I want you to come with us tonight." I made a fist with my right hand and covered my heart, promising sincerity the way we had since ninth grade.

"Then, I will."

We squealed and hugged. Jess abruptly stiffened and moved aside.

Will had been watching. His hair was wet, and he wore jeans and fresh bandages. He rubbed his clean-shaven jaw and pegged me with a grin. "It's settled then?" He winked as he made his way around the island to secure me in his arms from behind. "Elle, I'm starving."

I stuffed a slice of bacon into his mouth and ran my fingers over his silky jawline as he chewed. I traced the tattoo with my name on his arm. He kissed my butterfly. We both purred.

Ben tugged on Jess's arm. "We'll go into town and get Jessica's bags packed."

"We're leaving for the airport at six," Will said.

Jess watched us for a minute, her eyes intense. "Ells, do you want to go back to the house and get more of your things?"

I shook my head.

"She stays with me." Will's sharp words reminded me how insensitive he could be.

For me, he pulled from his buried reserve of tenderness. Most people weren't as fortunate. He was known to be an abrasive prick for good reason. But it was who he'd been from the beginning, and asking him to change wasn't something I would ever do.

Jess was able to see beneath a person's surface when given a chance. She'd figure him out when she saw how devoted to me he was, how hard he worked to make me happy.

Will twirled me around and connected our lips for a moment. "You never have to go back. Nothing in that house is worth revisiting a nightmare. We'll replace it. Buy anything you want."

Nothing left there held any real value anyway, not to me. Memories—the good ones, those subtle but endearing moments with my grandmother and sister—were all I needed to take with me. I carried those deep inside, and they'd never be lost.

"I want you to sell the house for me."

"What about this property?"

"This place too. Everything."

I would never delve back into the pain that had forever damaged my heart. There was no point, no reason to relive the horror when I had already moved on. Lissie and I would never stop grieving Isobel and Gran. We would always carry the loss in our hearts, but we'd do so in our new home, surrounded by the love of our new family.

Will nodded. "Done."

He understood, and he'd manage the business end of it. I'd never have to think about it again.

"What you did for Josh with the drugs—to protect him from an internal investigation—that was lovely, Will. Thank you." I kissed his cheek.

"It was a debt I needed to pay, baby."

"You should eat now, or you'll lose the strength you've regained. Then, you can take me for a walk on the beach."

With a smile, he pulled up a stool to the counter and opened a newspaper, and I set a warm plate in front of him.

Lingering longer than I'd intended, I bent and kissed his cheek again. Will was a man well suited for facial hair, and I loved it on his handsome face, but the silkiness of his bare skin was amazing on my lips.

"I'm going to hit the shower." I let down my hair and sauntered across the kitchen floor, tossing him a smile over my shoulder.

His fork hit the plate as he jumped up.

"You stay there and eat," I demanded.

"Witch," he said before sitting and filling his mouth with an entire fried egg.

fifty-two

Strolling along the shoreline at Lords Point was like walking through an old dream. I had been out of my mind for him from the moment he approached me on the pier. He had been my world by the time we walked on the beach together for the first time, but I never could have predicted how intense my feelings for him would become.

It was a gorgeous sunny day in October, and New England was bursting with its famed autumn colors. Cirrus clouds streaked across the horizon. The tide was low, and the Atlantic's surface was as smooth as polished glass. The nasal, rasping call of a snowy egret startled me. He had wandered to the mainland from one of the marshy islands to find a suitable female with whom to share his nest.

"Keep looking, mate," Will said to the white bird as it waded fearlessly into shallow water just four feet away. He squeezed my hand and grinned. "I found mine here."

I laughed from my gut, repaying the little egret with a scare of his own. My heart cherished every rare moment when Will could let go of responsibility and war. I locked each one in my memory's safe, as one would lock up gold and precious gems in an indestructible vault.

"Don't take his advice," I told the bird, now preening his curvy plumes. "He stalked me for years before making a move."

Will winced as he lifted me and kissed my mouth. "I don't regret it, Elle. I needed you strong. Look at you now. You're a beautiful force of will."

"The way you see me, the way you love me ..." My whisper trailed off as I smashed my lips to his. He opened his mouth and led us into a deeper kiss, and when we broke apart, breathless, I pushed my secret smile against his skin. "Put me down. If you open the wounds, we can't go home tonight."

We found a sunlit spot higher on the beach, near some boulders. He sat in the sand and pulled me onto his lap so that I faced him. I locked my legs around his lower back, rested my hands on his shoulders, and pressed my lips to his again. The fiery ruby on my finger connected with a ray of sun.

He commanded my gaze to his. "How long will you make me wait to marry you?"

I loved him insanely, and giving him the vows he wanted wasn't a concession. There would never be anyone but him. There was no reason to torment him.

"I need time to find the gown."

"What?" A smile dangled from one corner of his open mouth.

"You heard me. The gown, that's your waiting period. Then, I'll marry you."

His smile grew as he shook his head. "Fucking handful," he muttered. "What about all the other wedding things women do?"

"I don't care about any of that."

My mind functioned in an abstract manner. It wouldn't accept the intricacies of wedding planning. I liked the romance of weddings, but I would fail at organizing one.

He delved into my eyes.

"I'm serious. The gown is all I need, though it won't be easy to find."

"You're an artist, baby. Draw what you want to wear. Choose a design house in London, and we'll have it handmade."

He didn't know that I'd already put my vision on paper.

"You can't just force someone to make my wedding gown."

"I could, but I won't have to. Designers will fight for the opportunity." He winked.

"You can't see it before the wedding. Not even the sketch."

"I won't peek. Mum will be more than happy to oversee the rest."

"Okay, but Will—"

His smile faded. "What is it, Elle?"

"This is the second time you've left me. If you ever leave me again, for more than a few days to work in London, I will leave. I know I promised, but you can't do this to me a third time."

He hadn't left me, and my heart knew that, but the reasons for him going away made no difference. I couldn't be separated from him again, not like that.

He exhaled. "Okay."

"Okay?"

"Yes, I accept your condition. In fact, I made you that promise a few days ago. I have some conditions of my own since we've gone there."

"Are you mocking me?"

"I'm quite serious."

He was worth billions. Some of his wealth had been inherited, but he'd worked hard to earn most of it through his firm. Of course he would protect his assets. "I'll sign it, Will."

"I'm not referring to a prenuptial agreement."

"Oh. Well, what are your conditions?"

"My time in London is necessary. We'll get another house there, so you can go with me."

"Agreed." It wasn't a condition, it was fantastic. "What else?"

"Not so fast. Rules. You'll not be permitted to leave on your own for shopping or anything else. Not until I'm sure it's completely safe. Probably not even then. That means, you'll accept the protection of my men when I'm not with you. And there will be domestic employees."

I'd expected the protection detail, but I rolled my eyes at the thought of another live-in housekeeper. "One qualification regarding domestic employees. I don't want housemaids in our bedroom, and only Mrs. Bates at Eastridge. And no more segregated breakfasts. I understand the value of tradition, but that one is too much."

"Agreed," he said.

"What else?"

"The bishop of Chichester will marry us. I won't risk having the Crown or the government or even the Church disqualify our marriage the next time they're angry with me."

It was fitting since the bishop's diocese covered the same counties as Will's earldom.

I nodded. It made no difference to me who married us. "And?"

"You take my name. And I name our children."

"What?" I chuckled.

"Traditional names. No made-up names or twisted spelling deviations."

I swallowed another chuckle. "I accept your conditions. I have one more to add."

He narrowed his eyes.

"I get to be on top."

"No."

"Once a month?"

"No."

"That's hardly a compromise."

His forehead puckered with disapproval as he offered his concession. "On your birthday."

I giggled, rolling onto the sand. "Condition withdrawn. We'll allow it to happen organically."

It wasn't something I needed, and he knew it. His desire for dominance in bed wasn't a problem for me. In fact, once I'd understood his need to possess me, it turned me on. I knew his heart and what drove him, and I loved him beyond reason. Submitting to him hadn't taken away my independence. It had changed me, yes—it had set me free.

A spark of sunlight bounced around in his determined eyes as he claimed his position above me. "When you can overpower me, you can take the top." He demonstrated his power as he restrained my hands above my head and pushed his way into my mouth, taking all that was his with another one of his smooth, passionate kisses.

"I have."

"You cheated." He smirked. "How well did that work out for you, baby?"

We both smiled, remembering the time we'd spent in that little floral-papered guest room.

The muscles in his face tightened then, and his back stiffened. "The hell you live with is unbearable. I'll find a way—"

"Parker said you and Ethan hurt his family."

His mouth fell open, and his head jerked back. "What?"

I didn't say anything else. He needed a minute to grasp what he'd heard.

He turned his face from mine and cursed. "I didn't recognize him. The name …"

I thought of the confession he'd made months ago, that his lucrative business deals often had consequences for others. It was something I'd told him I could live with, and I would.

"I'm sorry, Elle. Christ, I've created more enemies, fucked up again, making it even worse for you. I'll work this out. I swear I'll make it up to you."

"I know."

There was nothing for him to make up to me, nothing to fix. But I knew Will, and for him to find peace, I had to allow him to believe otherwise.

I couldn't bring myself to ask about Parker's sister. I couldn't stomach the idea that there might never be an end to the nightmare, that there might be more pain. Selfish as it was, I wouldn't ask that question. But I would ask about mine.

"They knew." I hesitated, the words sticking to my throat. "They all knew Isobel wasn't my biological sister."

Will nodded. "Lewis confirmed it the night I found you with Parker. This hurts you, I know, but it also makes Lissie safer. She doesn't carry your blood at all."

I pulled an image of Lissie's innocent face into my head. He was right, it hurt me, but this truth guaranteed Lissie's safety. It was a blessing for our little girl.

"My brother knew as well, and he kept it from me. Ethan lied to me."

The pain in Will's eyes stung my heart, riled it. It reinforced my decision to keep the photo from him. Something was off, and I was instinctively desperate to protect him from it. If his brother had betrayed him with Simon Parker, if Isobel had been involved, I needed to find out how and why.

"I'm sorry. I know how much you loved him."

"I can't hate the lies we've been told, Elle, because they bind us. I will never feel regret for anything that binds me to you."

Will maintained our intense connection. Through our eyes, he measured my suffering and drew it inward, as he'd done in those dark days when we first arrived in England.

But this time, I did the same, combining his pain with mine.

I touched his cheek. "No regrets," I said. "I've never been happier, Will. The way you love me, the way I love you—that's what makes this hell we share tolerable."

He obscured his face in my neck and then nodded and kissed my butterfly. "You're amazing." His breath tickled my skin as he spoke, "We won't get a proper honeymoon, not right away, but when I'm certain it's safe, we'll go to Paris, Madrid, Rome. Whatever you want, it'll be yours. I'll do whatever it takes to give you the life you deserve."

"You know I'm not much good at travel anyway."

"I can get you to those cities without leaving the ground, baby."

We laughed against each other's lips.

"Let's go inside. You should rest, Will, before we fly home."

"There's only one thing I need before we get on that plane." He rocked his hips and tried to hide his pained grimace in a kiss.

I wedged my fingers between our lips. "You're the strongest man I know. Your strength is overwhelming, and it solidifies mine. It protects me in every way. But I want to be needed. Let me take care of you, just as you take care of me."

He kissed my fingers before moving them. "Don't you see? I draw my strength from you. My drive, determination, everything that's me is you. You are everything that hurts, everything that gives me pleasure. My desperation for you is an addiction, and it exceeds what words can express."

The way he loved me was inconceivable. Even more beyond reason was that I understood. Because I loved him the same way. I had opened my soul to his darkness, taking it into myself, capturing all of his heart, and he had taken part of my soul in return, owning all of me, all of my heart.

Our bond was primal, beyond explanation. Neither of us would survive it.

I twisted my engagement ring. "Until your last breath."

He smiled from his gorgeous eyes. "Until my last breath." He pulled me to my feet and treated me to one of his cocky winks. "Come inside. I'll show you."

As we walked up the rocky hill path, high tide swept in and sent the egret squawking away from his hunt at the water's edge. A breeze pushed at our backs and played in my hair.

We didn't make it inside. Instead, we made love on the double-wide chaise lounge, where he had first pressed his lips to mine. Will ignored the pain that the gunshot wounds caused. There was no line between dominance and submission. Every touch, every thrust, every tender whisper avowing me as his angel was deliberate and meaningful.

"I'll miss this place," he said, drifting to sleep.

I stared at his handsome face, as I had a few months before, and listened to the thundering crash of waves as they reached the shore and rolled back out with the current to rebuild.

He was doing nothing more than breathing, though it seemed as if he were anchoring the earth to its place in the universe and me to mine on earth.

Will was my place.

The sea became curt, a brisk gust of air flinging the blanket to expose my bare legs.

"Catch you on the other side," I whispered back.

I lay my head on Will's chest and closed my eyes.

His heartbeat was so strong.

"Help me protect him from their lies."

And then I swore to God that I would.

epilogue
CHRISTMAS EVE

WILL

Elle and I had settled on a private wedding at Eastridge.

Across the meadow, in an oak grove, I stood beside my brother John inside an old stone church, waiting for her.

Vibrant stained glass stretched out before me, depicting bible narratives and the coat of arms granted to one of my great-grandfathers.

The altar, elevated by three wooden steps with a red carpet running up the center, displayed a massive table made of the same Scottish oak that builders had used inside the house. The wide table legs featured ornate carvings. Pale roses, candlesticks, and the bishop's cloth for the marriage ceremony adorned the top.

Wisteria vines twisted throughout Christmas greenery hanging from the timber beams on the ceiling, cascading above our heads like mountain waterfalls flowing with fragrant blossoms.

Mum had outdone herself.

The bishop of Chichester gestured with his hand, catching

my attention, and bowed toward my mother. It was my prompt to seat her, which meant Thomas and Elle were on their way over from the house, and the ceremony was about to begin.

The two had grown quite close, and she'd chosen him to escort her down the aisle. With the excessive amount of activity on the estate and in town, I needed him to protect her as well. I trusted no one more than Thomas.

Floorboards groaned beneath my feet as I shifted my weight.

Waiting for her, waiting.

Earlier, Elle and I had exchanged provocative text messages while I entertained and she indulged in traditional bridal pampering. With each teasing message, I'd craved her touch more, ached to make her mine.

My mobile phone vibrated inside my inner breast pocket, my mind searching for the reason she was sending a message now, when she should've been holding my hand, becoming my wife.

I scowled over my shoulder at our seated guests, unlocked the screen, and read her text message.

I need to see you before
I'll come inside.

Everything had been fine when we parted after breakfast. Elle had insisted that I shouldn't see her again until she arrived at the church in her wedding gown.

Seven hours had come and gone, and I couldn't take another goddamn second without her.

I said to John, "She's outside. Give us a minute."

He put a hand on my shoulder. "Let her walk down the aisle, brother."

I'd been waiting for her for so long. No more.

Shoving his arm aside, I made my way between the rows of questioning faces. I glared at those faces with their silent, offensive inquiries as I walked past them.

Elle was more than I deserved, and everyone knew it. I could see it in their eyes. They wondered if she had backed out on me.

No fucking more.

I pushed through the grand mahogany doors and found her. My breath caught.

Angel. Mine.

Elle sat on a large gray horse and wore a white fur cloak over her gown, its fullness hiding everything from me except for her gloved hands and her face.

From what I understood, the horse was to pull a carriage. If I'd known sooner, I would have warned my mother. That kind of fairy tale arrival was too cliché for Elle. So, she'd changed it up to make it her own.

I stared at her for quite a long time, fighting to recover my breath, my thoughts. I swallowed hard and crossed the church garden, walking towards her.

Fallen leaves crunched beneath my shoes. The remaining foliage on our wishing oak fluttered in the stiff wind.

White ribbons swayed from the branches as large snowflakes fell from above and floated round her. The first snow of the season. Maybe the last.

One snowflake landed on the tip of her nose and another on her bottom lip. Envy gripped me. I wanted to be the one kissing her there, on her nose, her lips.

Elle removed the hood from her pretty head.

The sapphires and diamonds on her delicate silver tiara sparkled even with the sun hiding behind the winter clouds. But that wasn't the loveliness that captivated me.

It was her perfect smile that stunned me, ruined me.

A seductive combination of mischief and innocence marked her lips and revealed the desire in her green eyes, stabbing me in the heart, leaving scars there and on my brain.

Elle's words ended the silence. "Marry me, Will."

She reached out for me, daring to fall from the horse into my embrace, and a sense of calm washed over me.

Like those fucking snowflakes, the peaceful moment filling my soul with light was unexpected. I didn't understand how to preserve it or recreate it.

But as she fell into my arms, I realized she knew, and she would show me the way.

Before her feet touched the ground, I kissed her lips.

"Nothing can stop me, baby. I'm making you my wife right here, right now."

She whispered, "I can't wait to marry you."

THE EVENING PASSED RATHER QUICKLY, OUR RECEPTION AT THE house a lovely blend of dinner, dancing, and caroling.

It had been Elle's idea to get married on Christmas Eve. The woman who was the absolute center of my world preferred to avoid being the center of anything else, so she used the holiday season as a buffer to ease her discomfort.

I'd gone along with the idea because she was mine, and it made her happy.

Aside from those two things, there was nothing else.

Of course, Elle's plan to blend into the noise failed. She would always be the most brilliant light in every room, on every occasion, in every season.

I drank from another pour of the Macallan Fine Oak she'd given me while watching her. She stood a few meters away, in the center of the great hall, the distance enough to prevent me from hearing her, not enough for me to lose her lingering scent.

Inhaling to pull in every bit of her, I watched her eyes sparkle as she smiled, her pretty lips move as she talked with some other young women.

She had changed into a fitted, backless gown. Her long hair teased me, creating a veil over her bare skin, the blonde tips falling down to her arse.

So fucking beautiful.

She held a glass of champagne in one hand and Lissie's hand in her other. Her eyes met mine as she raised the crystal flute to her mouth for a sip of her favorite vintage.

Lissie's small face was beaming with curious wonder as she observed and mirrored Elle's graceful composure, her quiet exhilaration making it seem as if she'd fallen through a looking glass into an enchanting new world.

"Ease up, mate." Ben Scott could read me better than most. He added, "Ellie's anxiety seems well in hand today. She looks quite happy. And we all see how much she loves you."

"Yeah, it's not that." I knew she loved me.

I understood the gifts she'd given me, the sacrifices she'd made to spend her life with me. Only a woman with the fiery strength that Elle possessed could give all of herself to a man like me.

She was all in.

We were all in.

"It's been a difficult goddamn road for us. We're here, yet questions remain unanswered. She believes we need those answers, and that concerns me."

"All that shit is still going to be round next week, and I'll be here as well to help sort it out. So, as your third best man, arsehole, I order you to leave it and spend a few days in bed with your bride."

I grinned. "Fuck you, Scott. You know my brothers come first."

He gripped my shoulder. One of his rare, warm smiles covered his face. "Go on then. Take Ellie upstairs."

As if prompted by those words, the string quartet started

another set, transforming one of Elle's favorite love songs into an intimate musical ballad.

I put down my empty whisky glass and closed the distance between us.

To restrain my desire for her, to fight the urge to hold her against my body, was more than I could manage. I needed the rush that pulsed through my blood when we connected, when she became part of me. At the mere thought of touching her, my cock hardened.

But I gave her one last opportunity to choose me before I took what I wanted from her, possessed all of her. Although I didn't place a hand on her, I couldn't stop from imprisoning her within my space.

Her mesmerizing eyes locked on to mine from beneath her lashes.

Christ, how I loved her.

"You're more beautiful than you know, Elle. I'm at a loss. I can't come up with the words to tell you properly what it is I'm feeling."

She smiled and used the lapels of my jacket to draw her body in against mine. "There are no words for us. Just know that I love you madly, always."

Gone. She'd blown me away. Nothing could bring me back from that, from her.

My wife.

"Quite right, baby. There are no words."

She lifted her face to mine, offering me a taste of her sweet, warm mouth.

I accepted, finally allowing myself to touch her.

Gripping her arse and using my hold to press her against my erection, threading my fingers through her hair, securing the back of her head in my hand, I took more from her than she'd offered. With my tongue, I parted her lips and claimed the desperate kiss I'd been craving for hours, leaving her breathless.

I was an addict by nature, and she was my fix.

Elle understood my intense reaction. She'd provoked it.

"Let's get out of here, Will. Take me to bed."

I swept my beautiful wife into my arms.

"I can't wait to take you to bed."

the story continues

Thank you for reading *Twisted Beautiful Lies*.

Don't miss the rest story of this story! ***Her Lovely Lies*** is the edge-of-your-seat second part of this duet, and it's written in Will's point-of-view.

"So sexy your kindle will melt, and you
definitely won't see the shocking twists coming!"
★★★★★ Goodreads review

Get ***Her Lovely Lies*** now from your favorite bookseller or www.klclare.com.

Read the *Twisted Beautiful Lies* extended epilogue for even more of Will and Ellie's magical winter wedding—before and after he takes her to bed. Get the details at www.klclare.com.

about kelleigh clare

Ms. Clare is an award-winning, *USA Today* bestselling author. Before writing contemporary fiction, she was a human resources executive and a progressive voice on women's issues with a global coalition of bloggers. She also contributed to the successful startup of a *Forbes* and *TIME* recognized digital publication for women.

Sign up to receive news updates and get exclusive content at www.klclare.com/subscribe.

Follow @kelleighclare

also by kelleigh clare

HASTINGS BROTHERS NOVELS

Twisted Beautiful Lies (duet, book one)

Twisted Beautiful Lies: Extended Epilogue

Her Lovely Lies (duet, book two)

Two Pretty Lies (standalone)

Two Pretty Lies: Extended Epilogue

SAVAGE SYNDICATE NOVELS

Wicked Rivals

Merciless Empire

Cruel Vows

For more info, visit

www.klclare.com.

CPSIA information can be obtained
at www.ICGtesting.com
Printed in the USA
LVHW111955050422
715401LV00006B/231

9 781958 110096